# The Sleeping Beauty

# MERCEDES LACKEY

## The Sleeping Beauty

LUNA™

**www.LUNA-Books.com**

LUNA™

Recycling programs
for this product may
not exist in your area.

THE SLEEPING BEAUTY

ISBN-13: 978-0-373-80315-6

www.LUNA-Books.com

**Printed in U.S.A.**

To Terry Pratchett.

If I can be half as witty and funny on my best days
as he is on his worst,

I will be a happy woman.

# Author Note

I love comedy.

But comedy is nothing to laugh about. I know from listening to comics talk and reading their thoughts about it that comedy is hard, hard work. The best comedians study comedy, study timing and pacing, balance a fine line between "too far" and "not enough."

Terry Pratchett, for instance, has my undying admiration. He manages to sustain comedic writing on that narrow line for entire books; he doesn't rely on tricks like puns or pratfalls, and his books just flow from one great scene to another, loaded with terrific one-liners and dry, wry descriptions and little asides to let you know *he* knows that you are smart enough to get the joke and that he appreciates that.

Alas, I do not write comedy. I'm not nearly brilliant enough for that. I settle for "occasionally funny," with the occasional drop into *America's Funniest Home Videos* territory.

But I did have fun, a great deal of fun, with this latest Fairy Godmother book—the fifth in my Five Hundred Kingdoms series. Here we have a truly fractured set of fairy tales—when Sleeping Beauty gets hijacked by Snow White, then punted right off the field by the Siegfried saga. All three have sleeping princesses in them, which is how they manage to get crossed up, but how they *stay* entangled is what made this so much of a giggle to write.

I'd also suggest you listen to comedian Anna Russell's hilarious routine "The Ring of the Nibelungs (An Analysis)." You can find it online. I fully agree with her observations.

At any rate, I hope you find a laugh or two in this chapter of the Fairy Godmothers. Heaven knows there are few enough of them to be had these days.

# Prologue

"MIRROR, MIRROR, IN MY HAND, WHO'S THE fairest in the land?" Fairy Godmother Lily stared intently into the book-size, gilt-framed mirror she held cupped between her palms, and muttered under her breath, "And if you say *you* are, Jimson, I am going to hurl you so hard against the wall they'll be looking for your shards with tweezers for years."

"You don't need to get so appallingly aggressive, Godmother," the round, slightly green face in the mirror huffed. "I'm only the messenger."

"I'm appallingly aggressive because The Tradition has been gathering over this Kingdom in force for the past three weeks." *Ever since Queen Celeste died.* "I need to know who it's about to gather up and fling, like I am going to fling this damned mirror unless you give me a good answer!"

Though she expected it, the "good answer" would not be—

"Princess Rosamund, Godmother," sighed Jimson. "Cheeks, roses, check. Mouth, cherry, check. Hair, spun gold, check. Eyes, sky, check. Not even weeping buckets over her dead mother, sleeping little and eating less has changed any of that. And that indefinable something that means The Tradition is taking an intense interest in her makes her nothing short of radiant. If it weren't for the loss of her mother, she would be a prime candidate for the Beauty Asleep path. Still, that's relatively harmless…"

"Relatively? Leaving Eltaria unguarded with everyone asleep for a month, let alone years, would be a disaster." Fairy Godmother Lily groaned. That Rosa was the "fairest" was not what she wanted to hear. It would have been much better if it had been some shepherdess somewhere. Or even herself. She had been in charge of the Kingdom of Eltaria for three hundred years now. Unlike many of the Fairy Godmothers, the Godmother of Eltaria had been the *same* person all that time, rather than a different Godmother under the same name. Her longevity was aided in part by the fact that she was Fae on her father's side, and partly because the Fae themselves had made sure that Lily was granted extraordinary Gifts at her birth, even more than the firstborn Princess of any Kingdom, ever. They had known what she would become, and she had been trained for this since she was old enough to prattle. The kingdom of Eltaria was a very special case, and needed a Godmother who was skilled, vigilant and knew every trick in the Godmothers' book.

Eltaria was small, but tending it was a full-time job for its God-mother, because it was incredibly wealthy. The mountains that com-prised most of it yielded gold, silver, copper and gems in abundance. Where the farmers and peasants of other Kingdoms rarely saw a copper piece, here even the humblest shepherdess had at least one gold ring and a thin gold necklace with a locket of her true love's hair in it. Unlike most fanciful tales, the monarchs of Eltaria actually *did* dine on gold plates and drink from gem-studded cups.

Eltaria also had greedy neighbors. Often, the only thing that kept them from invading was the knowledge that if one did, the monarch would soon find himself facing off against the other three. The current King, Thurman, at whose christening Lily had presided, wore his Crown of State so seldom it had just been locked in the Vault, and his War Crown so often it had needed replating three times.

Thurman had married a darling little shepherdess he had met while out hunting in true fairy-tale fashion, thus neatly sidestepping the question of having to choose the daughter of one of his neighbors or the daughter of one of his nobles. One did not argue with true fairy-tale endings in this land, even though his choice somewhat disgruntled the small—and in Lily's opinion just a bit *too* inbred— Eltarian noble families. Nevertheless, fairy tales are fairy tales, and Eltaria was Eltaria, and no one dared to flout a choice approved by the Kingdom's Godmother. Lily did not intervene in the actual workings of the Kingdom often, but when she did, it was important.

It was not long before the new Queen became very popular in any event, for Celeste was sweet, practical, and clever as well as pretty. She did all the things a good and kind Queen is supposed to do, and more. She was a natural peacemaker. Among the peasants and farmers she was adored.

They had produced a single daughter, Rosamund. On Lily's advice, they had *not* had a public christening, which would simply have been the occasion for a veritable swarm of Wicked Witches, Dark Fairies, Evil Sorceresses and the like to decide that they had been slighted and come descending on the celebration to curse the poor thing. Instead, claiming, after the fact, the child's frailty at birth, they had had the priest waiting to perform an *immediate* christening before the child even got a chance to draw her first breath. With a completely *mortal* godmother, so that no blasted troublemaker could say that Lily had had foreknowledge and level a curse anyway.

Of course, no public christening meant no horde of Good Fae to come bless the child, but everyone agreed that the inevitability of curses, more curses and multiple curses, outweighed the loss of some blessings.

Thurman and Celeste, like all monarchs of Eltaria, and *unlike* most other Kings and Queens, were nearly as educated in the workings of The Tradition as Godmothers. They had to be. It was the only way that Eltaria had stayed intact for this long.

But of course, only a Godmother, or one of the Fae themselves, had the ability to sense that The Tradition was gathering to strike, and the power to command the sort of servants that could show them where....

"All right, show me where The Tradition is gathering thickest."

"I'm working, I'm working," Jimson grumbled. The Mirror Servant could see anything that was in view of any reflective surface, but that was a lot to sort through. Lily wished she could have her hands free to rub her aching temples.

If it had been possible to exclude The Tradition from every one of the Five Hundred Kingdoms, she would have done so in an instant. That powerful, yet completely unintelligent force of magic that the Fairy Godmothers called "The Tradition" quite literally made stories come to life. If a tale got told often enough, it became part of The Tradition—and the force then sought out those whose lives matched that tale closely in order to replay the story over and over again.

One might think that this was a good thing. After all, it meant that good, kind maidens, like Celeste, found themselves married to handsome Princes—that brave, penniless orphans slew dragons and won the hands of beautiful Princesses. And that was true.

But before the penniless orphan slew the dragon it had to decimate the countryside. The dragon might have been perfectly good-hearted before The Tradition drove it mad. The countryside generally was not improved by being decimated. Often many people suffered in the path of a Traditional Story on its way to its ending. It was also true that for every girl whose circumstances exactly matched those of, say, an Ella Cinders, there were dozens for whom the Prince in question was already married, an infant, a senile old man, a rake, a cad, or...would much rather marry another Prince, thank you. But The Tradition did not care, and would senselessly keep trying to force the poor girl and her "destined mate" down the "right" Traditional Path, generally to grief all around. Not only that, but with that much magical force building up around her, the girl and her destined mate would quickly become the target of however many Wicked Witches, Dark Fae, Evil Wizards or the like that happened to be in the neighborhood and in the market for a nice juicy dollop of magical power.

Which, of course, *every* Wicked Witch, Dark Fae, and Evil Wizard was on the prowl for. Always. It was easy enough to take someone around whom the Tradition was moving, and drain that power. The procedure, unless carefully managed by an extremely skilled, patient and highly ethical magician, generally killed, maimed, or mind-wiped the victim. Patience and ethics were not something dark magicians worried about. Not when it was easier to just rip the stuff away.

That, of course, was not the only set of problems The Tradition caused. Because not all—nor even most—tales had happy endings. For every Ella Cinders, there was a Bluebeard, a Laithley Wurm, and a Rakshasha. For every Gingerbread Witch, there were Babes in the Woods. Girls danced themselves to death. Wolves ate grandmothers. Little Match Girls froze to death in the snow. Mothers told their errant offspring about the Boggles that would get them if they weren't good—and lo! a child misbehaved, as what child doesn't now and again, and a Boggle got him.

At least as tragic were all the times that people failed the tests. The witch that held Ladderlocks captive generally infested the ground beneath her tower with brambles, and plenty of would-be suitors would fall into them to have their eyes put out and wander sightless for the rest of their lives. The palace of a Beauty Dreaming was always surrounded by poisonous thorns, and if a Prince's courage failed him, even a little, they would impale him and his sad corpse would hang among the vines until he turned to bones. If a Prince of the Kingdoms of the Rus failed to get the help of Zhar-ptica, he would adorn the garden of the Katschei as a statue forever.

Preventing the tragedies, steering the stories, finding a way to prevent the mismatched from becoming the victims of those who would drain that magical power, was the job of the Fairy Godmothers.

Like Lily.

But unlike Lily, most Godmothers didn't find themselves trying to stem off an entirely mortal invasion on a monthly basis on top of her other duties.

"Ah!" said Jimson, finally. And then…"Oh dear."

Before Lily could snap at him to explain himself, the mirror cleared and revealed a room she recognized—as she would recognize the public, and most of the private, rooms of most of the kingdom's nobles. This was the audience chamber of Duke Perrin, which was currently serving as Thurman's audience chamber, since at the moment he was there. Perrin's Duchy was right on the border with the Kingdom of Dastchel, which had moved troops to the border it shared with Eltaria as soon as the Queen died. Poor Thurman was not even allowed to mourn as anyone else would—

At first she had trouble understanding what she was seeing. The entire audience chamber was full of people in mourning garments in deference to the King, so three women in black and purple didn't stand out particularly.

Then her memory caught up with her, and she recognized three of the faces in the crowd.

In no small part because they were glaring at each other like the rivals they were.

"Nicolette of the Gray Forest." Dressed with deceptive simplicity, with wide violet eyes that looked utterly without guile, blond hair cascading to her hips, and a décolletage that was shocking in a mourning gown, Nicolette was widely acknowledged to be the most beautiful of the practitioners of the Dark Arts in this Kingdom.

"Asteria of the Ice Tower." True to her name, Asteria was aloof, cold and remote as a statue of snow. White hair and pale skin, eyes so pale a blue they looked like glacier-ice; the high-necked dress of dark purple made her hands and head look as if they were detached from her body in some peculiar way.

"Desmona of Ghost Lake." Of the three, Desmona was the most obviously an Evil Sorceress. Her black gown featured a spider theme, down to the glittering jet spiders—which might well be real spiders, enchanted—ornamenting her black hair. She openly carried her magical staff, atop of which a murky globe emitted the occasional sullen red spark in its depths.

She knew what they were there for, of course. And they knew it, too, throwing smoldering glances of sullen rivalry at each other. It didn't seem to have occurred to any of the three that she might be watching, because they were doing nothing to keep her from spying on them.

"Good job, Jimson," she said, putting the hand mirror down, carefully. She was going to have to act quickly.

But she hadn't been the Godmother of Eltaria all this time without learning to plan ahead. She ran to her Hall of Mirrors, generally the most-used room in her palace. Other Godmothers might be able to take the time to travel by roads or flying beasts or even the "All Paths are One," spell; in Eltaria things moved too quickly for that.

The Hall was, true to its name, lined with mirrors. All of them were shrouded in draperies, and each had a name above it. She pulled aside the drapes from the one marked "Perrin," and gazed into it.

Luck was with her. The King was using the Duke's private

chambers, which was where the mirror linked to this one already was. He was slumped over in a chair, his face in his hands, and the War Crown on the table beside him.

The magic was already in place, and keyed to her. She stepped through, from her Hall into the private rooms of the Duke, through a mirror mounted permanently on the wall. A gift from her to the Duke's great-great-grandfather. Just in case she ever needed to use it. She had to step down a little, and the leather sole of her shoe scuffed the wooden floor.

The sound of an unexpected footfall made Thurman look up; when he saw her, his face crumpled. She held out her arms to him, and he stumbled into them.

"My poor boy," she murmured, as he sobbed on her shoulder, as he had not dared weep with anyone else. He was the King. He could not cry for his Queen, nor show any weakness, not in public, and not with most of his Court. But she had known him since he was an infant; she was the person with whom the Kings and Queens of her Kingdom could be people, and not monarchs. "My poor, poor boy."

She let him cry as long as she dared, then pulled away ever so slightly. He felt that, and immediately straightened. He was, after all, a King, and he knew what her sudden appearance would mean. "Lily—what is it?"

"There are three of the Evils downstairs right now, waiting for you to show your face, and the moment you do, the enchantments will be flying thick and fast to ensnare you with all of the force of The Tradition behind them." She hated to do this to him, but there was no choice.

He didn't curse; Thurman was not that kind of man. But his face went to stone as he ran through all the possible scenarios in his mind. She saw him realize what she had, that there was no escaping this. The Tradition wanted him married, so that his daughter would have an Evil Stepmother, and there was an avalanche of force building toward just that.

Then she saw his eyes light up. She nodded. He had come to the same conclusion she had. She cast a spell over herself, changing her appearance utterly. Now she, too, wore mourning, a high-necked, black velvet gown, embellished with jet beads, her hair was as black as a raven's wing, her eyes as dark as the night sky, her skin as pale as milk. She looked precisely as she meant to—as another Dark Sorceress. The three below would see her and assume an unknown rival had stolen a march on them while they were jockeying with each other. Each of them would blame the other, and never think to work together to be rid of her.

The Tradition's power swirled and settled. It was satisfied. Rosamund would have an "Evil" Stepmother. He rang for a servant.

The man appeared instantly. King Thurman took her arm as the man stared in astonishment to see a woman in the King's private chambers when he knew that no woman had passed the door.

"Bring me Father Vivain," said the King. "I have work for him."

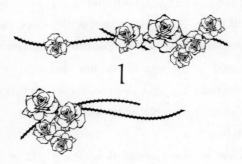

1

ROSAMUND'S HEART POUNDED AS FAST AS THE hooves
of the horse beneath her. This wasn't her sweet little palfrey, her
Snowdrop—the little mare had been sent away by her stepmother
without a reason, leaving only powerful, dangerous-looking black
beasts in the stables.

This was one of those black horses, strong and fast, and terrifying to ride. From the moment she snatched the reins from the groom,
threw herself into his saddle and smacked his rump with a riding
crop, she had known she was taking her life in her hands. This was
like being astride a tempest, or riding a boat over a waterfall. Her
arms were a mass of scratches, and every second was an eternity of
terror as she clung with all her might to his back.

But not half as terrifying as the Royal Huntsman, who was
probably on another one of these monsters, chasing her down. With
dogs. A pack of vicious, huge black boarhounds that had come with
the Huntsman when he'd arrived weeks ago. She knew about the
dogs, for sure; she could hear them baying behind her as the horse
raced through the woods.

She had to crouch low over the horse's neck, because the horrible thing wasn't paying any attention to low branches; she had been whipped twice across the face before she took this position, and it was a wonder she hadn't been blinded.

Not that still having her eyesight made any difference right now.

The horse was careering through the woods, and she couldn't tell if it was on a path or not. It didn't seem to care. And even if she had known where to go, she doubted it would have responded to the reins. This was almost suicide; the beast could stumble and fall at any moment, taking her with it, killing them both, or at least breaking bones.

But behind her was certain death.

It was that terror, the glitter of the knife in the dark passageway, the bruised arm where the Huntsman had seized her, the look of cold, bored evil in the Huntsman's eyes, that had driven her to wrench herself free, to run headlong to the stables, to seize the reins of the horse waiting for her stepmother's afternoon ride—

That terror was still coiled inside her, making her urge the horse onward.

She didn't know where the horse was going, but she had no clear idea where she should go in the first place, so that hardly mattered. She'd figure that out when she was safe from the Huntsman. She'd gotten away—so The Tradition might be moving in her favor now. She'd find rescue. Maybe a Prince or a brave woodsman or a bold peasant boy. Maybe a princely thief with a good heart. Maybe a Wise Beast. *Something* would come to help her, surely, surely.

It must. This was Eltaria. She would *not* think about all the stories where the Evil Stepmother won, where the princess was eaten or ravished and left for dead or—

The horse galloped onward, deeper and deeper into the woods, into the sort of forest she had never seen before.

Something *shrieked* off to the side, and the horse bucked and shied violently, as if it thought *she* was something that had leapt on its back and was about to tear its throat out.

She couldn't hold on. Red-hot pain lanced through her fingertips as her nails broke and tore off when the rim of the saddle was ripped out of her hands, and then she was flying through the air. There was a moment of clarity, and a strange calm—then she landed in a patch of brush that broke her fall. The horse went careering off without her. And now she heard the hounds again.

But they were following the scent of the horse, not her. And the horse had tossed her a good many feet away.

She burrowed her way into the bushes rather than running senselessly after the horse, which she had no hope of catching anyway. She managed to claw her way out of sight through the mass of twigs and leaves and into the musty gloom beneath the branches, then wiggled under the bushes like a rabbit in a warren, belly-down on the dirt and leaves until she was, she hoped, well away from where she had broken her way in, and still farther from where she'd parted company with the horse. And then, with her nose inches from the ground, she waited.

The hounds bellowed past in full cry, and she shivered, hearing the sound of hoofbeats on their heels. But they didn't stop, and the Huntsman must not have seen the signs of her being thrown. They raced off, farther into the woods, on the trail of the horse. She waited, sweat cooling and itching, insects crawling over her, until the sound of baying was nothing more than a muffled moan in the distance.

Then she struggled her way to the edge of the brush patch, staggered to her feet and listened, hard, to get a direction.

She had no idea where she was, of course. So any direction was a good one, as long as it took her away from the Huntsman.

She picked her way through the dense undergrowth as best she could, trying to get as much distance as possible between herself and her pursuers. She was tired, frightened, hurting from a thousand cuts and bruises. She had no idea where she was, no food or water, no shelter. And now, yes, she *did* hear the rumble of thunder above the trees. It certainly was going to rain.

Any minute.

Could things possibly get any worse?

*Don't think that!* she told herself sharply, thinking of bears—wolves—not-so-princely thieves. This wasn't a bad thing. The rain would wash away her scent. The hounds and the Huntsman would not be able to find her. She just needed to find someplace to get out of the rain. And pray that The Tradition didn't want to make a Fair Corpse out of her—

She couldn't help it. She started to cry. It shouldn't be this hard; didn't everyone in the family study what The Tradition was going to do? Shouldn't they have been able to stop this? She stumbled against an old oak tree, put out her hand to steady herself and found it was hollow. Like a frightened rabbit, she crawled inside.

It wasn't fair. It just wasn't fair. Why did her mother die? She had been so *good;* she'd never done anything to deserve to die!

But of course, the part of her mind that was always calculating, always thinking, the part she could never make just stop, said *and if it hadn't been that, it would have been something else. You just turned sixteen. You know what that means in The Tradition.*

Oh, she knew. Sixteen was bad enough for ordinary girls. For the noble, the wealthy, The Tradition ruthlessly decreed what sort of birthday you would have—if you were pretty, it was the celebration of a lifetime. If you were plain, everyone, literally *everyone,* would forget it was even your birthday, and you would spend the day miserable and alone. Traditional Paths went from there, decreeing, unless you fought it, just what the rest of your life would be like based on that birthday. For a Princess, it was worse. For the only child who was also a Princess, worse still. Curses or blessings, which might be curses in disguise, descended. Parents died or fell deathly ill. You were taken by a dragon. Evil Knights demanded your hand. Evil Sorcerers kidnapped you to marry you—or worse.

It wasn't fair. And it didn't help that she knew exactly what to blame.

She cried and shivered and hiccupped and cried more, sneezed and shivered and cried. She wanted her father, but her father was back at the border with his army, having delivered his new Queen ceremoniously to the palace. She wanted her mother, but her mother was in the Royal Cenotaph, and Queen Sable was—

Was an Evil Stepmother, was what she was. She had *nothing* in her wardrobe but black! Oh, she *said* it was out of respect for the late Queen Celeste, but this was Eltaria, and someone who wore nothing but black was either a poet or an Evil Sorceress, and Rosa hadn't heard Sable declaiming any sonnets or seen her scribbling in velvet-covered journals.

And besides, not three hours after the King had left again, Rosa had gone spying on the new Queen, and had seen her actually *talking* to some disembodied green head in a mirror! So that pretty much clinched the Sorceress part! And who else but an *Evil* Sorceress would have been talking to a disembodied green head?

That had been enough for her, she'd avoided her stepmother completely after that, and lived in dread of what was coming. She avoided needles, the spindles of spinning wheels, anything sharp and pointed. She kept away from balconies and only ate what she'd seen everyone else eat. She'd locked her door at night, set traps to trip up anyone coming through the window or down the chimney and had so many charms against demons and the like hung up in the canopy of her bed that they rattled softly against one another in the darkness. She'd done everything she could think of—

But she truly had not thought that a servant, no matter how sinister, would dare to raise his hand against her.

She was so cold…so cold she ached with it and jumped every time lightning struck near, which was horribly often. And every time she thought she couldn't cry anymore, a fresh shock sent her off again.

Why had her father done this? She didn't know; at times it was as if he was two different people. There was the wonderful Father who sometimes turned up without warning to teach her how to make her nightmares stop, who gave her rare, enchanted toys, like the tiny kitten that never became a cat and would go curl up on a shelf when you told it "time for bed." Then there was the King, who was always away at war, and who treated her with the grave formality of a complete stranger.

*Of course he did,* said that voice in her head. *If you were the beloved Princess, The Tradition would make your life, your fate, even more horrible.*

Where was Godmother Lily then? She'd come to the funeral, but why hadn't she healed Rosa's mother? Why hadn't she kept her father from marrying that witch?

She could remember her old nurse saying something, though. *It doesn't always take a spell to turn a man's head and wits.*

Just as Rosa thought that, she felt movement at her back.

And what had been, she thought, the solid wood behind her abruptly vanished.

She squeaked, frightened, confused—had lightning knocked a hole in the tree? Had it been so rotten it was now falling to pieces?

But then she felt *hands!*

They were grabbing her, seizing her, hauling at her clothing, her hair, her arms!

She screamed, kicked, tried to squirm away, scrabbled frantically at the edge of the hollow to pull herself out and run—no matter that it was running into the storm. That didn't matter a bit when there were dozens of *hands* trying to grab her! But these hands were strong, rough, and grabbed her with grips of iron, bruising her arms, pulling her hair. She screamed again, tried to writhe, and suddenly her head was enveloped in harsh, fetid, mildew-smelling cloth.

She screamed again, fought, hit, kicked, but was pulled backward and down. She continued to fight, trying to grab for things blindly, caught what felt like roots and had her hands torn away from them.

Then there was a tremendous blow to the back of her head, and she saw stars and for a little while, lost consciousness.

When the stars and the dazzle cleared away, she felt herself being half dragged, half carried, and when she tried to wiggle free, knew immediately she had been trussed up like game. There were ropes around her upper arms and chest, more ropes tying her ankles and wrists together; two or three people had hold of her shoulders, but her heels were dragging along a dirt surface, and every so often one of them lost his grip and let her fall. She couldn't smell anything through the mildew of the bag, but it was cold and dank, like a cave.

A long time later, or so it seemed, as she collected a whole new set of bumps and bruises, she was summarily dropped on a stone floor, and the cloth was pulled off her head.

She looked up. She was in a rough stone-walled room, with seven people in it besides herself. Two of them had lanterns. She didn't have to look up very far, her captors were all very short and the two lanterns they had were more than enough for her to see them clearly. They were very dirty little men, with long beards of various colors, beards that had bits of stone and moss and probably food in them. Their rough clothing, made of what looked like canvas and leather, was ragged and in dire need of mending. No matter their short stature; they were all heavily muscled and looked very strong.

This was, of course, because they were indeed very strong, stronger than most human men. She knew what they were, of course. They were Dwarves.

Dwarves did a great deal of the mining here in Eltaria. They had an uncanny feeling for rock and earth, where the best stuff was, and how to get it out without killing themselves or anyone else.

She had seen Dwarves before, quite a few of them in fact. When they got mining concessions, it was on the basis of sharing the wealth they extracted with the Crown as well as a tithe to their Clan, and the quarterly presentations of the Crown share were actually considered a sight not to be missed. The Dwarves would turn up in amazing outfits, entire gowns made of plates of metal scarcely larger than a head of a pin for their women, chain mail that looked like knitted silk for the men, and jewelry that never failed to make jaws drop for both sexes. Beards and hair were combed, braided, perfumed and bejeweled. They were truly gorgeous.

Not this lot. They were filthier than any living being Rosa had ever seen. They hadn't so much as a copper chain around their necks, nor a garnet earring. And they stank. She doubted that their beards had ever seen a brush.

There were, of course, renegade Dwarves; there were bad Dwarves just as there were bad humans, or virtually any other race. There were Dwarves who didn't want to hand over a share of what they found to the Crown or tithe to their Clan, and dug their hidden mines furtively. Of course, because they didn't hand over the proper share to Crown and Clan, that meant that they couldn't sell their takings in the open market, which meant they had to sell it all clandestinely. That meant they got a fraction of the price they would have gotten if they'd been honest. They also went in fear of some honest Dwarf happening upon their mine, and taking it over in a mining concession by Crown fiat.

It looked as if these seven were that sort of Dwarf.

Which, for Rosa, was good news. It meant they wouldn't immediately take her to the Queen.

And since they were men, it was unlikely that they would recognize in the somewhat battered remains of her clothing, the signs that she was at the very least, nobly born. Men didn't know much about clothing, at least, not when it was modest, and not all showy velvets and satins. She just might get them to believe—

"Help me!" she blurted, looking up at them. "I'm running away from my stepmother! She hates me! She wants to do horrible things to me! I'll do anything if you'll help me!"

They erupted in laughter, raucous laughter that sounded like rocks banging together, slapping each other on the back and grinning evilly. "A Bargain!" they shouted. "A Bargain is made!"

Five of them turned, proving that there was a way out of this room, and lumbered on ahead up a staircase carved out of the rock wall that she hadn't seen until now. Two of them seized her, roughly cut her bonds from her, and then shoved her, stumbling, up the crudely cut stone staircase. They continued to shove her through what looked like a cellar—and a meagerly appointed one it was, too—then up another stone staircase to come out into—

A kitchen. A perfectly ordinary kitchen, if an extraordinarily filthy one. A dirty, sooty fireplace with two iron cranes for pots in it and a spit above the smoldering fire that currently was empty. A big wooden table in the middle, laden with wooden plates, cups and bowls, most of which could use a good scrubbing. A big iron sink with a pump, various bags, boxes and kitchen implements. Stone floor, stone walls and one tiny window.

And there were the other five, with tools in hand, waiting, and before she knew it, she had a shackle around one ankle, a chain leading from it to a big metal ring on the hearth. "Take a look around, ugly!" said the one that seemed to be the leader. "This'll be yer home from hence! Yon chain will reach anywhere in the house, if ye're careful, and ye'll be a-cookin' and a-doin' fer us now."

And with a sudden sinking of her heart, she realized what it was she had gotten herself into. She was to be, in essence, their slave.

There had never been anything in The Tradition like *this!* There was Snowskin, but...the Snowskin's saviours were good kind creatures, not horrible things that took her as a slave!

As the chief of them—he told her importantly that from now on she could call him "master"—shoved her toward the hearth and ordered her to make porridge with the bag of oats next to it, she could only comfort herself with one thing.

She wasn't dead, and she was still a Princess. Sooner or later, The Tradition would move again. She would just have to be ready for it.

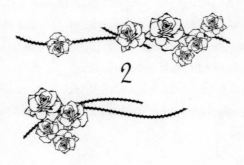

2

LILY SHOOK THE MIRROR, FRANTICALLY. *"Where is she?"* she screamed, making maids on the floor below jump and look for a place to hide. The moment when she knew that Rosamund was missing had coincided with the onset of a terrible storm. The torrents of rain and volleys of thunder and lightning had only made her covert search more frantic.

And it had to be covert, because she dared not drop her persona of "Queen Sable" to show any real interest in the Princess.

*"I don't know!"* Jimson screamed back, the green face contorted with emotion. The Mirror Servant might occasionally be snippy and even snide, but Lily would have been the first to say he took his duties very seriously. "I can't *find* her if she's not near something that reflects!" A bolt of lightning, striking right outside the palace, and the simultaneous barrage of thunder punctuated his scream, making the maids decide that the work could wait until morning and flee to their rooms to cower in, or under, their beds. The thick palace walls prevented them from hearing the words clearly, but Queen Sable shrieking at someone—and being answered—in a room they knew no one else was in was not a good sign.

Lily jumped as the bolt hit, feeling almost as if it had hit her. After a frozen moment, she put the mirror down, carefully, and just as carefully walked away from it.

She knew that Jimson couldn't find anything that wasn't reflected; she'd known that for hundreds of years. She also knew that Jimson was just as eager to find Rosa as she was. The Mirror Servant had been with her as her helper longer than anyone else she knew, and was patient and kind and forbearing with her out of all reason. She knew that screaming at him didn't help. She knew all of these things, but it didn't stop her from wanting to scream at him. She was in a panic, and she wasn't going to solve anything if she couldn't get herself under better control.

This was a disaster. This was the worst disaster in Eltaria in three hundred years. No Godmother of this Kingdom had ever *lost* an entire Princess.

"If it's any help," Jimson said wearily, "she is still the fairest in the land." Even if he couldn't see her, there were still some things that worked. He could still tell that she was out there, alive, and unharmed enough to trump Lily's beauty.

So Rosa was still alive at least. Lily took many deep breaths and forced herself to calm down and *think*. "All right, the most logical point of trouble is the Huntsman," she said to herself as much as to Jimson. "What's he doing?"

"He's not in his quarters." When the man had turned up with his hound pack, ostensibly as a wedding present from Duke Perrin, Lily had taken the precaution of putting reflective surfaces everywhere he might conceivably go. "He's not in the stables. He's—he's in the woods. With the pack."

Lily was reasonably sure that Perrin had not sent the man, but she was also reasonably sure that Perrin would say that he had. There were many ways to ensure the Duke would *think* he had sent this most peculiar present—anything from coercion to a spell that gave a false memory. The spell would be the most likely; while Perrin was warded by his Palace wizard against magic that would harm him, there was nothing about the memory of having sent a valuable servant and a dog pack as a wedding present that would cause *Perrin* any harm.

There were pitfalls to relying too much on magical protections. There was only so much that magic could do—especially when The Tradition was forcing a path. Unfortunately, Perrin was a man who did not think long or deeply about anything that didn't interest him, and when it came to magic, it bored him.

So chances were, the Huntsman was a planted agent for someone, and it would be impossible to prove it. There was no telling when or how the manipulation had taken place, nor by whom, and rather too late to worry about that now.

"Can you see anything useful?" she asked immediately. "Can you tell where he is, other than in the forest?" Thurman's Palace was—of course—on the edge of an enormous woodland that stretched for miles. It would not have been a proper setting for tales if it had not been. All sorts of Traditional Paths started in Palaces and ended in Woodlands, and vice versa. Even if the Palace had once been in the heart of a city, here in Eltaria The Tradition moved so strongly that eventually *something* would have happened to change the very landscape.

"Not really. Bits of him in the bridle brass. Bits of dogs and woods in the bridle brass. A lot of storm in the bridle brass. The question is, why would he be out in this weather?" Jimson's mouth pursed shrewdly. "The Princess is missing, and the Huntsman is miles away in the forest? In a storm?"

"That is a very good question, which is probably answered by 'because he is chasing the Princess.'" She rang immediately for a servant; one came, cowering. She'd had to maintain the illusion that she was Evil by a fierce and intimidating manner, though she hadn't actually *done* anything to any of the servants. Poor things, she felt so sorry for them. Queen Celeste had been a gentle and considerate mistress. She could console herself by reminding herself that if she was terrifying them, at least *she* wasn't making their lives a living hell the way a real Evil Stepmother would have. "I want a count of the horses in the stable immediately. Get the grooms to do it. Tell me if any are missing, and which ones."

The man left and returned very quickly; he must have gone himself, for his green livery was rain-soaked and his hair was plastered to his head by water. He made a profound obeisance and stayed that way. "Two horses are gone, Majesty," he said, his voice a little muffled by the fact that he was still in a deep bow. "One is the Huntsman's, and one is your usual ride." She noted that he did not also mention that the Huntsman and his pack were gone before he backed out of the room. Already the servants were rebelling in small ways, telling her only what she had asked about and no more. While this was good, since it meant they were much more likely to be very loyal to Rosa, it meant she was going to have to be very precise in what she demanded of them.

Lily put the mirror down and began to pace; though her body moved restlessly, her mind was curiously calm. "I can still feel The Tradition putting pressure on the situation, so we can assume something or someone will come to her rescue."

"Or try to kill her again," Jimson said glumly.

"Well we can deal with the Huntsman—does the man have a *name?*" she added irritably. "At any rate I am fairly sure I can find a way to tie him up, at least temporarily…in fact, I know exactly how." She felt just a little satisfaction at that. "I'll put him to looking for her, and partner him with someone trustworthy. I'll have to do this carefully, so it doesn't look like my idea, but I think I can manipulate things in our favor." She ran over the list of Thurman's best

men in her mind. "Hodges and May. They are both Captains of the
Guard and technically outrank him. I can reinforce that by putting
them in charge of the search effort. He won't be able to shake them,
and they're suspicious of me—well, of 'Queen Sable.'" She rang for
the servant again. The poor man. He was going to get a back injury
from spending so much time bent over in a bow.

"I want to be informed as soon as the Huntsman returns," she said.
"And gather the Guard. Princess Rosamund must be found."

This was Eltaria. Rosa was an Eltarian Princess who studied The
Tradition. So Rosa had known all of her life that there were some
skills an Eltarian Princess needed to have that…were not generally
in the curriculum of a Royal or even a Noble.

She knew, basically, how to clean clothing and a room, how to
mend garments, how to plain-sew as well as embroider, and how
to cook very, very basic food. She could not make bread, but she
could make griddle cakes. She could make porridge, soup and stew.
She could milk a cow or a goat. She could cook game over a
campfire after cleaning and skinning it herself, and she could start
the campfire herself. She could spin, and in a pinch, knit and weave.
She knew how to hunt, of course, and shoot; most nobles knew
that. But she also knew how to set snares and traps, choose wood,
find edible plants and knew a half a dozen mushrooms that were
safe to eat.

In short, she had most of the skills her mother had. After all her
mother had been a shepherdess before she was a Queen.

An Eltarian Princess never knew if The Tradition was going to
decide to dump her in the middle of nowhere and force her to fend
for herself.

And now, faced with a filthy kitchen, and seven sullen "masters,"
she needed those skills.

In her mind, she started giving them names. The biggest, she called "Bully," because he shoved everyone around, not just her. The eldest was "Deaf," because he was, or nearly, but since he didn't speak at all, and none of the others spoke to him, it didn't seem to matter; pushing and pointing pretty much conveyed everything that needed to be said. There was "Sly," who could never look at anyone straight on; "Surly," whose every other word was a curse; "Angry," who was too out of sorts even to curse, and just glared; "Lumpy," who, when not eating, just sat and stared into space; and "Coward," who deferred to everyone except her.

"Need meat," Bully said when they were on their second bowl of the stuff. He glared at Coward, who cringed. "Ye didn't get meat."

"'S the storm, see? Can't check the traps inna storm!" Coward whined. "What'f I get struck by lightnin'?"

"What if I shove me foot up yer arse?" snarled Bully. "Ye got one job, tha's traps. We need meat. Dwarf gotta have meat t'dig. Tha's yer job, cause yer shite at diggin', ye lazy sod."

Coward sank down in his chair and whimpered into his bowl. Bully indicated to Rosa that he wanted more by the simple expedient of flinging the empty bowl at her and grunting at the kettle.

They pretty much ate the kettle bare, left the dirty bowls and spoons on the table and shuffled off to some other part of the cottage. To sleep, she presumed. She gathered everything up and started cleaning—the two kettles first, and since it didn't seem that they minded a bit of ash in their food, the second one got filled with coals from the fire to have its insides burned out.

It didn't appear that the Dwarves cared what they ate or when, so she did what was easiest: she took the clean kettle and filled it full of water and dried peas with some salt and set it to cooking all night for pease porridge. They could eat that in the morning. Right now, she was too tired to think past morning. Her hands were a mess; she was filthy, bruised, exhausted, wanted to sit on the floor and howl with fear and grief; and at the moment, the only thing good about her life was that the Huntsman wasn't going to be able to kill her.

Tonight, anyway.

In the morning, the Dwarves woke her with the sound of their thumping and quarreling. With that warning she had the bowls full of pease porridge waiting on the table for them, even though she was sleepy and muddleheaded and so stiff and sore from sleeping on the stones that her eyes leaked tears with every stab of pain. They said nothing to her about the food, which she knew wasn't particularly *good,* which just told her that their own cooking must have been pretty bad.

Then again, judging by what she'd had to scrape out of the bowls, it was stuff that the Palace cooks would have beaten an apprentice for making, just before throwing him out the door onto the rubbish pile.

If they noticed she was crying, they said nothing about that, either.

When they were full, they stomped out of the kitchen and headed into the cellar, all but Coward, who went out the door into the forest. So their mine must be below the cottage, and they reached it by the cellar. How had they found her in that tree? Was it an extra way in that they had been checking? Did they seize her thinking she was a thief coming to loot their mine? It couldn't have been a very good one, since the really good mines were all in the mountains; she wondered what they were mining. But she didn't wonder for long; there were a lot of other things she needed to get done right now. She had to find out just what her options were, here.

She explored the cottage as far as her chain would reach, which took her just outside the kitchen door and to every room in the cottage. There had been a kitchen garden there, next to the door, once. There were at least a few hardy herbs still struggling. Mint, of course.

Nothing killed mint. She could just reach a few feet away, as far as the outhouse, but at least that meant she could start a garden midden for garbage. She had the sinking feeling she was going to need it.

She quickly discovered that absolutely nothing in the cottage, not the heaviest tools or the sharpest chisel, made the faintest scratch on the loop of metal on the hearth, the chain or the manacle. She hadn't really expected them to, since she doubted that the Dwarves were so stupid as to leave the tools to free herself in the reach of their captive, but it was disappointing anyway.

They'd told her to "clean," but given the state of their house and themselves, it appeared that their idea of what was acceptable was set to a standard a lot lower than hers.

Good.

She got a stick, picked up their discarded clothing with it, started a fire in the kitchen garden with a big cauldron of water over it and boiled the entire lot. That was as much in the way of laundry as she intended to do. She did sweep, and swept everything out the kitchen door to the place where she was making a midden, because there was a prodigious amount of petrified or rotting food, bones and other nastiness. She had no intention of scrubbing the floors, or *anything,* unless they ordered her to, or she just couldn't stand it herself. And she wasn't using the outhouse; the stench in there was enough to knock a person over and suffocate her. Instead, she made her own place to go discreetly behind some overgrown bushes.

The storeroom actually proved to be somewhat valuable. There were a lot of things in there that looked as if they must have belonged to the previous owner of the cottage, now broken and tossed aside. Some real bedding, for instance, which was moth-eaten and tattered, but was better than sleeping on the bare stone floor. She boiled it, too; heaven only knew what was living in it. And wedged on a shelf, there was a cookbook. She leafed through it, and figured she might be able to manage some of what was in it.

By that time, the stuff she had spread in the garden to dry was ready to take in. She left all the clothing in one pile and the blankets in another; let them fight it out among themselves who belonged to what.

Coward returned with some scrawny hares at that point. He tossed them on the kitchen table and dived for the piles, greedily picking through them before claiming what looked like the best of a bad lot of rubbish for himself, changed with no thought for modesty and demanded food.

She gave him leftover pease porridge. He didn't complain, gobbled down three enormous bowlfuls and went back out again, leaving her to gut and skin the game herself.

To make it go as far as possible, she made soup, managed unleavened griddle cakes without burning too many and spread the leftover pease porridge, which by now was a paste, onto them. She took her bedding in from the garden, but left it piled in a corner behind the broom and some buckets, because she had a good idea that if they saw it, they'd take it. She also ate first, at least of the griddle cakes, with some of the stewed rabbit meat. Coward turned up again with more game, squirrels this time; he looked with longing at the soup, but this time didn't demand any, though he did grab greedily for griddle cakes. She didn't stop him. He was still stuffing himself when the other six came stumping up the stairs. Bully had a very small bag at his belt. He smacked Coward with the back of his hand when he saw the smaller Dwarf was eating.

"Wha?" Coward sniveled. "I din touch yon soup!"

"See ye remember not ta, then," Bully sneered, and sat down at the table.

She brought bowls of the soup—the squirrel wasn't completely cooked, but they didn't seem to care—and the griddle cakes for as long as they lasted. They had no leavening, no milk, no eggs in them, being more like flat unleavened bread than cakes, but again, the Dwarves didn't seem to care. They ate everything she put in front of them.

Once again, they gobbled everything down and left a mess behind. By the time she was done and had set another kettle of pease porridge up to cook overnight, she was ready to weep with exhaustion. She dragged her bedding out onto the hearth, and made a more comfortable bed there than she had the night before.

And then she did weep. Because how would anyone ever find her out here? Who would come here, even if The Tradition led them? Who would see she was pretty beneath the layers of filth that were going to build up on her? Keeping clean was going to be impossible. And if they did, how would they get her free without cutting off her foot? There was nothing in the Snowskin Tradition about the princess being chained—or having to cut off her foot to get free!

No, this was a new twist, and a horrible one, and right now there seemed to be no Path, Traditional or otherwise, out of it.

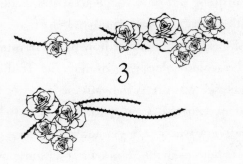

3

*"I'VE GOT HER!"*

Jimson's shout woke Lily from her fitful doze. She had fallen asleep in the chair while Jimson searched for the missing Princess, combing through every reflective surface in the general vicinity of the buildup of Traditional power that he and she could sense. Now she knuckled the fog out of her eyes and leaned forward. "Where?" she demanded.

"It's in the forest. I can place it on a map for you later. Not many reflective surfaces there, I'm using a knife and a water bucket." The image from the bucket wasn't very useful since it showed mostly ceiling. The one from the knife wasn't much better; it was fogged and distorted.

"Ah, I have some more options. Cups."

The glimpses Lily got of the Princess as she filled those cups made her wince. Bruised, hurt, poor child—her hands were a mass of scratches and cuts, the nails broken and torn. She was filthy, too. Her hair was full of twigs and bits of leaf.

Not as filthy as the creatures appropriating the cups, though. The glimpses she got of matted, fouled beards, yellowed teeth, snarled hair and filthy faces made her grimace. The reflection from the knife gave relative heights, proving that girl's captors were Dwarves. But...not the sort of Dwarves that Lily was used to dealing with.

Lily frowned. This was unexpected...perhaps. It looked as if more than one Traditional tale was getting tangled up here.

And the tales were warped and twisted. Those foul little creatures were not the kindly helpers of the proper Traditional Path; the Snowskin Path brought creatures that might be ugly but were always nurturing and kind. *Brutish* was the most charitable word to describe the things that were being reflected now. The way they were treating the Princess was entirely terrible. Rosa had spirit, and Lily could not imagine her staying there unless she was being held in some way.

Meanwhile Jimson was searching for every reflective surface he could find near her, trying one after another so they could get a better idea of what was going on there. It was beginning to look as if they were not going to find anything useful, until—

"Ha," Jimson said quietly, and suddenly a crystal clear—if somewhat warped, as if it was being viewed through a bubble— image of what was the filthiest kitchen Lily had ever seen appeared in the mirror she was holding. "Fly's eye," Jimson said. "Best we're going to get."

Well, the little brutes were definitely Dwarves, probably digging an illegal mine. The Tradition was definitely at work here, however badly twisted, for there were seven of them; seven was the right number for a Snowskin Princess. The fact that Rosa's looks didn't match the Snowskin Path didn't seem to matter this time—a Snowskin had "cheeks white as snow, lips red as blood and hair black as ebony," and Rosa was *much* more in the line of a Princess Dawn with her rosy cheeks and golden hair. Well they would have been rosy if they hadn't been smudged with dirt and tears, and it was getting hard to tell she had "locks of gold" what with all the bits of forest snarled in them. Lily's wince turned into a cringe; the poor child was definitely the worse for wear. A Princess, even one with Rosa's unorthodox schooling, was ill-suited to being a servant and cook. She was indeed bruised, dirty and looked exhausted. And behind her trailed a long chain, binding her to the hearth.

"Find me where that cottage is," Lily said grimly. "I want to get to her before the Huntsman tracks her down."

If this was the Snowskin Path there was a logical approach that would compel The Tradition to throw a lot of power on Lily's side to make this right again—what was more, when Lily broke her disguise, it could be as herself and not as the evil Queen Sable. That should make it possible for her to get the girl safely away before revealing that she was also the Evil Stepmother. It was pretty obvious now that The Tradition was moving in such force that Lily needed Rosa to understand the deception that she had been perpetrating as Queen Sable. She had only met Rosa a handful of times, all on formal occasions, in order to keep herself as the mysterious Rescuer just in case such a thing would be needed, and to make sure Rosa never felt she could depend on Lily to save her at any point, but a Fairy Godmother was the sort of person who made a lasting impression.

"Have you seen enough for now, Godmother?" Jimson asked.

She stood up. "I have," she said. The reflection disappeared, and one after another, more glimpses flashed across the mirror's surface. Jimson was tracing a path back to the Palace, from reflection to reflection. When he finished, he would have a clear way to the Dwarves' cottage that he would read to her. She in her turn could transfer it to a map.

Meanwhile she had preparations of her own to make. A second transformative spell—probably best to make it part of a cloak—something that might break that chain…and something to use if she couldn't break it. Whatever path The Tradition was trying to force, it didn't much matter. Both ended in a spell of sleep. It was a great pity there weren't any Princes lying idly about for this moment, but she would manage. Without a Prince and a kiss, the thing was harder to break, much harder, but not impossible.

She stepped through the mirror to her own castle, where she had everything she could possibly need, taking Jimson's mirror with her.

As soon as she stepped across the frame, the castle resounded with a beautiful bell tone, announcing her arrival. She hadn't gotten more than both feet on the carpet of the Hall of Mirrors when she was swarmed by her Brownies, all of them in their typical earth colors.

Brownies were, traditionally and Traditionally both, the servants and helpers of the Godmothers. Being half-Fae, Lily got more than her share of would-be aides and companions. This time she was glad of it, for the ingredients she would need for the sleeping potion were best when gathered fresh.

Brownies were smaller than Dwarves, of a similar build, but less muscular. They tended to look quite pleasant, jolly even, with round little faces and cheerful expressions. So when her crowd of helpers swarmed her, Lily was still more than tall enough to see over the heads of all of them, and direct who to fetch which component.

When they were all gone, leaving her alone for the moment, she pressed one hand to her forehead, trying to concentrate. "Plans," she said, half to Jimson. "We need plans. We can't just keep solving one crisis after another. We have to anticipate what might happen—"

For once, the Mirror Servant's voice was not bored, nor heavy with irony. "My dear Godmother," he said fondly, "you and I have worked together for many years. Centuries, in fact. If you can do without my services while you make your potions, I will try to anticipate all the paths that might be walked, and uncover as many possible solutions for each as I can."

Lily held up the mirror and gazed with astonishment at Jimson's disembodied face. "You would do that for me? After all the abuse I've heaped on you lately?"

Jimson laughed. "When one is trapped in mirrors for so many centuries, one learns which reflections are the true ones. You are the kindest Godmother I have ever served, as well as the one with the most difficult and trying Kingdom to keep stable, and I can tell when it is frustration speaking. Just put me down here, where I won't be distracted, and make your potions and disguises." The corners of his eyes crinkled a little as he smiled. "If you will trust me with this, it will be a pleasure to act as an advisor instead of a mere—reflection."

Lily sighed with relief. She had long known that Jimson was far more than an "ordinary" Mirror Servant; for one thing, she had inherited him, rather than creating him, and he was much, much older than she was. But now, it seemed, he was showing yet another side of himself that she had not expected. "I'd kiss you if you weren't on the other side of the glass," she declared. "I promise never to threaten to smash you again."

Jimson chuckled. "Now there is a reward indeed!"

There was another row of mirrors here, each reflecting a different interior. These did not have to be left covered, since no one but herself and her staff would ever see them. It was a pity they were all one-way, but having that many mirror-passages concentrating their magic within the walls of a single building was dangerous enough without making them work in both directions. She stepped through the one that deposited her just outside her workroom and put Jimson's mirror on a table just outside the door.

Just as the workroom of a worker of darkness stank, the workroom of a Fairy Godmother generally was awash with heavenly scents, and Lily's was no exception. Because each Godmother was a little different, each used a different "signature" base for her potions, and each worked her magic in different ways, you could often identify one of them merely by the scent of her room. Not necessarily the potions themselves, because by the time you got done concocting, the potion was often odorless and tasteless, but definitely the scent of the room.

In Lily's case, the main note was the cool sweetness of April Lilies. Beneath that was mint, just enough to keep the lily scent from being cloying; lavender to cut it further; and a hint of Elflock, which only grew in the Fae realms. Most of her potions used that formula for a base. For Lily, the scent was always that of home, her own comfortable and secure castle.

She stepped inside the room, which was actually two rooms divided by a wall, both heavily warded and shielded against interference of any kind, and against what went on within them. Neither room had windows, and both were lit by an enchantment on the ceiling itself. The Potions Room looked like the still-room in any noble house, save only that there was a great deal more of the apparatus than was ever in such a room——glass vessels, small ovens, crucibles, alembics, beakers, glass pipes, funnels, little charcoal braziers over which a single item could be simmered.... Walls and floor were stone, impervious to just about anything that could end up tossed against them. Sometimes there were accidents; a bit of miscalculation, and the next thing you knew, you were looking for a broom. Sometimes...well, sometimes Lily's temper got the better of her, and when things had gone wrong repeatedly, as they sometimes did...a broom was definitely in order.

The other room, entered through a door in the Potions room, was also stone-walled and stone-floored, and completely bare, except for the three magical circles inlaid in the floor. The outer one was gold, the middle, silver, the innermost one, electrum. They were not complete; there were bridge-pieces that could be placed in the empty groove in the floor to complete and seal them. This was a great deal more certain than drawing your circles out in chalk and hoping you didn't scuff them—because there could be something you would contain in there that you really would not want to get out. Or something outside the circles that you really did not want to get in. Lily had not been in either case very often—only a handful of times in three hundred years—but those times had been more than enough to cause her to be happy for such sturdy precautions.

In the right corner was a mannequin, in the left was a cupboard that contained the items Lily needed for spell-casting, and that was all that was in this room.

Now a sleeping potion was one of the easiest to concoct. It was also one of the most common. Virtually any common village witch could make one, and make a good one. There were perfectly good reasons to administer one to someone, if they were unable to sleep.

Of course, that was usually not why someone wanted one. Spouses wanted to be able to sneak out on their mates. Thieves wanted to make their jobs easier. Courtesans wanted to render their customers unconscious to rob them. The list of good reasons was shorter than the list of bad ones, so most of the trade in such things was confined to the…less than scrupulous. Nevertheless, it was something that was in Lily's arsenal, too.

Be that as it may, it was not a sleeping potion, as such, that was wanted here, not this time. At this point, it looked as if the easiest path to manage was the Snowskin Path, rather than the Beauty Sleeping Path. Therefore, what she needed was a potion to simulate death. And that was a far, far more difficult thing to manage.

In the Snowskin tale, the heroine was rendered insensible by a poison of some sort, and it was only the intervention of The Tradition that kept it from actually being fatal. It took a *lot* of magic to do that, more magic than even Lily had at her disposal. So she was going to have to simulate what was wanted, the hard way.

You had to slow breathing and heartbeat to almost nothing. Which was fine, a perfectly reasonable and not *terribly* difficult thing to do. Except that you had to do it without damaging the person you'd given the potion to. The human body—or most any body for that matter—does not like trying to exist on very little air or without the blood flowing at the right pace in the veins. Terrible things can happen when a magician does that without thinking; the poor victim ends up, once revived, with damage everywhere. Mostly, damage to the mind. You not only had to slow the breathing and heartbeat, you had to slow everything else down, so that the body no longer needed that much to live on.

So, strictly speaking, you weren't making a sleeping potion, or even a "this looks like death" potion. You were making a slowing potion.

And that was very, very difficult indeed. You would think with so much magic about such things would be easier! But more often than not, magic only complicated an already-knotted situation.

This was why most of the time, when these things were applied as curses, they were done so as spells rather than potions, with a trigger and a possibility of a release. The "Beauty Dreaming" for instance—that was a simple sleeping spell, no need to feign death there. Touch a finger to the object, draw blood—that triggers the spell, instant sleep. There it was, simple. And because, by the way that The Tradition worked, if a release had not been built in, The Tradition would *put* one in there. The Tradition did not like absolute curses with no way out. The more powerful the curse, the more likely it was that The Tradition would arrange the commonest release, that the Prince passes all the trials, and kisses the Beauty, and all is well.

The potion was going to take some time to brew. Well enough, during that time she could go impersonate the Evil Stepmother impersonating the Helpful Old Woman. Right now, Rosa looked like five miles of bad road. Under all the bruises and dirt, she still was the fairest in the land, but only The Tradition would have been able to tell that. All well and good, but to make the sleep spell easier to lift, she was going to have to *look* like the Beauty Asleep.

Lily shook her head as she selected the components for her base, and began compounding. It was a wonder that more Godmothers didn't go mad.

However, not so bad really, because the Helpful Old Woman would be doing the work Rosa was supposed to be doing, making it possible for her to get a good bath, clean herself up, heal up all the bruises and look like a Princess again. Rosa would have to *feel* like a Princess for everything to work just right.

Hopefully the Dwarves were inclined to ignore anything that didn't affect them.

She set up the workbench in the middle first, then the ones against the walls, with three stations on each of the wall benches, and four on the bench in the middle. The Brownies began arriving with the ingredients, and Lily started the thirteen separate components that would eventually be combined to make her slowing potion. Oh, and of course every one of those components had a cantrip or a minor spell that had to be cast on it, and you had more cantrips to cast when you combined them. And they had to be combined at the right time. And the right temperature. And it went without saying, in the right order.

She left it all simmering or chilling or bubbling away, with a Brownie team keeping an eye on it all. The first lot would be ready tomorrow.

Time for her illusion cloak.

She placed a plain cloak on the mannequin as she carefully concocted the illusion she wanted associated with this cloak. First, the general shape of the body under it—round, matronly, sturdy. Since she could see through the vast majority of illusions, she clearly saw the mannequin under what she was doing, but atop it, she also clearly saw the shape of an old peasant woman's body. At this stage it looked a great deal like a doll made of dough.

She tinted the dough with a healthy skin color, weathered and rosy. This was the stage at which most people began to be unnerved, because her creation was starting to look too much like a person for comfort.

Next, she added the clothing—it would be much easier not to do that, since she had so many costumes in her extensive wardrobe that it was a step she could easily skip, but she also wanted the Traditional impact of throwing off the cloak and revealing her true self. It was just another way of making The Tradition do what she wanted.

So she added another layer over the skin-colored body—a set of worn, sturdy leather shoes; heavy woolen stockings; a patched linen petticoat; the fustian skirt, also patched, over that; and a clean, crisp, embroidered apron over that. Then the clean, slightly threadbare linen blouse, the embroidered black felt vest. She walked around it, examining it from all sides. Kalinda, who had done this many times before, did the same.

"It's very solid, Godmother," the little Brownie said, then moved in to check closer. Lily's vision of what was *really* there showed Kalinda reaching out and fingering air; her vision of the illusion showed her checking the weight and feel of the apron, the skirt, the blouse and the vest. You actually had to know how these fabrics felt and acted in reality to replicate them in illusion. The simplest illusions, and the easiest to break, were the ones that acted only on the eyes. The best extended to all senses. Kalinda sniffed.

"Smells just right, too, Godmother," she said with satisfaction. "Just perfect. Like you'd washed it all and left it to dry in the sun, then put it away with some lavender."

"Excellent. Hands now, I think."

"Right-oh." Kalinda held hers out as models.

Kalinda was a Brownie accustomed to hard work, and her hands showed it. There were tiny scars, the nails were groomed but uneven and the thumb was a bit chipped. The skin was brown, there were calluses in the right places from using household implements, and the middle two knuckles of the right hand were just a little scraped. Lily replicated all of that for her illusion.

Now the head. First, gray hair, long, neatly braided, fastened up on the top of the head in a sort of crown. Over that—because in this kingdom no respectable married woman or widow went with her head uncovered—a faded red kerchief, tied under the nape. Kalinda checked those details for feel, while she went to work on the face.

She tried never to duplicate the face of someone living, but she *had* been alive for three centuries, and she had met a great many people in that time. So she considered her options, and chose an old woman who had been the nursemaid for Prince Sebastian some two hundred years ago.

She stepped back and examined the kindly face she'd created, adding a few more wrinkles, a couple of moles that hadn't been on the original's face, and making the forehead just a little lumpy. There. This was the point where people sometimes back uneasily out of the room, because this *looked* like a person, only one without any life.

Then Lily untied the cloak, swirled it around her shoulders, and tied it in place.

She didn't feel any different, but when she looked down at herself, she saw the illusion like a transparent layer over her own body. She walked, bent, jumped a little, trotted back and forth, until Kalinda nodded.

"It's solid, Godmother. Unless someone stronger comes along to dispel it, you should be all right."

Lily breathed a sigh of relief and pulled the cloak off. "In that case," she said, "it's time to get to work. Back to the Palace. Queen Sable needs to cement her hold over the Kingdom, or The Tradition will probably do something on its own."

Siegfried von Drachenthal considered himself to be a very lucky Hero, so far. Hero, because, well, he did Heroic things: slew dragons—only the evil, plundering, destructive ones of course, and only the ones that couldn't be reasoned with—defeated wicked knights, drove out bloodthirsty barbarians, destroyed rampaging giants and killed every manner of monstrous beast that your average village was having problems with. He hadn't rescued any Princesses yet…but there was a reason for that. He *had* come to the aid of a prince or two, a lot of counts, one duke and assorted adventurers. But not Princesses. On the whole, he was trying to avoid Princesses, just on general principle. He could not afford to have the wrong sort of Princess fall in love with him.

At the moment, having crossed over the eastern border of a mountainous Kingdom he was hacking his way through the undergrowth of a forest that seemed to go on for an awfully long way. There were all sorts of rumors of war in this area, and war was a good way to do heroic deeds without the complications of princesses or even maidens in distress.

The first woman that young Siegfried had ever seen was one of his aunts. So was the second. And the third. And the fourth.

And, truth to tell, every other woman up to the point where he left his childhood home of Drachenthal. When your mother and father are also your aunt and uncle, things tend to be complicated that way. When both are half-godlet, and both blessed and cursed by other gods, things get even more complicated.

Such things generally lead to a life of Heroism and Doom. The Heroism part was enjoyable enough. It was the Doom part that Siegfried wasn't too fond of. Doom was generally painful, and there was never anything good when it was over, unless you were a religious fanatic who was really looking forward to the afterlife.

"So, this Kingdom is rich?" he asked his companion, a little, brown, nondescript bird. Heroes didn't usually have any interest in birds, and the names and categorization of them were generally limited in a Hero's education to "good to eat," "not good to eat," and "singing while I have a hangover, kill it with a rock."

Birds don't snort, but the bird, which he just thought of as forest bird, since that was where he had met it, made a derisive chirp. "This Kingdom is rich in the way that Eitri's Forge is a little warm."

"Well, that's good," Siegfried said with relief. "Hero work doesn't exactly pay well. Maybe if I smite enough of whoever is on the side of evil, they'll give me a reward."

Now those who are destined for a life of Heroism often begin it precociously early, often as a mere baby, with little events like strangling great serpents in the cradle—the Hero's cradle, not the serpent's. Siegfried had been no exception to that. But from everything he'd learned since, the rate of his Heroic development had overshot all others by leaps and bounds. Where other Doomed Heroes waited until their beards had begun to sprout, their voices to descend to rich baritone or melodious tenor, and they began to manifest a distinct interest in Females before slaying their first evil, gold-hoarding dragon, Siegfried had done so much earlier.

Age ten, to be precise. The age when Girls are, Traditionally, Icky. Besides, the only Girls he knew were his aunts.

So, when he tasted the Dragon's Blood and suddenly could understand the language of all of the birds and animals, and when the little forest bird began talking sense to him instead of merely shouting "Look! Look! Look at meeeeeee!" he paid attention rather than merely making use of it as a glorified guide.

"Oh I wouldn't take *that*," the bird had warned as he reached for a particularly enticing golden ring. It was a beautiful thing. It glistened in the sunlight as if it was made of liquid, and it called to him. It whispered to him....

But it was, after all, a *ring*. Jewelry. Girlie stuff. So—"Why not?" he had asked the bird.

"Well, since you *ask*," the bird had replied, with incredible ebullience in its voice, "I'll tell you why!"

So he learned, well beforehand, that the ring would lead to power and glory—but also to a rather horrible death, being stabbed *in the back* of all wretched things, and worst of all...by a Girl. Not an aunt, but that didn't make it any better.

"Now on the other hand, if you just dip your sword in that blood and have another taste, you'll learn something worth knowing, and your sword will never break!" the bird had caroled. So he did. And he *did*. He still carried that sword; he'd been a very large boy at ten and strong for his age, as befitting a Hero, after all.

And at ten years old, Siegfried of Drachenthal learned that he had been a game piece all of his life in the metaphorical hands of The Tradition. That he was supposed to go and wake up a sleeping woman, that they would fall in love, and that this was going to lead to an awful lot of unpleasant things. And that if he didn't somehow find a way around it, he was Doomed.

At ten, Doom didn't seem quite as horrid a fate to try to avoid as a Girl was. But it seemed that by avoiding that one particular Girl, in those particular circumstances, who would be the first woman he had ever seen who was not an aunt, he would also avoid the Doom. So he did. He got away from Drachenthal, had the bird scout on ahead so that the first woman he ever saw was not his aunt but someone's lively old granny, and began searching for a way to have a Happy, rather than a Tragically Heroic, ending.

At twenty, the idea of a Girl all his own seemed rather nice, but

Doom was definitely to be avoided. He had begun to think about this, rather than just merely avoiding all sleeping women in fire circles wearing armor. Other Heroes ended up with Princesses, castles, happy endings, dozens of beautiful children. Why couldn't he?

The bird had been of the opinion that he ought to be able to, if he could trick The Tradition into confusing his fate with some other sort of Hero's. That sounded good to Siegfried. The other thing at twenty that was starting to have appeal was the idea that he could settle down somewhere. At the moment, the height of luxury for him was a reasonably vermin-free bed in a reasonably priced inn with decent meals and a good strong ale. He would look at palaces and castles and wealthy manors and sigh; the only time he ever saw the inside of one of those was if he'd been invited to a victory celebration, a recruitment—which half the time was into the service of evil, which was right out—or by someone who intended to kill him. So, it was two chances in four that he was going to get to enjoy a sumptuous meal, and not have to fight his way out of it before he got the first bite of roast peacock.

"So, in order to hoodwink The Tradition, all I have to find is someone blond, asleep in a ring of fire and flowers, who is *not* a Shieldmaiden demigoddess, and wake her up?" he was asking the bird, as he hacked his way through the underbrush with his ever-sharp, unbreakable sword.

"That's the basic idea," the bird said, fluttering from branch to branch beside him. "Really, if you were desperate enough, you could just find a nice little goose-girl, ask her to lie down for a quick nap, set the turf on fire and shake her awake to see if that worked."

"Do you really think it would?" he asked hopefully. He was getting rather tired of running from his fate. He'd had to flee at least six Kingdoms in the last year, six times he'd been wandering about a perfectly nice forest, looking for evil to conquer, and suddenly—*bang*—

there would be a clearing in front of him, with a stone slab in the middle of it, adorned with a beautiful sleeping woman dressed in armor of the gods, surrounded by rings of magic fire and flowers. He was beginning to wonder if it was the same woman every time, and The Tradition just kept moving her.

"I'd say it's worth a try. I think the wench with the bronze bosoms is stalking you." The bird was very cheerful about it. Then again, the bird wasn't going to share his Doom if he accidentally woke the woman up. "And you know, you *could* always give up the heroics and be a blacksmith. You'd be quite good at it. You've had the best teachers."

He had; Dwarves. They were about the best blacksmiths in the entire world, barring gods. And given what his fate was, he would really rather avoid gods. He'd forged his own sword from the remains of the one that his father had carried, in fact, the same year he slew the dragon. But—

"I don't know the first thing about horseshoes, or plowshares, or all those things farmers need," he replied, sadly. "I'd be a middling blacksmith for those purposes, and I really don't like it much. I like being a Hero and I'm good at it."

The bird chuckled. "And modest, too, just like a real proper Hero. No wonder Cast-Iron Cleavage is trying to get you to wake her up."

Siegfried shuddered. That last escape had been a very narrow one. "Where are we, anyway?"

The bird cocked her head to one side. "A rather nice little place," she said. "I believe it's called Eltaria."

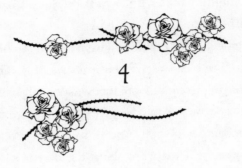

4

ROSA HAD NEVER THOUGHT OF HERSELF AS being weak—in fact, she had taken a great deal of pride in being able to keep up with the most enthusiastic of the hunters, the most energetic of games players, in the Court. When her mother had given her all those lessons in commonplace tasks, nothing had ever been beyond her strength or endurance.

The few times she had given the idea any thought, she had been quite certain that she would have no difficulty whatsoever in being able to work side by side with any of the servants in the Palace, do their work, and be no more worn out at the end of the day than they were.

By her second day with the Dwarves she knew how wrong she was.

Even though she was doing the barest minimum that she could get away with, the work she was doing was hard, backbreakingly hard. It had never looked that hard when the servants were doing it. She was exhausted by the time the Dwarves went to their beds, and fell asleep immediately. She was tired within a few hours of getting up in the morning, and everything ached.

The Dwarves had produced more clothing for her to clean and mend today, hauling it out of chests where it had been so long that the folds were actually stiff. She was listlessly spreading the boiled shirts out on bushes to dry, when something entirely unexpected made her look up, startled.

"Hello the house!" called a cheerful, slightly cracked voice. "Anyone here?"

For a moment, she didn't know what to do. Then she answered. "In the back garden?" Her own voice was hoarse, and sounded strange to her; it was so rough and full of fear it sounded as if it belonged to someone else.

Around the corner of the cottage came a perfectly ordinary-looking old woman, one with a sweet and kindly face. She wore the sort of clothing peasants did: patched and worn, but very clean. She carried a basket over one arm—and Rosa could not for a single moment imagine where she had come from.

But when she spotted Rosa, her hand flew to her mouth, and her eyes widened in consternation. "Oh deary me!" she exclaimed, hurrying over to where Rosa was standing, dumbfounded. "Those wretched, wretched Dwarves! Wicked things! What have they done to you, poor child?"

"I—ah—"

The woman put her basket down, words pouring out of her in a perfect torrent. "I talk to my bees you know, bees, terrible gossips they are, but usually accurate, and today they told me, yes they did, that the Dwarves had a new servant girl, and I couldn't imagine anyone serving the likes of *them* on her own, or at least not without being tricked into it, and they wouldn't part with a groat so they couldn't have *hired* a girl, so I hurried *right* over to see what I could see, knowing that she'd be all alone during the day, and I said to myself, 'Maggie, you must see what they're doing to the girl, if there even is a girl, and see if it's a Dwarf girl or a human one, and how she managed to get tangled up with *those* Dwarves,' so I did, you see, and here you are and here I am and good *gracious* look at you, you poor thing!"

As she spoke she was fussing over Rosa, looking at her cut, bruised, and now-burned hands, patting her hair away from her face, tugging at her dirty clothing. "I...was running away and they grabbed me," Rosa managed, finally, a certain alarm rising in her, for she thought she recognized this situation as a Traditional Path—but how could anything be worse than the situation she was already in? "I asked them for help, and told them I'd do anything—"

"Ah, and the horrible things called it a *bargain,* did they?" The old woman frowned. "They would, and they'll use that to hold you here as long as they like. Well! I'm Old Maggie the bee lady. Aren't I, my sweets? And good little things you were to tell me about this poor, poor little wench!"

While she had been speaking every bee in the garden had left what it was doing to come circle about her as if the old woman was some kind of enormous, fragrant flower. She held up her index finger, and one of the bees landed on it, vibrating its wings to make a buzzing that almost sounded like speech.

"You *are* my brave little workers, so you are," she said tenderly. The bee flew toward the old woman's face, making Rosa flinch, and touched its head to the tip of the old woman's nose before flying off. The rest of the bees went back to their business.

And a thought managed to make its way up out of the depths of Rosa's exhaustion-fogged mind. *No bee will abide in the presence of evil.*

So whoever, whatever she was—this "Old Maggie" was a friend.

Rosa burst into tears.

About an hour later, for the first time in days, Rosa was feeling better. Old Maggie chattered nonstop, making it almost impossible to get a word in, but that wasn't so bad, because it meant Rosa didn't have to say anything herself.

As for the rest, Maggie had taken charge of the entire situation. She'd tested Rosa's manacle and chain herself, said a very ladylike curse and pronounced herself "fair gobsmacked," which Rosa assumed meant she was baffled. Out of the basket had come a lovely little loaf and end of ham, a pot of honey and the sort of salad that a woods-wise person can make if she knows what's edible—a great deal of watercress, some crisp roots, a little sorrel, some tender goosegrass and a few edible flowers. That alone would have convinced Rosa that the old woman was what she seemed to be. She could not begin to imagine her Stepmother recognizing any of that, much less knowing it was good to eat.

Now all that food was inside Rosa; she sat combing her hair, working the tangles and knots out with a comb that Maggie had produced from a skirt pocket, while Maggie "Set the kitchen to rights."

It looked almost like magic. Truly. Somehow Maggie had gotten the ancient mop, which was as stiff as wood, to soften. She'd gone into the cellar and returned with a dirt-encrusted box which she declared with glee had soap in it—and so it did. She had already scrubbed the table, the sink and the counter, and the grime had just dissolved away. It was rather hard to tell, because the wood and stone were so stained and blackened that they didn't look much different, but if you touched them you knew the difference. Now she was doing the same with the floor.

"This soap is nasty stuff, my duck, strong but nasty," she chattered. "Wonderful for floors, but not so nice for you, pretty. Old Maggie will just—"

Then she stopped, tilting her head to the side. A bee had just flown in the open door and was buzzing at her. Her face took on an expression of alarm.

"My land, one of those horrible Dwarves is coming!" She bustled over to Rosa, but Rosa was already on her feet, shoving the comb into her pocket. Her mind seemed a thousand times clearer now, and it was obvious what she needed to do. She took the mop from Maggie, and Maggie whisked out the door.

A few moments later, Coward bumbled inside. He looked about and grunted, threw the morning's catch on the table, shoved her roughly aside and helped himself to the remains of the porridge in the pot on the hearth. When he had eaten it all and scraped the pot clean, he went out again. A short while later, Old Maggie reappeared and took the mop from Rosa.

"You just get your poor hair unsnarled, pretty," she said, head bobbing. "And you leave the rest of this mopping to Old Maggie, and after your hair is set to rights, I'll be cleaning while you deal with those poor conies. Tomorrow I'll bring you some *nice* soap so you can be getting yourself clean."

Being clean again sounded heavenly; Rosa worked industriously at the tangles in her hair so that Old Maggie wouldn't start cleaning the rabbits herself. The closer she got to her head, the fewer tangles there were, so by the time Maggie was about two-thirds done, she was at the butchering. And Maggie kept chattering.

"Trust me, my duck, we'll work on getting that shackle off and getting you away. But that takes doing, and Old Maggie will have to be at some hard thinking, and you, too." The mopping was done, and so was the butchering. The two of them added the meat to the simmering vegetables; after some consideration, Maggie threw in a couple handfuls of flour.

"That'll thicken the broth so it's more stew and less soup. Fill them up and make 'em less likely to beat you." The old woman held out her hand for the comb, and with a sigh, Rosa handed it to her. "You might boil those shirts with that soap. They won't look any better, but they'll stink less. I'll be back in the morning, ducky, yes I will. Old Maggie keeps her promises!"

The old woman moved faster than Rosa would have thought she could. She was out the door and out of sight around the front of the cottage before Rosa got into the garden.

Her throat got tight for a moment when she realized she was alone again. She might have cried…

But she fought back the tears and straightened. *Some* sort of help had finally come. It wasn't a handsome prince, or a brave shepherd, or a wise hunter. But it was help, and it was welcome, and if Old Maggie was just a little crazy, she was also very clever. A handsome prince probably wouldn't be able to beat the craft of her shackle, either, and would have done nothing about the floor, her hair or her empty stomach.

On the whole…if The Tradition had finally elected to do something for her, it could have done a lot worse than Old Maggie.

Rosa went and got a spoonful of that harsh soap, stirred it into the kettle outside and put the shirts back in as the old woman had suggested.

Siegfried von Drachenthal stood over the remains of a boar roughly the size of a horse—or rather, leaned against the spear that was still sticking out of said remains. As Heroing tasks went, it had been an average one, but that didn't mean it hadn't been a tough fight. He was looking forward to a big flagon of mead and a slice of this fellow, nicely roasted and served with applesauce. And a bath. Definitely a bath.

The peasants whose lands had been ravaged by the Black Boar of Brimsdale approached with commendable caution. They hadn't really believed it when Siegfried had promised he would kill it.

The astonished looks on their faces were quite gratifying.

"You slew the beast!" the village mayor said, gaping at it, then him, then it again.

"I said I would." He shrugged. "It's what I do."

"How can we ever repay you?" blurted an old woman whose fields had been ruined. "You've done what the King would not!"

"Could not, Mother Crey," the mayor admonished. "The King can't be in two places at once, and there's war a-brewing again. He'd have come if he could. He's done so before, and you know it well!"

Now Siegfried straightened, and let go of the spear. This was news to him, and truth to tell, good news. Here he had been doing this King a disservice by assuming he was just a neglectful monarch. But a war—that meant more work for a Hero. And it was a good reason for the King to be busy. "War, you say?"

Many heads nodded. "We've greedy neighbors," the mayor said bitterly. "They'd like nothing better than to swallow us whole—"

He looked as if he was going to make a good long speech, but Siegfried raised his hand to stop him. "Then this is what you can do to repay me. Give me a good meal, a soft bed and provisions, then set me on the road to the King's hall. And tell me about this war while we eat."

The peasants gaped, as if they couldn't believe they were getting off that lightly. The mayor especially had a look on his face like a stunned calf. "But—"

Siegfried patted him on the shoulder. "There's a good fellow. I am a Hero. This is what I do. And right now, I am a hungry Hero and one in great need of a bath, as well. So let's have a feast and you can tell me about your land and its troubles. Besides—" he laughed "—Kings can afford to pay better than farmers. I shall tell him about the Boar, and let *him* reward me."

Now he was speaking words they understood; well of course he was going to claim a big reward, but it would be from the King and not from them. With a shout of approval, some went for a cart to carry off the Boar, while the rest carried Siegfried off in triumph to the Inn where the bird waited, perched on the rooftop, singing happily.

The next day, as soon as Coward left for his rounds, Rosa went out into the garden. This time Old Maggie was preceded by a veritable cloud of bees that swarmed around the garden and through the cottage before vanishing. Maggie appeared a moment after they had left.

"They're my little clever guardians, ain't they, then?" Maggie said triumphantly. "And if they *find* some nasty old Dwarf a-lyin' abed, well! All *he'll* think when he sees bees is that they're a-swarming, and all he'll think to *do* is to hide himself under the blanket lest he get stung!"

She cackled, and Rosa managed a laugh, herself.

"Now!" The old woman had a much bigger basket this time, strapped to her back. Out of it she pulled an old, threadbare, but immaculately clean shift, which she handed to Rosa, and a chunk of pinkish-purple soap. "Off with them clothes, pretty, and put this on. Into the cauldron with them and a piece of this—" She handed Rosa the soap. "No need to boil, just get the water warm, like, and then we'll stir, stir, stir."

Rosa scrubbed and rinsed, scrubbed and rinsed; wished she could wash her hair, too, but at least it wasn't matted up like a wild sheep's wool. Finally, as she put the shift back on over skin so clean it felt new, she asked, "Have you heard any news? I heard that the King has a new wife—"

"I only hear what the bees tell me, and they don't care for Kings nor Queens, no more what they do," Maggie said dismissively. "Nor should you. Kings and Queens and their doings ain't for the likes of us."

Disappointed, Rosa agreed rather weakly. The two of them got to work on the minimum that the Dwarves were likely to expect, which was finished in plenty of time for them to take the slightly damp clothing, mend the tears with needles and thread that Maggie produced from her basket, and for Rosa to put it on again before Coward made his lunchtime appearance.

Maggie returned when he had gone, handed Rosa a meat-and-vegetable pasty, and gathered up the soap, the shift and the comb.

"You look as good as new, don't you, pretty!" she exclaimed, as she helped Rosa braid up her hair in a more tidy fashion. "And Maggie may have some good news for you tomorrow, yes she might! So keep your pretty head down, and don't call attention to yourself, and we'll see what the morning brings, aye!"

Once again, she whisked around the corner and out of sight before Rosa even got a chance to ask what she meant.

The potion was done. Tomorrow Lily would see if the time was right to reveal herself twice over. Tonight, thanks to the bespelled soap, Rosa was safe, still looking like the filthy thing that she had been yesterday. That wasn't a powerful spell and it *would* wear off; the trick was to make sure it didn't wear off until after the Dwarves got rid of what they thought was a dead girl.

Lily went to bed torn between anticipation and apprehension. With all of the potential of this situation, it wouldn't take much to unbalance it. She only hoped that she and Jimson were fast enough to get The Tradition to work with them, instead of against them.

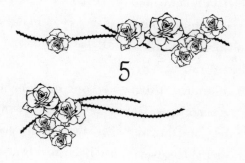

5

LILY WAS VERY GLAD THAT SHE HAD A GREAT deal of
experience behind her, for she could not imagine trying to juggle all
of this two hundred years ago—or even only a hundred.

She was back in the Palace, in the persona of Queen Sable, who
had somehow not gotten around to telling the King that his
daughter was missing. Or so everyone thought, for everyone
seemed to be sending clandestine messages to the King at the
northern border.

In actuality, she *had* told him the moment that she knew where
Rosa was. She'd gone in person, assured him that she had the situation in hand and that Rosa was safer with her seven Dwarvish guardians than she was in the Palace, where someone was certainly trying
to murder or abduct her. She had lied a little. She'd not told him the
conditions that Rosa was in. Eventually, she supposed, it would have
to come out, unless she could enlist Rosa in perpetuating the lie, but
for right now it was better that he had in his mind the Traditional
picture of the happy Princess playing at housekeeping amid a throng
of adoring Dwarves. And since *she* was the Evil Stepmother, there

would be no danger of an old woman slipping her a poisoned comb, a strangling necklace, or a fatal bit of fruit or candy.

So the messages to the King were all going unanswered and unheeded, which only cemented the certainty of the rumors that she had placed a spell on him. This was fine. This was perfect, in fact. The Tradition would be satisfied with that, if such an insensate thing could be said to be satisfied.

The search continued, although no one had gone as far afield as the Dwarves' fetid cottage. The horse had been found, lame, wandering in the forest, and that was where the search was concentrated. No one, not even the Huntsman, had been able to trace back to the point where Rosa had parted company with the wretched beast. The storm that night had obliterated every sign. Lily had the shrewd notion that with the distance Rosa had tried her utmost to put between herself and where she had last seen the Huntsman, as well as the distance traveled underground by the Dwarves, it was extremely unlikely that anyone would ever have found her.

Of course, she had made certain of that now. Spells of confusion for the hounds worked wonders. So did false traces.

Her sturdy Guard Captains were sticking to the Huntsman as if they were all members of the same devoted family. His frustration was cheering to watch.

The interesting, and somewhat alarming, aspect to all of this was that he had not approached *her,* nor even tried. This meant he was almost certainly working for someone else; that was a very dark cloud on her horizon.

In the meantime, the Kingdom still needed to be governed, and the King was too busy facing down another army on the border to handle the day-to-day matters. And if Queen Sable was not beloved, she was certainly as good an administrator as Queen Celeste had been. She was rather better at quelling disputes among the nobles:

all she had to do was bend a cold and faintly murderous glare on the offending parties, and suddenly everyone remembered more important business.

The administrative tasks, thank goodness, could all be handled by her Brownies. They were good at that sort of thing, and they enjoyed it. Perhaps it had something to do with being able to issue orders that the Big Folks had to obey!

Thanks to Jimson keeping an eye on almost everyone through anything that reflected, she knew who was likely to give her trouble at any given audience. The murderous stare was the best weapon in her arsenal, and she used it freely today. By the time she dismissed them, there wasn't a soul who would have dared to offer a petition, complaint or even a comment. The Lesser Audience Chamber was as silent as a tomb.

"Is there any more business?" she asked. No one spoke up. "Very well. This session is concluded. May King Thurman be successful in preventing war, and if he cannot prevent it, may he be victorious. All hail King Thurman."

The courtiers and petitioners mumbled a response of "Hail King Thurman," and quickly shuffled out.

She breathed a sigh, and hurried back to her rooms. It was time to become Old Maggie, the Bee-Woman. This was perhaps the easiest disguise she had ever donned, other than the complicated illusion itself. She liked bees, and bees liked her. Best of all, perhaps, bees never caused her any problems.

She stepped through the mirror in the Queen's Chambers into the Hall of Mirrors, picked up the cloak and the basket with the potion bottle in it from where she had left them and stepped through a new mirror, a temporary one, that she had set up just for this purpose. She stepped out of an identical mirror incongruously leaning against a tree. How it got there, she had no idea; the Brownies had managed it for her, as the Brownies managed so much for her. They had their own rules and their own magic—if she was able to give them a day or so to do their work, they could accomplish amazing things. If not, though— well, that was where the ingenuity of a Godmother had to come in.

She shook out the cloak and pulled it on, feeling the persona of Maggie settle into place. The bees began to gather about her immediately. They told her with their dancing that the Dwarves were all gone and Rosa was alone.

She sent the bees on ahead of her, made her way down a mostly overgrown path, and came around the corner of the building. Rosa's face lit up to see her, and she felt a lovely warmth to see it. If they managed to get through this, she knew that she and Rosamund would have an especially close relationship, perhaps making up for the fact that she had held aloof for all of Rosa's childhood.

Rosa looked as if she was on tenterhooks, and well she might be. "I believe I have a solution," Lily said gravely. "But first...you should know I have been deceiving you, though never with malice."

She whipped off the cloak. Rosa gaped at her, blinking. "God-mother Lily!" was all she could manage. She stared, as if she couldn't believe it. "But—oh. Yes, of course. You're trying to force the Tra-ditional Snowskin Path, right?"

"Exactly. Which is why I am also Queen Sable."

If the revelation that Old Maggie was really Godmother Lily had been a shock, this left Rosa reeling.

"There were three women vying for the title of Evil Stepmother while your father was staying with Perrin," she continued, as she watched Rosa try to absorb this revelation and process it. "Three gen-uinely Evil Sorceresses. No matter how much Thurman was pro-tected, it was clear that sooner or later someone was going to take him down that path. So I became just what The Tradition wanted."

"You married my father?" Rosa said incredulously.

"In name only." She smiled wryly. "Is all this making sense to you?"

Rosa suddenly sat on a stump. "I—think so," she replied after a moment. "This is all very sudden."

Lily spread her hands wide. "We were swiftly running out of time to act. This was a joint decision."

"It would have to be." Rosa looked dazed. "Is Father all right? Is there a war? Is—"

"Your father is as well as he can be, there is no war yet, and I've kept him informed as soon as I knew where you were and what was happening to you."

Relief spread over Rosa's face. "Well, I assume you can snap the chain? Break the manacle lock?"

Lily shook her head. "Unfortunately, no. When a Dwarf makes a chain to hold something, believe me, it stays held. They have a magic with metal that even I don't dare meddle with. But I do have a plan to release you, one that will follow the Snowskin Path."

Rosa made a face, but didn't object. "Well, I am glad you told me. I think if I had suddenly found myself paralyzed, I'd have gone mad. The Huntsman was bad enough." She frowned a little more. "But if the Huntsman isn't yours, who does he belong to?"

"Something I am trying very hard to find out," Lily replied. "But let me explain what I have in mind now. The Dwarves will come home and find you dead. After they make sure this isn't a trick, they won't want to have a corpse on their hands, and I fully expect them to unchain you and dump you somewhere in the forest. I'll be watching them. I'll have you taken to a safer place, and lift the spell. We'll decide together what to do from there." It looked as if Rosa was taking this much better than Lily had dared to hope. In fact, the bees were calmly circling both of them, visiting the flowers among the weeds, yes, but keeping them in a protective ring. A good sign. She sat on the grass near Rosa. "If I'd had any notion that the

Huntsman was going to attack you so soon, I would have put more effort into keeping a watch over you, or told you what was going on."

The girl smiled wanly. She was certainly game, and resilient. "And if you had, something else would have happened. I've had a bad time, but it could have been much worse. It was Dwarves who found me. It could have been robbers, who wouldn't have thought me too ugly to touch."

Lily shuddered. "From this moment on, I pledge you, you will be entirely in my confidence. I'd also like you to wear this at all times." She pulled a bracelet out of her pocket and handed it to Rosa. Hanging from the fine silver chain was a piece of obsidian cut *en cabochon*. By Eltarian standards, this was a mere trinket, the sort of thing a milkmaid could own. The back of it had been polished to a mirror finish. Rose examined it curiously, then put it on. "As long as you wear that, I can find you."

Rosa nodded, and fingered it nervously. "So—what do I do?"

Lily took out the potion. "Drink this. That's all. The next time you see me, you'll be free, and we'll plan what we should do from there."

Rosa's hand shook, but she took the bottle, screwed up her face and drank it down. Before she even reacted to the pleasant taste, Lily cast the net of the sleeping spell on her, the strands of it sparkling a little in the sunlight. She caught the girl as Rosa started to topple over, and laid her gently on the grass.

Lily did not trust to the reflective properties of the little pendant; she left a fragment of broken mirror propped among the weeds of the garden, in a position to reflect Rosa's image. With that in place, she escaped the scene, returning to her larger mirror. She took Jimson's mirror out of the basket, and settled down to wait.

"You timed things well," Jimson remarked, as the Dwarf that Rosa called Coward shambled into the garden, rabbits dangling from one hand, then stopped and frowned.

"Wake up, lazy ugly!" the Dwarf shouted. "No time to sleep!"

When Rosa didn't respond, his face grew red with anger. He stormed toward her and kicked her. Lily winced as Rosa's body rolled over, head lolling. The Dwarf drew back his foot to kick her again, then realized that there was something very wrong. He bent over, felt her face and cursed.

Rabbits forgotten, he lumbered for the kitchen and the staircase down into the cellar and the secret mine.

Sometime later, all seven of the Dwarves emerged from the kitchen, to Coward's babbling and gesturing. Bully cuffed him into silence, and went to examine Rosa himself. By this time, her body was getting cold.

After assuring himself that she really was dead, Bully vented his spleen in a round of cursing, blaming Coward in part for the loss of their house-slave. Coward cringed away, as Bully stomped angrily around the garden, cursing the Dwarf, Rosa and anything else he could think of.

Finally he threw up his hands. "Got to get that thing out of here," he said with exasperation. "Spent all day digging, last thing I want to do is dig a hole. You, and you—" He pointed to Coward and Angry. "Haul it away, dump it in a ditch."

"Who'll make supper?" Deaf whined.

In answer, Bully spun him around and marched him into the kitchen, with the rest following.

"Are you marking their passage, Jimson?" Lily whispered, as Jimson switched the view from the fragment of glass to the pendant around Rosa's neck.

"Easily, Godmother. Best go bring your Brownies through. I doubt they'll bother carrying her too far." She could almost hear Jimson's lip curl with contempt. "I must say that I have seldom seen seven beings less inclined to do anything more than the barest minimum they need to get by."

"Nor have I." She stepped through her mirror to find six of her strongest lads waiting. Now, breaking the spell was going to require more dancing around what The Tradition was trying to do. The Tradition dictated that where Snowskin was laid out in state—and eventually awakened—should be technically within reach of where the Dwarves lived, so they could all go mourn her, periodically. Never mind that this lot was far more likely to give up their illegal mine and form a kitten-rescue society than go and mourn over the body of a virtual slave. The Tradition had to be satisfied. So Lily couldn't bring Rosa back to the safer environs of her own Palace for this; it all had to be done in the woods. Also, The Tradition dictated it be in a forest glade where beams of sunlight could illuminate her lovely form. This also somewhat limited where she could do her work.

Never mind. It was worth all the fuss and bother, since so far, all that fuss and bother had managed to keep Rosa alive.

Unfortunately, Siegfried's triumphant leave-taking from the village of the boar had been marred when he ran across the only thing he feared, lying in a meadow just outside of town.

His Doom. The sleep-charmed Warrior Maid in her ring of fire. He had fled in the opposite direction as if an entire clan of dragons were after him. It was a good thing he'd had the bird to guide him, or he would have gotten completely lost in this forest.

"You don't suppose I could find a Prince about to awaken a Beauty Asleep and trade girls with him, do you?" he asked her. If only it were that easy! "You know, get him to leave the Beauty alone and come wake up the Shieldmaiden for me? Or maybe…do you suppose I could just hunt around for a wandering prince, then when You Know Who turns up again, shove *him* across the fire?"

"That's a puzzler. No one's ever tried," she replied. Then—"Hark!" The bird was always saying things like "Hark!" and "Lo!" and when it did, Siegfried generally found it advantageous to peer ahead up the trail…or as in this case, into the clearing they'd come upon.

And at first he thought it was Doom-Woman again, because yes, there was the ring of magic fire, and the ring of flowers, and the stone slab. But before he turned to run, he took a closer look.

It wasn't a woman on the slab; it was a really beautiful maiden. She *was* blonde, but she wore a gown, not armor. She didn't look frail, but she also didn't look like the sort that would be inclined to don armor and go whack at things on a daily basis. And she was asleep. He could scarcely believe his eyes, or his luck.

"Get her, Siggy!" chirped the bird, and nothing loath, he was halfway across the clearing before he noticed the sorceress.

And the other man.

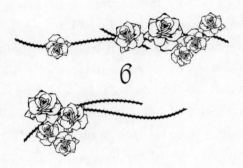

6

NOW WAS THE MOMENT TO DO SOME REAL magic. The spell to nullify the slowing potion was actually a lot more like a religious ritual, since it involved a great many symbolic components. First, Rosa had to be on something like a bier, to symbolize death, which was in turn a symbol for slumber.

One Princess on a stone slab, courtesy of some extremely strong Brownies.

She had to be illuminated by rays of sunlight, which symbolized the first rays of sunlight at dawn and the spring sun that brought the earth to life.

One Princess, bathed in a beam of sunlight streaming down through the surrounding trees.

There was the ring of rose petals and violets around the slab, which was supposed to symbolize the quickening of the earth in spring.

There was the flower crown for Rosa, which was supposed to symbolize any one of a hundred Goddesses of Spring, who would emerge from their winter slumber.

To symbolize the slowing effects of the potion, ideally one would want something that hibernated. Snakes and frogs were the easiest.

After some consideration, she used a serpent-shaped ring on her finger, and one on Rosa's.

She would create a circle of fire around the slab, to invoke both the cleansing power of fire to burn the potion away and the awakening power of the sun's rays.

And lastly, sprinkled all over the rock were various cleansing herbs, and the grit used to polish metal, which symbolized the cleansing of Rosa's body of the potion. Just for good measure, symbolizing itself, Lily had added the actual antidote to the potion, which would counter it, if the person in question had been awake and able to swallow it when they tasted it…which would have taken about a week.

They didn't have a week. Lily needed to get Rosa back to the Palace. If the King fell in battle, or even died of natural causes…it would be a race to figure out what to do next, at the very least, and having the actual, legal heir there would buy them some time.

She had just lit the ring of fire and begun the incantation part of the spell, when she spotted the two men, one on either side of the clearing—and the moment she saw them, they spotted each other.

The one on the right must have been from the north, farther north than Eltaria's northward neighbor. He was kitted out in the "hearty, fears-nothing" style that a lot of them favored up there—bronze breastplate, greaves and armbands, and not much else in the way of armor, short-sleeved brown leather tunic and leather trews that didn't quite match, brown fur boots, a huge broadsword slung on his back instead of at his side as was common here, and no shield. He was blond, with his hair just on the attractive side of shaggy, a ruggedly handsome face with a square chin, high cheekbones and a broad forehead. He was also tall, incredibly muscular, and with that powerful aura that told Lily "The Tradition is going to pound this lad into his Fate like a blacksmith pounding a horseshoe." And if it weren't for the fact that there was acute intelligence in those guileless blue eyes, she would have dismissed him without a second thought except for how to get Rosa awake and out of there as quickly as possible, because he was going to be a complication. A Prince most likely. And not a stupid Northern Barbarian one. But probably a penniless one. A complication, and one she and Rosa did not need right now.

The first thing that struck her about the other man was the look in his eyes; the minute she saw him, she knew. *This one is trouble.* "Trouble" of the rakish sort. There was a merry devil in those green eyes, and the carefully tousled look of his long brown hair, the dashing set of his battered hat, only reinforced what instinct told her. For the rest— he was as rakishly handsome as the other was ruggedly handsome. He was somewhat lighter in frame than the blond, but then, nearly every man she had ever seen would be. His clothing had been very, very good once, but had seen a lot of hard wear. So, another Prince, probably, but one just as penniless as the first one. And on top of that, the sort of fellow who brought a swarm of problems in his wake. Another complication, and more dangerous than the first.

Had The Tradition at that moment appeared before her in a material form, Lily would happily have beaten it with a stick. Here they were, drawn in without a doubt by The Tradition itself, and without a doubt they both wanted Rosa. They wouldn't listen to reason and how many *more* problems were they going to create besides the ones they brought with them? She didn't know *which* Paths they were following, and inserting themselves into all the problems of this Kingdom could bring down disaster on everyone!

The two men saw her, then saw each other. Since she looked like herself, she was clearly not a threat, and for the moment, they dismissed her. But both of them recognized a rival when they saw one. Their reaction was instantaneous; they both rushed for the stone slab where Rosa was.

When the blond recognized that the dark-haired one was likely to get there first, he put on a mighty effort, jumped like a horse heading over a fence and threw himself in the air. But not at Rosa; at his rival.

He managed to tackle the man just as he was about to cross the circle of fire and both of them went tumbling into the underbrush.

Lily continued the spell, because the last thing she wanted for either of these fellows was to awaken Rosa with a kiss. Once awakened by her spell, Rosa would be much less vulnerable. Out of the corner of her eye, she watched the two men wrestling each other; they rolled around on the grass like a couple of boys—*this is more like a tussle than a serious fight*. It seemed that neither of them wanted to hurt the other, so their efforts were confined to one attempting to get free and the other pulling him down. They weren't even trading blows. And there was a lot of shouting from both of them. The blond seemed desperately to be trying to make a bargain of some kind. The other was having none of this, yelling "Bugger off! I saw her first!"

Lily was not going to allow any of this to distract her, and she had three hundred years in spell-casting behind her to give her every ounce of the discipline she needed. She sketched sigils in the air with her wand and punctuated each with a twirl that sent a swirl of dustlike sparkles soaring through the air. This was something of a signature touch for her; it was a characteristic of the magic that most with Fae blood had, for Fae magic was visible even to ordinary folk. This was why stories were full of references to "fairy dust." As the men wallowed and shouted at each other, she concentrated on her magic, as drift after drift of sparkling power wafted over Rosa, and the scent of roses, violets and lilies intensified.

She finished the spell with a final arc of power that hung over Rosa like a rainbow dissolving into mist; she knew that it had worked when she saw Rosa's chest move. A few seconds later, the sleep spell wore off by itself.

For one moment, the men were silent, and in that silence, Rosa coughed.

Both men froze at the sound. Their heads turned as if they had been pulled by the same string, and they stared at Rosa, who was just raising her hand, slowly to her head. Her eyes weren't open yet, but her eyelids fluttered. Lily sighed in relief. Whatever happened now, the men were both too late for The Tradition to make a hash of this.

Evidently however, they didn't know this, or else they thought they were still in time to work the Traditional awakening. Both scrambled for purchase on the slippery grass. The dark one was just a bit faster than the blond. He squirmed away and leapt desperately for the groggy Princess, leaving the other grasping at where his heels had been.

Rosa did not so much fall asleep as...well, drop into oblivion. Her last thought, as she felt something very strange start to happen after drinking the potion, was to wonder, *was I tricked by Queen Sable into believing she was Godmother Lily, who was impersonating Queen Sable, who—*

Then, there was nothing.

Next, like a very heavy wagon being pulled by straining horses finally starting to move, hair by hair, she was *aware* the way a plant was aware, then her thoughts slowly formed again, floating up out of the dark pool of nothingness, following the path they'd been on when she stopped thinking altogether.

*—was pretending to be Old Maggie, who was really—*

She coughed, and her spinning thoughts came to a dead stop. So she hadn't been tricked? She realized she was awake again, and lying on something hard and flat, laid out neatly with her hands folded on her chest. She felt warmth on her skin that felt like sunlight, smelled flowers, heard someone running—

And then, out of nowhere, felt a mouth mashed against hers and a pair of hands on her breasts.

There was a single moment of feeling strangely *tingly* and an unfamiliar pleasure that warmed her in a way the sun did not.

But only a moment. Then she was galvanized with outrage. Her eyes flew open; all she saw was the cheek and brown hair of someone she certainly *did not* know, who was taking liberties that no one other than a husband had any right to take. Rage added to outrage. She did the only thing possible for a spirited young woman under such circumstances.

All in an instant, she made sure of where his groin was, which wasn't at all difficult considering how he was sprawled all over her. And she brought her knee up into it with all her strength. She was someone who had spent all of her life dancing, riding, walking, not a weak little thing that spent her days reclining on a couch, embroidering or listening to gossip. Her legs were strong, very strong.

The person taking the liberties was actually propelled over her head and off to the side by the force of the blow. As soon as his weight was gone, Rosa scrambled off the place where she had been lying. She tumbled from what turned out to be a stone slab and leapt to her feet, looking around herself for a weapon of any sort. She didn't see one, but she did see the Godmother, whose right eye was twitching, and who had both her hands over her mouth, her wand sticking out at a comical angle.

Rosa staggered over to her side, and turned toward her attacker, but it was obvious that he was in no shape to take any further liberties, and probably would not be for a good while. He was alternating between gasping and groaning and was curled up in a fetal position with both hands tucked between his legs. She felt a moment of intense satisfaction, seeing him like that. Served him right, taking liberties with a girl he thought couldn't defend herself.

Stifled laughter was leaking between Godmother Lily's fingers.

Surprisingly, Rosa felt a laugh bubbling up inside her, too, and she had to fight to suppress it.

There was a heavy, sorrow-filled sigh to her right; she glanced over, and realized there was a fourth person in this forest clearing.

A very blond, very large man picked himself up out of the grass and flung himself at her feet, babbling at her. She tried to sort out what he wanted, but his accent was so thick she couldn't understand a word he was saying. For a moment, Rosa wondered if she had gone mad, and this was all some delusion or other. Or maybe Coward had hit her over the head and this was some sort of brainstorm. Why else would she be standing in the middle of the forest with the Kingdom's Fairy Godmother and two men she had never seen before, one of whom didn't seem to be able to speak reasonable Eltarian, the other of whom was a libertine?

But his words definitely had an effect on the Godmother. She stopped trying to stifle her laughter and sobered, but as the blond man tried to grasp her hand she stepped back and snapped, *"Silence!"* Rosa's eyes widened. Granted, she had not seen Godmother Lily all that often, but she didn't ever recall the Godmother using that commanding tone of voice before. Nor one so overflowing with irritation.

The blond shut up abruptly, his guileless blue eyes going very wide indeed, and Lily strode over to Rosa's victim. She made a perfunctory gesture with her wand, one that didn't produce any of the usual fairy dust; and the man stopped groaning and slowly began to sit up.

"I—" he began.

"Shut up," snapped Lily. "Here is an order. I do not, ever, want to hear a sentence from you beginning with 'I' again. You very nearly ruined everything. So did you," she added to the blond, who dropped his chin and looked up at them both with a hang-dog gaze. She contemplated them both; her expression softened just a little, looking at the blond. Rosa looked from one to the other of the men. On the one hand, she wanted to feel sorry for the blond, and he hadn't yet done anything to her, but on the other, that was all she knew about him. For all she knew, he and the other man were confederates. She supposed that there might be a good explanation for why the dark-haired man had been doing what he had. She couldn't think of one— all right, granted, she had been asleep, and the Beauty Asleep was supposed to be awakened with a kiss, but it wasn't supposed to be *that* sort of kiss. "Both of you, get up," the Godmother ordered, looking frighteningly stern. "Stupid, interfering—I don't know why you're here. I don't know where you came from, but since you managed to insert yourself into this situation, you are coming along with us. I strongly suggest that if you do not care for this option, you pick yourselves up, start running and hope I don't feel like lobbing any curses at you. You might, *might,* be useful. But I am going to use you for target practice if you foul things up again. They are bad enough as it is."

Rosa almost gaped with astonishment. She had never, ever heard the Godmother talk like this! *Did* Godmothers ever actually curse anyone? Was that allowed? Why was she so angry with them? If The Tradition had brought them here, surely that wasn't their fault... was it?

Evidently neither man was intimidated enough to turn around and run. Either that, or for whatever reason, they had both decided that sticking with Rosa and the Godmother was very important. That probably meant that either The Tradition was beating heavily on *their* doors, or they saw an opportunity.

As soon as the blond was standing, a small, brown bird landed on his shoulder and twittered at him. The man listened for a moment, then spoke in a voice still heavy with an accent Rosa didn't recognize, but at least she could understand him this time. "Aye, I agree. Maybe we had just better go find a kindly little shepherdess."

She blinked. Had he been talking to the bird? And why would he need a shepherdess?

Lily fixed the big blond man with a glare that made him wilt. It was rather funny, actually, to see such a big man almost cringing in the face of the wrath of such a small woman. "Follow me," she barked. "And don't dawdle." That didn't make much more sense to Rosa than the man talking to the bird. A moment ago, Lily had told them to run...

Well they hadn't run, so perhaps Lily thought she was stuck with them.

The Godmother stalked off into the trees, her lace-edged skirts swishing with indignation, down a path that looked as if it had only recently been beaten into the grass. Rosa followed her closely, the men at a discreet distance. She was suddenly conscious of the fact that her gown was definitely the worse for her adventure, and that the "bath" she had had was a sketchy one at best. Fortunately it seemed that the aroma of the flowers, and not something a lot less pleasant, was what was lingering around her as they passed single-file through what was a very wild forest. The trees towered above them, fifty feet in the air, at least. It was gorgeous, actually, with golden beams of light slanting down through breaks in the foliage, lighting up the peaceful, green gloom. It was hard to believe that this was the same forest that had so terrified her in the storm.

At the end of the path was a huge wooden cart pulled by two glossy brown draft horses waiting in a primitive track, a couple of ruts in the grass that led through a kind of tunnel through the trees. The rear of the cart was full of very small men in earth-colored clothing. Rosa was extremely happy to see the cart, but she wondered just how the two strangers were going to take being told to ride in the bed with the tiny people. They didn't look like the sort who would take to that.

"I don't suppose either of you have horses?" Godmother Lily asked wearily, as she paused beside the cart with her hands on her hips. The two men shook their heads. She fixed them with glares again, as if she somehow suspected they had come without mounts on purpose to annoy her, then held out her hand to one of the men in the cart. "Mice, please," she said.

*Mice?* Rosa thought at first. Then she remembered. She grinned a little; if the men were not familiar with the Ella Cinders tales, they would have yet another surprise in store.

The little fellow reached under the seat, and brought out a little wooden cage with several mice in it. Rosa had thought that all mice were gray, but these seemed to also be black, brown, and some even had splotches of white. The Godmother started to reach in, when the mice squeaked and the blond spoke up.

"Excuse me, Lady Magician, but the brown one with one white foot says he would like to come out, and the fat black one says that he is up to my weight?" The man sounded very doubtful when he said this, and the Godmother looked at him, startled, then reached into the cage and let a brown and a black mouse climb up on their own into her hand. She put them on the ground, and waved her wand in a complicated pattern over the two mice. Little drifts of sparkles fell from the tip of her wand, like dust sparkling in a sunbeam. She swirled this stuff around and over them, and as she stepped back they began to grow and change.

Rosa watched with glee; for all that she had lived her entire life in Eltaria, and knew The Tradition better than any other girl her age except a Godmother-in-training, she had not seen much magic. She had certainly never seen the spectacular things that a Godmother could do when the power of The Tradition was behind her. Now, before her very eyes, in a few moments, the mice had transformed into horses, complete with saddles and bridles. The black one was the size of a draft horse, and the brown one with one white foot pawed the ground and bent his long neck into a graceful curve.

Their manes and tails flowed right down to the ground in silken falls
of shining hair. Now, having ridden real horses, Rosa was only too
well aware what a stupid idea that was—to allow a horse's mane and
tail to grow that long. On a real horse, they would be full of dirt and
leaves and burrs in no time at all and take hours to comb out again.
But of course, these were not "real" horses. These were, more or less,
the perfect idea of a horse, the most exaggerated dream of a horse
that there could be.

The two men were going to look positively shabby astride them,
but, oh well. Too bad for them.

She glanced over at the men; both of them had eyes as wide as
an owl's. So they weren't used to magic, either. Or at least, not this
sort of magic.

"Haven't you ever seen a Fairy Godmother do her magic before?
Don't stand there all day, get on!" Godmother Lily didn't quite snarl,
but her expression was very close to that of someone who was about
to take a head off. She tapped her wand against her side, impatiently.
The eyes of both men went to the wand, and Rosa had the notion
that they were wondering just what else she could do—to them—
with that wand. "And don't think you can steal one. I can have it back
to a mouse before you can say 'knife.'"

The big man knuckled his eyes and looked again. When the horse
was still there, he shrugged and mounted. The dark man approached
gingerly, while Lily continued to tap her wand against her knee with
growing impatience, he felt the horse all over as if he was making
sure in his way that it was real, and then mounted. Lily helped Rosa
onto the wagon seat, climbed up herself, took the reins from the little
man on the wagon seat, and they were off.

Lily cast the "All Roads Are One" spell as soon as the wagon was
underway. The wagon was necessary; they had needed to pick up the

mirror she had left near the Dwarves' hovel. But she was glad that they had it for another reason, because she and Rosa could easily have used the mirror to go straight back to her Castle or the Royal Palace. She wanted the time to work out what she was going to do before they appeared at the Palace in front of all the people that would be there. That was another good reason not to mirror-walk straight back there. Rosa's reappearance was going to have to be an event, not a mystery.

So. Should she stay in the persona of Queen Sable, or not? Finally she decided to ask for a second opinion.

"Arnott, hand me Jimson, would you?" she asked the Brownie in the back with her supplies. This was actually not so bad, really, since she'd had to send the Brownies to collect the mirror anyway. You couldn't leave a magical door like that just lying about, even if she was the only one who could use it, and she was the only one who could break the spell on it.

Arnott got Jimson's mirror out of the padded box she'd placed it in. Rosa eyed the little bit of glass oddly; Lily decided she was going to have to ask Rosa about that, along with a few dozen other things. She gave the reins of the horses back to Kole, and took it from him. "Mirror, mirror, in my hand—" she began.

"Still Rosamund, Godmother." Jimson's green face appeared, making Rosa jump and squeak. Jimson smiled broadly and bobbed a little, in what passed for a bow when you were only a head. "Ah, and there she is. Greetings, Princess. It is a pleasure to see you face-to-face, so to speak, and a greater one to see you safe and sound and in good health."

"Ah...hello," Rosa stammered, looking a little confused that he recognized her. "You aren't a demon, are you?"

"Nothing of the sort." Jimson smiled encouragingly at her. "I am a Mirror Servant, and my name is Jimson. I find out things for Godmother Lily. Many of the Godmothers have Mirror Servants. They find us extremely useful." He turned his attention back to Lily. The two men, who had been riding behind the cart, craned their necks to see what was going on.

"Right now, what I need is advice and an opinion," Lily told him. "We seem to have picked up a pair of stray Princes, and I am not sure what to do with them. I am also not sure if I should arrive as Queen Sable when we return to the Palace, or merely deliver Rosa as the Godmother as if I had been the one to accomplish the rescue, then drive away and vanish, and have Queen Sable appear in due course to greet her return."

"The latter," Jimson said immediately. "The Huntsman might still approach you, hoping to strike a separate bargain. You'll lose that advantage if Queen Sable appears as a rescuer. It seems to me that it is extremely important to keep the Huntsman unaware of the fact that you are not the Princess's enemy. Nor is the Huntsman the only one that I think should be kept in the dark. If there are any more agents of treachery among the Court, either I will overhear them, or you'll smoke them out as Queen Sable. But if you become the Godmother, everyone who is aware of Mirror Servants will know to beware of reflective surfaces. And even if they don't, they will assume some other magical means of spying. You'll never learn a thing. You certainly won't learn who sent the Huntsman after Rosa."

She nodded. It would take some rather fancy footwork, but the disguise of Old Maggie could serve once more rather neatly. "What about our two problems?" she asked. "We seem to have acquired a pair of figurative Princes, if not actual ones. I'm sure The Tradition puts them in that category."

She held the mirror so Jimson could look back over her shoulder.

"Hmm. The Tradition is thick around the big one, not so much around the other. I am going to hazard my professional guess that, yes, they are at least technically Princes, that the dark one is nothing more than a younger son, but not a *youngest* son. He looks to me as if he is rather too old to be out on his first quest. He was likely kicked out by his father to find himself a Princess, and I'd guess fancies himself as a rascal. He has *probably* been getting bribes from the fathers of those Princesses he had gone courting to go away, and using that to live on, and lately the bribes have been very few." Lily lowered the mirror. Jimson looked up at her. "As for the other, he's Northern, he may be Prince by blood but actually owns nothing, and I'll have to see what I can find out later. I actually don't have any advice. I have several courses of action, but no real advice. You could send them to the King to make use of, assuming they will actually be of some use. You could give both of them horses and money to go away. Or you could let them stay. Letting them stay *would* have the advantage of confusing The Tradition about Rosa. There aren't supposed to be two Princes, only one. They are wildly unalike, so The Tradition will be further confused about which Path to take for Rosa. On the other hand, something could turn up to force the Path, and you have been trying very hard to keep that from happening."

Lily weighed the advantages of all of those possibilities in her mind. Here she had assumed that having yet another Path coming into conflict with Rosa's would be a disaster. But as Jimson pointed out, it could be advantageous.

What won out, in the end, was the ability to further confuse The Tradition. While the dark-haired rake was negligible in that regard, with the kind of power she could now see besetting the blond on every side, having two really strong Traditional Paths clashing would only be good for Rosa. Three Paths, really; Rosa could still fit both Snowskin and Beauty Asleep. And if need be, Lily could throw in some other Traditional Path to really mire things up.

She thanked Jimson and handed the mirror back to be put safely in the box. A few moments later, the vague forest track opened up, the tree tunnel became a lane lined with beautiful beeches and oaks and the worn ruts became a well-tended gravel road. Recognizing that the spell had worked, and they were close to the Palace, she stopped the wagon.

She stood up on the wagon seat, held the wand over her head and made several complicated passes with it, concentrating on what she wanted to do. A kind of explosion of faint, sparkling "dust" erupted out of the tip of the wand, fountaining up, then raining down on them. She rather liked the effect, so she had never tried to tone it down; it reminded her of miniature fireworks. And as the plumes of fairy dust drifted down and touched them, the wagon, horses, Brownies, Godmother, and Princess changed.

The wagon became a grand carriage, ridiculously elaborate, all in lily-white and gilt. In keeping with The Tradition, it was gently rounded, with metalwork done in graceful tendrils like squash vines, and metal leaves and blossoms. The horses became blinding white, with bobbing feather plumes on their foreheads, and their harness. Their manes and tails were braided up with gold and satin ribbons, the leather harness was spotlessly white, with gilded fittings. Rosa's stained and battered gown became gold-embroidered, pink satin that billowed out around her like a rose blossom in the very latest style. The Princess herself looked as if she had come fresh from the hands of her maids. Lily's own gown became heavy white silk samite, with trimmings in a deep cream, a long train and flowing white sleeves that would trail behind her on the ground when she walked. Utterly out-of-date, of course, by several hundred years, but people expected that sort of eccentricity of a Fairy Godmother.

And the Brownies all became liveried footmen in uniforms of white and gold. Unlike Lily's gown, their uniforms were in the very latest style for such things.

Two of them helped Rosa and Lily off the driver's box and into the carriage, which was lined in gold velvet and had luxurious cushioned seats. Lily took the opportunity to glance back at the two men, and chuckled at their expressions. Their eyes were bulging so much they looked like frogs. Very startled frogs. Like...Frog Princes?

Then, as she sat down, she started laughing. Rosa looked at her askance, but she only shook her head. It would take too much explaining, even to Rosa, for her to understand why Lily was so convulsed because, besides everything else going on, there were two Frog Princes following them.

Word that the strange, opulent carriage was coming sped on ahead of them; those that remembered what the Godmother's carriage looked like told everyone else. People began to appear at the side of the road, curious, excited, staring until their eyes nearly popped out of their heads. And as they passed, those same people began running along behind, so that the closer they got to the Palace, the more of a procession they were leading. By the time they arrived at the Palace Gates, everyone knew that the Kingdom's Fairy Godmother was coming, and Rosa knew that no one doubted it was because the Princess was missing.

They expected her to solve the problem, of course. It was going to be a great surprise for them to discover the problem was solved.

Meanwhile, in the carriage, Rosa listened carefully as her Godmother explained what she should do, and why.

"Once I've driven away, go ahead and dawdle, try to give me as much time as you can. It won't be hard, your loyal supporters will be pressing on you on all sides—answer every question, even if it means repeating yourself twenty times. Wait for Queen Sable to make her appearance and then *you* take over the situation. The Tradition will expect you to be meek and self-effacing. Don't be. Act like your mother."

Rosa nodded, and whatever Lily saw in her face, it made her smile. She thought for a moment. "Mother would have been gentle, but firm. Polite, but quite clear." She pondered a while longer. "Do you want the Huntsman to flee, or stay? I can lie about him, or tell the truth, but if I tell the truth, he'll probably do his best to escape."

"Stay, if possible," Lily replied instantly. "I would like to see what he does next, and now that we know he is an enemy, and you know what I am, I can make sure you have a protector at all times."

"Then I'll say that I was attacked and fled, but never saw the attacker's face. And that once I was on the horse, it ran away with me." She nodded decisively. "I hesitate to tell any other story because he will know I am lying and wonder why. This is close enough to the truth that he might be cautious, but assume that I am telling everything I know."

Lily gave a nod of approval, and Rosa felt warm and proud. "One way I can keep you safer is to keep you with me more. I'll drop suggestions that I don't believe you, that I think you ran off on purpose as a kind of temper tantrum, and it will look as if I am keeping you from your loyal folk out of spite. To keep this from getting boring, I am going to start you on Godmother training."

Rosa gave a gasp of surprise and delight; Lily smiled. "Now mind, I have no idea if you can ever become an actual Godmother, or if you'll be able to work any magic at all when this is over and you *stop* getting so much Traditional power focusing on you. But there are a number of simple spells I can teach you that you'll be able to use now, and there is a great deal of information I have that you need. If you have the native ability, which I think you do, I can also train you to see magic—that is, the power twisted into spells that are on things and people." Her smile broadened. "It won't hurt. You already know a great deal about The Tradition. And if it happens that you *do* become a Godmother, well, that is even better, if you ask me. It's been a long time since a Queen was also a Godmother, but if any kingdom needs two, it's this one."

Rosa's smile was rueful; after the initial moment of excitement wore off, she realized just how much more complicated her already complicated life was about to become. "I wish I didn't agree with you so much."

When the carriage pulled in through the gates of the Palace, it was practically mobbed. When Lily was handed down, the crowd became so quiet that Rosa heard the cooing of the pigeons on the roof above them, and the scuffling of feet in the gravel as people in the crowd moved restlessly.

But when she turned without saying a word, and Rosa herself stepped down, the crowd erupted in a roar.

Lily merely smiled, sphinxlike, waited for a few moments and motioned to her footman. The footman handed her into the carriage, and she drove off. The two Princes sat on their horses, the dark one looking disgruntled, perhaps because he hadn't gotten the credit for a rescue, the blond one looking lost.

Rosa remembered what her mother had done in situations like this and made the same hand motions Queen Celeste had to ask for quiet. It worked for her as well as it had for her mother; she got instant quiet—not quite dead silence, but more than enough for her to be heard. "I know you are all wondering what happened, and how I came to vanish. On my way to my quarters on the day of the great storm, I was attacked in the passage nearest the stables," she said, in a firm, clear voice. As those around her gasped, she continued quickly, "Whoever it was meant to kill me, for I saw the flash of a knife in his hands. I did not see my assailant's face—he must have been wearing a hood or a mask. I fled, hoping to find a Guardsman or a footman, with my attacker in hot pursuit. I saw a horse standing ready, and I did not even think. I simply flung myself into the saddle and rode for my life. I intended to try to pull up once outside the gates, but the horse was too strong, and ran away with me. Once we were deep inside the forest, he was frightened by something, and threw me, and I landed hard and fainted. The thunderstorm revived me. I found a cave and lived on the mushrooms and berries I found until the Godmother found me again, for I was mindful of what my mother had taught me."

The last was an outright lie, and she hoped that it wouldn't lead to a problem later. Well, that was more or less what she probably would have done if the Dwarves hadn't found her first. And she didn't want to mention the Dwarves. She had the feeling they would be very bad enemies. Better to let them fester in their hovel, never knowing who they had played host to, eking out a bare existence from their wretched mine, at least until their law-abiding kin found them.

She glanced at the Princes. If they were a little confused about her version of the story—or at least, as much of it as they knew—they didn't show it. They were, in fact, waiting very politely and quietly. And since the Mirror Servant had advised that they be kept around, she wove them into her story, too.

"We encountered these gentlemen on the road, who had learned of my plight and were searching for me. Because of such gallantry, the Godmother advised that they be rewarded. We offered them the hospitality of the Palace, therefore I beg you show them to the guest quarters and make them comfortable."

The dark one looked a little better satisfied with that. The blond was whispering to his bird, which flew off to join the pigeons on the roof.

As soon as the coach was out of the gates and out of sight, Lily ordered the Brownies to pull it off the road and set up the mirror. Swiftly, she returned the horses to their mouse state, the coach to a squash and the Brownies to themselves. By holding their hands as they crossed the threshold, she was able to ensure that the mirror spell allowed the Brownies through it; a tap of the hilt of her wand shattered the mirror and the spell with a single blow. Then, with a wave of her wand, she reduced glass fragments and wood to merest dust. There would be nothing here that anyone could use, magically or otherwise. She hated doing this, it was a dreadful waste of a mirror, but didn't want to put the Brownies to the effort of taking it home, and she hadn't wanted to leave even a trace of her magic back where the Dwarves might possibly come upon it. Just because someone couldn't *use* something, it didn't follow they couldn't identify where it had come from.

She'd learned to take precautions like that a very, very long time ago. Never leave anything magical about unless there was no other choice. Such things had a Traditional tendency to turn up in the hands of people who only used them for mischief.

Then she shook out Old Maggie's cloak, tossed it over her shoulders, picked up the box with Jimson in it and trudged toward the Palace as if she had every right to be there, heading for the servants' entrance.

No one stopped her; most of the servants and all of the Guards were up at the front, in any case, and very few people ever trouble an old woman who is carrying a box and looks as if she knows where she is going. She nodded to a few people, as if she knew them. That was another way to make people leave you alone. They nodded back, vaguely. Once she was in the Royal Wing, she ran up the back stairs to the hall of the Queen's Chambers, which were locked from the inside. She tapped on the door with the hilt of her wand and murmured the countercharm, "Open locks, whoever knocks," and the door unlocked for her with a *click*.

She let Jimson out of his prison and hung him for the moment on the wall, pulled off the cloak and folded it away, to be returned as soon as possible to her own Castle. Or, possibly, loaned to Rosa. Being able to look like an old woman might be very useful to the girl.

Then, she put on the much more powerful illusion that kept her in the form of Sable no matter what she was wearing, and resumed her disguise as the Queen.

She just stood in the middle of the room, composing herself, slowing her breathing. She reminded herself of who she was supposed to be, settled into the personage of Queen Sable. At last, without hurrying her steps, she made her way from the Royal Wing into the more public parts of the Palace, and descended the Grand Staircase, arriving near the great door just in time to hear Rosa tell her altered story. She nodded to herself with approval. There was nothing in it that anyone could disprove, except for the part about the Princes. She was pretty sure that neither of the young men wanted to irritate the Godmother by giving the lie to anything Rosa said, especially not when going along with the tale gave them free run of the Palace as a guest.

She waited until a servant came toward her, leading the two Princes up to the guest quarters. She stopped all three of them with an imperious gesture.

"Who are these…men?" she asked, looking down her nose at them. She wasn't sure yet if she was ever going to let them know that she was also the Godmother. It wasn't likely that the blond was another enemy agent, but the dark one? She couldn't as yet tell, and was going to ask Jimson to be very particular about his investigations. "And where are you taking them?"

"The Princess ordered me to take them to the guest quarters, Queen Sable," the servant stammered.

"And their names?" she asked again, knitting her brows.

The servant cringed a little, and looked terrified that he didn't actually know who they were.

Predictably, the dark one answered first, reaching for his battered hat and sweeping it off his head in a low bow. "Prince Leopold of Falkenreid," he said, radiating a deliberate charm. "At your service, in all things. It is a privilege and an honor to be granted the hospitality of Eltaria."

She narrowed her eyes at him. He doubled the charm. She sniffed, to indicate that she was immune to it, and turned toward the blond.

"Prince Siegfried von Drachenthal," the blond said, drawing himself up with commendable dignity, then bowing just enough to show respect. "Your hospitality is appreciated, but I shall soon be on my way if you have no need of me. I prefer to earn my way with my sword. I heard there is war—"

"There is *possible* war," she replied, with as little expression as she could manage. "There is no actual conflict—as yet. Nevertheless, I shall send word to the King. It is possible he can find a use for you, either or both of you. In the meantime—" she made a slight gesture onward "—please enjoy the hospitality of the Crown while you remain in our land." Her expression made it very clear that she would do her best to see their visit was as short at possible.

They passed her; she stopped the servant again. "See that they have more suitable clothing," she said, with cold disdain. "And baths. We shall have them to dinner with the court. We would rather not be confronted with vagabonds and barbarians at our table."

The servant nodded frantically, and she let him go.

*The dark one is going to take it all as his due. I'm not sure how this Siegfried is going to react.* But it was interesting that Siegfried had offered his sword immediately. If Leopold was living on his charm, Siegfried was clearly living by his arms. Someone like that could be extremely useful here, so long as he kept his role to that of bodyguard.

*He certainly rides well enough. If Jimson decides he's safe, it might not be a bad thing to have him go with Rosa whenever she has to leave the Palace.*

She descended the rest of the way to the courtyard, where half the inhabitants of the Palace still mobbed the Princess. As people caught sight of her, however, they went very quiet, until at last the entire throng was as still as they had been when she as the Godmother had descended from the carriage.

She stepped toward Rosa, and the crowd parted silently to let her pass.

When she came face-to-face with the Princess, Rosa stood up to her bravely, although she was just a little pale—no doubt because she still was not quite sure that under that cold exterior was the Godmother. Lily lowered her lids and looked at her with slitted eyes.

"Well," she said. "We are pleased to see you safely restored to us. We shall hear your entire tale in private, we think. Such things are not for every ear."

Rosa straightened immediately, and at that moment, Lily could see her mother live again in her. "Of course, my lady," she replied, using the appellation "my lady" to make it clear to anyone who understood the protocol that she was naming herself as the Queen's equal. "We have every intention of disclosing all details to the King's Consort." Again, Rosa used the royal "we" to show she was standing up to the Queen; Lily was, after all, only the Royal Consort. She had not actually been *crowned* Queen here. Technically Rosa was as much Queen as she was. Lily had been proud of her courage before; she was doubly so now.

She took Rosa's arm, and gazed about at the rest with the glare of a basilisk. "In the meantime, return to your duties," she said coldly, raking her eyes across the entire crowd. "There will be a cask of wine in the servants' kitchen and another in the Guardroom with which you may drink to the safe return of King Thurman's beloved daughter."

Pulling Rosa along, she made her way back up the stairs to the Queen's chambers, called for wine and cakes, then dismissed all the servants and locked the doors.

Only then did she drop the cold demeanor, though not the disguise, and take a chair. Rosa was still standing, looking uncertain.

"It's all right, dear, sit and have something to eat," she said in her normal voice, and Rosa immediately relaxed. "Jimson?"

"What can I do for you, Godmother?" the Mirror Servant asked, his green face appearing in the glass.

"Our twin burdens have finally told me their names. He of the weighty regard of The Tradition is Prince Siegfried of Drachenthal. The one I wouldn't trust around a susceptible chambermaid is Prince Leopold of Falkenreid."

Jimson chuckled, as Rosa sighed and shook her head, plopped down into a chair in a most unregal manner, and seized two cakes and a glass of wine.

"I'll discover what I can, Godmother," the Mirror Servant replied, and vanished.

Lily helped herself to wine, and patted Rosa's hand sympathetically as she reached for a third cake. "I'll let you go have a real bath and get into clothing that isn't an illusion in a little bit," she said. "Or better yet, a nightdress. If I were in your place, I would soak until the water got cold, then wallow in the feather bed until I fell asleep. And I'll give orders that you are to have an early supper in your rooms, and we will let the gossip wonder if I am punishing you, or if you are rebelling against me, or if you were more worn-out by your ordeal than you appeared. Then I'll make sure your father knows that you are all right and back home."

"Oh, thank you!" Rosa said gratefully. "I'm near famished. And I could sleep for a—" she stopped herself "—for a good night's rest."

Lily nodded with complete approval. Rosa was swiftly getting the knack of thinking on her feet; she had clearly remembered in time that The Tradition just might decide that with two Princes in attendance who might be able to kiss her awake, it would be a very good idea *not* to say things like "I could sleep for a year." She was coming along nicely and her training hadn't even begun.

Her mother would have been so proud of her....

"Then let's just relax and enjoy our brief respite," Lily replied. She felt The Tradition hovering over them like a thunderstorm that hadn't yet decided when to break. "I do not think we are likely to have another anytime soon."

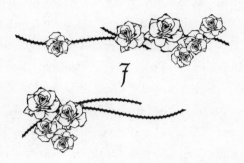

7

"UGH," ROSA SAID, LOOKING AT THE VISCOUS, dark contents of the tiny flask that Lily had handed her. "What *is* that?"

Thurman was still on the border, though it was looking as though he could return soon. Rosa would be very happy when he arrived. Privately she had vowed to do whatever she could to help him through his own grief.

They were in the Queen's Chambers, and "Queen Sable" had shooed everyone out. She motioned Rosa to a comfortable chair and handed her the flask. The stuff in it looked black. It didn't slosh, it oozed. She wondered what the Godmother expected her to do with it.

"Dragon's Blood. Not the herb, the real thing. You need to drink it." Lily turned back from the sideboard with another glass, this time of a white wine that Rosa knew from experience had a very sharp taste. She shrugged apologetically at Rosa's appalled expression. "One of the first talents that a Godmother needs is the ability to understand the speech of animals. Tasting Dragon's Blood allows you to do that. One taste allows you to understand Magical Animals, like unicorns or dragons, and Wise Animals, like my mice and Siegfried's little bird. A full drink allows you to understand the speech of all animals. And that much will also allow you, if you have the ability in your bloodline, to see magic, as I described to you."

Rosa thought about that for a moment. "Can I just have a taste now and decide if I want a full drink later?" she asked, looking unhappily at the murky, dark liquid. Just looking at the stuff made her feel sick. The King could understand the speech of animals, and when she was very small, he had told her silly stories that had made her laugh in rare moments of peace. The "speech" of real animals, unlike that of "wise" ones, generally wasn't all that enlightening. "I'm not sure I want to wake up every morning, listening to the doves under my window babble about nothing like a lot of silly girls gossiping."

Lily chuckled and shook her head, taking a seat beside Rosa. "On the one hand, I sympathize, but—no. Two reasons. One, it is rather difficult to get Dragon's Blood, since most dragons are not entirely friendly. Not that one could blame them, what with having to dodge heroes all the time, but dragons are difficult to find at the best of times, and it's something of a nuisance to the friendly ones to keep being asked for a bit of blood, so out of courtesy we try to limit our requests. The other reason is that the blood has to be drunk relatively fresh, within a couple of days of being obtained, or it does go off, so to speak, and we've not found any way to preserve it. I had to call in a great favor this morning to get it, and made quite a long journey by mirror to Godmother Elena to bring it back myself. So, you might just as well get it all over with at once. Hold your nose, dear, and take your medicine."

The liquid seemed to get darker even as she stared at it. It was about the consistency of honey, if honey could look malignant. Rosa gulped, braced herself and tried to toss it down in one fast gulp.

It was horrible. There were no words to adequately describe the sensations, which began even before the awful stuff touched her tongue. It had all the musk-laden pungency of a dead snake and the smell filled her head even as she tipped the vial into her mouth. It was worse than anything she had ever had before. So bitter it made her tongue curl up in a vain effort to escape the taste, so fiery-hot she felt sweat explode out of her forehead, so powerful that her eyes filled with tears and she had to fight to keep from throwing it up. Everything about it made her body scream, *"No!"*

Somehow she managed to swallow. It burned from her mouth all the way to her stomach, leaving her throat feeling as if someone had passed a red-hot poker down it. She gasped, and Lily put the glass of wine in her hand in the hope that the wine might cool the fire. She drank the glass as fast as she could—she couldn't breathe anyway— and that gave her enough relief that she was finally able to pull a shud-dering breath into her lungs. The wine—which after the blood was utterly tasteless, like water—managed to cut through the fire and cool it, leaving only the bitter, oily taste behind.

Lily handed her a napkin and another glass, which she drank more slowly. After the first two sips, the bitter taste began to wash away, and she was able to get a flavor of something other than the blood. Or, not a flavor, precisely, but the idea that this liquid was something sweet, sherry perhaps, though it was hard to tell with the undertone of the dragon's blood still overwhelming her senses. She realized then that her eyes were leaking tears of pain, and that she was as damp as if she had stood in front of a furnace. She wiped her streaming eyes, finished the glass of whatever-it-was, and as she tried to clear the fog of tears by blinking furiously, Lily put a third cup into her hand. This was hot water mixed half-and-half with honey and some sort of fragrant herb cordial, and it succeeded in clearing the taste from her mouth, her nose and her throat.

Strangely enough, her stomach was not in revolt. This was possibly because every other part of her body that had come into contact with the awful stuff *was*. Possibly because her poor stomach still didn't realize what had been dumped into it. Or possibly because the blood had never actually gotten there, and instead had coated her throat and mouth.

She was very glad she had been sitting when she drank it. She was not entirely certain her knees wouldn't have buckled under the onslaught. She sincerely hoped that Lily would not ask her to drink or eat anything like that, ever again. The experience was enough to make her rethink wanting to be trained as a Godmother.

But Lily must have guessed her thoughts from the expression on her face. "I promise you, that is probably the worst thing that will ever happen to you in your training," Lily said in sympathy, patting her hand. "Eventually something will happen that you will need the gift of animal speech for, and you will be very, very glad that you have it. As for the rest, there is a great deal that you won't have to learn, because you already know it. The very existence of The Tradition comes as a shock to most new Godmothers-in-training, and they have to study for a good deal of time before they have the depth of lore that is already at your command. I can tell you already, because I am of Fae blood, that the Fae will accept you as a Godmother, should we decide you actually need to be one. And unlike Champions, Godmothers don't have to keep undergoing ridiculous ordeals every time one turns around. Our idea of besting a dragon is not to chop it into bits, but to get it to sit down to tea."

Rosa laughed weakly, and finished the honey drink. As her senses cleared of the noxious stuff, she was able to relax as she had not expected to since her mother's death.

The Queen's Chambers had always been the most welcoming in the Palace. Only the outermost room had the air of formality one would expect from a Queen. The rest—the bedroom, sitting room, and tiny supper room where she and her mother had often played silly card games long into the night—were decorated in a very curious but comfortable fashion. They looked *exactly* like what they were—the rooms of a country shepherdess with impeccable taste and an unlimited amount of money to spend. All the furniture was solidly built, and solidly comfortable; whitewashed oak and woven willow for the most part, with bleached muslin cushions stuffed with goose down. The white marble fireplace always had a nice fire in it. Wood-paneled walls had been whitewashed, then tinted pink, with a touch of gilding. There were sensible lamps instead of ostentatious candelabra.

Rosa had feared that Queen Sable had turned these rooms, once a haven, into a nightmare, despoiling them with expensive, spindly furniture and things too fragile to even look at lest they break, or worse, into a gloomy cave furnished in black velvet and plum satin. To discover that it was really Lily here, and that the rooms had been untouched, was a little like getting part of her mother back.

"Well." Rosa coughed a little. "What is there for me besides a near poisoning?"

"First, what we are doing, which will certainly set some tongues wagging." Lily smiled. "Simply being closeted together without anyone seeing what we are up to."

Rosa had kept to her rooms for two days after returning, mostly because she discovered she was a great deal more worn-out than she had thought. She had bathed until she finally had the last of the filth out of her hair, from under her fingernails, scrubbed off her skin. She'd slept an amazing amount. And she had eaten far more than she would have thought, too; mostly fresh fruits and lovely, lovely salads, but when Lily had suggested a nice bit of roast beef she had eaten such a great slab of it that the ladies of the Court would have been scandalized had they seen it.

"I put about the truth—that you were recovering from your ordeal," Lily added. "Of course, since I was the one who said this, most people didn't believe it, and thought I had locked you up. I suspect that only the fact that your servants could come and go freely stopped the rumors that I'd had you murdered in your bed."

Rosa nodded. This morning for the first time ever she had turned up for Morning Court, and had defiantly taken her place beside Queen Sable, something she had not done since the Queen had arrived. The Queen had given her a cold stare, but then, the Queen gave everyone cold stares, and there wasn't a particle of difference between this one and the one she bestowed on someone she *really* did not want to hear petitioning her. They sat side by side on matching smaller thrones—the larger one for the King had been removed to the back of the dais—listening to petitions. Breaking fast, of course, was done in the private apartments, so this was, officially, the first time the two of them had been together since Rosa's return. The Lesser Audience Chamber had been so full of frozen politeness that it was amazing icicles weren't hanging from the noses of the courtiers before it was all over.

"It was all I could do to keep from laughing during Court," she said with a grin. "You do know I was deliberately imitating you, don't you?"

Lily chuckled. "We believe," she said, a deep chill in her voice, "that the petitioner should reconsider his position. But we would like to hear the opinion of the Princess Royal."

"The Princess Royal has no opinion," Rosa replied, with the same distant manner and chill. "Except that the Royal Consort is a stranger here, and thus, may have the analytical distance required to asses this situation." They both laughed.

After Morning Court was the large meal of the day, dinner. This was the meal at which everyone who was anyone had to turn up, unless he or she was ill. When Rosa entered at the same time as the Queen, and the two sat side by side at the high table, it caused an immediate stir, because again, Rosa had not sat at dinner since the Queen had been installed. Dinner was a piece of balletic extravagance that only a country as wealthy as Eltaria could afford. There were seven courses, and each course had several dishes. One was not expected to eat everything, or even to taste most of the dishes—though Siegfried had made good inroads on many of them. Rosa wished she could have been there to see the reaction of the two men the first time they had been presented with such bounty.

"What happened at the first dinner—with our tagalongs, I mean?" she asked.

"Siegfried's eyes nearly jumped out of his head. I had put them on either side of me and he muttered something about not expecting the feast day in Vallahalia. Leopold was...impressed. But he spent most of the feast trying to impress *me* by pretending to be casual about it all."

"At least Leopold didn't try to pocket the knives and forks," Rosa said drily.

After dinner—which took place in absolutely uncanny and unnatural silence, since virtually everyone was waiting and watching to see what Rosa and the Queen would do—the two had stood up simultaneously. The Queen announced, in a stern voice, "Princess Rosamund will be pleased to attend us in our chambers. Alone."

Rosa had bowed stiffly and replied, "It pleases us to do so." Her manner had made it very clear that she was doing so only because she felt like it. The moment that they had exited, the Dining Room had erupted with the buzz of speculation.

Once the two of them were safely behind the locked doors of the Queen's Chambers, however, they had nearly collapsed with laughter. They held each other up, giggling helplessly, and every time one of them would manage to get herself under control, she would glance at the other and go off again. Once they had wiped their eyes and settled down, though, it had been time to get down to business, and the first order of business, it seemed, was drinking that Dragon's Blood and obtaining the gift of tongues that would come with it.

"Now, about the gift of tongues—it will also help you get through strange accents and even muddle through languages you don't already know," Lily said, as she uncovered Jimson's mirror. "Not as clearly as with animals, but human language is much more complicated than animal language. Siegfried had a nice dose of Dragon's Blood after killing a particularly nasty one when he was just ten. That's why Siegfried can actually bumble through Eltarian without having learned it before he crossed the border."

Rosa was a little distracted at the moment, because she was hearing two things from the birds outside in the garden, one set of information layered over the top of the other. She heard the perfectly expected birdsong from them. But she also heard a tangled jumble of other things. From the robins, "I'm here! Here! Here!" From the larks, soaring above them all, "Look at meeeeeee! Look! Look!" From the meadowlarks, farther out where the stables were, "My place! Mine! Mine!" And from the starlings, squabbling over the kitchen midden, "Gimme, gimme, gimme!"

"It's working already," she said, and made a face.

Lily watched her, and nodded sympathetically. "You will get used to it, and you'll soon be able to tune the nonsense and useless things out. Meanwhile allow me to introduce you to a most intelligent little source of information, the one who actually told me about Siegfried and the dragon." She went to the window and whistled, holding out her hand. In no time at all, a little brown bird whisked off the roof and alighted on her outstretched finger. The bird tilted its head to the side and chirped. What Rosa heard, under the melodious chirping, was, "I don't suppose you have any of that lovely cream cake, do you, Godmother?"

She nearly jumped with surprise.

"Of course I do, little friend," Lily said fondly, and brought the bird into the sitting room, where she let it hop onto the table where a slice of crumbled cake was waiting in a white porcelain saucer. The bird happily stuffed herself—the voice that Rosa had heard had definitely been female—and Lily waited patiently.

"I tend to believe in serving my guests dinner before I interrogate them," she said to Rosa, drily. The bird looked up and gave a wink, before going back to the cake crumbs.

When the bird was at last full, it hopped onto the back of a chair and regarded them out of intelligent black eyes that sparkled like two beads of jet.

Rosa stared at her, fascinated. Her fingers itched to touch those tiny feathers. "I don't suppose…you'd let me stroke you, would you?" she asked tentatively. "I've never stroked a live bird before."

"Have you any nasty lotions on your hands?" the bird sang. "Or perfumes, perfumes are nasty. too. Oil is bad for my feathers."

Rosa shook her head.

"All right then." The bird waited for Rosa to hold out her hand, and hopped onto the finger that Rosa offered. Her claws felt very light, very delicate, like two bits of thistledown that had contracted a little to hold on, and to Rosa's surprise, they were quite warm. Carefully, she stroked the bird's head with her other index finger, just barely touching the amazingly soft, smooth feathers for a while, then growing bolder, carefully, gently scratching with index finger and thumb, as she would scratch a young kitten. The bird closed her eyes in pleasure and very nearly purred. "Ooh, you do that very well," she trilled. "I like you. You're as nice as Siegfried."

"That's a fine recommendation," Lily chuckled. "Now, would you be so kind as to tell us all about Siegfried's past? Where does he come from? Who are his parents? And how on earth did he get The Tradition so interested in him?"

"He comes from the Kingdom of Drachenthal, which actually has no King, just a great many Clans that are constantly fighting with one another, and a lot of foolish, quarrelsome gods. His father and mother are brother and sister, and the children of a god and a mortal," the bird sang. "I don't really need to weary you with all of the details. The gods of his land are rather dim, and they don't think very far ahead. They actually take pride in acting on impulse, as if that was particularly heroic. They make bargains with each other and with magical races without thinking of consequences, and The Tradition only compounds all of the difficulties that rushing about doing things impulsively causes. Well! Just as an example, the gods are always messing about and siring children on mortal women, and then become surprised when their goddesses aren't happy about this. Then the goddesses want to punish the women for violating the vows of marriage, and the gods want to protect their leman and— it just gets very, very messy."

Lily rolled her eyes. "Which only makes me a great deal happier that we at least are not burdened with *that*. Gods are best at a distance, and not meddling with mortals. Do go on."

"Well, Traditionally, this would make him a Hero. Which he is. It would also make him just as dim as his grandfather-the-god and his father, who couldn't even recognize his own twin sister and fell in love with her and made things even messier, if you can imagine it. Actually Siegfried is *not* dim, not at all. He is really quite clever, so when he tasted Dragon's Blood and heard me talking, he actually stopped to listen and ask some intelligent questions. I was able to warn him about The Tradition and what his fate would be if he didn't do his best to avoid it. When he heard that, he didn't just bluster something useless about Death and Glory, he actually *listened* to my advice, and then took it. I'm quite fond of him, really. And he's kind. Even when all he has is a crust, he makes sure I have enough to eat."

"Well," Rosa said, cautiously, "Traditionally speaking, that *is* one of the marks of a true Hero. It might not all be him…"

The bird tilted her head. "I like you. You are smarter than you look. But no, most of it is him. Traditionally the Heroes of Drachenthal are mighty of thew, small of brain, and not kind at all. Usually when one of us magical birds tries to warn them, they turn around and try to kill us with rocks." The bird paused. "Of course, the fact that we can only get their attention when they have hangovers might contribute to that."

"So just what is this fate he keeps trying to escape?" asked Lily.

The bird's words turned lyrical, as her eyes half closed and she sang the tale. "Asleep on a stone in a ring of fire is the Goddess-Shieldmaiden who sheltered his mother from the wrath of the god-her-father and allowed him to be born. She is awaiting the kiss of a Hero, for only the kiss of a true Hero can awaken her from her slumbers. When he kisses her, she will belong to him, and thus will begin his fate! Love! Death! Doom! And *Glory!*" The bird ended on an upward spiraling trill, standing on the tips of her toes, her eyes completely closed.

Then she settled back down again, flipping her wings to settle them. "Sounds nice in a song, not so nice in reality. The Shieldmaiden happens to be another aunt, which is rather awful, right there. Poor Siggy, until he got out of Drachenthal it seemed the only women he *ever* saw were related to him! It's the usual messiness of cursed treasures—we managed to avoid that part—and then more messiness that would follow on rescuing the aunt from the sleep spell. Curses of forgetfulness, betrayal, jealousy, murder and suicide. The Drachenthalers all think this sort of thing is grand stuff, and they don't seem to have *quite* the same problem with incest that other kingdoms do, but from my point of view…" She fluttered her feathers with contempt. "If they didn't wrap it all up in magic and saga and a lot of self-inflated ego, it would be pretty tawdry. Fortunately, Siegfried, although he does enjoy being a Hero, is not terribly fond of Doom and Death and he has a healthy dose of common sense. So since there is nothing particularly Heroic about leaping across a ring of fire and kissing a sleeping girl, he's been avoiding girls-sleeping-in-fire-rings-wearing-armor as if they were carrying plague."

Rosa blinked. "I'll admit that I am not very widely traveled, but are armored wenches in fire rings very common in the countryside?"

"You haven't been with us." The bird sighed heavily. "I'm beginning to suspect that the Drachenthaler gods are constantly moving the wretched wench and planting her in our path. Or The Tradition is. We are hardly a fortnight in some places before she turns up."

"That's very possible," Lily confirmed.

"I had this notion that if we could find a girl that was *almost* a match for Burning Helmet, or whatever her name is, we could trick The Tradition into leaving him alone and he could settle down with a nice wife and some ordinary Heroics. We've been trying to find a girl-sleeping-in-a-fire-ring who is *not* a Goddess-Shieldmaiden, nor wearing armor, for quite some time now, but we haven't been having a great deal of luck. And in fact, the Doom-fraught one has been cropping up more and more frequently." The bird sighed, and regarded Lily with sad eyes. "You see, that was why, when he saw your Goddaughter the Princess, we got so excited. There was just enough about the situation to satisfy The Tradition so that it would leave him alone, and enough that was unlike that he wasn't going to end up playing the rest of the tale out."

Well, although Rosa had a great deal of sympathy for the poor nearly Doomed Hero-lad there was one thing she objected to. "I don't particularly *want* to 'belong' to anyone," she protested. "Especially not forced into it by The Tradition."

Lily looked quietly pleased at that. The bird fluffed her feathers. "Well," she sang, with just a touch of irritation, "you can't blame the lad for trying to escape the simplest way possible. It isn't as if *he* has a Fairy Godmother to help him. Only a lot of gods who only make things worse."

"You have a point," Rosa admitted. "Well then...I suppose he can stay, and if we find a Burning Maiden adorning one of the sheep fields, I'll send someone to cover her up or something."

"He's large, strong, and a Hero," Lily pointed out, pouring a saucer full of water for the bird, who drank some daintily. "If anyone tries to hurt you again, he is pretty much honor-bound to chop them into small bits, since he has accepted your hospitality."

"Well let's hope that he chops them up pre- rather than post-my-mortem," Rosa said. "Now, what about the other one?"

"I can't help you there," the bird murmured. "We never set eyes on him before he and Siegfried collided in the clearing." She eyed the saucer. "That's just big enough to bathe in...."

Taking the hint, Lily moved it to the window ledge where the bird could splash and sing to her heart's content, then fluff and drowse in the sun afterward, safe from cats.

"In that case," the Godmother said, returning. "We can move to our other source of information. Mirror, mirror, on the wall—"

"Who is the cleverest of them all? Myself, of course," Jimson replied, his green face fading into view. "I am so clever, I impress even myself."

"Impress us, then," Rosa chuckled, as he winked at her. She had gone from being terrified of the "demon in the mirror" to becoming as fond of him as Lily was. Or—she cast a glance at Lily—perhaps not quite that fond, given the tender look the Godmother was giving to the creature. But certainly fond.

"Prince Leopold von Falkenreid," Jimson intoned. "Absolute dead middle of the five sons of the King of Falkenreid and the one his father was quickest to toss out of the *Schloss* with a horse, a sword and a hearty slap on the back."

"And is there a reason why?" Lily asked. "Drinking? Wenching? Gambling? Seduction of cloistered votaries?"

"Popularity," Jimson replied.

Lily blinked. "Surely I didn't hear you correctly? His father wanted to be rid of him because he was popular?"

"Let me show you." The mirror cleared, and then showed a young man a few years older than Leopold, perhaps twenty-five, doggedly inspecting troops. He...was not handsome. He was not particularly *fat*, but compared to Leopold, he was rather, well, lumpy. Leopold wore even the shabby outfit he had arrived in with a panache that made it look as if it was better than it was, and the fine garments that had been loaned him looked as if they had been made for him, and were flattered that he considered wearing them at all. This poor fellow in the mirror could never be described as anything but stodgy.

"This is the heir to the throne, Leopold's eldest brother, Theodore. No one dislikes Theodore, but he arouses no particular enthusiasm, either. He's not a bad fellow, and he's not dim, in fact he has a very good mind, but a good mind isn't the sort of thing you can trot out to show to the populace. He has never, in his entire life, done anything wrong. He has a plain little dumpling of a wife, who has produced three little dough-lumps of children. He is faithful to her, to his father, to his church."

"Whereas Leopold?" Lily asked.

"Has riotous parties in taverns, is frequently found abed with women who are no better than they should be, organizes street battles between factions of students from the University and once rode his horse into church because he said the beast needed the blessing more than he did." Jimson's face appeared again. "And while the leaders scold him, rail at him and hold him up as a bad example, the general populace adores him. He's more popular with the Army than anyone but the King. He is absolutely loyal to his older brother, mind you, and does not *want* the throne—"

"It would be too much work," Lily said wryly.

"Possibly. He is willing to work hard when he sees a reason to. When part of the city burned down he was out there in the street with the fire brigades, and when it was out, he was known to climb up on ladders with a hammer himself. He is loyal to a fault, he always keeps his word when you can get him to give it, and as far as I can tell, he has never purposefully hurt anyone. But the King absolutely despaired of poor Theodore getting any recognition for his hard work and many talents as long as Leopold was around. So, he booted him out."

For the first time since she had kneed him in the goolies, Rosa felt sorry for Leopold. It seemed a hard thing that he should lose his home and his place just because people liked him too much. After all, it wasn't something he could turn off.

Maybe he wasn't the sort of rake she had first taken him for.

"Since leaving, his popularity has continued to be more of a curse than a blessing," Jimson continued. "Although the fact that he hasn't mended his rather wild ways has not improved his position in the eyes of the various Kings and nobles whose daughters he has courted." Jimson waggled his eyebrows. "I must say, though, I am tempted to speculate that this is on purpose. Every one of those kings and nobles has offered him sums of money to go away as soon as their daughters began to demonstrate a real interest. If he really doesn't want to settle down…"

"I had the same thought myself," said Lily.

"I would shrug, but I have no shoulders," replied Jimson. "At any rate, there you are. All I know about the gentleman in question. At the least, I would say, he is unlikely to seduce the chambermaids, although if *they* attempt to seduce *him,* there will not be much cleaning done in his room. He is otherwise, so far as I can tell, a polite guest. Riotous drinking will take place in taverns, which is where he will sleep it off. Fights will not be held on the Palace grounds. The Ladies of Nightly Entertainment will be entertaining away from the Palace. I do not think he could ever be recruited to harm the Princess. However, I cannot speak for him letting something vital slip while in his cups."

Lily nodded. "So, I do not believe that he should be entrusted with the fact that Queen Sable and Godmother Lily are one and the same." She sipped her wine. "Thank you, Jimson. You are, as ever, a wonder, and I do not tell you that nearly often enough."

"Ever at your service, Godmother." Jimson's face faded, and the mirror reflected the room again.

"I'd like to keep them here, Godmother," Rosa said hesitantly. "I see more reasons to extend our hospitality than reasons to send them on their way. "

"And I agree with you." Lily replied, and was about to say more, when someone pounded on the door to the Queen's Chambers with a desperate urgency that made both of them jump.

*"Doom!"* trilled the bird, and flew out the window.

8

LILY AND ROSA STARED AT ONE ANOTHER, AS THE pounding began again. There was absolutely no doubt that whoever was out there was not merely knocking to see what he could stir up. "Your Majesty!" a tired voice shouted. "I bring urgent news of King Thurman!"

A Royal Messenger could be bringing good news—or bad. In either case, they needed to assume the roles of Evil—and possibly irritated—Stepmother and Rebellious—but cowed—Princess. Quickly Rosa composed herself and folded her hands in her lap. She watched Lily's expression completely vanish, leaving only the emotionless mask of Queen Sable. There was no need to do anything else, for not even here had she dropped the illusion of her disguise. When Rosa nodded, and schooled her own face into an expression of sullen unhappiness, Lily rose and passed through the private audience chamber, then opened the door.

A Royal Guard messenger, tired and covered in dust, all but fell inside. The servant who had accompanied him quickly backed away and hurried down the hall out of earshot. What Royal Messengers had to say was not for the ears of mere servants. "Majesty—please,

I beg you, you must at all costs summon the Prin—" The Messenger stopped when he spotted Rosa in the other room, and nodded. "Good. You are both here."

Rosa knew then; she knew it by the man's white face and shaking hands. So, she expected, did Lily, who motioned her to come stand beside her. She rose from her seat and made her way slowly to the door. She did not have to manufacture an expression of dread. "Go ahead," Lily said, her voice steady.

The messenger took a deep breath and composed himself visibly. "I bear grave news, and was directed to give it to your hands only. His Majesty, King Thurman, is no more. His physician believes the cause was natural, but he and the chief Magician of the Guard are testing to be sure. Before he died, he named you, Queen Sable, as Queen Regent until the Princess comes of an age to rule at twenty-one." The messenger's voice was harsh; it was impossible to tell if it was from the dust of riding so hard and so fast, or from grief. Perhaps both.

Rosa felt strangely distant, as if this was happening to someone else. It almost felt as if she were an actor in a play, with all the lines memorized and the outcome predetermined. And of course, on one level...it was. The Tradition again. The beautiful orphaned Princess, besieged by enemies...was The Tradition now trying to force her down the path of being rescued by a Hero, or down the one where she became the spoils of the victor?

And it seemed strange, when she had wept so much for her mother, that she should feel so little grief for her father. Then again...she had known her father so little. It was her mother she had known and adored, her mother who had gone counter to every bit of protocol and acted as the nursemaid and teacher to her own child.

And now she was an orphan. Exactly as The Tradition would like it. With an Evil Stepmother who had been appointed guardian over her, and who would now answer to no one if she vanished. Perhaps

The Tradition now wanted her to be bartered off to the enemy by that same Evil Stepmother, never to see her home again. Of course *that* Path was an ugly one, too. The Evil Stepmother would trade Rosa off in return for the enemy's promise that *she* would be crowned Queen of Eltaria for as long as she lived. Which would be—probably not very long, for The Tradition dictated treachery on the part of the enemy. Then the enemy would have both Kingdoms without a struggle. And Rosa would spend the rest of her life a virtual, if not an actual, prisoner.

It was a good thing that the Evil Stepmother wasn't what The Tradition dictated....

"What does the King's physician believe?" she heard Lily ask, as she stood there woodenly. Lily's voice was still steady and seemed to come from a great distance.

"That the late King perished, worn down by duties, crushed by loneliness and a broken heart," the messenger said, in tones that implied *he* believed this, but that he did not believe that *she* would.

Why hadn't Godmother Lily gotten some sort of warning? Or at least some knowledge that the King was dead?

But Rosa knew the answer, of course. The Tradition. This sort of thing was supposed to come as a complete surprise, even to a Godmother. Therefore, it had.

She bowed her head for a moment.

Lily, however, was still every inch Queen Sable. "We assume you have the requisite proclamations?"

"I do." The messenger started to open his sealed dispatch case, but Lily stopped him.

"Hold your hand. We will summon the full Council and the Court so that you may present the proclamations there." When the messenger nodded, Lily's voice took on a tone of heavy irony. "We would not have anyone claim that we somehow substituted false or forged papers for the ones you carry. Go to the Great Audience Chamber and await our pleasure."

The man clicked his heels together, saluted stiffly and left, his footsteps sounding heavily on the wood of the corridor. Lily rang for the servants, and kept ringing, until she had a phalanx of them waiting just inside the door. "There is grave news. Summon all of the Councillors to the Great Audience Chamber, and all of those of the Court that you can to await our pleasure. Inform them that they must be there immediately." With that, she dismissed them, and when they were gone, closed the door and put her back to it. She looked searchingly at Rosa. "Are you going to be all right?" she asked quietly.

Slowly Rosa nodded. The feeling of being at a distance was fading. This was real, yes. This was real. She would never see her father again. "It's...not like it was with Mama," she replied, feeling a distant grief, as distant as, perhaps, her father had been. "I never really knew him well."

Nevertheless, Lily came to her and held her for a moment, and that released whatever had held back the tears. Rosa let herself cry a little on the black-clad shoulder, cry for the father who had appeared to tell her stories, the man with eyes that worshipped her mother, the man who had somehow known the few times that Rosa had wanted something very dearly, and had always seen that she got it.

"I have seen so many of you come and go," Lily murmured, stroking Rosa's hair. Her voice sounded terribly weary in that moment. "That is the curse of the Fae-blooded. We see our friends fade and die while we go on and on...." She sighed, and Rosa thought she heard a grief that the Godmother refused to give voice to, buried in that sigh. "I think the physician is correct. When I saw him last, Thurman was a shell of himself. Maybe, with me in place to be Regent, he felt it was safe for him to...slip away. But more likely, I think, is that all of this was too much for a human to bear, and once he felt he had achieved a brief peace again, that grief and duty simply broke him between them, and his heart failed, in both senses."

Still crying a little, Rosa nodded, the velvet of Lily's bodice soft against her face. But soon enough, the tears were gone, and she lifted her head. Lily let go of her and handed her a black silk handkerchief. The Godmother searched her eyes, looking for strength, Rosa guessed. She raised her chin and determined not to give in to weakness.

"Are you ready?" Lily asked. "Really ready? This is the beginning of the worst either of us has ever faced. I've never served the Kingdom when things were this bad. Everything is going against us. You know that this is going to mean all those armies are eventually going to descend on us and tear us to pieces unless we do something before they find out Thurman is dead. You know The Tradition has all manner of paths it will try to force us down, and very few of them end happily for you."

Rosa nodded, wiping her face, feeling cold fear creeping over her. "Please tell me you have an idea," she begged.

Lily nodded. "In fact," she replied, "I do."

The Godmother faced the assemblage of the full Court and full Council, standing impassively while the messenger presented his news and his proclamations. She watched every member of first the latter, and then the former, stiffen and go white-faced as they realized just what Lily and Rosa already knew. This Court was full of all manner of men and women, and none of them was prepared for this. Thurman and Lily together had always saved them.

All those greedy neighbors would look at a Kingdom governed only by a woman and a girl, and they would assume that neither knew anything of warfare. They would gleefully decide that this was, at last, their chance to take the rich plum. Every leader of every enemy would think that if he just moved swiftly enough, he could take the prize uncontested. And they would descend in strength.

They'd have to. It was, after all, The Tradition.

Meanwhile it would be Eltaria that would suffer. It would be very tempting...in fact, nearly a necessity...for the Eltarian forces to withdraw to the cities to hold out while their neighbors beat each other into powder. At worst, all five of the neighbors would pounce, with armies, and proceed to fight on Eltarian land. And strategically it would make the greatest sense for the Eltarians to preserve their cities and populace, then emerge to battle the much-weakened winner.

Strategic sense, yes. And that assumed that none of the neighbors would have the same idea, which was not likely. So this could mean up to two years, maybe more, of trying to hold off enemies, besieged in the cities, and waiting for the chance to eliminate the last one.

Even if by some miracle of arms or diplomacy, they won free of this, the country would be ruined for a decade at least. The countryside certainly would be. Fields would be destroyed under the feet of battling armies, looters would take everything they could get their hands on, people would be displaced from their homes, and the destruction and chaos would leave hunger and disease in its wake. Eltaria's wealth was in its mines, but those would go untended while armies raged across the face of the land. What would be the point of taking anything out of the earth by great effort, when as soon as you got it to the surface someone would take it away from you? The once-wealthy country would be reduced to poverty within months.

But Lily had a plan...a plan that would, with any luck, keep those armies within their own borders, and prevent armed conflict altogether.

While the Court had gathered, she had sat calmly and written a message, then magically duplicated it a hundred times. It was simple, stark and to the point, and ready to be sent out via a hundred fast messengers as soon as she got the Council to bend to her will.

And now, faced with utter disaster, the Council as one man turned to her. No matter what they thought of her, she had established her authority in their minds as well as by the King's final proclamation. She knew what they were thinking. That it was true that she might be an Evil Sorceress, and was at least a scheming ice-vixen who had somehow finagled the King into wedding her, and might have every intention of murdering the Princess. But she was, no doubt, also the cleverest person in this room, and they knew it, and they also knew she would do nothing about the Princess until she knew that the Kingdom itself was secure. After all, she *wanted* this Kingdom and its wealth. If she had been in league with any of these enemies, she would not now be standing before them with the Princess at her side—she would be standing before them with one of the five enemy leaders by her side, and an army surrounding the Palace. No, she wanted this kingdom for herself. For now, she needed the Princess, in order to keep someone beside her who had the popular support of the people and most of the Court, so Rosamund was safe for the duration.

As for the Councillors themselves—they were men who were used to advising on trade agreements, on internal disputes, not matters of war. Thurman, his father before him and his father before *him* had saved them from that, working with Lily, or taking the entire burden of the threat of war upon his own shoulders and those of his generals so that the Councillors could concentrate on internal matters. The balance had held until now, but this—this was enough to break it, as impulse backed by The Tradition overwhelmed and prevented any second thoughts. Anyone with military experience was with the army now. Those here were faced with something they could not cope with.

She cleared her throat, and looked decisive. The room was utterly silent, as every pair of ears was turned to hear what she might say.

"The Kingdom of Eltaria is now in the gravest danger it has ever been in its history," she said, with icy calm. "There is no point in pretending otherwise. We must act, and we must act swiftly, and yet, as you know, faced with the certainty that most, if not all, of Eltaria's enemies will descend on us at once as soon as word of Thurman's death reaches them, it is a fact that we do not have enough men and arms to oppose them directly. But I have another plan. I have prepared a message to be sent to every ally we have, every ally we *might* have, and yes, even to the rulers of those countries who are now our enemies. Here it is." She held up the first copy of the message and read it aloud.

> "Salutations, from Sable, Queen Regent of Eltaria, and Rosa-mund, Princess Royal of Eltaria. Our husband and father, King Thurman, has been taken from us, to join his beloved Celeste in the Fair Fields of the afterworld. We stand alone against the world, and we are but women, unaccustomed to rule. There-fore, send us your sons, that we may choose husbands from them, and once again place Eltaria under the firm, guiding hand of a King. Two candidates are here already. Let there be a hundred, and let there be tests and trials, that all may see the choice was fair."

She folded the paper. "Signed, et cetera. This is our only hope of keeping the wolves from the door. From this, they will not know that the two 'candidates' are from distant lands that have never heard of Eltaria." She nodded at Siegfried and Leopold, who looked torn between wishing to express the proper sentiment of sadness at the death of King Thurman, and the happiness at the fact that they had actually been *named,* in public, as candidates for the Princess's, or even the Queen's, hand. "This is not something they would have considered, for Thurman has, for years, refused all offers for Rosamund's hand. Thrown off balance by this, they will pause to think rather than attack. This will only benefit us. They cannot yet have information about our guests. They will think only that one of the others has stolen a march on them by attempting to take the easier route of marriage to the riches that lie beneath our soil. And while they are pausing, the sons of the others, second, third and youngest, will be descending on us, for this is a very rich portion for a prince who is likely to otherwise have nothing. By the time our enemies gather their wits, it will be too late to attack. The Palace will be full of princes of every sort. Attacking while this throng of Royal Sons is here means that they will be at war with the kingdom of every prince endangered." She allowed herself a thin smile. "We will have protected ourselves behind a screen of exceedingly valuable hostages, hostages who put themselves into our hands of their own free will. Eventually, we are sure, they too will add sons or nephews to the throng."

She watched the faces. There was some doubt—not a great deal, but some—but as the Councillors murmured amongst themselves, she saw doubt swiftly turn to agreement.

"This will be expensive, of course," she pointed out. "A hundred Princes to entertain—this will not be without cost and effort. But it will be a fraction of the cost of a war, and will not result in the decimation of Eltaria and poverty for decades to come. And, all things being considered, might ultimately result in a fine King and ruler for this land."

She watched them consider that for a little. These old men were not easy contemplating a land without a King. To their mind, strength was only found in the male. Well, fine. So long as that manipulated them into doing what she wanted…she would use any weapon that came to her hand.

"Do we have the unanimous agreement of the Council?" she asked, in tones that implied that she was going to do this, even if they didn't agree.

But she knew her men of Eltaria too well. The younger men might have been willing to fight, but these old, staid, lazy men, full of themselves and their fortunes, who had been defended from the outside for far too long, looked into the face of disaster and knew they would not survive it. The nods that answered her question were shaded with emotions ranging from craven eagerness, to weary assent, but every man there was happy to let her try this scheme.

And after all, if it failed, *she* would be the one they could point to as the cause of failure.

She made a mental note to infuse some danger into Eltaria from now on, at least for the ruling class. These folk had been safe and soft for too long, and she had been so busy protecting the royals and the peasantry that she had forgotten the wealthy and noble. But that would be for the future. They had to survive the present, first.

"Very good," she said. "We wish you all now to return to your places. Assume the garments of mourning. Pray for the souls of the King and Queen. Prepare to receive our beloved King Thurman's body here for the state burial of a hero, for a hero he truly was, protecting all of you from this grave danger for all of his life, so that it remained invisible to you. You may go."

They went, with no show of reluctance; they simply filed out. Some, she was sure, who were unconvinced of her ability to save the country, were already planning how to make their wealth as portable as possible in order to flee within hours or days. Let them go; they would not be anyone that this land needed. Some would be trying to figure out how to buy their way into the good graces of whatever conqueror came. Those were fools; a conqueror would merely take, then crush, for what need did he have to share? That, too, was fine; there were mirrors in every house, and Jimson would soon determine who they were.

First things first. Lily summoned the messengers, twenty of them.

Each one was given explicit instructions and sent out on the King's—now her—swiftest horses. Five would go to the near neighbors, fifteen to allies. That left eighty more copies…which would go out by yet faster means.

Birds. Thurman's grandfather had established a network of communication with trading ambassadors well out beyond the neighboring lands, with emergency messages being sent by pigeon. If anything was an emergency, this was. She had reduced these copies to the size that pigeons could carry, called in the Bird Master, and sent them to be spread as far and wide as possible. Not just Princes would come. Obviously. But the worst adventurers could be sorted out and sent away.

She was relieved that Siegfried and Leopold had not lingered; she didn't want to deal with them just yet.

Instead, she took Rosa with her back to her chambers, and again dismissed all of her attendants, but left a heavy guard on the door. Not that she couldn't defend herself but…better safe than sorry.

She felt weary, impossibly weary. And her work had only begun. This was, in every sense, the worst crisis she had faced in her entire three hundred years as Eltaria's Godmother, with no discernible ending in sight.

*Damn, you Tradition,* she thought, a little bitterly. *Why don't you move so that a Godmother can always win?*

Rosa looked as frozen as Queen Sable's demeanor; after a glance at her pale face, Lily decided that some things could not wait. "Sit down, love," she said, guiding her to what had been Celeste's favorite chair and pushing her down into it. "We still have a long day ahead of us." She had to shake her head. "Heaven only knows what they are going to think of the way you and I are locked in together, but it can't be helped."

Rosa looked up, and her face took on some expression again. "Probably that you are lecturing me. Should I start acting cowed and puppetlike?"

She considered this. "That's not a bad thought, at least for now. Not *too* unlike yourself, however, or they'll think I've stolen your soul or some other nonsense. Now, I want you to sit there and think of what I might need to help me out with your courtiers, while I tend to some other matters."

She opened the mirror to her own Palace and stepped through. Normally she would never have expended this much magic, but between Rosa and Siegfried, there was enough to be profligate, so she might as well use it. Perhaps if she could drain enough of it off, this kingdom would manage to avoid attracting a powerful Evil Magician along with everything else.

Her Brownies heard the news in silence. "I don't trust the kitchens for now, not until I can afford to have Jimson spy on the help. So I want food and drink for us, and—" she looked for, and found, the four Brownies who tended her wardrobe "—I want you Gayna, Tris, Latti and Mira, to bring your tools. I'm going to need some special things and quickly." The Brownies sped to relay her orders. In an amazingly short time, they returned, with what might, to other eyes, have been a strange series of burdens. Trays of food and hot tea, but also the tools of a seamstress.

She brought them through the mirror, and before Rosa had any idea of what was happening, turned them loose on her. While they fed and measured her, held up bits of fabric to her face and buzzed around like a flock of fat brown quail chasing bugs, she turned to Jimson's mirror.

Jimson, of course, already knew what had happened, and his wordless look of sympathy warmed her deeply. "Tell me what you want, and it will be done, Lily," he said simply, without the honorific. "If I have to, I can collect enough embarrassing information on every important person for twenty Kingdoms around to coerce them into—"

She held up her hand. "I've another idea altogether," she replied.

"I plan to make this a real contest, but I am going to need a lot of help. I'd like you to speak to as many of the other Godmothers and magicians as you can reach and ask them to speed the Princes who want to come here on their way, by whatever means they can. I honestly don't care what they do, if they want to hand-deliver a boy, then do so. The sooner they get here, the better, and honestly the more fuss there is, the better. I want our enemies to be caught utterly off guard by how swiftly we moved."

"Done," Jimson replied immediately. "What else?"

"As repugnant as this is, set a watch on the nobles and the staff in the Palace, the kitchen in particular. We can afford deserters, but not traitors."

"Easily done," said Jimson, and chuckled. "You know, Godmother, *we* have apprentices, too. This is just the sort of thing to put them to. We don't often get carte blanche from a Godmother to do a wholesale watch. It will be good practice for them."

"I need you to think as you never have before, and see if the other Godmothers can and will help with this, as well. We are going to need some real trials here. Hard ones, but not fatal ones. Trials that require a lot more than brawn. Honestly—" She paused and rubbed her aching head. "Honestly, this is going to have to be a set of trials that *sets* Tradition, not just follows it."

Jimson's head bobbed. "You don't intend to marry any of these princes yourself, do you?" he asked hesitantly.

"Good God, no!" she exclaimed. "Oh no...I only added myself to the letter so that we'd get those who would otherwise hesitate by reason of age. The only reason I am continuing on here as Queen Sable is to protect Rosa. And truth be told, if it weren't for those wolf packs on the borders, she wouldn't need any protecting." She sighed. "I hope, I really do, that what comes out of this is a Traditional love match."

"I'll settle for a strong, clever, kind man I can like, who will care for my people as I do, Godmother," said Rosa herself, coming up behind Lily, wrapped in one of Lily's own black velvet dressing gowns, and carrying a little tray with tea and scones on it. "Now, it's time someone tended to you, or you'll spin yourself out into nothing. Right, Jimson?"

"Well said, Princess," the Mirror Servant replied, bestowing a look of approval on her so hearty that she blushed, and Lily smiled.

"Beset on all sides," she mock-complained, then sat down and took the tea from the Princess. "None of this would be necessary if your neighbors had Godmothers, you know," she observed ruefully.

Rosa looked thoughtful. "That might be another reason for me to take over some of the Godmothering here," she said, slowly. "If I can manage some of the day-to-day matters in this Kingdom, perhaps you could…well…interfere a bit with the neighbors."

Lily raised an eyebrow, but it was a good thought. "You know more than you've told me," she said, narrowing her eyes.

Rosa shrugged. "Mama wanted me educated in everything. She always said it was nothing more than a lot of village politics, just on a bigger scale."

"She wasn't far wrong," Lily replied wryly. "Well then. That's for the future. Let's survive this first."

By the time they were finished, it was dark and they had gone through several pots of tea and two meals. And Lily had a fairly good idea of which allies were trustworthy, which were trustworthy only if they were bought, and which would stay bought, once bought. Within the Kingdom itself, she knew which of the Councillors were loyal only to their purses, which were weak-willed, which were strong-willed, and those few that Celeste had known were motivated by something other than selfishness and could be trusted, no matter what befell. This had not much mattered in Thurman's time, but Rosa and Lily between them decided that it was time for a bit of a shake-up on the Royal Council. At the moment, while she didn't much mind that these men were soft, Eltaria couldn't afford anyone who put his own interests first.

"Not dismissal, though," she warned Rosa. "That makes for enemies. No, we'll find them appointments. Make them the heads of things that don't matter, but a position that comes with a meaningless title. We can make them Lords of some brand-new Order, give them spurious duties and send them home."

But Rosa shook her head. "No, sending them back to their estates, that would be a bad idea. That will look like disgrace, or exactly like it is, that they are being shuffled off."

"Hmm," Lily said. "Then this, perhaps. Let them stay here if they want, and preen and posture. In fact, we could probably use them...if we set them up as a War Cabinet and feed them with misinformation, then see if that misinformation turns up elsewhere, we'll find out which of them is actually corrupt instead of just venial. Thank you for that observation."

"Mother taught me to pay attention." Rosa managed a wan smile.

"So she did."

Lily had always known, when she had begun helping and aiding Celeste—among several other little girls—as a possible consort for Thurman, that the girl was special. Even as a youngster she had been a peacemaker and a problem solver among her peers. When she grew into lovely maidenhood, she had continued that among even the elders of her village. But she had never quite realized how deeply Celeste's craft went.

"Your mother was quite the manipulator, wasn't she," Lily observed without rancor.

Rosa considered that judiciously. "Well, she used to say that she was very well aware that she *had* that power, so it was up to her to use it for good, to counter the ones who used it for bad." She shrugged. "I suppose I am, too, since she taught me how to use it wisely."

"I most fervently hope so," Lily replied with feeling. "You are going to need to, in order to handle the plague of princes about to descend on us."

She was interrupted by Jimson. "Lily, your fellow Godmothers have been informed, and offer as much help as you think you need. Even in setting up and executing the trials. Many of them are arranging for the Princes and other would-be suitors to get here by means of 'All Paths Are One,' and a few of the young men will be delivered by the Godmothers or magicians themselves. Oh, and the Brownies are finished with their task and would like you to let them through."

"Task?" Rosa said, but Lily had already gone to the mirror to usher through the parade of Brownies nearly invisible beneath piles and piles of clothing.

"I have gowns——" Rosa said hesitantly, looking at the heaps of fabric that the Brownies were setting down on every available surface. "More gowns than I generally wear, in fact."

"Not like these," Lily replied grimly. She picked up a lovely mourning gown and handed it to the Princess, who frowned at the weight and the thickness of the bodice. "This isn't just stays…"

"Armored bodice," said Lily with a sigh. "Good against knives in the dark, and possibly even axes. You'll have to set a new fashion for high collars, I am afraid. An armored bodice isn't much good if it doesn't cover the chest. Your riding habits are further armored against arrows. But on the positive side, you won't need corsets when you wear these."

The Princess nodded, but she had gone a little white.

"There are also knives where the bodice busk would be, and slits in the skirts for you to reach through to get more weapons. *Not* the sort of thing your seamstresses would know how to make, nor would they do so as quickly as my Brownies." Lily picked up another gown, then put it down with a sigh. "And this should have been such a lovely time for you…suitors vying for your hand, you the fairest flower in the Court…Thurman and Celeste watching you dance at balls so full of pride and happiness they—" She found tears in her eyes. "If only—"

"It's not your fault!" Rosa said fiercely. "No Kingdom ever had a better Godmother than you! It's the blasted Tradition, that's what it is!"

Lily took a deep breath. "Thank you," she said, simply. "I hope you are right. But even if you are not, the fact remains that we must deal with what is on our plate as best we can." Then she smiled a little, taking in the Brownies, Rosa and Jimson, who had appeared to gaze anxiously out of his frame. "And no one could ask for better friends."

9

SIEGFRIED HAD BEEN A LITTLE OVERWHELMED at the luxury of the rooms he had been given. Actually, he had been a little overwhelmed from the moment he'd seen the Godmother turn the cart into a coach.

Yes, he had seen magic. After all, his mother and father were half god. He'd reforged his father's sword in a Dwarven forge. He'd fought and killed two dragons. He'd tasted Dragon's Blood, and getting the gift of tongues was certainly magic.

But…not magic like this. Not magic that casually turned one thing into something else. The bird had been kind enough to explain Godmothers to him. He wasn't sure his people had a Godmother. For that matter, he wasn't sure that his land counted as a Kingdom; there were no Kings, only Clan Chiefs. And the gods seemed to interfere much, much, much more there than they did in places that had Godmothers.

He was beginning to have suspicions about his gods. He was beginning to think they were just another kind of Fae Folk. Very, very powerful Fae Folk, but ones who were quite shortsighted and not particularly bright, with a penchant for meddling like a lot of old grannies. Why else would they act pretty much like thickheaded warriors without the common sense of a goose?

But at any rate, this new sort of magic had fair made his eyes bulge. And then, they got to the Princess's Palace.

Now…he'd spent most of his time, a good eight years of it, wandering in the wilderness of just about every Kingdom he'd been through. Leaving home that young was unusual, even for a Hero, but he hadn't had a lot of other options—and at least, wandering in the wilderness was relatively safe. On the whole, cities made him feel like a bumpkin, and on the rare occasion he'd done some hero business for a noble or a King, it was generally when he'd followed rumor to a war, or had encountered one of those nobles or Kings wandering on their own in the wilderness. Mostly, when he'd been entertained, it had been in remote stone castles that were not a great deal different in the sort of things you found inside them than the Clan houses he was used to.

So when he saw the sort of affair they were riding up to, he'd been taken a bit aback. He had to keep reminding himself that if you measured worth in terms of deeds, he was just as good as anyone who lived in a place like this.

And that had held him right until the servant brought him to his rooms and left him there. Rooms! In the plural!

He had spent most of his life before he had left his land sleeping out-of-doors, or in a cave, or at best in the sort of one-room Clan house shared by most of his people when they were gathered under the protection of a Clan Chief or a petty lord. Oh, they were big places, really big. Big enough to house a hundred or more. But it was all one big room, with a hearth fire in the center and a smoke hole above it. Impressive, if you were used to tiny cottages, yes, and large, definitely, but they were nothing like the buildings in these lands, and the idea of a bit of space carved out with walls for just one person was laughable.

After he had left his homeland, well, it had been the occasional room in an inn, where people mostly slept several to a bed, the occasional bunk in the barracks of some notable for whom he had done heroic service, or the occasional cottage, pretty much identical with the ones back home, where he slept on the floor next to the fire in the middle, because as the warmest place, it was the one first offered to guests.

Otherwise he slept out-of-doors, or in a cave.

He had never had an entire room to himself—unless you counted a cave as a room—much less several.

This was the first time he had spent any length of time with the high-ups of any kingdom in a setting other than a battlefield. The bird had coached him on how to behave, or he would likely have covered himself with embarrassment. The bird on his shoulder didn't seem to give them any pause at all, which was a great help. Then again, half of the dandies, half the old ladies, and half the young ones were toting around a fluffy little thing that they said was a dog, or were followed by whole clouds of the yappy creatures. He had to be very careful where he put his feet. It was a good thing that they seemed better trained than the dogs at home, or he would have had to be very careful about where he put his feet for an entirely different reason.

He hadn't been in those rooms long enough to get over the shock of them when one of the servants turned up with a big pile of clothing for him. Another shock. All his life, he had had two sets of clothing, the one he was wearing and the one he had just cleaned. Now he had...well, a great deal, and someone was always whisking away what he took off to clean it for him!

He did like the clothing; it was much like his own, without the armor, and was very practical. The stuff of which it was made was certainly the finest leather and linen he had ever set eyes on. The leather was so soft to the touch it felt like the finest swansdown, and the linen was like warm water on the skin. He'd seen other men here, who were not servants and not Guards, wearing much the same sort of thing, so he knew he was not being mocked subtly. It seemed to be the clothing of choice for a sober sort of man. Well, that was all right. He supposed he could be considered a sober sort of man. He would not have wanted all the nonsense and folderol that the other fellow, Leopold, was wearing.

He *did* know good table manners, however. He'd picked that up fairly soon after passing out of the Clan-lands and into a real Kingdom. And he also knew how to manage polite conversation—which was pretty much talking about nothing, when you came down to it.

But he could manage that. The way he managed, even if he didn't understand half of what the other person was on about, was that he simply looked grave, paid close attention, and when their intonation and body language told him they were asking for his confirmation of something they already believed, he nodded gravely, and said either "yes" or "no" as fit the question. And when they looked at him for a simple comment he would nod again, and say "indeed."

So he had himself a bath—his people were fastidious about baths; they bathed all the time, even in winter, or they'd have been eaten alive by lice and fleas. He was very partial to a good steam bath with an ice-water plunge after. He put on the clothing and went out into the hall, then followed the sound of people until he came to where everyone was gathered—gathered to await dinner, he finally understood. People at this court seemed to wait a great deal. But then, they seemed to have very little to do.

Within hours he was reasonably popular. The bird said they found him a good conversationalist, which meant, he supposed, that they liked the way he listened and agreed with them. The young women found him fascinating. Maybe it was because all their young men were so spindly. But the few times anyone flattered him, or tried, about his strength, he simply looked somber and said, "Size and strength are not the answer to everything. Cleverness can overcome strength nearly every time. A small clever man can almost always best a strong, dim one." Or, "I cannot take great credit for having a strong father and a sturdy mother."

As a result, he got fewer black looks from the young Eltarian men than he might have, and a reputation for commendable modesty.

He also made no attempt to follow up on the interest of any of the young ladies, and devoted himself as much as possible to making friends with their elders. The black looks rapidly diminished to nothing.

Not that this was from anything other than self-interest in his part. He certainly did not need any smoldering resentment here, and while the young ladies were attractive, he very much doubted any of their fathers would be interested in acquiring a penniless north-lander as a son-in-law, however heroic he might be. At any rate, there was only one young woman he was interested in, and that was the Princess. What with that Godmother about, she could be counted on to have rings of magic fire at her disposal. And she might even be persuaded to put on a breastplate for the purpose of being awakened. So far this was the most promising alternative to his Maiden of Doom he'd encountered yet. Provided that she was reasonably interested in having a penniless northlander as a husband, she was certainly comely, definitely practical and had a commendable fighting spirit. These were all good things in anyone, woman or man. Now, since her father was apparently away, trying to stave off a war, if Siegfried could just manage to find out if the Princess found him sufficiently interesting, he had a number of options to think about. The most promising, and the one that made the best use of his talents, was to go off to join her father, and challenge the champion of the other side to single combat. He'd lost count of the number of champions he'd defeated in single combat. The only times he'd lost was when he hadn't listened to the bird, and he'd wound up fighting on the wrong side. The bird liked his chances this time.

It was possible that the father might not care for penniless northlanders, but if that penniless northlander saved his kingdom for him, from everything Siegfried could tell, he was pretty much obligated to offer the Princess in marriage.

So that was good.

Leopold, on the other hand, was seemingly in his element, which was more than worrisome. He was equally popular with the young ladies and young men, he dressed the way they did, spoke the way they did and knew how to keep them entertained. In the two days after they all arrived, while the Princess was incommunicado, and all that they saw was that dreadful black-clad glacier of a Queen, he fitted himself right into the very center of things. If there was a big group of people laughing about something, you could be sure he was at the heart of it, telling an amusing tale. He was always in the middle of games—generally not winning most of them, but Siegfried had the shrewd notion that this was on purpose. Siegfried worried that when the Princess finally did appear, Leopold would be far more attractive to her than he himself was. He certainly wasn't going to force himself on her as a suitor. That was not fair. And if she did favor Leopold over him, it would complicate things immensely.

Of course, as luck would have it, when she did finally recover from her ordeal and make her appearance, there was no chance for either of them to put themselves forward before everything went straight through the ice and into the frozen river.

Because the very first either of them saw her, it was standing next to Queen Crow while the woman delivered the news that the King was dead, and that she and the Princess were now the rulers.

To say that the people of the court reacted like a flock of spooked sheep was to give less credit to sheep than sheep deserved.

At first, Siegfried couldn't understand why they were acting as if the world-snake had let go of its tail and was about to come eat them all. Granted, it was very sad that the King was dead, and he felt very sorry for the Princess, but there was no need to carry on as if you had just seen the Fedris-Wolf and Vallahalia was in flames.

Then the bird explained it all, and their reaction made sense. Quite a lot of sense, provided you were senseless to begin with.

And cowardly.

And you regarded the King as if you were toddling babes, and he was father who kept the Fedris-Wolf away.

On the other hand...from what the bird said, he really had kept a metaphorical Fedris-Wolf away.

Still, they acted, well...rather stupidly. Despite the fact that Queen Glacier had a very sound plan—and having hostages to prevent other people from acting stupidly was *always* a good plan, as his people knew very well—once the court had been dismissed, a good half of the people in it reacted with varying degrees of panic. A few actually rushed off, declaring wildly that the only sensible thing was to flee and fling themselves on the mercy of one side or another. Now, since in Siegfried's experience such mercy was generally non-existent, and since a would-be conqueror could as easily—and with far more profit—declare them to be agents of the enemy, take all their valuables and fling them into a pit, this showed very poor planning on their part. He did try to remonstrate with as many of them as he could, out of sheer pity—for some of them had rather nice daughters and not-so-terrible sons who had not made fun of him to his knowledge. Some of them listened and managed to calm them-selves and their families down. Others did not. One declared hys-terically that he was going to disguise himself and his family as gypsies in order to escape. Siegfried attempted to explain that gypsies were not much welcome in *any* kingdom, and that in all events, such a disguise would be quickly penetrated, but the fellow was in no mood to listen to him. He ran off declaring he was going straight to a gypsy camp and buying himself a wagon before anyone else got such a good idea.

Siegfried had to console himself with the knowledge that he had tried, he really had, and with any luck the fellow would not get more than a day away from the city without discovering that he did not know how to manage a wagon, or drive a team, did not know how to make a camp, and no one in his family knew how to cook over an open fire, or indeed, knew how to cook at all. That did not even begin to cover all the difficulties of passing a wealthy, well-born family off as gypsies.

At least some gypsy family would certainly find themselves much the richer out of this. And, being gypsies, they stood a very good chance of slipping across the border with every penny intact.

Still, he did manage to talk sense into some. As he spoke, reasonably, calmly, as he would to a bunch of terrified children, some of his calm communicated itself to them. "The news cannot yet have reached your enemies," he said. "And when it does, it will still take them some time before they can move their armies. Have any of you ever been with an army?"

He looked around, took in the soft hands, the arms that had never actually borne arms. Oh there were plenty of people who *had* at this court, but they were not here, among the ones that were panicking. So, no. They didn't even have to shake their heads. No, of course, they had not.

He racked his brains for a practical comparison. Wait...he recalled some of the young ladies lamenting that they were going to go to a "summer home" soon. That implied moving, twice a year. That would do. "Well, think about how it is when you need to move your whole family. Yes?" He saw brows furrowing as they tried to imagine how rounding up the family, servants and all was anything like moving an army. "An army is like that, only a thousand times bigger. A much more complicated thing to get going in one direction."

"But disciplined!" said one man, voice breaking pitifully. "All the generals have to do is issue orders, and things get done without any arguing!" Siegfried looked at his rabbity face. No wonder he had been sitting in a chair despairing, instead of panicking and trying to flee. It sounded as if he already knew he couldn't get his family to agree on anything regarding an escape until it would be too late.

"Yes, but they need to be fed. They need to get their provisions together. Yes?" His expression prompted reluctant agreement. "Then they need to get their equipment. Armies need arrows, bowstrings, spare bows, spears, spearheads. They need horseshoes and horseshoe nails, spare reins, spare wagon wheels. They need blacksmiths and farriers and *those* people need supplies. Then they need to be sure of their supply lines, because they certainly cannot take everything they need with them, and they certainly cannot live off their *own* land because their own people will object to that. So getting them moving takes time." And he pointed out, carefully, that the Queen's messages had not yet had a chance to reach their intended hands, much less produce Prince-hostages. "Prepare to flee if you must," he told them calmly. "But I intend to remain. I expect we will be seeing more Princes soon, and the more that arrive here, the more difficult it will be to attack us without getting other Kingdoms declaring war."

His calm, he thought, did some good at least, even if his arguments weren't all that convincing. Eventually, the remaining people dispersed to meet up with their families and retainers and decide what to do.

He had sent the bird off to his rooms as soon as all the panic began; he did not want someone to swat her accidentally, and although he could have used her advice, he was a little uneasy about the notion of people watching him talk to her. *They* couldn't understand animal speech, and it might make them less inclined to trust his sanity. As soon as he was alone, and the Palace had settled for an uneasy night, he went to see if the bird was still awake. She was, though very sleepy. Still, she fluffed all her feathers and got herself alert willingly enough for him.

"I didn't even have to sing 'Doom!'" she observed. "They were already singing it for themselves. Which is a bit silly, really. There isn't any sign of Doom. But tell me what else happened."

He told her everything he had learned since he had sent her back here. It was not much, but he was a careful fellow and had learned that the more the bird knew, the better her answers were.

She listened just as carefully as he laid out what he had gathered up, and he wished that the Godmother was still around so that he could ask her questions, too, but about the bird. Or perhaps, if he just asked the bird directly, she would answer them. Not her name, though; he wouldn't ask that. He always called her just "Bird," and she had never offered a name, which only made sense. Names were Power, and she was a tiny, relatively helpless thing and very magical. Giving away her name would give power over her. Perhaps she'd tell it to him one day, but only when she was ready.

Those questions were going to have to wait for now; there were much more pressing concerns to worry about.

The bird bowed her head, and her little eyes grew very bright with the intensity of her concentration. "So," he said, "do you think you and I should leave?" She had told him to leave other situations before this, when it was clear there was nothing that he could do to make them any better. He always had—although, granted, those had generally been times when the troubled situation did not involve war or potential invasion, merely political or emotional conflict. He was not good with those sorts of things. Among his people, a diplomat was someone who talked to his opponent *before* hitting him with an axe, rather than afterward.

This time she surprised him. "Before I say anything, what do *you* want to do?" she asked.

He furrowed his brow. "I think…I should stay. I know this makes no sense. I should leave. I'd have no difficulty getting into another country quickly enough. I am good at skulking and hiding, I know more than enough to avoid any trouble on the border, and I wouldn't be going by road anyway. But I want to stay. The little Princess is brave, and deserves help, and while I am only one, maybe I can help simply by being calm while others are throwing their hands in the air and bleating." Then he shrugged. "Besides. I am a Hero. It is the sort of thing that a Hero does. And if it all goes into the frozen river, I can fling her over my shoulder and escape with her. Perhaps once we were safe she'd agree to have a nap in a ring of fire so I can wake her up."

"Well put," the bird said. "I wanted to see if you were still thinking like a Hero, and you are." She fluttered her wings and gave a trill of approval. "There will probably be a great many things you can do to make things better. You can certainly make things better if you stay, and better still if you agree to take part in the trials for the Princess's hand."

He felt immensely cheered at that. "I'm glad to hear that. I'm rather good at trials, and I like the Princess…" He felt his ears growing a little warm, and he stopped himself there before he said anything else.

The bird nodded. "Here are the reasons. You are a foreigner, and if anyone would have a reason to flee and no reason to stay, it would be a foreigner. If you stay and are calm, people will take heart from that. As for the trials, well, as you said, you are a Hero, and this is nothing new to you. And I know The Tradition. That will be a tremendous help to you. I will tell you this, as well—if anyone can save this Kingdom, it will be that Princess and her Godmother. I cannot tell you what the chances are, because all the signs are jumbled, but if anyone can do this, they can." The bird laughed. "In fact I expect that there will be a fine lot of candidates for the trials here by tomorrow. This sort of thing is fairly stiff with The Tradition, and there is so much magic wound up now that getting them here will be the easy part, and the Queen will have bought herself some time."

Somewhat to Siegfried's surprise, and to the utter shock of the rest of the Court, the Princes that the Queen had invited started arriving at the first light of dawn. It had to be magic: there was no other way they could have traversed even Eltaria, much less the vast distances that they *had,* in so short a period of time. Immediately, people began talking about the intervention of Godmothers in order to bring the Princes here. Several Godmothers, not just their own.

The bird had said that they would be here, but the first arrival at dawn came as a surprise to Siegfried, because he had never known anyone in these lands of wealth or birth to be up that early unless they were on a battlefield. *He* was, of course, and the servants were. Otherwise during his few days here he had had the entire Palace to himself until nearly midmorning.

And yet, before the sun was even on the horizon, a chariot—a *chariot!*—pulled by a pair of briskly trotting, snow-white mules, came rolling up to the front courtyard. Attracted by the unexpected sound of hooves and wheels, Siegfried hurried there in time to see the vehicle turn into the courtyard and pull to a halt in front of the big bronze front door.

It was driven by a queenly woman in a columnar, ivy-green gown, entirely unlike anything the women wore here. He didn't get more than a glimpse of her, though, because the chariot wasn't even at a full stop when a young man in half armor with a bow on his back and a sword at his side leapt out of it. The woman blew a motherly kiss at him; he smiled, put his hand on his heart and bowed to her. With a wave of her hand, the woman slapped the reins on the backs of the mules, who cantered off in a cloud of dust.

And it appeared that the young man was expected, for the great door opened; the chief servant of this place—the bird called him a "major-domo"—appeared, greeted him gravely and ushered him inside.

He was the first of a procession of Princes. They arrived alone, afoot and threadbare, with no clear idea of how they had gotten here, but knowing that there was a Princess to be won. They arrived mounted, in shining armor without a speck of dust on it. They arrived with entire entourages and their own pavilions. There were fops that had never cut their own fingernails, and seasoned fighters bearing weapons with worn hilts and scabbards. There were ugly Princes, and Princes so handsome that they made Leopold look ordinary. There was even a frog that *said* he was a Prince, but he got turned back—or so the bird told Siegfried—since he really didn't qualify yet. When Siegfried found out about the poor frog, he trudged a mile down the road looking for the creature, but it had disappeared. He just hoped it had found somewhere else to go and had not been eaten by something.

In three days, there were more than fifty Princes in the Palace, Siegfried and Leopold were sharing one room of his three-room suite, and there were two princes in each of the other two rooms. The rest of the guest quarters of the Palace were similarly crowded. There was a field set aside that was full of pitched pavilions, both those that had been brought by the candidates and those that had been put up at the Queen's orders. There were even, so Siegfried had heard, plenty more without any claim to royal blood who had shown up for the trials. The bird said that they would be allowed to join, too—after all, The Tradition was full of tales of commoners who rose to thrones by winning Princesses.

And, it appeared that Queen Glacier's plan had worked, for there was one Prince from each of the five neighbors of Eltaria. Three were sons outright of the ruler in question, two were nephews. Messages had come from the watchers on all of the borders. The armies had withdrawn, and the Eltarian army brought King Thurman's body home.

There was a very impressive funeral, which Siegfried was able to see quite well, since he was a head taller than almost anyone else. There was a great deal of singing of massed people—the bird said it was called a "choir," and this was quite a new thing for Siegfried. His people had skalds, who recited rather than sang, and very raucous drinking songs. On his travels, he had listened with great pleasure to bards, minstrels, jongleurs and ladies who were said to be accomplished singers and musicians, but he had never heard massed, disciplined voices before. It was very moving. He actually found himself with stinging eyes several times, even though he did not know the dead King. He rather wished there had been more of that and less of talking. The god here, if he understood the speeches aright, was considered to be very far away, and everyone who was good got to go to a lovely place that was completely unlike Vallahalia—more of a great sky-garden than a feast-hall and a battlefield. Then again, while these folk did enjoy their feasting, they didn't seem to enjoy fighting nearly as much as Siegfried's people did, so Vallahalia probably wouldn't be much to their liking.

Finally the speeches and the singing were over, the King was put into a stone box in the god-hall instead of being set on fire, and the funeral was over. The bird, which had been on his shoulder the whole time, being very quiet, fluffed her feathers and stopped looking like a bird-shaped ornament. Some people milled about, talking about the dead King, while the throng of Princes remained to talk, retired discreetly to their quarters, or their martial exercises, according to their natures, and Siegfried pondered which group it would be better for him to join, though he was inclined to the most active choice.

That was when Leopold drew him aside. "Care to get away from this lot with me?" the man asked, rather too casually. "I know a good tavern."

Siegfried considered this. "Does it have plain food? Meat that is meat, and not hiding under a sauce?" He was getting just a little weary of the stuff these people ate. "And a good strong beer?"

Leopold smiled. "And no little dogs yapping around at your heels."

Siegfried snorted. But it was to cover what the bird was saying, because this had all the trappings of some sort of trick or trap. It might not be, of course. Of all the people here, Leopold knew him the best, and he'd not seen nor sensed any falseness about the fellow. But it paid to be careful.

"It's fine," the bird sang. "I don't feel any treachery from him. I think he wants to talk."

"All right," Siegfried agreed. "But I pay. And when my money is gone, we leave. I don't want to be chased by your creditors."

It was Leopold's turn to snort. "I'm not the sort to think I don't have to take care of my reckoning because of my blood. I always pay my due. I just do it with other peoples' money." He sighed melodramatically. "Lucky at dice, unlucky at love."

"So you say." Siegfried smiled. "Lead on, then. I already made my bow and condolences to the Princess and the Stormcrow before all of this. I don't think we'll be missed."

"Stormcrow?" Leopold asked.

"Black Glacier. Frozen Obsidian. *You* know." Siegfried shrugged. "The Bird of Ill Omen. She Who Is All In Black. The—"

"Oh, right." Leopold eyed him curiously. "Are your people generally so poetic?"

"Cautious," said Siegfried. "If you speak something's name too often, it might come looking for you. I don't want *that* to come looking for me."

"Ha! Point taken."

Leopold led the way toward the gardens that the courtiers strolled in, and which now were packed full of Princes and courtiers, supposedly being sad about the late King but actually abuzz with speculation. There would be trials for the Princess's hand, of course, that went without saying; it was the reason they were all here. But *what* trials? This sort of thing was unprecedented. There had not been a gathering of Princes like this for—well, in living memory of anyone who was here, and the Princes were a far-flung lot indeed.

The path Leopold took, however, skirted the edge of the gardens, then went behind all the lovely plantings and flower beds, shrubberies and fountains. Clearly it was one used by the gardeners. It led out of the pleasure gardens and into the practical ones, the vegetable and herb gardens. And from there, into the orchards; the particular plot of trees they were in was laden with little green apples.

The orchards ended at an extremely high wall; Leopold pulled out a key and unlocked the door. He motioned Siegfried through.

On the other side of the wall was a city.

Siegfried was astonished; he'd had no idea there was such a thing so near the Palace; all he had ever seen was the side that fronted on the forest. It was a big city, too, houses crowded so closely together that there wasn't enough room to put your hand between them. The door dropped them straight into the middle of it, the wall looming on one side of the street with temporary stalls all along it, a row of houses and shops on the other. Leopold emerged from the doorway and locked it behind them, put the key in his belt-pouch, and stood for a moment, grinning at the street and the traffic on it, breathing the air deeply.

"Now this is my sort of place!" the young man exclaimed, and slapped Siegfried on the back. "Come on, admit it, that Court is enough to put you to sleep, with gossipy hens shrilling in one ear and self-important asses in the other!"

"Well," Siegfried admitted with a slow smile. "Yes it does. But this does not suit me, either. I am not fond of cities."

Leopold looked surprised, then motioned to Siegfried to come with him. "Why not?"

Siegfried walked along beside him, keeping a wary eye out for trouble. Thieves often made the mistake of seeing a big man who moved deliberately as being an easy target. They always discovered their mistake. Depending on how old the thief was, that discovery could come at the cost of a broken finger, broken wrist or broken arm. "I'm not comfortable being in a place this crowded that is not an army camp," he said. "I'd rather be in the wilderness, or a small village. It's a matter of...knowing I always have to watch my back for trouble." He shrugged, saw a very young pickpocket approaching, and swung his foot out sideways to knock the boy's feet out from beneath him just as the lad reached for his belt-pouch, sending the child facedown in the road. Leopold raised an eyebrow as Siegfried walked on, leaving the young thief sprawled in the dust behind them.

"You're better than I thought," the Prince said. "Not as dumb as you look."

Siegfried shrugged again. "There are thieves in my land, too," he pointed out. "They are just usually a lot more obvious about it. Thieves where I come from tend to come straight at you, and bash you with something heavy. There's nothing subtle about trying to hit you with a club. The subtle dangers are from the wildlife. But once you learn what to be alert for—"

The child was back. Persistent. Possibly thought the tripping had been an accident. This time Siegfried waited until the fingers were on the pouch. Then, fast as a snake, he had the child's wrist in his hand and hauled the thief up by one arm until his face was level with the child's.

The boy dropped the tiny knife he was going to use to cut the pouch off Siegfried's belt. Leopold caught it. The boy's face was white.

"When I was your age," Siegfried said, carefully, so that the boy would be able to understand every word even though the Hero knew he had a thick accent, "I had already killed two poisonous serpents twice as long as I was, a wolf four times my size, a bear as large as I am now and a man. I had a necklace made of their teeth. Yes, even the man. In my land, someone caught trying to steal is killed. Now, I have learned that this is a land where it's not a good thing to kill every man who annoys you, so I am going to let you go. First, because you are not a man yet and there is no glory in killing you, and second, because killing you would disturb my friend. But I suggest that you find another line of work, because the next person who catches you with your hand on his money might not have a friend along, might not be as concerned about glory, or might have a hangover."

By now, they had collected a small audience that watched and listened in silence.

He dropped the boy, who landed on his rump, turned without looking to see what the child did and walked off in the direction Leopold had been going. The crowd, seeing that there was no more entertainment coming, dispersed.

Leopold ran a couple steps to catch up with him. "Clever."

"Not very. I've only discouraged the young and the less skilled. Now the most skilled will think I am a challenge." Siegfried sighed. "And I will have to break some bones. That probably *will* discourage the rest. It is difficult to ply the trade of thief with a broken hand, and weighing the odds of small profit from me against high probability of not being able to cut purses for a month, they will leave me a—"

He reached behind himself and caught the wrist of the hand on his belt-pouch. It felt adult, so without even looking around, he twisted and jerked upward. He felt the bones breaking as he did so, and dropped the man before the fellow even started to scream with the pain.

"—lone," he finished. "Well, that took less time than I thought. This must be a very sophisticated city." Behind him, a man sat in the dust of the street, holding his wrist and hand against his chest, howling with agony. Siegfried had gone for the maximum amount of damage this time. It was possible the man would never be able to lift a purse again. "That's good. It means word will spread quickly. You were saying, Prince Leopold?"

10

LEOPOLD GRINNED. "I WAS ASKING WHY YOU didn't like cities. Obviously it isn't because you can't take care of yourself here. So, is it a matter of needing to be absolutely alert all the time?"

They pressed up against a wall to let a wagon pass, then resumed walking.

Siegfried nodded, very pleased with Leopold's understanding. "Exactly so. I know the wilderness. I know it so well that I do not have to think about when I may be less on guard and when I must be completely on guard. In a small village, everyone knows everyone else, and I can tell by how they react to each other who cannot be trusted and who is harmless. And an army camp is disciplined and busy. A busy man does not have leisure to make trouble. Discipline keeps each man in his place, and when he is out of that place and up to no good, he stands out. Besides, in an army camp, a lawbreaker knows that troublemakers are going to be harshly dealt with. Army laws are harsh ones, you see. Thieves generally are hung on the spot."

"I suppose I have the same instincts—or maybe training—in the city that you have in the wilderness," Leopold said thoughtfully.

"Interesting. Well, you will be safe enough from thieves in the tavern we are going to, if that makes any difference to you. Bar fights, maybe not. If a fight breaks out, the owner will eject the fighters if he can and guard the stock if he cannot, and then it is every man for himself. Card cheats, probably not—the owner doesn't care if someone cheats others in his establishment. But the owner has a charm on the place that keeps cutpurses and other thieves out."

Siegfried raised an eyebrow. "I have never heard of that, but it is a wise thing, if possible."

"Oh it costs him a pretty penny to get it renewed every month, but he told me that what it brings to his door in extra custom more than makes up for the cost." Leopold grinned up at him. "Think about it. If you were alone in this city, how much more for a room would it be worth to you, if you knew that anyone who was going to rob you couldn't get into the building?"

Siegfried mulled that over in his mind. "Quite a bit, actually. It would let me sleep sound of a night. A good sound sleep is worth more to a fighter than anything other than a good full meal."

They continued on in relative silence—relative, because a city is never quiet—with a wary eye on their backs on Siegfried's part, in case the fellow with the broken wrist had stupid friends. This was a fairly clean city; someone came along with a cart, scooping up droppings, quite frequently. And unlike places he'd seen where people just tossed nasty stuff into the gutters and waited for the rain to wash it away, it seemed that no one tossed anything into the street here.

There were just so many people…the only other time he was crowded like this, it was on a battlefield.

"And here we are." Leopold gestured at a building, which had the usual signs of a tavern and inn on it. A hanging sign above the door with the name of the place—which Siegfried could not read, since the gift of tongues granted by the Dragon's Blood didn't extend to the written language—and a picture, a pair of crossed arms with a crown, which probably meant "The King's Arms." Down one side of the door frame were carved images of a wheat sheaf, a bunch of grapes and a beehive. So they served beer and ale, wine and mead. Down the other, a loaf of bread, a bed and a horseshoe. They served food, served as an inn where travelers could stay, as well as a tavern, and they had a stables. Above the door, a hammer and a leaf.

They would admit and serve Dwarves and Elves.

Those were signs he hadn't seen too frequently outside of his homeland.

"Dwarves and Elves?" he said aloud.

"Is there a problem?" Leopold asked, brows knitting as he paused on the threshold.

"Not at all, I learned forging from a Dwarf. But I have been through some Kingdoms that don't believe they exist." He entered as Leopold held the door open for him. "And I was in one that considered them to be anathema."

"I have, too. But this is a land whose wealth is based on mining, and where there is mining, you'll find Dwarves." Leopold nodded at a table full of them off to one side, all of whom looked up as they came in. Siegfried saw their eyes light up with purpose. "Um," Leopold added, seeing the same thing. "I think they know what we are. They'll probably want to talk to us—"

Before he finished the sentence, one of the Dwarves had already pushed his stool away from the table and was heading in their direction.

"—once they've made up their minds about it. Greetings and sound stone to you, friend," Leopold finished, addressing the Dwarf. "What can we do for you?"

The Dwarf looked up at both of them. He was very well dressed, though not in the height of Dwarven elegance, Siegfried noted. His clothing was of leather, and not unlike Siegfried's own, with light mail over the top of it. Light by Dwarven standards, which meant it was as fine as knitted silk, but would hold off the blow of a broadsword in someone like Siegfried's hands. Siegfried tried not to salivate at the sight of it.

His brown beard was neat, braided into a club, without being or-namented at all; his hair was pulled back and braided into a similar club. He had the usual hammer, which served a Dwarf as weapon and tool—and a club. That was fairly typical for a Dwarf among humans; no one with any sense picked a fight with them, so they felt quite safe going about without edged weapons on their persons.

"You're one of the Princes come to Court, aye?" Dwarves were direct. Very direct. *Blunt* would be an understatement. Siegfried liked this about them very much; it made discussions much easier.

Leopold nodded. "And you would like to hear what's going on straight from the Prince's mouth?" Siegfried smiled at Leopold's manner, for it was exactly what he would have said. Leopold was good; he went straight to Dwarven manners. "Well, talking is thirsty work. I would be partial to a good yard of ale, and my friend Sieg-fried here—"

"Mead for me. Aye, I am willing to sit and talk. And I should maybe like some plain food, if the talk goes long enough." He shrugged.

The Dwarf nodded. They tended to have faces a cardsharp would kill for, with the ability to keep just about everything they felt behind their beards. But this one looked a little more relaxed at discover-ing that the two humans weren't going to play what Dwarves called "word-mincing" with him. "Then join us, and well met."

Siegfried was actually rather good at reading Dwarves, which came from being apprenticed to one. There were anxious faces around the table, which should have come as no surprise. After all, a war would be terrible for them. Not because they couldn't get out of the Kingdom—they could probably tunnel their way out if they had to, and it was unlikely that anyone would be able to stop them. But war would effectively close their mines. Even if the conquerors permitted them to continue operating, there would be enormous new taxes, and even larger export tariffs, and who within the country would be prepared to buy what they brought out? There were no Dwarven armies here; there was nothing to stop a conqueror from doing whatever he pleased.

So war would be as much a disaster for them as it would for the rest of the Kingdom. What did surprise him was that they were coming to people like Leopold and himself for their information. He would have thought that they would go straight to the source—the Queen—rather than get information secondhand.

Then again, maybe they didn't trust the Queen. Given what he'd been hearing, they were probably right not to trust her.

Uncharacteristically, the Dwarves waited until the order had arrived before hunching over in a conspiratorial manner and fixing both of them with earnest gazes. "All right, what's this Queen got in her head?" the one who had accosted them asked. "The King, rest him, dies, and there's looking like an invasion any moment—"

"Bad for business, that, very bad for business," one of the Dwarves muttered.

"Then of a sudden, there's armies pulled back, and the Palace is full of Princes and adventurers—"

"Actually the adventurers are being put up in army tents on the drilling field," Leopold interrupted. "Or the barracks, if they're lucky. No princely pedigree—" he waggled his fingers in a shooing motion "—no bed in the Palace, nor pavilion in the garden. Rank does have its privileges."

"Yes, yes, yes," the Dwarf replied impatiently. "The point is, *what's going on?*"

"The Queen must have studied my people," Siegfried replied,

when Leopold said nothing. "She invited the lot of them to come, Princes got direct invitations, adventurers apparently smelled what was up and were allowed to join in. She told them they could all make a trial for the hand of the Princess, implied they might make a trial for hers, and now she's got a city full of hostages."

The Dwarf cast him a sharp look. "Northlander, are you? Aye, you'd know that ploy when you saw it then. Well. That's a sharper notion than I'd have given her credit for. But how long will it work?"

Leopold shrugged. "Who's to say? Don't forget there's that Godmother to reckon with. The longer the Queen can hold things off, the more time the Godmother has to do something about all of this."

"Oh, aye, the Godmother." The Dwarf pulled on his beard. "Not sure what she can do about an army——"

Siegfried shrugged. "I'm a Hero. I can challenge the champion to single combat, assuming they'll appoint a champion and he'll take it."

"Aye, aye, that's one way..." The Dwarf who had spoken chewed on his lip. "But what if they don't?"

Leopold leaned back a little and looked utterly relaxed. "Well, that would be a problem, then. But look at it this way—this Queen is clever. She sends out invitations for hostages. That's all well and good, but the first ones show up at *dawn* the next day! You don't get that without magic help. So the Godmother here is meddling in this, as well. Maybe more than just her. Hmm?"

"I saw the first one arrive with my own eyes," Siegfried said thoughtfully. "Looked like a Sorceress bringing him, not a Godmother. Actually, if I were making a guess about it, and you were to push me to tell that guess...looked as if it was his mother leaving him to try his luck."

They *all* gave him an odd stare, and he shrugged. "Prince can't have a Sorceress for a mother? Or maybe a sister? The thing is, where there's one like him, there's probably more—if not mothers or sisters, then, well, patrons. Friends. Ties, that's the point, ties to magicians. Yes? Bad idea to meddle in the affairs of magicians. Unless you like eating flies."

"Or think that your crown would look better with all your hair burned off." Leopold chuckled. "There you are, not only do we have hostages with fathers with armies, we have hostages with friends and family that can turn you into a newt. That will be enough to make the neighbors pause, I should think."

The Dwarves made thoughtful sounds and contemplated their beer. Siegfried kept eyeing their armor, and thought wistfully that if he only had the tremendous sum it would take to buy a coat of that chain mail, now would be the time to strike a bargain with them.

But he didn't. And there was no use even thinking about it. Gods got armor like that, not mere Heroes like him. Not unless they got a god to give it to them. Granted, his parents were half god but...his grandmother was more likely to send a thunderbolt to kill him than give him armor, and his grandfather was the one trying to set him up to marry his aunt and have that Colorful Doom descend on him. Dwarven chain-mail was no compensation for getting hacked to bits.

Or a King might give him such a thing. Kings could afford it, too.

Maybe if he ended up having to challenge a champion from one of the enemy armies, he could ask for a coat of that mail from the Queen. The good thing about chain mail, of course, was that it didn't have to be made and fitted to you; it was easy enough to have a general size, and just as easy to add some or take some away, so he *could* just ask for a Dwarven coat and it would turn up the next day. He had made chain mail in the past himself—the Dwarf that had taught him had said it was important for him to learn "the patience of the metal"—but nothing like as fine as this. Sadly, he had outgrown it long ago, and at the point where it had become too small, he hadn't had access to a forge to make the rings to extend it. Nor, truly, the time to do so. With regret, he had bartered it for the breastplate, greaves and arm-guards he had now.

He forced his mind from the beautiful mail with an effort.

Leopold was deep in discussion with the Dwarves, about trade in gems and metals and how all of this might hurt them. Siegfried was surprised at first, but then he noticed something. Leopold was giving the impression of being knowledgeable, but what he was really doing was letting them talk, which they did with great enthusiasm and at great length. Leopold merely waited until they ran out of things to say, then asked a leading question based right out of the last things they had said. That set them off again, and like spirited horses with the bit between their teeth, they galloped on for a few more miles.

Siegfried accomplished much the same thing with his nods and "indeeds" among those people at the Palace. But not nearly as cleverly. Leopold really was getting a lot of information.

Finally the Dwarves were completely relaxed. They called over the serving boy—Leopold looked vaguely disappointed that it was a boy and not a wench—paid the reckoning and got up. "You're good lads," the chief of them said, as two of his fellows slapped Siegfried and Leopold on the back. "Best of luck in the trials. We'd bet on ye, but Dwarven folk don't bet." Siegfried had been ready for the slap and braced himself for it, but Leopold, like most folk who had never had much close contact with Dwarves, was not prepared for their strength, and nearly went over into his food. The Dwarves knew very well that they could catch the unprepared in this way, and were always hoping for it. This was the essence of Dwarven humor.

So it was Siegfried who gravely thanked them, while Leopold got his breath back. They trundled out, and it wasn't until some moments later that Leopold stopped gasping. Dwarves really were very powerful.

The bird was laughing. Leopold leveled a withering glance at her. That only made her laugh more.

"Is your pet laughing at me?" he demanded.

"No, no," Siegfried lied with a straight face. "She's just singing."

But the bird stopped laughing. "Pet?" the bird said in outrage. She fluttered her wings and hopped with anger. "Oh...just wait. Next time he wants to impress one of those maidens, I'll fly over and drop a p—"

"Don't even think about it, bird," Leopold said, looking straight at her. "I know you must be thinking about dropping something nasty on me. I can tell by your expression. I have many, many feline friends."

The bird actually spluttered.

"Now, both of you, please," Siegfried said, alarmed now. "Leopold, yes, the bird is very clever. Smarter than I am, truth to be told. She has been giving me a great deal of help for some time now, purely because she is kind, so any threat to her, I take quite seriously." He inclined his head to the bird, who was somewhat mollified by that. "My friend, Leopold has done us no harm, and you must admit that you were laughing at his misfortune, which is not fair."

Leopold nodded.

"Now. Let us have peace among ourselves. Leopold, I do not believe you wished us to come here because you are fond of the ale. Or at least, you did not ask *me* to come here because you are fond of the ale. Yes?"

Leopold gave the bird another sour look. "True enough," he agreed, grudgingly. "I wanted to talk to you away from the hundred-odd pairs of ears back there. Now, besides being a prince of whatever far-off northern place you come from, you are some sort of wandering do-gooder, right?"

Siegfried thought about that definition. "I suppose that is as close as anything else," he agreed. He explained to Leopold about Heroes, and the sorts of things they were expected to do. Then he explained about the Shieldmaiden of Doom without going too closely into The Tradition. For one thing, he wasn't sure Leopold would believe him, and for another, he wasn't sure the Godmothers wanted that sort of thing bandied about. It worried him sometimes that *he* knew, but since no one had struck him with lightning, he supposed it must be all right.

However, telling someone else might bring on the lightning bolts, and that was no better than any other form of Doom. So instead of telling Leopold about The Tradition, he framed the story in terms of a prophecy. He borrowed heavily from the sagas of his land, saying that the bird had directed him to a witch who had done a foretelling for him after he had slain the dragon, tasted its blood and could understand her.

"Not bad," the bird said when he was done. "I think I even believe it."

"So, you see, I am trying to find a maiden who is something like this demigoddess, near enough to satisfy the prophecy, but without things ending up like a saga," he finished.

Leopold grinned. "You mean, ending up with murder, suicide and general all-around disaster?"

"That is a good summation, yes," said Siegfried. "Although since my murder would start the last lot, I would not be about to see it. And since I would get stabbed in the back, I wouldn't even have the satisfaction of my spirit going to Vallahalia and watching the rest. "

"We can't have that," Leopold said firmly. "Now, you were right about why I asked you to come here with me. You and I more or less started all of this together, and whether or not you believe in fate, we seem to complement one another. So what I have in mind is a pact between the two of us, yes? However these trials go, whatever we do, while there is still a lot of competition, we help each other. When it gets down to ten or so left, then we can talk about it more, but for now, you and me against the rest of that lot."

Siegfried thought about it. He couldn't see a flaw in it as long as Leopold upheld his side.

"It's a good plan," the bird said grudgingly. "And he means it. Well, he means it right now. Whether he'll hold to it…I can't say. He's a bit of a rogue, I just don't know how much of one."

"What's more, if in the end, when it is down to you versus me, if you don't win the Princess, I'll help you find a wench asleep in a fire circle even if I have to get a goose-girl drunk and set fire to the turf myself." Leopold grinned but there was no doubt he was in earnest.

"I'm positive he'll hold to that," the bird said instantly. "He might even tempt you with it. Of course, if the Shieldmaiden shows up during all this, *you* might tempt him with *her.* She is very comely, after all."

"All right, it's a bargain," Siegfried told him. "It's a fine thing, Leopold, and I believe that we can help each other without conflict. My thanks."

The bird fluffed her feathers. "I forgive him. Tell him I'll try not to laugh at him anymore and I promise not to poo in his hat."

Blinking, for the bird had never once given him permission to tell anyone that she wasn't an ordinary pet, Siegfried did so, then cautiously took a sip of his mead and waited for a lightning bolt to strike him down.

Leopold grinned. "Ha. I knew she had to be a Wise Beast," he said in triumph, the emphasis and meaning clear in the way he said "Wise Beast." He did not mean a human that had been transformed into a beast, nor yet an ordinary animal that had been enchanted. He meant one of those rare creatures in animal form that had the understanding and intelligence of a very intelligent human indeed—rather more intelligence than a good many humans, and no few gods, if you were talking about the gods of Siegfried's home of Drachenthal.

Siegfried stared at him. "How do you know about such things?" he asked.

Leopold stretched and leaned back. "Let me tell you about my great-grandfather and his boot-wearing cat," he began, and signaled to the serving boy. "But first, another round."

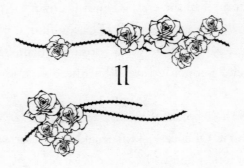

11

"TRIALS," SAID LILY, TAPPING HER LIPS WITH her quill pen. "We are going to need rather a lot of them." It had been a week now, and no more Princes were trickling in, although new adventurers were still arriving. The bunks in the barracks and the tents on the drill-field were all filled up, and the contenders were either having to supply their own tent, find accommodations in the city or take their chances in the forest. This was proving a great boon to the farmers roundabout the city, as the adventurers—since they had *not* been invited—were being fed, but on the most basic of rations, army-bread. And at that, the General Provisioner of the Army was taking advantage of this to clear the warehouses of army-bread that was anything from two to ten years old. You could easily drive nails with it. "And lucky to have it," the General huffed, when someone dared to complain. "No one asked you here. You're free to go. You're free to buy food you like, if you can find it. You've leave to hunt in the Royal Forest. Stay clear of the Common Forest. Our people need to eat, too. And…by the way, the Royal Forest has… Things…in it."

Not surprisingly, even of the adventurers, there were not a lot who were willing to hunt the Royal Forest after that.

It was a good thing for all of the small farmers thereabouts, who were nervous anyway about crops being trampled into mush if there was an invasion. They were harvesting as soon as anything looked remotely like ripe, hauling it into the city and selling it to these fellows.

It was a good thing for some enterprising women, mostly the wives of bakers, who for a fee would take this stuff that none of these men knew how to cook, cart it away in the morning, and come back with it in some edible state in the afternoon.

It was a very good thing for the taverns, since most of the adventurers opted to save their coin, eat the bread and use the coin to drink with.

However, this state could not persist forever, and it was time to get on with the tests before the mob got out of hand.

"We have rather a lot of Princes," observed Rosa, looking down at the crowded garden, which was full of the visitors. The Palace population had doubled. It was a very good thing that Lily could call on the resources of her own Castle to help feed them. The Chief Palace Cook was not arguing when the number of dishes he managed to squeeze out of the kitchen at every meal mysteriously doubled by the time it got to the dining hall. "Not to mention the adventurers, woodcutters sons, clever shepherds, goose-boys and odd brave little tailor or two."

"True. Hmm." The tip of the quill went tap-tap-tap against Lily's chin. "If this were an ordinary set of trials, things would be different, my dear, but although I would like to be fair to all of them, this *is* a competition to prove who is the best suited to not only being your husband, but to ruling Eltaria. Frankly, if one of the drill-field lot even places among the finalists, it would be a miracle. And if such a miracle occurs, it will do so without my being fair to them. Sadly, while I would love to present your hand to a sweet young man who is blessed with all manner of graceful skills, none of those skills will serve when staring down an enemy army. So perhaps we should look at the situation in that way." Lily made a note. "So, we need to concentrate on the skills of a King whose War Crown is rarely off his head. The King of Eltaria does not have to be one of the finest of warriors, exactly, although it would help, but he should know his way around a battlefield..."

"Let's start with something simple. Father was always having to get on a horse in full armor and get to one of the borders in next to no time." Rosa stared down at a particularly foppish fellow, who looked as if he would faint if presented with a warhorse, much less the armor. "So, a race. In full armor, on a warhorse. That should eliminate about a third of these fellows at least. But I don't think we should place too much emphasis on the winner, just use it as a way to eliminate people. Perhaps have a cutoff time."

Lily put the pen down and went to join her at the window. She smiled. "We may lose most of that third as soon as they hear what the first trial is."

"And then, when they get to the end of the first half of the race, they should have to—" Rosa thought carefully. "They should have to herd three sheep into a pen, still in full armor, then gather a dozen eggs wearing gauntlets, lay them out in a straight row without breaking them and gallop back to the finish line. That comes as close as I can think to how father used to have to organize stubborn allies and arrange all the camps before he got any rest." She thought a bit more. "I think we should allow them to use any means they have to herd the sheep and move the eggs. That would count as assigning responsibility, the way father did. So using magic or hiring someone to do it for them should count. Except that, like father, they won't know in advance where the point of the racecourse with the sheep and eggs is, and the longer they spend waiting for whoever they hired to come, the farther back in the race they'll be. If they ride their helper double, the horse will tire and that will put them farther back. We should have someone do this to find a good average time that it takes, then allow a bit more for the cutoff. I can't think of any way that anyone can cheat on that trial, can you?"

"Good!" Lily went back to the table and finished taking notes. "No, I can't. That business with the sheep and eggs sounds utterly nonsensical, and as such, it follows all the Traditional requirements for this kind of trial. We'll supply armor to those who don't have it, of course. And horses. I can magic all that up without any effort at all, thanks to all the Traditional power we have built up here." She noted that, as well. "The mice will hate me."

"Actually I think the mice will be amused. They seem to have very good senses of humor. Did you know Siegfried's bird knows all about The Tradition?" Rosa had spotted the big Northlander, off to one side with Leopold, and, as always, the little brown bird on his shoulder. The two seemed as thick as thieves of late. Really, so far as she could tell, they were becoming friends, which was interesting, considering how they had met.

"Yes I did. And I believe that she told Siegfried about The Tradition, as well." Lily gave her a sidelong, unreadable glance. "Which would certainly save a great deal of time and education if he should happen to win these contests."

"Do you think that's at all likely?" Rosa asked, feeling her cheeks grow hot. She wasn't supposed to have favorites, but so far, the Northlander and the roguish Leopold were ahead of any of the newcomers.

"One never knows," Lily said enigmatically. "I'm trying to hedge this about so that whoever does win, is exactly what Eltaria needs. If ever there was a crisis in this kingdom, this is it."

"Quite right, too," replied Rosa stoutly, her cheeks cooling immediately—and her heart sinking a little. "This is no time to be taking anything else at all into consideration. But..."

Lily looked up from the list she was making. "But?"

Rosa tried not to think too hard about a few of the candidates she'd seen. Oh, they probably would be eliminated quickly—but— "But what if the one who is best for Eltaria is...horrid?"

Lily gazed back at Rosa with a sober expression. "I don't know, dear. I can do a certain amount by making sure they don't cheat. But you are right, it is possible for someone to win these contests entirely honestly and still be a nasty piece of work. I don't know how to prevent that. I can only promise that I will try."

Rosa nodded, and turned back to the window, watching Siegfried and Leopold. She shouldn't have favorites. It wasn't right. But that didn't prevent it from happening. Rosa had been quizzing the Northlander's bird remorselessly about both men. The bird obviously was going to sing—literally—Siegfried's praises, but she grudgingly admitted that Leopold seemed to be a decent fellow, too. He and Siegfried had entered into a pact to help each other, which she had no intention of telling Lily about. It wasn't strictly within the rules, but it wasn't against them, either. There were other cases of such things, although normally the two men in question were lifelong friends, or even brothers. So Traditionally, it was sanctioned.

She had already decided that she was going to help them covertly as much as she could. After all, Traditionally, the Godmothers helped their favorite candidates, and there were all sorts of other helpers, not only Traditionally, but right here and now, from sorcerers to animals both ordinary and Magical.

So if they could, she could.

She left Lily writing out the list for the trial, comparing it to the list of those who had applied to compete and what they had brought with them. This was not as tedious as it might have been, since Jimson was helping her. She would call out the name, and Jimson would see if the fellow in question had brought a warhorse and armor. If he had, Jimson would give it a good look-over and tell Lily.

Just as she was slipping out, she heard the first disqualification.

"Adrian of Beau Soleil." Lily called out the name. There was a long, long pause, and Rosa hesitated, palm against the panel of the servants' door, to listen—because such a long pause from Jimson generally meant something was up.

"Regretfully disqualified, Lily," said Jimson, just as Rosa was starting to grow impatient.

"What?" Lily exclaimed. "Why?"

"The Prince is, in fact, a Princess," Jimson said solemnly. "And while under other circumstances I would have been willing to let this pass, we did distinctly invite only Princes, and I do not believe that Rosamund would be in the least interested in co-ruling with another of her sex."

"Definitely not," Rosa muttered to herself and slipped out the door.

She had already written out what the first trial was going to be on a small square of paper, and she had purloined Lily's "Old Maggie" cloak. Now she pulled it on, used the servants' stairs and doors and went down into the garden and along the gardeners' path until she got to where the two men were sitting, watching some of the others. Leopold wasn't flirting with any of the women of the Court, because at this point the women of the Court were quite spoiled for choice, and there wasn't one of them that didn't have her own particular Prince to be flattered and cajoled by. Rosa eased through a gap in the hedge and came out behind and between them.

"Hist," she whispered. "Don't be turning around. I'm a friend. But I don't want everyone to see you're talking to me."

Of course they both moved their heads stiffly to try and see who was talking to them. That was why she had stolen the "Old Maggie" cloak. What they saw was a brisk old woman, not the Princess.

"All right, friend," said Leopold out of the corner of his mouth. "What can we do for you?"

"It's what I can do for you," she replied, with a laugh forced out of her by tension. "Unless you've no use for knowing what the first trial will be."

There was a long silence, in which, at first, she was afraid she was going to be refused. But then Siegfried spoke up, his voice a thoughtful rumble.

"No one gives this sort of secret away——" he began.

"Except in tales," she interrupted. "And here you be, in the middle of a tale. Say, you've earned it. I'm sure ye've done a mort of good works in the past. Say, there's someone partial to you in the Palace, maybe some lady who's taken a fancy to you. Say or think whatever you like, but Old Maggie thinks you won't be the only ones getting help. So you might as well have it from me."

The men exchanged a quick glance. "Well, there was that first Prince I saw, and he had a sorceress bringing him. I doubt she's confining herself to just giving him a ride," said Siegfried doubtfully. "And I'm sure the others have all manner of charms and things. Magic armor and swords...maybe more, too."

Encouraged, she thrust the square of folded paper into Siegfried's hand. "Ye have a friend in Old Maggie," she said, and tried to simulate a cackle. "Old Maggie will see to it." She failed miserably, managing only a giggle, and on that note, she slipped back through the hedge. Now to get back upstairs and return the cloak.

On the whole, she thought that her performance had been rather good. The giggle was only a little slip, and whoever said old ladies didn't giggle? They wouldn't suspect a thing.

"That was no old lady," Siegfried said solemnly, before the bird could. "I've never heard an old lady that sounded like that, ever."

"Not with that voice," agreed Leopold. "It was a good disguise, though. Magic, do you think?"

"Probably. This kingdom is thick with it. Practically nothing is what it seems to be." Siegfried unfolded the paper and looked it over. Unfortunately he had the same difficulty he'd had with the Inn sign.

He couldn't read it. This was very frustrating. He looked at the bird.

"Don't look at me," the bird said cheerfully. "I can't read. Period."

Mutely he handed it to Leopold, defeated. "What do you make of this?"

"Well, this sounds normal enough," Leopold began. "A race in full armor on a warhorse. That's better than a footrace in full armor."

"Much," Siegfried agreed, but then Leopold exclaimed in dismay.

"What?" he said with outrage in his voice and incredulity in his gaze. "This is insane! What kind of a contest is this? What does this have to do with—with—well, anything?"

"What is it? And keep your voice down." Siegfried drew Leopold with him behind the hedge. Leopold had crumpled up the paper in his fist, he was so upset; now he smoothed it out again and shook it at Siegfried, as if the Northerner was somehow to blame for what was written there.

"It says here that at the end of the first stage of the race, we're to herd three sheep into a pen—three *sheep?* Are they *insane?*" Leopold looked very much as if he wanted to punch something. "Is this some kind of joke? Are they trying to make fools out of us? What kind of a test is that? And then, as if that isn't bad enough, we're to gather up a dozen eggs while wearing gauntlets—"

But Siegfried nodded wisely, because he could see the sense in it. It was like all the seemingly tedious chores he'd been forced to do by the Dwarf who had taught him forging and the old man who had taught him fighting. They seemed tedious and as if they had nothing to do with the task he was supposed to be learning, but when he looked back on it all, he'd been strengthening his muscles, getting coordination and learning patience. Oh yes. Patience. "The eggs? That's to prove you've got patience. If you rush things, you'll break the eggs, and you know they'll take points off your score if you do. The Dwarves made me do that. The trick is that you don't pick them up. You put one hand flat, then roll the egg into it. Then you put it down like this—" He mimed cupping his hands together, then carefully separating them so that presumably the contents settled slowly into place.

Leopold looked momentarily convinced, then he looked down at the notes, and exploded again. "But sheep! *Sheep!*"

"You were herding sheep," Siegfried observed.

Leopold looked at him as if he had lost his wits.

"When the King died and these silly court people were panicking. They acted without thinking, in their minds, running in circles. Like sheep, frightened by wolves." Siegfried shrugged. "You were herding sheep."

"That was a meta—that was diff—that was—" Leopold stuttered to a halt, and stared at Siegfried.

"That was what you did. And you herd real sheep the same way." Siegfried nodded. "Unless you have a dog to help, that is. The dog is fast enough to herd them by frightening them just a little to make them move the way he wants them to. You watch a herd-dog—he acts like a wolf, barks, jumps—they run away from him. But a man alone can't move that fast, so you don't frighten them more than they already are. In fact, you don't frighten them at all if you can help it. You just get them moving and stand where you don't want them to go, blocking them from going there, then move slowly and keep them moving. The one thing sheep want to do is stay together, so if you can get one moving in the right direction, they all will go. If your horse is well-trained, you can do what a dog does. Or you can lead them if you can manage to find the one you can lead. But you don't chase them, because that will only frighten them more and make them harder to herd." He took a deep breath. "And that's why herding sheep really is showing something important. That is what a leader does. He gets sheep to do what he wants them to do by giving them no other choice, but does it in a way that does not frighten them."

"But that——but I——" Leopold opened his mouth and closed it a few more times. He scratched his head, looked around for a bench here on the servants' side of the hedge and sat down in the shade. "You're...right."

Siegfried nodded, then added casually, "Of course, the shepherds will be there on the side, with their dogs. I see nothing in this that says you cannot go to them and give them money to herd the sheep for you. Or I suppose you could hire a shepherd and a dog and take them double with you on the horse. That is also what a leader does. He finds people that know how to do what he needs done, then he puts them in charge of doing it so he doesn't have to."

Leopold stared at him, then burst into laughter.

Siegfried patted his shoulder. "Do not say it. I already know. I am smarter than I look."

Leopold shook his head. "All right, let's just look at this thing and figure out what needs to be done and how we can do it better than the rest of them. We don't have horses, but this says they'll supply them. I don't think there will be any advantage to anyone there. I'd bet a round of ale that the Godmother had a hand in this, and that she'll be making mouse-horses."

"Magic armor, too." Siegfried considered this. "I have armor. You don't. Mine is light, compared to some of the foolishness I have seen people trying to wear around here. You could ask for light armor too, but..." He considered. "Now that I think about it...there could be a problem with this. I am fairly certain that at some point we'll have to fight. And I am fairly certain that at that point, if we made a specific request for this trial, they will give us the same armor we asked for the first time and make us fight in it. These sorts of trials are full of things to catch you like that."

"Hmm. I see your point. Riding in armor is no joke. But if you pick light armor for this, you'll be stuck with it when we fight. If you pick heavy armor, you'll be laboring at this trial." Leopold sucked his lower lip. "Unless—"

"Unless they allow us to pick whatever we want?" Siegfried brightened, thinking of the one thing that would serve both purposes.

They looked at each other in glee, and said, simultaneously, "Dwarven chain mail!"

"I have wanted a set of that since I first saw it," Leopold said, matter-of-factly. "My father, the King, has a set. It's been passed down in the family for generations."

"I would seriously consider trading my mother for a set," Siegfried replied fervently. "I would definitely trade my father. Of course, given that my father was not noted for thinking very far ahead, that would not be a good bargain for the Dwarves."

"You'd better not consider trading me," the bird twittered in his ear.

Both men chuckled at Siegfried's quip about his father, then sobered. "Well, assuming they have thought of that already, and have already decided what sort of armor those who don't have any are going to get..." Leopold pondered. "This might not be a question of winning the race so much as not being eliminated."

"A very good point." Siegfried nodded. "It's the whole thinking-ahead business. People who *race* to the midpoint could get themselves into trouble. Arriving exhausted to deal with the sheep and the eggs..."

Leopold shook his head. "It won't be pretty. So, as long as we don't actually fall off in the race, and we look as if we are making an effort, that ought to be enough to keep us just ahead of the middle of the pack."

"The middle is not a bad place to be," Siegfried pointed out. "If you are not a leader, no one is shooting at you."

Leopold's glance sharpened. "You think that might happen?"

Siegfried nodded toward the other side of the hedge. "All of the Princess's enemies sent young men to this trial. I very much doubt that they are concerned with anything but winning, and making sure that what they do to win is done quietly enough that no one suspects them. And besides the obvious candidates, those enemies could have covert agents, as well, placed not to win for themselves, but to make sure that their own Prince wins." As Leopold's mouth dropped open, he shrugged wryly. "Just because my people are sometimes dim, it does not follow that they are not cunning and treacherous. Remember, the keeping of hostages is routine in the north."

"I have the feeling that before this is over, I am going to be more grateful to you for your insights than you are for mine," Leopold said ruefully.

Siegfried smiled. "That depends on which of us wins the Princess."

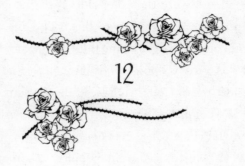

12

SIEGFRIED RECKONED THAT HE AND LEOPOLD would not be the only ones to get advance notice of what the first trial was going to be; they were only the first. And he was right. A full day before it was to take place, it was an open secret. And there was not a shepherd or sheepherding dog to be had neither for favors nor money for miles around. It seemed that the first thing that came to most of the clever candidates was to take an expert riding doubled with them on the horse, on a pillion pad behind the saddle.

Siegfried, on the other hand, went out and talked with sheep.

Or rather, he listened to sheep.

They were, on the whole, just about as dim as most birds—or the men of the north. But he spent a morning paying very close attention every time they wanted something. By afternoon, he had a good idea of what they liked. He had thought they were grazers and ate grass—well they did, but it wasn't what they preferred. They preferred things with leaves and flowers. Clover was a favorite, but any leafy, sweet plant would do. In fact, that was a great complaint of the flock that he listened to; there were bean plants they would dearly have loved to get at, and at least once an hour they would drift over to the fence, lean against it longingly and complain that it hadn't gone away.

It was after supper by the time he hiked his way back from the pasture, but Leopold had promised to meet him at the tavern, and by the time he got there, Leopold had ale and a good meat pie waiting for him—the kind you picked up and ate, rather than the messier sort you had to carve up and fuss with.

"So, I hope you learned something?" the Prince said, as Siegfried bit into the tasty crust.

He nodded, but waited until he had stilled the complaints of his stomach before answering. "I have a plan. Sheep like clover and bean plants. We'll carry bunches of bean plants in flower with clover at the center. When we get there, we'll just lure them into the pens with those."

"You think that will work?" Leopold held up his hand. "Never mind, forget I asked. You're the one who can understand animals. If the sheep said they like beans, then they like beans. I've been working out a way to deal with the eggs."

"Oh?" Siegfried was glad of this. There was always a chance that metal gauntlets would still be too clumsy to handle the eggs. And the rules specifically said that gauntlets had to be worn.

"The rules say nothing about using tools. I picked up what we need in the market this morning." Leopold held up a wooden spoon and a small dustpan, the sort that careful housewives used to collect crumbs from tabletops, to go into the chicken feed.

"Oho!" Siegfried grinned around his pie. "Roll the egg into the dustpan with the spoon, use the spoon to guide it into place in the line. We are clever fellows."

"I'm sure the smart ones will figure out something similar. Or use magic." Leopold shrugged. "One race isn't going to win this set of trials."

\* \* \*

"Well, this should be interesting," Lily observed to the Princess, as they watched the candidates milling about and getting themselves lined up for the start of the race. She felt relatively relaxed; word from the borders was that all the armies had withdrawn—though not completely. At least they weren't bivouacked close enough that it would be an easy march to invade. "It's certainly proved lucrative for the local shepherds." It was an absolutely lovely day; the sun shone down with a warmth that was pleasant in a summer gown, and would soon be hideous for anyone in armor. There was a brisk breeze that no one in armor would feel. The scent of the Forest—green with a hint of something blooming deep within the shelter of the trees—was in the air, which none of the candidates would appreciate, poor fellows, because they would be far too busy concentrating on the trial.

Rosa giggled; about twenty of the sixty or so riders had someone up behind them—obviously shepherds. The lucky ones had a couple of pretty little shepherdesses, and their dogs, tireless little fellows who could run all day and easily keep up with a horse, were sitting patiently at the horse's heels. The unlucky ones had taciturn old men with older dogs in their laps. All of the dogs were of a small, shaggy, black-and-white variety that was the only sort of dog she had ever seen tending sheep. As she and Lily had guessed, of the hundred or so princes who had first arrived, a good half had decided that they would either take the penalty of not being in the first trial, were not in the least prepared for a race in full armor and what that implied about the difficulty of the rest of the trials—for some of them had not bargained on trials that might actually require fighting something—or were not interested in taking part in a contest that began with so little dignity. The Palace was a good bit emptier this morning. It probably would get even more empty when those still competing or those waiting on the sidelines realized that things were only going to get worse from here.

Of the adventuring types...well, they weren't out here right now, but the requirements for them were more stringent. They either would take this first trial, or forfeit and leave. Their race would be tomorrow, but already the tents were emptying. A great many of them simply could not ride a galloping warhorse, or even ride any sort of horse whatsoever, and that disqualified them immediately. Sadly, that was most of the clever shepherds, and a great many of the sell-sword mercenaries, who typically were infantry, not knights or cavalry. Rosa felt a bit sorry for them, but not so sorry that she was going to allow people who had turned up uninvited any sort of leeway. Lily was in agreement here.

It wasn't as if anyone could claim she just didn't want to marry a commoner, either. Not with her pedigree...

The starting line was well away from the Palace, on common grazing land that anyone could use, and many city folk had a beast or two out here, tended by herders whose wages were shared among all those who used his services. Even in a wealthy land like Eltaria, meat was not the sort of thing you had on your table every day if you were a common working man. The animals generally grazed there were milk cattle, geese and goats; these had been herded off to one side so the race could take place. It would follow the edge of the Forest, rough land that wasn't much good for farming, so no one's crops were going to get trampled. That had been a great concern for both Lily and Rosa; how was it fair to destroy someone's livelihood just to have a race? Yet there was no way to have that many men pounding around on horses on a road. Once they had decided on the form of the trial, the hardest part had been finding a good place to hold it.

In the interest of fairness, or at least the appearance of it, Lily had

decided to supply everyone with the same mouse-horses and magically created armor. She and Rosa were the only ones who knew
where these things came from; it was possible that the ability to just
produce that many trained mounts and suits of armor on a moment's
notice might give their enemies something to think about. But that
was only one of the reasons; given the rough ground, neither of them
wanted to risk a horse stepping into a hole and breaking something.

A mouse-horse, being a Magical Beast, might step into a hole, but
if he did, he knew to roll so he didn't break a leg. And hopefully the
rider knew to leap off if the horse went over. He might end up lying
on his back, unable to get up, like an overturned turtle, but if he
knew how to fall, he wouldn't break anything of his own, either.

The muttering and sounds of restless hooves on turf began to die
away as the candidates sorted themselves out into a line. Finally the
milling stopped. All eyes were on the majordomo, splendid in the
royal livery, who had a flag-boy beside him, a blue-and-white banner
held high and floating bravely in the breeze. The tension mounted,
and from where she sat, Rosa was able to make out the majordomo
smiling a little.

He tapped the boy's shoulder. The flag dropped.

They were off, pounding away in a flurry of hooves and flying
clods. The noise was louder than anything Rosa had ever heard
before, louder than thunder. The earth trembled under her feet, and
the air filled with the scent of fresh earth and bruised grass. A clear
number of faster riders surged ahead of the rest. All those carrying
double immediately dropped back; so did the most timid riders, as
the more aggressive shouldered their way through the pack. Before
they were out of sight, the pack had gotten strung out, and it was
possible to single out individual riders and identify them. Siegfried
and Leopold, easily picked out because of Siegfried's height, were a
bit ahead of the middle.

"What on earth do that Northlander and the scoundrel have tied to their saddles?" asked Lily, shading her eyes with her hand and peering as they all vanished into the distance. "Some great shaggy bundle of green. I couldn't make out any details."

Rosa could only shrug; she had seen whatever it was, too, and had been just as puzzled by it. "It looked like bushes. I can't imagine why they would have bushes with them, but I'm sure they have a plan."

"I would be surprised if they didn't," Lily replied matter-of-factly. "Well, time to go to the next stage. I confess, I am looking forward to this." She turned around and went into a small pavilion that had been set up with a guard to mind it. Inside was nothing but one of her mirrors, but no one would know that but the two of them. She set the spell, and led Rosa through the mirror.

They came out of a second one in another small pavilion set up at the middle stage.

The race was going to be long enough that overeager riders would exhaust even mouse-horses, which only had the stamina of real horses—but the mouse-horses had more sense than a real horse and could not be goaded into overextending themselves no matter what you did. So if the mouse-horses pulled up here tired, they would be trotting, or at best cantering, the return route. At this end of the course, there was an enormous sheepfold made of stakes with thorn-bushes impaled on them—in it, the flock of sheep drifted from one side of the fold to the other, baaing and bleating.

There was more than a hint of pungent wool on the breeze.

These were white-face sheep, although Eltaria supported flocks of both black and whitefaces. Far enough away from the full sheep-fold to make it a challenge were the small pens, attached to another, empty sheepfold. These were the pens that the candidates were supposed to get their sheep into, and once they did, gates would be opened in the back of the pens to let the sheep into the other fold.

Along the back of the space between the two folds were the baskets of eggs for the egg-challenge. In theory it didn't matter which you did first, but the smart ones would see how crowded and chaotic the sheep situation was before they decided.

They stood now on a bit of a hill set out with the shade-pavilion; in the back of it was the mirror behind a dividing curtain. The front of it held a pair of chairs and a table that provided a viewing stand for Rosa and Lily. There were already servants here—Brownies disguised as ordinary human servants—with cold water and fruit. "I would willingly have killed someone for all this when I was in the forest," Rosa said, looking down at the food, the comfortable chairs, being careful not to mention the renegade Dwarves.

"We have to look the part, dear," Lily replied, taking a fan from the servant and fanning herself with it. "Appearances are important. You don't know who is watching. We must show that we are vitally interested in the outcome of this trial."

Rosa took that as the cue and warning that it was, and nodded. There truly was no telling who might be listening. Unless Lily took magical precautions, which in and of themselves would betray that she was, in fact, a magician, it was very easy for another magician to eavesdrop on everything they said and did here. Some would be friendly, some merely opportunistic, and some unfriendly.

When the first riders came over the hills, their horses were, predictably, tired—not quite stumbling with exhaustion, but not far from it. The mouse-horses were not going to put up with that sort of abuse on the return leg, and all the speed that the riders had gotten on the outward leg would be lost as their mounts took their time getting back.

And now came the part that Rosa had been looking forward to. She had not really laughed much since her mother died. She and her mother had shared so many things, and laughter was high on the list of the things she missed. And—all right, she knew she was going to be laughing *at* those hapless Princes, and that was not kind—she needed laughter desperately.

As she had known it would be, as the trial unfolded before them, it was not just funny, it was hilarious.

Three of the first men to arrive had brought shepherds with them, the lightest of the lot, two girls and a boy and their relatively small dogs. The shepherds jumped off the rumps of the horses without being told; the little dogs looked eager to get to work. The shepherds at the big sheepfold released about two dozen sheep, which looked bewildered at suddenly finding themselves without the fence around them; the dogs went to work, each of them cutting out three sheep and driving them expertly toward the little pens, while the Princes went straight for the eggs.

But although they had thought through the sheep problem, they had not thought about the eggs, nor the difficulty of handling them in heavy metal gauntlets. Very shortly all three of them were cursing and covered in bits of shell and spattered egg. Their return trip was going to be quite…fragrant…as the raw eggs aged ungracefully in the heat.

Rosa only hoped they weren't getting egg inside the armor. That would be rather nasty.

Meanwhile more riders were appearing with every moment, and more sheep being released, and the ensuing chaos as riders left their horses at a run, only to be confronted with a sea of swirling sheep, was hilarious. It was a giant white wooly whirlpool, in which every sheep had only one urge—not to get away from the flank of its neighbor.

Some just stood and stared. One very large man had evidently decided that the only way to deal with the problem was to tackle it as he would another unarmed warrior. Which was to say, he was tackling the poor sheep.

Or to be more precise, he was trying to. Sheep, it appeared, were able to evade tackles fairly well, and he ended up facedown on the turf time and time again as the flock swirled away from him. When he finally did manage to seize one, he caught it firmly around the middle and hauled it up off the ground—except that the poor thing was upside down, bleating pathetically while he tried to ignore the fact that he had a smelly sheep's rump right in his face. Doggedly, he hauled the bleating, struggling, unhappy animal to the pen, dumped it in and went after another.

Another fellow had the idea that he was going to toss a loop of rope over each sheep's head and lead it to the pen one at a time. This was, in theory, a good idea. The problem was the sheep were not cooperating. He'd get the rope almost over the beast's head, and it would toss it off again. He kept trying to get closer and closer to it, talking coaxingly, but what he was cooing to them were the vilest, funniest epithets Rosa had ever heard. Evidently the sheep's father, mother and grandparents for the last hundred years had gotten up to some interesting assignations if you believed the incredible words emerging from this man's mouth.... It was a wonder this beast still looked like a sheep.

"You really shouldn't be listening to that," Lily murmured, her eyes sparkling with suppressed laughter.

Other men were just attempting what the big man was doing, and the herd swirled faster, in further confusion, sheep leaping over each other in alarm as armored men lunged at them. Finally some of the men realized that once the designated three sheep had been herded up for those who had the foresight to hire shepherds, those shepherds no longer had a job to do. In other words, there were an increasing number of shepherds standing around laughing at them.

But shepherds standing around were shepherds who could be hired now. At least the sheep got a chance to settle down, as the princes converged on the shepherds and began desperate bargains with them, the bids rising higher and higher as each one tried to get *his* sheep to be the next in line.

Then more riders arrived. One, an extremely handsome fellow— Prince Desmond, Rosa thought—clearly had some magical charm to help him; he simply walked up to three sheep and touched them, and they followed him as if they were lambs and he was their mother. She narrowed her eyes and concentrated, and sure enough, she saw a sort of green-brown glowing tether reaching from their foreheads to his hand. Magic. Another had a different sort of charm; he flung some sort of dust at them, and wherever the dust fell, a sheep fell asleep. This wasn't magic, per se…it must have been some sort of herb. He put halters on three and led them to their pen; the stuff didn't last long, since the rest of the sheep woke up pretty quickly once he was working on the eggs.

Oh yes, the eggs. Some of the men had clearly thought the egg problem through and had brought various things to pick up and move the eggs with.

Others…had not. And they waited like hungry ducks, watching the wiser fellows, ready to beg the use of their tools when they were done. Rosa made a note of who took pity on his fellows and gave them the tools, and who did not. "I'd like to add a point for whoever shares his egg-things," she said quietly to Lily, who nodded. "Not penalize for not sharing, but reward for generosity."

"That's a good idea," the Godmother replied, and designated a Brownie to keep track of just that.

Prince Desmond, interestingly enough, had neither tools, nor trouble. Rosa wondered if he had another magic spell to keep the eggs from breaking. If so, it was so minor she couldn't see it from this distance. Well, that was not against the rules, and it was a good idea…though it also made it impossible to say whether he would have shared or not.

Then up rode Siegfried and Leopold, who dismounted and took down those bundles of greenery from behind their saddles, and immediately it became clear what the bushes on the backs of their horses were.

Fodder.

"Interesting," Lily said quietly. "I would have expected them to try hay, which sheep will only eat in the winter. But those are bean plants, which sheep love."

"Do you suppose that Siegfried went and listened to sheep to find out what they like?" Rosa wondered aloud.

"I would not be in the least surprised." Lily leaned forward and watched them keenly. Leopold and Siegfried, instead of going to the milling, frightened flock, went to the sheepfold and asked for six sheep that were not in a panic to be released. And as the gate was opened, they stood side by side and thrust the bundles of fodder in the sheep's surprised faces. Then, still side by side, they backed away. The sheep were hungry, the men were not acting like predators and the bean blossoms must have smelled delicious. They managed to lead all six sheep, step by careful step, across the space between the sheepfolds and into the pens. While not as fast as the shepherds and their dogs, it was efficient, and clever.

Then they went and dealt with their eggs, just as efficiently, using a spoon and some sort of scoop. When they were done, they generously gave the tools over to two of the other Princes without even being asked.

"Very kind," Lily murmured.

Then just as calmly as they had arrived, the two men got on their horses and galloped off. A slow gallop, meant to eat distance without tiring the horse. Rosa felt like applauding.

But the distraction of new riders turning up and trying even more ploys on the hapless sheep was too much, and she turned her attention back to the trial. Several of the men finally decided to be herd-dogs themselves, banding together to chivvy all their sheep at the pens at once. Which was fine, and a good idea, but the pens weren't made for more than three sheep each, and the wooly idiots all tried to crowd into one, met the fence, panicked and began leaping over each other's backs to get out again.

It became very clear that eventually what was going to happen was that, short of more magic, or someone who actually knew what to do about the sheep, the Princes were going to keep paying the shep-herds to take care of the problem for them, and there were going to be enough discarded implements to get the eggs moved into their lines. Rosa glanced over at Lily, who nodded. They used the mirror to get back to the one set up at the starting line, which was now the finish line.

There were already some of the first arrivals there, with the clerks that Lily had left in charge. These were not the ones who had arrived at the sheepfolds first; their mouse-horses were not exhausted and they were mostly clean of egg. Prince Desmond was among them, standing a little apart from the others, his expression pleasant but unreadable, as he waited for his own horse to be brought to him.

"When this is over, those shepherds back there are going to be able to hire more shepherds to do their work for them," Leopold said to Siegfried, as they rode toward the finish line. "In fact, their dogs are going to be able to hire dogs!"

"And a flock of their own to mind." Siegfried chuckled. He was in a very good mood. He and Leopold had gotten through the first trial in good order, and now that they were on their way back to the finish line, he was extremely pleased with where they were. The mouse-horses seemed pleased, too; they loped along at an easy pace, just about a slow gallop, only a little warm and not at all winded. In fact, he and Leopold were passing the occasional rider whose mouse-horse was refusing to get above a trot, horses whose necks and flanks were spotted with dried flecks of foaming sweat. "I think they may be the ones who made out the best out of all of us."

"You're probably right. Still, I have to say, this was not so bad when we used our heads. And your business with the fodder worked a treat." Leopold grinned at the Northerner, who grinned back.

"We could have moved twice the number of eggs with your spoon trick." Siegfried had no trouble returning the compliment. "All things considered, we should do very well in these trials if they are all going to require us to use our heads. You and I are rather good at that."

The horses made a snorting, snickering sound.

Leopold laughed. "Face it, we are geniuses." Then he sobered. "This gave me a good chance to measure our real opponents, actually. I think I've pinpointed five of them that could give us some serious trouble, and I don't mean mere honest rivals...." He shook his head. "I don't much like them. They are clever, no doubt of it. They all thought to hire shepherds. But they went at this as if we were all on a battlefield, and I'm not entirely certain they didn't do some bashing in the pack on the race-leg out. Grigor is as cold-blooded as a snake, and Karl looked like he was ready to kill three of the sheep and chuck the carcasses in the pen."

"The rules didn't say the sheep had to be alive...." Siegfried replied, and shook his head. A chill passed over him, as if the sun had gone behind a cloud for a moment. "I get the feeling that if that one had thought of it, there'd have been mutton before you could say 'knife,' and never mind the shepherd. I expect to see some more trouble out of Karl. And we should watch our backs carefully anytime he is near."

Leopold rode on in silence for a moment; they were far enough from any other riders that the only sounds were the pounding of their own mounts' hooves on the sod, and their rhythmic blowing as they galloped. "Themas and Peder might kill each other. Did you see the way they glared at each other? Fairly made my blood run cold."

"And Stenoth looked like he'd kill the lot of us if someone offered him enough to do it." Siegfried patted his horse's neck, more to comfort himself than anything. Karl might murder you in a conflict, but Siegfried had the impression that Stenoth would be willing to do so in the dark, when you were least expecting it, if he thought he'd profit from it. "That made *my* blood run cold."

"Desmond seems like a good chap. Look, there's the line—" Leopold waved ahead of them, where a faint line of color against the green of the commons had resolved into a line of tiny figures.

"Desmond seems much better than the five. Look, they've brought the carriages up already to the finish line." Leopold pointed at the distant crowd at the point where they had started, and sure enough, the carriages that had brought them all here were pulling up to take them back to the palace. "Hmm. We'll have to share with four other fellows, the way we did when we came in." And since Leopold and Siegfried were still in the front half of the middle group—

"There's going to be a lot of egg-going-bad about." Siegfried slowed his horse to a trot and looked down at its ears. "So, mice, would you be willing to take us all the way to the Palace so we don't have to put up with that?"

The mouse-horse he was riding flicked his ears. "As long as it's at a walk," the Magic Beast replied, sounding amused. "We'd have to walk back there anyway, since we aren't going to be restored in front of everyone. That would be giving part of the game away."

Leopold's mouse-horse glanced over at Siegfried with an amused glance. "I wouldn't want to be in those carriages. How did you know we were mice?"

"A little bird told me," he laughed. The mouse-horses snorted.

"Don't worry. I've no intention of telling anyone else. The Ice-Queen is also the Godmother, isn't she?"

Leopold stared at him as if he had gone mad. "Where did you get the idea that the Queen is also the Godmother? That's pre—" Then he stopped, blinked and sucked in a breath.

"Bloody hell," he said. "That's clever. That is damned clever. That is astonishingly clever. It lets the Godmother run all this without anyone knowing she's doing so. No one can cry 'cheat.'"

More than clever, as Siegfried well knew, and not just because it allowed the Kingdom's Godmother to appear to be aloof from this. It might be one of the reasons why the Princess was alive. The bird had been telling him about The Tradition off and on for years, but this was the first time he'd been able to use some of the things she'd told him to sort out someone *else's* situation. That was why he'd first realized that the Queen could not possibly be as evil as she seemed. If her stepmother really *had* been a Traditional Evil Stepmother, Rosamund would not even be there. The Queen would be the one making the choice of consort, Rosamund would probably be dead. And probably the trial would be much, much smaller, limited to the five enemy princes, and going on for quite some time as she played them against each other.

"How did you figure that out?" Leopold asked him, his eyes narrowing. "And don't tell me a little bird told you."

"I'm astonished. I think you're getting smarter!" the bird sang from above them. She dipped her wings in salute. "I think I may be a good influence on you!"

"Well…" Siegfried felt rather embarrassed, as not only was Leopold staring at him, the ears of both horses had swiveled to catch what he said. "Partly it was because the Princess isn't nearly as intimidated in her presence as she should be, and partly that the Queen isn't doing the sort of things I would expect if she really was bad. Do you know what I mean?"

"Not…really…"

Siegfried rubbed his eyebrows, because with the helmet on he couldn't reach his hair to run his hand through it. "I'll tell you what. Let's get to the Palace, get rid of this armor and go find a good bathhouse. I'll tell you there." He cast a slightly nervous look at the crowd they were rapidly nearing. "You never know who's listening."

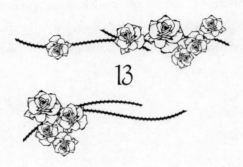

13

SIEGFRIED'S PEOPLE MIGHT HAVE BEEN barbarians by some standards, but they were quite fastidious about cleanliness. Every Clanhouse had a bathhouse attached, and bathing was not a luxury; it was needful. In the winter, the bathhouse was one place you knew you could go to get warm when you were half-frozen, and when your clothing tended to be made of wool and fur, it was a good idea to deflea and delouse them and yourself quite regularly. Bathhouses, as Siegfried knew from experience, were excellent places to have a conversation that you didn't want overheard. The bath attendants would cheerfully put you to soak or steam, and then leave you alone, especially in summer. The walls of a bathhouse were thick to keep in the heat, and usually made of stone or entire logs, which had the effect of preventing most eavesdroppers from listening through walls.

The bathhouse attached to The King's Arms was no exception, with walls at least as thick as Siegfried's arm. It had several small rooms with two tubs in them rather than one big soaking pool, but that was the only way it differed from most of the others Siegfried had seen. The idea was that you scrubbed down, the attendants doused you with buckets of water to clean off the soap, then you soaked in the hot tub. The tubs were very much like oversize barrels, and you soaked in hot water up to your neck in them.

Siegfried would have preferred a northern-style steam bath, but this would certainly serve to soak out the aches of riding. He knew how to ride of course; he just didn't do it often. Drachenthal wasn't suited to horses, so he hadn't actually learned until he left his homeland, but even after he had learned, he preferred not to travel in the saddle. He tended to lose horses, actually. Or rather, people tended to shoot them out from under him. He would get fond of the one he had, only to have someone decide that the best way to get rid of the big blond hero was to kill the horse under him. It got disheartening after a while.

He was just settling in for a nice quiet soak, prepared to think about nothing for a while, when he was interrupted by Leopold taking him at his word and bringing up the subject of the Godmother again. "So," Leopold said softly, "tell me what gave you the idea that Queen Sable was the Godmother."

Siegfried eased himself back in the water, bracing against the side of the tub. It was hard to pinpoint exactly where his suspicions had started. "The name, maybe. It's just a small thing, but it was what made me wonder in the first place. It was...too obvious. Too blatant. Who names their daughter 'Sable'? The name is both the color black and a nasty little weasel that lives in the north. King Thurman was supposed to be no fool, and you would think he would see someone named Sable and avoid her at all costs. He wouldn't marry her. And if someone was named Sable, whether she was born with that name or took it on herself, and if she wanted to marry King Thurman, you would think she would know that and use another name."

Leopold considered that, as the steam from the water rose up around his face. "All right. That's got some logic to it, although I think you could be reading far too much into a name. What else?"

Siegfried couldn't blame him for being skeptical. Leopold wasn't able to understand the bird, and it was likely he was having second thoughts about leaping to the same conclusion. He would have to be very careful about mustering his arguments. "It seemed strange to me in retrospect that the Godmother rescued the Princess, delivered her to the gate, then vanished, and only then did Queen Sable appear." Time to elaborate on that statement. "I would have thought that the Godmother would have stayed to have some sort of confrontation with the Queen, warn her that the Princess was under her protection. Wouldn't you?"

Leopold examined his nails critically before answering. "I could think of reasons why she wouldn't, but...they seem a bit specious, since the Godmother here seems to be pretty powerful."

"It seemed very odd that she just drove off," the Northerner persisted. "And the more I thought about it, the odder it seemed that we never again saw her, even though her magic was clearly everywhere." He closed his eyes for a moment and tried to think of examples before Leopold could challenge him. "The mouse-horses. Why would the Godmother give the Queen mouse-horses to use in the trials? That made no sense at all. The idea for the first trial was a smart one, but there was no reason for the Godmother to supply mounts for it. If the Queen was a powerful sorceress, and those were her mouse-horses, why didn't she...do more?" He groped for more examples. "It was a great many very small things. The Godmother and the Queen are exactly the same height. I'm good at measuring those things by eye. The Godmother and the Queen have exactly the same accent, yet the Queen is supposed to be a foreigner. They have the same inflections when they are angry."

He glanced over at Leopold, whose long hair had gone wild in the steam, curling around his face in tendrils. He wondered if Leopold was listening to all this and thinking he was a loon. Leopold nodded.

"Then there was the Princess. When she arrived, she wasn't out of her rooms for two days, and when she did appear, the Queen took her off to the Royal Suite and was locked up with her when the messenger came. After that, she's been spending most of her time at the Queen's side. And you would think she would be terrified, being locked up with the Queen for hours at a time. The Queen is older. She has a commanding way, and a young woman like that can only stand up to a woman like the Queen for so long. You'd think she'd be cowed, getting meeker every day." He waited for a response from Leopold.

The Prince scratched his head thoughtfully and stared off into space for a moment. "She wasn't. Even I could see that. She didn't seem properly frightened, in fact, it seemed like she was—they were—"

"Acting together." Siegfried nodded. "It looked to me as if they were pretending they didn't like each other, but they didn't go any further than that, because people here already don't like the Queen and they'll think anything bad of her that you suggest. But the two of them, when it came to getting things done, didn't argue. The Queen didn't even give the Princess an insult now and again, or sneer at her. All she did was keep up the glacier facade, and even that didn't hold up if you looked at her closely."

Leopold pulled a face. "You are still making sense. I didn't even think about it, but then, why would I?"

"Why would anybody? People see what they expect to see." Leopold mustered his thoughts, splashing some hot water over his face to rinse off the sweat. "Then they put together the first contest. I was wondering, when they said that it didn't matter if the contestants didn't have a horse or armor, because they would supply them, if somehow we were going to do this thing in small groups over the course of several days. Because there just weren't enough horses in the Palace stable for all of us, and armor doesn't grow on trees. But no, they say it's going to be one big race, and suddenly there's enough horses for all of us, and matching armor out of nowhere, all the same."

"Magic," said Leopold. "Could have been the Queen—"

"But she had never done anything like that before. That's not small magic. Transforming, creating out of nothing—that's big. If the Queen could do things like that, what does she need with a little Kingdom like Eltaria? No, that's Godmother magic. But where's the Godmother? Nowhere." Siegfried returned Leopold's nod. "So you see. Then I realized the horses were the same ones we rode here on. Exactly the same. I'm big, and there aren't many horses, transformed or not, that are up to my weight."

"Still— " Leopold looked as if he was about to agree but still had a reservation or two about Siegfried's conclusions.

So Siegfried drove his argument home. "But what clinched it was when I saw the Queen and the Princess at the starting line, watching, and then when we got to the middle section and sheep part, there they were again, watching. *Maybe* they could have gotten faster horses than ours, but we would have seen them passing us. They couldn't have gone by horse, so they had to go by magic and the Godmothers are the only people I ever heard of that could do that." He had to smile as Leopold accepted his clinching argument.

"Do we tell them?" the Prince asked instead. "Do we tell them that we know what the Queen is?"

He shook his head. "Not unless something comes up and she needs to know that we know. It gives us an advantage. I like advantages. I like—" he was about to say "the Princess," but stopped himself in time "—the idea of knowing things no one else knows in a situation like this."

"The bird might tell—" Leopold began, then shrugged. "I suppose you can ask it not to."

"And I will." Siegfried ducked farther down into the hot water.

"Tomorrow. Right now I want to soak until all my aches are gone, and then I want to sleep past dawn."

Leopold rolled his eyes and laughed. "Past dawn! Shame! Civilization is making you soft!"

Siegfried threw a handful of water at him.

The Palace ballroom, which had many doors that opened up on the garden, had not been in much use over the past few years. Every time Celeste intended to hold a ball, it seemed, the enemies on the border decided it was time to rattle sabers again, and off King Thurman would go.

All that had changed, and although there was no ball taking place, the ballroom was no longer closed up and dark. Tonight, as on the past several nights, it was lit with thousands of wax candles, and all the doors were standing open wide to a wonderful night breeze coming in from the garden. The garden itself had been illuminated with torches, their light reflecting in the water of little ornamental pools and tiny fountains.

All of the sons-nephews-grandsons of the neighbors were still in the running, and as a consequence, the borders were still clear, and Godmother Lily had told Rosa not to worry for now. So she was trying not to; trying to actually enjoy some of this.

The much-thinned ranks of the Princes milled about the garden and ballroom, while a single minstrel played in one corner. There was wine to drink, and there were still lovely ladies to flirt with, and none of those lovely ladies but the Princess had been present to see what fools they all had made of themselves at the sheepfolds. Princess Rosamund moved among them and her courtiers, congratulating and commiserating in turn.

At the moment, things were not going as she had planned or hoped. She had looked in vain for Siegfried and Leopold; they were nowhere in sight, and she felt a twinge of disappointment. She told herself again that she wasn't supposed to have favorites, but it didn't really help.

Then she heard her name in an unfamiliar voice. "Princess Rosamund." Just as she was turning around on hearing a little stir from the garden, hoping she might finally catch them coming in the door, one of the crowd in front of her detached himself from the people he was talking to, moved into her path and bowed a little.

She returned the bow with a gracious nod. It was a good thing she had early on learned the trick of pinning names to faces quickly, for she had his name on her tongue before he had straightened. "Prince Desmond. You did well out there, and I understand from all that I saw you were particularly deft in the middle stage." She did not say that Siegfried and Leopold had been just as quick without the use of magic. That would not have been politic, and besides, this was the first time she had seen this particular young man except at a distance. He certainly was worth a closer look.

The Prince in question was undeniably good-looking.

He was built as well as any of the candidates, and better than some. Wide shoulders did not strain the velvet of his tunic; it was fitted to him too well for such a tailoring mistake. A sash-belt with an ornamental sword hanging from it showed off a narrow waist without making it look as if he was *trying* to do so. Good, muscular legs inside formfitting moleskin breeches made it very clear that Desmond rode, rode well and rode often.

As for the rest of him, blue eyes glittered at her from a face that was just saved from being too pretty by a good square jaw. A comma of black hair over one eyebrow saved his short ebony locks from being arranged a little too perfectly. He smiled charmingly, and had very white teeth. "If by that, Princess, you mean to imply that I had magical help, yes I did. There was nothing in the rules forbidding it." His smile broadened. "In fact there wasn't much in the rules at all. Very wise. If you'd forbidden anything, plenty of people would try to violate the rule, someone was sure to cry foul, and we would be running the same race for the next fortnight. The shepherds would appreciate it, but not the sheep, and certainly not us."

She shrugged. "It isn't as if you all are without resources, and the trial is supposed to weed those who have little from those who have a great deal to offer. I must find out just what resources those are, and how clever you are with them. My people have a saying, 'Never buy a pig in a sack.'"

"I think that's a universal," said Desmond, then cocked his head to the side in a curiously charming gesture as he shifted his weight to his other foot and she fanned herself. "That is a rather earthy sort of saying."

"I am a rather earthy sort of Princess," Rosamund replied, throwing him a challenge. "My mother was a shepherdess, after all." There were those that would find that a distinct handicap. *Let's see how he reacts to that.*

"Was she?" He chuckled. "My grandfather made clocks. As a hobby, but they were rather good ones. We think he probably would have made a better clockmaker than a ruler. He certainly would have been happier as a clockmaker. There is something to be said for being happy in what you do." Desmond's smile didn't waver. Well good, he wasn't going to run screaming because she was half commoner.

"Do you expect to get similar magical help with the rest of the trials?" she asked. "It would be useful to know that, from my perspective. Resources, after all—was this just a onetime charm, or do you have someone you can call on at will? I suppose you already know that since we know some of you will be using magic, we're concocting contests where magic won't help." *I hope,* she added mentally.

"Oh, I would expect that. You've already shown how clever you are, just by staging all of this— " his gesture took in the room full of Princes and the gardens beyond "—in order to hold off the wolves that would have descended when your father died. I admire your skill and your wit, Princess, and your ability to think when pressed and pressed hard. You have enemies ready to swoop down over the borders and swallow you whole, so you manage to get almost a hundred hostages to come to you and put themselves willingly in your hands. Very good strategy. I couldn't have managed better myself."

For a moment, it seemed as if the two of them were encased in a bubble that held everyone else out. He gazed into her eyes with a hint of challenge. She raised an eyebrow at him. "You don't approve?"

"Oh, I very much approve. I wouldn't be here myself if I didn't approve." His smile never wavered. "There are plenty of available royal ladies out there who don't have the sense to save themselves or the wit to figure out how. They rely on men to do all that for them. They don't interest me."

"And I do?" She was getting charmed, despite trying not to be. She couldn't help it; that last came out with more than a hint of flirtation in it.

"I wouldn't still be here if you didn't." He gave her a bow, and the moment passed, the invisible bubble evaporated, and people were moving into their space as they talked. "But I am keeping you from the rest of your guests. I understand that protocol must be observed here. It wouldn't do to be seen talking too long with any particular fellow among us. You can't have favorites."

But his knowing smile said *not even me, even though you'd like that.*

"Quite right." She gave him a nod, and softened it with a smile. "Best of luck in the next contest, Prince Desmond."

As she moved on to the next guest, a waft of breeze carried the scent of roses in from the garden and she found she was still smiling, the disappointment over not seeing Siegfried quite, quite gone.

\* \* \*

Lily collapsed in a chair beside the cold fireplace, which in summer was filled with flowers. Once the last of the spells had been broken, she felt as if she had been carrying every one of those Princes across the finish line on her own back. It had been a very, very long day, first transforming, then releasing all those mouse-horses, conjuring and dismissing the armor. Even with nearly unlimited Traditional power pressing down on this kingdom like swollen-bellied rain clouds, the work had still taken its toll on her. A hot bath had helped, and after a light supper Rosamund had volunteered to be the gracious hostess, and Lily had blessed her for the few hours alone. She'd not gotten many of those of late, and she surely missed her privacy and the comfort of her own Palace.

This was the most time she had spent in the company of anyone other than her Brownies in decades. Godmothers generally worked alone, and Lily was no exception to that rule. She had forgotten how wearying the constant presence of mortals was. Especially when she had to keep up her disguise of Queen Sable. They seemed to be everywhere, and they all wanted something of her. Her Brownies were exquisitely sensitive to her moods, and knew when to leave her alone. The human servants…weren't. If she didn't periodically lock her door, she'd never keep them out.

But now the doors *were* locked, the windows were open, there was a lovely breeze coming in off the garden, and the people who crammed the Palace full betrayed themselves by nothing more annoying than a distant murmur, like bees. She sipped at a glass of sherbet.

"Have you had any luck with the Huntsman?" she asked aloud. And Jimson, as she had known he would, answered her.

"He has been very circumspect, Lily. He's scarcely moved from his quarters except to conduct his duties. I don't understand it. In short, he gets up, he eats, he goes out to hunt, he comes back laden with game for the royal tables, he eats, and then goes to sleep."

She frowned. That was unexpected. She had thought that surely he would have made contact with one of the Princes—whoever had paid him to dispose of Rosa. She wouldn't have thought he'd have given up so easily. "Somehow I don't think we frightened him. Do you?"

"No," the Mirror Servant said flatly. "I do not." Then Jimson sighed, and Lily thought she detected a distinct note of guilt in his voice. "I believe he has been ordered to keep quiet, possibly by one of the candidates our neighbors sent, although how he got those orders, I don't know. I thought I was watching him very closely. I am sorry. I must not have been watching him closely enough. This is on my head."

"It's not your fault," Lily replied, waving off the apology. "You've been every bit as busy as Rosa and I have. For all we know, the Huntsman's orders came in a note left in a kennel, and catching him looking for that would have taxed anyone. It's not as if I haven't had you doing the work of three Mirror Servants—even with the help of your Apprentices—" She paused when Jimson coughed discreetly. "What is it?"

"Oh, I have been watching the Huntsman personally," Jimson replied, "I hope you do not think I delegated that—"

"I know better than that. Don't be ridiculous, Jimson. I work you harder than any Godmother has ever worked someone, and I know I can always rely on you to do what you say you will—no one could keep up with me but you! I really do not know what I would do without you, especially now!" She smiled over her shoulder at him, and he flushed a slightly deeper green. "If you need more apprentices for this, then get them. Let them handle things that are tedious and less important. I need you for the clever things." She got up and moved to the chair facing the mirror. As another breeze wafted through the room, she lifted the hair off the back of her neck to let the cooling air get to it. "Speaking of clever things, the next contest should be something where magic is not going to help. There were too many of those young men using charms—and I don't think that the King of Eltaria should place too much reliance on magic—except for mine." She sighed. "And mine is not infallible."

Jimson frowned, his brows furrowing. "That isn't going to be easy. You can forbid the use of it, but that doesn't mean they won't cheat. Finding a task where magic is useless will be a tall order."

"I've been thinking about this a little." She sipped her sherbet and pondered the question. "We could make it strictly a test of intelligence, a chess tournament, perhaps. Though I am not sure that would serve if not all of them know chess. Or solving a puzzle? That's Traditional."

"Don't make it untying a knot," Jimson replied, making a face. "There's a Traditional answer for that, which leaves you without a knot to be solved by the rest of the candidates. And they can't all chop the thing to bits."

She twined a strand of hair around her fingers, thinking. "A maze, a puzzle… we would have to put some sort of negation spell on them so that magic couldn't be used to solve them. Besides, that seems too…small." She shook her head. "Am I not thinking spectacularly enough?"

Jimson nodded. "Whatever we do, if it is a public trial, it must be flamboyant. The Tradition expects that. Remember, the more we satisfy The Tradition, the more power will be available to you. And whatever we choose, we need to make sure it has something to do with testing the capabilities of a potential king for this country."

"I can't see how puzzles or mazes would be relevant, then," Lily sighed. They needed a contest and they needed one soon, or their enemies would see this for what it was—an attempt to stall for time. "What would be relevant?"

"Finding a way to get what you want without having to fight," said Jimson wryly. "That would be relevant, considering that Thurman managed to fend off fights more often than he actually engaged in them. Traditionally, one of the tasks in a trial is to fetch something with a dangerous guardian. Could we have them get something for us? Don't we have a dragon up on Sharpstone Pass? Don't dragons have the ability to nullify magic?"

"Some of them do." She frowned, thinking. She hadn't had much to do with the Sharpstone Dragon in a century. Even when she had, he hadn't spoken more than three words, and one of them had been "No." Still, he was perfectly happy with his monthly tribute of sheep, no one really wanted to use the Sharpstone Pass, and the only people who ever tried to come through there were generally up to no good. "I don't want him hurt. He's a very effective deterrent on that pass. The question is if he would be willing to cooperate. You know that he is not going to want to part with any of his hoard."

"What dragon ever does? And even if we gave him things for them to….oh…" Jimson suddenly became very alert. "I think I have a plan. But as you say, we would have to see if he will cooperate. Is there anyone we can send so that you don't have to go?"

Lily drummed her fingers on the arm of the chair for a moment. "Perhaps. Perhaps. Can you see if Godmother Elena is able to talk? I need to find another dragon. Sharpstone won't talk to me, but he will to one of his own kind."

Jimson beamed. "Immediately, Lily!"

14

SIEGFRIED AND LEOPOLD SLIPPED BACK INTO THE
Palace by the servants' entrance, after an evening spent trying to
puzzle out what the next contest might be at the King's Arms.
Neither one of them wanted to mingle—again—with the rest of the
candidates as was the custom after supper, to tell the truth. The
regular evening gatherings were already getting rather tedious to
both of them. Nothing ever happened, except the endless subtle and
not-so-subtle jockeying for information and status. In fact, what
both of them wanted most to do was get some sleep. It only occurred
to Siegfried, just as he was drifting off, that the so-helpful old lady
might be waiting in the garden again to give them hints about what
the next contest was. But of course, at that point it was too late to
do anything about it.

In the morning, they went together to the dining hall, got food
and took it out into the gardens to see if the bird was about. She was,
but she didn't have any good ideas, either. She happily shared their
breakfast, but that was all. "I was asleep last night," she explained
needlessly. "And besides, it's not a good idea to spy on a Godmother.

They are sometimes swift to anger, and I am easy to transform. I like being a bird. I wouldn't like being a toad."

Lacking anything else to do, they separated to see if they could get more information that way. Leopold joined the Princes idling in the garden, Siegfried joined the ones idling in the stables and the practice grounds. From everything that Siegfried could see, no one else had any clues, either. Many tried to guess, of course. A good many decided fearfully that it was likely to involve fighting. Even more came to the same conclusion, but regarded the prospect with a great deal of enthusiasm. This meant that the practice ground was thick with young men sparring with each other by midmorning. The ladies of the court found this much more appealing to watch than their needlework. There was a rough stand of sorts set up, with a canvas shade to keep the sun off, just outside the fence. Since this was a practice field normally used by the knights of the court, there was often a lady watching, but this might have been the first time in a very long time that the stands were full.

Siegfried joined them, but only to keep his hand in and stay fit, not because he thought they were right. Leopold did not join them, but leaned on the fence to observe with several other men. Siegfried did not think he was doing this because he was lazy, as some of the others said in voices they thought too low to carry. When he was resting, he watched Leopold watching them. Analyzing the fighting styles of others was, oddly perhaps, not what he was good at. But then, his people were not themselves noted for subtle fighting styles—and his own style was, truthfully, to rush in like a great bear and attempt to batter his opponent into unconsciousness, or at least submission, within the first dozen blows. But Leopold was watching all of the other Princes very closely in a carefully-not-watching way as they fought. Siegfried had hopes he was going to get an earful about how the others measured up, and even higher hopes that Leopold might be able to coach him through some changes to his own fighting.

When Siegfried was satisfied that he had gotten enough of a workout, and several of his fellow Princes were nursing the bruises he had given them with winces and rueful glances, he joined Leopold at the fence. The Prince wrinkled his nose as Siegfried approached. Siegfried moved downwind.

"I know. I stink." The Northerner made apologetic motions with his hands. "I'm going to get cleaned up, and then it will be time for dinner."

"I don't know how you can even think of dinner after doing something like that," Leopold mock-complained. "Considering how many blows you took, you should be sick by now."

"Because a little exercise makes a man hungry," Siegfried replied. Then quietly he added, "Studying their styles, I hope? It's not as if I can't adapt, but I need coaching. A lot of coaching."

"Indeed I was, and if you and I need to fight them, they are going to be even more bruised than they are now, because I am a very good coach." Leopold shared a conspiratorial grin with him.

"I'm glad to hear that." Siegfried was gladder than ever that he and Leopold had cooked up this alliance. The more time he spent with the handsome devil, the better he liked the man.

"And hope that you don't ever have to face Desmond." Leopold sobered. "He is not someone to underestimate. He's got the same reach you do, he's as strong as you are, and he's quicker."

"I'm not glad to hear that." Siegfried frowned. This was not the sort of thing that boosted his confidence. But—these fellows were usually trained in very specific styles, and Siegfried came from a land where anything was fair—

"And don't think fighting dirty will help. He'll fight dirty, too." Leopold might have been reading his mind.

"Bah." Siegfried vaulted over the fence, and the two of them headed in the direction of the Palace, Siegfried carefully remaining downwind.

They parted at the Palace, Siegfried to go get a quick wash at the stable, where there were pumps, Leopold to collect rumors. But what he collected was not a rumor, but a fact, and he caught up with Siegfried while the latter was still shirtless and toweling off his hair.

"After dinner the next contest is going to be announced," he said, with suppressed excitement. "And that's all anyone knows. But it is definitely official. I heard the Queen herself confirming it."

"So whatever it is, either Old Maggie thinks we can handle it without advance warning, or she took her services elsewhere," murmured Siegfried, a little disappointment in his voice.

"Or she didn't know, either. I would bet on that." Leopold seemed very sure. Siegfried wasn't nearly as certain. But—well, he should give the woman the benefit of the doubt, he supposed.

The announcement had spread like wildfire, and the Queen and Princess looked down at the restless men at the very full tables with enigmatic smiles. Finally when the last of the food had been cleared away, the Queen arose.

"We are pleased to announce the second contest of the trials," she said without any preamble. "We think it will prove something of a challenge."

As she spoke, servants began bringing in baskets lined with white silk cloth—and curiously, they all wore silk gloves. Siegfried's brows furrowed, as he stared at them. *What on earth*—why would they need to handle what was in those baskets with silk? Were the items that delicate? Was the contest to keep from breaking them?

"Our servants are going among you and handing you small, valuable objects. They are all made of gold. Please take one, and hold on to it while the rest are distributed." There was something very odd about the gleam in the Queen's eyes.

Sure enough, the servant that was working their table handed Leopold a strange neck-chain, and Siegfried a gold ring. And the moment he touched it, he got a familiar mixed feeling of danger and desire from it. And a tingle. It was the same sort of feeling that he had gotten from—

*"Doom!"* sang his bird at his shoulder. He stared at her in alarm. Oh surely, surely no one had gotten hold of *that* ring and brought it here! Then she trilled a chuckle. "Only, not the doom you think—"

By that point every one of the Princes had his object and was holding it, wearing varying expressions, ranging from boredom to bafflement.

"Each of you has been given a cursed object," the Queen said with apparent relish.

*I knew it!* He wanted to throw the ring as far away from him as he could, but he knew it was too late now. *That* was why the servants had been wearing silk. Silk insulated you from magic.

"Now we assure you," she continued, her voice strengthening to carry over the sounds of outrage and surprise. "We assure you that they are merely inconvenient curses, not fatal ones. Some of the curses will cause some discomfort, some will cause embarrassment, and some will change your behavior, which will probably also cause embarrassment. Still, you will want to get rid of these things. And that is your contest—you are to rid yourselves of these objects as quickly as possible. Only you are not to merely discard them, nor give them to whatever magician you have in your employ, nor fob them off on a Dwarf. You won't be able to in any event. The object will return to you unchanged unless you meet the very specific condition required. No, there is only one way and one place you can go to be rid of these things."

She smiled. Siegfried groaned. He knew what was coming, knew it instinctively. After all, what was the one thing that was almost immune to magic and loved gold more than Dwarves did?

"You must place your object in the hoard of the Dragon of Sharp-stone Pass. And you must do so without harming the dragon in any way. He is useful to us. If you hurt him, you forfeit. There will be a Marshal there to make sure you abide by this." She gazed down at the Princes. "You may persuade him, trick him, slip the object into the hoard without him knowing, bargain with him—the possibilities are endless. As long as you don't attempt to harm him, anything is fair. Time is flying, gentlemen. Time is flying. The curses have not yet come home to you, and the dragon is a good distance away from here. And the longer you dally, the more likely it is you will find out personally just what curse your object carries."

"You are a sadistic woman," said Rosa, from her vantage point in the window overlooking the garden. The garden boiled with activity, like a nest of ants that a child had stirred up. Behind her, Lily chuckled.

"Don't blame me, blame Jimson. It was his idea," she replied. "I merely agreed that it was a good one, since we specifically wanted a task that couldn't be helped with magic. Even Sharpstone was amused, once Gina explained things properly to him."

"Gina?" Rosa asked, her brow wrinkling. "I don't recall that name. Do I know anyone named Gina?" She turned to look at Lily. She realized at that moment that they were beginning to look like a mother-daughter pair—both in the black of mourning, both in garments made by the same Brownies.

The only difference was that Lily had a far more revealing bodice. The protective one that Rosa was wearing was a lot more comfortable than she had thought it would be, but the high neck had the curious effect of making her look younger than she actually was, which annoyed her once in a while. Usually when she was trying to get one or another of the Princes to see her as *her,* and not the prize-to-be-won.

"Not directly. She's a dragon, specifically, a Dragon Champion. One of only two that I know of, although, who knows—" The God-mother shrugged. "I would expect that the other dragons are studying this, and there may one day be more. Dragons take a long time to decide if they are going to do something—almost as long as the Fae. At any rate, your indirect connection is that Gina is the donor for your dose of Dragon's Blood. She and her mate are extremely friendly and helpful to the Godmothers, and I was able to contact her again through Godmother Elena. Sharpstone is not particularly friendly to humans, but I thought he might be willing to listen to our proposition if we made it through another dragon."

"I can see that a dragon would be happy to add to his hoard, and all of those things are made of gold, so that would make them attractive to him, as well." Rosa nodded and turned back to her perusal of the garden. Things were getting quite interesting down there, more so by the moment. "What I don't understand is why he would be willing to have so many cursed objects near him. I would think even a dragon would need to worry about curses."

Lily laughed as she replied. "The reason is why this entire scheme works so very well for all of us. Sharpstone won't be any more concerned about those curses than he would be about fleas. He is one of those powerful old dragons whose very presence nullifies any magic but his own. It's something a dragon acquires over time, just like increasingly tough scales, which is why the older a dragon is, the harder it becomes to kill even with a magic weapon."

Rosa turned away from the window to see that Jimson was more or less looking over Lily's shoulder at her, both of them looking, not smug, but commendably pleased with themselves. "I didn't know that!" she exclaimed. "Is that why really old, wicked dragons need *blessed* weapons to kill them, rather than magic?"

"Indeed." It was Jimson who replied. "And that is half the reason why he is willing to take in cursed articles. The curses are negligible to him. He is so powerful he could nullify a hundred times more than we'll send him. But as you wisely pointed out, the objects themselves are gold, and there is nothing that a dragon of his sort loves better than gold."

Lily smiled. "The other half of the sum that makes him willing to work with us is that fairly soon word will spread that his hoard is full of cursed objects, and it won't be possible for anyone to tell which are cursed and which are not. Would *you* try stealing from that hoard under those circumstances?"

Rosa had to laugh at that. It would be a very, very foolish person who would take that sort of risk—first to have to face an old and powerful dragon, and then assume that you might be infected with not just one, but many curses. Unless you had someone along with you who could do a wholesale curse removal... "I don't think so! And anyone who would—well he'd have to be so stupid he would deserve what he got. But where did you get all those cursed objects?"

Lily smiled ruefully, and shared a glance with Jimson. "Well, that comes under the day-to-day tasks that a Godmother does without really thinking about it. Things with curses on them turn up all the time, and when I find out about them, I generally take them away from the owner, because my control of Traditional magic is powerful enough to allow me to do that. Most magicians just can't command that kind of force—it's relatively easy to take a curse off an object before the curse has infected anyone, but it's a lot harder to negate the magic that binds the object and the curse to a person. Because we Godmothers routinely put these sorts of minor curses on people that need a lesson, Traditionally it's easier for us to bind and unbind curses and cursed objects."

Rosa nodded. "Witches would be good at setting them and taking them off, too?" she hazarded.

Lily gave her an approving glance. "Better at setting than taking them off, but yes. It's The Tradition, again. Wizards and sorcerers of all sorts are very poor at it, followed by sorceresses. Those with the most success are witches, and if you *really* want to make things skewed in your favor, it's best to make the witch look as ancient, gnarled and warty as possible."

"That's rather hard on pretty witches." Rosa giggled.

"I must admit, I'm glad that particular part of The Tradition doesn't apply to Godmothers." Lily smoothed the hair back from the side of her ageless face with an unconscious gesture. "When I get these things away from people, I can store them in a place that's shielded, where they can't hurt anyone. Sometimes they're useful to have around in case I need to teach someone a lesson, but mostly they gather dust in safe bins in the cellar of my Castle, because I either don't know or can't tell what it was they did. I have not only the ones that I collected down there, I have the ones that my predecessors gathered, and not all of them left careful notes." She walked over to join Rosa at the window. "Frankly, I wasn't going to give the Princes a choice, but I did have a modicum of pity for the adventurers. I told them what they were going to get, and that they could decline and leave. We lost a goodly swath of them, as you might imagine."

It was easy to tell some of the curses from up here. There was one poor fellow that seemed to be cursed with clumsiness; he couldn't pick up a glass without spilling it or an object without dropping it. People were giving him a wide berth. "What if a Prince just can't get Sharpstone to take his wretched object?" Rosa asked after a while.

"In a week or so I'll offer the ones who are still left the option to take their chances with Sharpstone or admit defeat and allow me—the Godmother version of me—to take their object and curse away and forfeit the trials." She raised an eyebrow. "I'm not entirely unfair or without pity."

They both watched the Princes below. Lily had not been trying to bluff them into hurrying their plans when she'd told them that time was fleeting. Besides the Curse of Clumsiness, several curses were already manifesting...

Boils, mostly; it seemed to be a very common curse. There were faces dotted in soothing salve, and necks and hands covered in bandages. Rosa felt very, very sorry for the poor fellows, because not only were none of these curses going to go away, until they finally decided to dare the dragon, it was only going to get worse.

Leopold and Siegfried stared glumly at one another. By nightfall, their curses had manifested. Siegfried's was the most...obvious. "Well," said Siegfried. "I can say this much. It's unique. And it's not as painful as boils."

Two toads and a frog fell from his lips.

That is, they *appeared* to fall from his lips; they actually manifested two inches away from his mouth and fell. He caught them expertly— he'd had a lot of practice by now—and tossed them in a bucket.

Anytime he spoke, frogs and toads fell from his mouth. Real, live frogs and toads. He had no idea where they were coming from.

It didn't happen when he ate, breathed or yawned, only when he spoke, and the curse didn't seem to care if he shouted or whispered. The moment a word passed his lips, he got an amphibian. Sometimes more than one. He *really* did not want to approach the Princess with this happening. He didn't think she was the kind to squeal at a frog, but it wasn't pleasant to try to talk to someone and have slimy things raining down on your shoes.

"I'll trade you," Leopold replied glumly. His curse apparently had been bad luck—but only at gambling. This had him in deep despair, for gambling was not a trivial pursuit for him. "I don't have a father feeding me great stacks of money, Siegfried! I make my living gambling! Technically *this,* going after the Princess, is a gamble! If I don't get this thing off me, I won't have a chance of winning her!"

Obsessively he threw a pair of dice over and over again, and each time they came up ones.

"I'm pretty certain trading doesn't work, Leo," Siegfried replied, catching the toads as they fell. "Two of the others tried it and they ended up with both curses. And their original objects returned to them anyway. I think they have this tied up pretty neatly to prevent us from doing anything but face the dragon or give up." He took the bucket to the window and turned the toads out onto the lawn, where they hopped indignantly away.

So far, only three of the Princes had left for the mountain, which was something of a surprise to him. Curses were nothing to be sneezed at, and he wanted his taken off as soon as it could happen. The irritating fact was, if Leopold hadn't been obsessing over the loss of his gambling luck rather than figuring out what to do about the dragon, they themselves would have been halfway there by now.

He began to wonder if the bad-gambling-luck was the actual curse, or just a kind of side symptom of what was really afflicting his friend. This wasn't like Leopold at all. He was usually overflowing with optimism, not moping.

Looking at Leopold's tragic face, Siegfried made up his mind. This was ridiculous. He couldn't go on like this—not because having toads and frogs raining out of him with every word was all that bad, but because if he had to listen to Leopold moaning anymore, he was going to kill the man. It was time for him to take charge of the situation.

He put down the bucket, advanced on his friend and hauled him unceremoniously to his feet. Holding him by the collar, he shook Leopold vigorously and set him down again. "Enough!" he said. "It won't be the end of the world as long as we go do something about it!" Five more toads landed on the floor.

Leopold sagged back down onto the chair, and looked up at Siegfried in dazed shock. The Northerner stalked over to the arms rack, grabbed his sword and belt, and Leopold's, and threw Leopold's at him. Reflexively, Leopold caught it. With a jerk of his head and a grunt—which only produced a hapless little tree frog—he stalked out the door.

Leopold caught up with him at the door of the stables. Siegfried thankfully didn't have to say anything when he got there; the grooms were already waiting to saddle up horses for whoever turned up. It didn't look as if they were getting mouse-horses this time; what the grooms pulled out for the two of them were plain, sturdy brown beasts of the sort you might see pulling a farm cart. There evidently was a standard kit ready and waiting: saddlebags with provisions and a map to Sharpstone Pass. A glance at the map gave Siegfried one bit of good news; the Pass wasn't more than two days away.

Wordlessly, they mounted up and headed down the road on the map. It was easy enough to follow, and they spent an entire day in unwonted silence. It actually wasn't bad at first, if he didn't look back at his friend; Siegfried was used to traveling alone, and with Leopold hunched morosely in the saddle, obstinately refusing to do anything other than sigh, he might as well have been alone.

Still, having that giant lump of gloom trailing behind him began to wear on him after a while. Siegfried managed to keep from having to say anything until they found a spot to camp for the night—which was near enough to a stream that the poor creatures he was producing would be able to get to water easily. Only then did he open his mouth.

"Are you done whining like a sulky brat?" he asked, producing a veritable flood of amphibians. It caught him by surprise; had the curse saved up an entire day's worth of toads to spill out as soon as he spoke?

"I think it's more than just losing my gambling luck," Leopold finally said, sounding—well, not at all like himself. Strained, but with something more under his voice. Panic, maybe? "I have this horrible urge to write poetry and learn to play the lute...."

Siegfried stopped catching frogs and chucking them in the direction of the water to turn to stare at his friend in absolute horror. Write poetry? Learn the lute? The Queen had warned them that there might be some curses that changed you—but—this could be bad. This could be very bad. "Please don't tell me you want to dress all in black," he said, aghast, as a couple more frogs dropped to his feet.

Leopold nodded, a haggard wariness coming over his expression. "Black...of course I want to dress in black. It suits the deep night of my soul. What rhymes with shadow?" he asked, then looked appalled. "I don't believe I just said that...."

In the back of Siegfried's mind, a tiny treacherous thought arose. It was obvious that Leopold was turning into one of those morose poet-princes, the sort that slouched around their Castles by night, slept by day and spent all their time trying to be Artistic and do what bards did, only do it half as well, if that.

*If I don't do anything, if I just leave in the morning without waking him, he'd never get there himself. He'd either go back to the Palace or just sit here moping. I'd get rid of him without ever actually doing anything to him—*

Immediately, though, he stepped on that nasty thought and pounded it into submission. That was wrong; it was completely wrong. He and Leopold had promised to help each other, and he was not going back on that promise. Besides, Leopold as a poet? He wouldn't inflict that on the world; it was too cruel.

No matter how tempting it was.

The bird was perched on a dead branch he'd driven into the ground near the fire where he could keep an eye on her. He hadn't spoken to her since he'd started this frogs-and-toads nonsense, but if anyone would have advice, it was likely she would. She was drowsing, having eaten some cake crumbs and a few insects she'd caught. He tapped gently on her branch, and she opened one eye.

Before he could ask for advice, she was already giving it to him.

"Try talking to him. The dragon, I mean," she said, and closed her eye again, settling back into her drowse.

*Try talking to him? What kind of advice is that? It's a dragon!* he thought indignantly. He was actually reaching for the branch to shake it, when he stopped himself.

Maybe that wasn't such a bad idea.

After all, the Godmother'd had to talk to the beast herself to get him to agree to this—though why a dragon would want cursed gold in its hoard—

*Wait, of course it would. If people think the dragon is sitting on a lot of cursed objects, they won't try stealing anything.*

All right then. They'd try talking to it. What was the worst that would happen?

*The worst that would happen would be we're stuck with these curses. No. No, I refuse to let that happen. I absolutely refuse to let that happen.*

He glanced over at Leopold, who was hunting through their saddlebags.

"What are you looking for?" he asked with irritation, producing two toads and a big bullfrog.

"Paper. And something to write with. I thought of a rhyme for *shadow*."

It was going to be a long night.

The next day, Leopold was in the depths of despair because he didn't have anything black to wear, and there was no rhyme for *ensanguined*. Siegfried had to push him to do anything, he lost his temper multiple times, and another flood of toads marked every word.

That was when he got more avian advice. "You might not have noticed," the bird observed, "but the angrier you get, the more hoppers you produce. Maybe if you concentrate on feeling sorry for Leopold, you'll be able to take two steps without squashing a frog."

Siegfried stared at his bird blankly, then slowly nodded. He couldn't imagine how he had missed that simple fact, but there it was. He concentrated very hard on feeling grateful to the bird, and sorry for losing his temper. "Thank you. I'm sorry," he said humbly, and was rewarded by dropping a baby toad scarcely the size of a beetle.

"You should be," the bird said smugly. Siegfried's temper flared again, but he reined it in and managed to get Leopold to saddle and bridle his horse and swing up into that saddle without having to say another word. Now his best hope was that he could just get them to the pass and the cave without Leopold deciding to start composing sad songs instead of poems. He wasn't sure he would survive songs.

So far there were only seven Princes on the way to the pass. Desmond was in the lead—he'd gotten the rather common curse of boils, and they'd broken out all over his face. Almost as soon as the affliction had occurred, he'd gotten his horse and ridden out.

With the collusion of Jimson, Rosa was watching him, and Siegfried and Leopold, in Jimson's mirror. Normally it was a good week of hard riding to Sharpstone Pass, but Lily had taken pity on the poor fellows, and she'd cast the "All Paths Are One" spell to shorten their journey. Their map routed them all over an obscure little trail that almost no one ever used, which they would encounter early on their second day. It was drawn to look like a shortcut, which would guarantee that they would use it. That was where the spell had been placed.

Prince Desmond, however, had been so desperate to rid himself of his affliction that he had pressed his horse onto that path late in the evening of the first day. As a consequence, at this very moment, with a pack on his back, he was climbing up one of the mountains at the pass—

Not the mountain that the dragon's cave was in, but one opposite it, which puzzled her more than a little.

"What do you think he's doing?" she asked Jimson.

"I confess myself baffled," the Mirror Servant replied, as the mirror showed Desmond making his way up a narrow goat track. "Utterly baffled. I thought maybe he was going to talk to Gina and ask her to deliver the object, which is perfectly within the rules, but no. Wait, look, he's settling down—"

And so he was. He removed the pack and pulled out a crossbow and a handful of blunted bolts, arrows that had a round ball-like head. With practiced ease, he cocked the bow, inserted a bolt and took aim at the entrance to Sharpstone's cave.

"Oh, of course!" Rosa exclaimed as the bolt fell short. "Oh, that's clever. As soon as it's in the cave, it's part of the hoard, of course. And with the head blunted, those bolts wouldn't do more than bruise a man at the distance he's shooting. If they hit Sharpstone, he probably wouldn't even feel it."

"Likely not. It *is* clever," Jimson agreed. They both watched as the Prince sighted on the cave, made sure of his target by getting three bolts in succession inside the entrance, then took his object—a gold coin—and affixed it to the front of the blunt head with beeswax. This was risky; if he fell short, he was going to have to climb down, find the coin, climb back up and try again. Finding the coin was going to be the trick. There was a lot of mountain out there....

As Rosa held her breath, he sighted and let fly.

The bolt sailed in through the mouth of the cave, just under the upper rim.

"Oh, well done!" Jimson exclaimed, as a moment later Prince Desmond's plague of facial boils began to fade. "Good shot!"

"I hope some of the others think of that," Rosa said. "Let's check Siegfried and Leopold."

They left Desmond clambering back down the mountainside and found the Northerner and his companion within sight of the pass. The two of them were still on horseback, but the track was right in the mountains now. Pines clung to the steep slopes on either side of them. Siegfried was on the lead horse, slumped over the saddle, looking miserable. Leopold—was singing.

He wasn't good at it.

"My heart is wrapped in endless night," he warbled dismally. "And something, something, something blight. And in despair my soul is led—"

"Your mother dropped you on your head!" the bird sang scathingly.

Siegfried choked on a laugh. Evidently, that wasn't misery; that was a valiant attempt to keep from falling out of his saddle with laughter. Rosa didn't have to hide hers, nor did Jimson.

"My spirit weeps in awful dread!" Leopold howled, oblivious to the effect he was having on his audience. "Oh, love shall never-more be mine!"

"I think your brains were soaked in brine!" the bird sang.

"So drown it in a mug of wine!" Siegfried countered, and a frog hit his horse's neck and leapt off into the brush at the side of the path.

"I moan, I sigh, I do repine!" groaned Leopold. "Oh love, sweet love, will never be!"

"Because she kicked you in the—knee!" The bird caroled. Siegfried choked.

Leopold stopped singing and glared at them both. "You're ruining my art!" he whined.

Rosa convulsed with laughter, her sides aching and her eyes watering, to the point of having to gasp to catch her breath. Jimson snickered.

"Leopold," Siegfried said, in a placating tone. "Vibration. Ava-lanche. Please." He managed to produce only one toad, which

followed the frog, as he pointed upward at the loose slip area above
the trail, a tumble of boulders that didn't look in the least stable.

"Oh, all right," Leopold grumbled. He slumped down in his
saddle, looking for all the world like a surly adolescent in a state
of high sulk.

"Oh, poor Siegfried," Rosa gasped, wiping tears from her eyes.
"How did anyone ever produce a curse that complex? And more to
the point, why?"

"I have no idea, Princess," said Jimson. "None. I don't remember
Lily ever picking that one up, so either she got it before I became
her helper, or it was in storage from her predecessor. But I must
admit, it is a work of art of the highest order."

By this time the two men had spotted the cave and the narrow,
winding path that led to a final difficult scramble over a rock field
up to it. And Sharpstone, possibly having been awakened from his
sleep by Desmond's arrows, was just oozing his way out of the cave.
The dragon looked down at them from his heights and sneered.

Sharpstone was a long, lean, snakelike beast, a sort of bronze-black
in color. His scales must have been the size of dinner plates. No teeth
were visible when his mouth was closed, but since his head was easily
twice the size of a horse, he might not need huge fangs to kill
someone; he could just swallow the offending party whole. His eyes
were a dull gold, and had a sardonic look to them.

He stretched out on a ledge to watch them, as they edged up the
path, and then scrambled over the last several hundred feet of loose
rock and boulders to get to him. From his posture, Rosa got the
feeling that he was really enjoying their struggles and was in no
hurry to put an end to the fun.

He waited until they stood panting before him before he
decided to speak.

"Go away," he hissed, his eyes narrowing with pleasure at thwarting them. "You bore me." He had maneuvered himself so that his considerable bulk blocked the entrance to his cave so they couldn't just throw their cursed objects in.

"I'd appreciate it if you would hear us out," Siegfried said testily.

Five frogs and a toad dropped down onto the rock at his feet, tried to leap away and plummeted to their doom.

Sharpstone's eyes widened at that. "Why should I?" he replied, and tilted his head to the side in anticipation of Siegfried's answer.

"Because perhaps it wouldn't hurt you to be nice for a change?" Siegfried snapped. And a cascade of toads followed the first lot, and like the first, bounced pathetically over the edge.

Sharpstone's head came up. All the way up. And as his pupils shrank to the size of pins with excitement, he goaded Siegfried again. "I see no reason to be nice to a couple of idiots who are too stupid to find some easier way to get rid of their problems," he said gleefully. "Go away! I can't be bothered with you!"

Siegfried's temper snapped. He unloaded an angry lecture on the dragon, who paid no attention whatsoever to what he was saying. Instead, he kept his eyes delightedly fixed on the waterfall of toads, frogs and even an occasional snake that poured from the air in front of Siegfried's lips and rained down the side of the mountain.

Meanwhile, Leopold, who couldn't understand the dragon and was clearly bored with the entire situation, had wandered away until he found a boulder stable enough to sit on. There he slumped, until inspiration struck him again. Well, inspiration, or something else…

He picked up his song of misery just as Siegfried's invective ran out. "Oh, death, come wrap me in your wings!" he sobbed. "In deepest darkness my soul sings! I will not fear the Reaper nigh! Oh take me for I want to die!"

Now Sharpstone turned his attention from the frog-fall to the tuneless troubadour. His mouth gaped open in astonishment.

"Eat him, would you?" the bird said crossly from Siegfried's shoulder. "Put him out of our misery."

"Sadness fills my life with pain! I cannot go on again! Darkness falls across the land! Come to me and take my hand!" Leopold's eyes were clamped shut as he bleated out the words, caught up in a transport of creation. Or something like creation.

The dragon listened, with his mouth gaping, until he couldn't restrain his mirth any longer.

His sides heaved. He began to snort, then gurgle, then belch out smoke and chortles.

"It's not that funny," Siegfried said crossly. More frogs, two of them, joined the others over the cliff. The dragon kept laughing, then fell over on his side, rolling on his ledge as he howled with laughter.

Leopold stopped singing and stared at him. Siegfried grew red-faced, but kept his jaws clamped tightly shut. Perhaps he didn't want to be responsible for the death of any more amphibians.

Finally Sharpstone's laughter subsided somewhat. The dragon clawed himself upright, raising his head weakly, wheezing. Little plumes of smoke leaked from his nostrils.

"Oh…First Egg," the dragon gasped. "I haven't laughed that hard in centuries." He coughed a tiny flame or two. "Shells and stone…" He shook his head. "All right. You've earned it. You've earned it. You've given me endless entertainment here, so you've convinced me to take your cursed baubles." He held out a massive claw, "palm" up. "You needn't try and trick them into my hoard, nor do any more convincing, nor do me a further service, nor offer me something precious to take them. Put them here. I accept them."

Instantly, Siegfried ripped off the gold ring he was wearing and dropped it in the dragon's claw, then scrambled over to Leopold, and over the latter's protests that "he was just getting inspired," ripped the gold chain from his neck and deposited it in the same place.

The moment that the gold of the chain touched the dragon's claw, Leopold went scarlet. He didn't say a word—he simply scrambled to his feet and started down the mountain as fast as he could go without killing himself.

"Thank you," Siegfried said to Sharpstone.

"My pleasure, literally," the dragon replied, then wheezed with laughter a bit more. "Thermals! I'm going to put these things somewhere special and find a way to pass them off on some other unsuspecting booby in a century or two! That was worth double your weight in gold!"

And with that, the dragon turned around and oozed back into this cave. Siegfried followed Leopold down to where they had left their horses.

They rode in silence for a few minutes, until Leopold cleared his throat, and spoke.

"If you ever," he said, quietly, but venomously, "tell anyone what I was doing? And most of all what I was singing? I. Will. Kill. You."

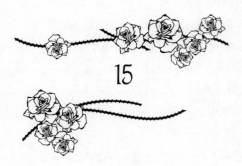

15

THE CONTEST OF THE CURSED OBJECTS HAD taken its
toll on the young men vying for Rosamund's hand and Kingdom.
Rather than face a dragon they didn't have the skill to persuade, didn't
think to offer a service or gift to, couldn't hurt and weren't allowed
to kill, many of them had given up, declared their forfeits and waited
to be relieved of their afflictions. It had been rather sad, actually, to
see the poor lads queued up when the Godmother had put in an appearance to take their curses away. It had been even sadder to see
the procession of the dejected leaving the Palace as they had packed
up and departed with figurative tails between their legs.

Most of the adventurers hadn't even tried. Uninvited as they were,
now they left unheralded. The tents emptied, the bunks in the Guard-
house went back to their rightful tenants, the tents were packed up
and put away, and there was nothing left to show of the horde of
hopeful suitors than the trampled-down grass and the burn-rings of
their fires. A handful of the adventurers remained, all quartered with
the Guards, and Siegfried had a notion that this handful might try to
remain, not as suitors, but as new members of the Guard.

The Princes' numbers had been reduced to thirty-one. That was still more than enough to serve as hostages, especially since it still included all of the enemy candidates, but it made the Palace a lot less crowded. Siegfried and Leopold were still sharing quarters, but they had the whole suite to themselves now, and Siegfried had moved his sleeping arrangements into the second room. Someone had even found him an old bed somewhere that he could use. The sun came in that room first thing in the morning, but that scarcely troubled him, since he was still up with the dawn.

The easy part was over. Now things could begin in earnest.

And now, they both instinctively understood, the competition was going to get a great deal more serious. And probably more hazardous.

While the Godmother would not purposefully make the contests deadly, there was no telling what might happen from here on. And Siegfried knew, though Leopold did not, that there was another factor to what could happen in the contests.

The Tradition. Depending on the Path you were taking, The Tradition might raise the hazard to Potentially Fatal.

The Godmother had to be aware of that, as well; she had proven herself to be as sharp as splintered glass so far, and Siegfried didn't see *that* changing anytime soon.

But Siegfried and Leopold had something else to worry about besides the contests.

It appeared that they had real competition for Rosamund's attention in the form of Prince Desmond, for now that the ranks had thinned, Desmond was moving his campaign forward.

"Good evening, Princess." As Rosa entered the ballroom, she felt, for the first time since the hordes had descended, as if there was actually room to move and breathe in there. Her ladies were not as happy, of course, since there were no longer so many Princes to flirt with and be flirted with in return. Her gentlemen were much happier; they had a fighting chance to get their ladies' attentions back.

The Princes were much happier, since there was less competition, though none of them was quite as bold about approaching her as this man was.

Rosamund turned, and smiled faintly at Prince Desmond, who smiled back. "Good evening, Desmond," she replied, and self-consciously tucked a strand of hair behind her ear. When in her presence he never looked less than perfect, and that triggered an urge in her to be the same. Even though she knew now that this perfection was nothing more than a carefully cultivated facade, it still induced that urge.

To look at him, you'd never know that a few days ago he had been scrambling desperately up a goat trail, covered in dust, face swathed in bandages. In fact, it was impossible to picture him scrambling up a goat trail. It was impossible to picture him in any sort of setting but this one.

She even felt a little embarrassed at having spied on him like that, as if she had used the mirror to watch him in his private rooms. He would hate it if he knew; no one who created a facade like his wanted anyone ever to see him at less than perfection—even though she had watched him demonstrating a high order of cleverness and skill.

He was, of course, oblivious to her thoughts. Instead, he offered her a single flower with a little bit of a flourish. It was one she wasn't familiar with, about the size of the first joint of her thumb, a creamy white color, with five ruffled petals around a tiny pink heart.

A spicy scent wafted up to her from it, and she felt her eyes widening in delight. The scent was not familiar, either, and she thought she knew every meadow flower that there was. "Thank you!" she said, taking the curiously shaped little white flower with the scent that was all out of proportion to its size. "What is this?"

"To tell the truth, Princess, I have no idea." He chuckled a little, his lids dropping down over his eyes to give him a slightly sleepy and very relaxed expression. "There was a woman in the flower market selling them. No one paid any special attention to her or her flowers, so I assume they are common, but I never encountered a scent like that before, and I thought you might like it. She assured me that one small flower will dispense its perfume all night long."

Rosamund slipped the stem in among the laces of her bodice. "Thank you for thinking of me," she said. "I prefer scented flowers that are not so showy to scentless ones that produce enormous blossoms. The trouble with many of the lovely flowers in the Royal Garden is that they have no scent. The plantings were established in my great-grandfather's time, and I would dearly love to remove some of them for choices of my own. But I'm not supposed to ask for change, or the chief gardener will get into a huff and sulk for days, which, apparently, is a disaster."

There was an odd moment, like a flicker of chill across his face, that startled her. *What did I say to strike a nerve?* she wondered, but then as quickly as it had come, the expression passed and she could not be certain it had ever been there at all. How strange…what on earth could that have meant? Was he a gardener in disguise? Was he under the impression that even a gardener could intimidate her? Did he not approve? Did he think that a ruler should have absolute power over servants? Did he think her weak?

Did he not understand she was joking?

"How often we are the slaves to our own servants," he said lightly. "Or perhaps, slave to custom. There are probably good reasons for what seems like a ridiculous condition. Perhaps the beds are so well established that removing the plantings would take an enormous amount of effort and ruin the design of the garden for a decade." He waved a hand in the air. "I am merely maundering and getting far from the subject I wished to broach to you. I was wondering if, now that there are fewer of us, I might challenge you to a game or two of cards in the evening? Not just with me, of course, but with whoever

happens to wish to play. It would be a little more mentally challeng-
ing than walking around and around the gardens, as enchanting as
they are." There was a certain sharp look to his gaze, as if he expected
her to refuse, and intended to persuade her.

However, she was perfectly willing to agree without the persua-
sion. Of course, she wasn't going to let him know that. That would
spoil the game. "I think that might be arranged," she replied noncom-
mittally. "I will see what I can do."

He bowed again, at just the right moment, and backed away. As
always, he did everything at just the right moment. She wondered how
he did it, even as she moved on to other guests. But from time to time,
as the scent of that little ruffled flower came to her nose, she smiled.


While Rosa circulated among the Princes, Lily and Jimson were
plumbing ideas for the next contest. All the windows to the Queen's
chambers stood wide-open to catch every hint of breeze that there
was, for now that there were not so many suitors, the sound of
distant conversation was far less than the drone of a few bees.

It wasn't a question of being able to stage contests—it was a
question of having one that everyone could complete. Like the
famous knot-puzzle that had been "solved" by a slash of a sword, it
wouldn't serve anything to have one man finish the task in a way that
left all the others sitting on their proverbial thumbs.

And there was the matter of what they were going to test.

"What about intelligence?" said Jimson. "We don't need to stage
every contest in public. And not that the first two tests didn't
require intelligence, but I was thinking of solving something that is
more obviously a problem. Something that requires logic and
analysis and thinking."

Lily nodded and fanned herself with a sandalwood fan as she
reclined on the cool satin of her favorite divan from this room. Since

there was no one but Jimson and the servants to see her, she had rid herself of the overpowering weight of the gown and petticoats and corset, and was in a light and frothy wrap designed to be bearable for summer. It was getting very warm now; Midsummer Day was almost on them. "Well, there's the old classic of separating different sorts of grains or seeds," she suggested. "And that can be done in all sorts of ways. If you have animals to help, if you have magic, and if you are clever enough to get sieves with holes of three sizes."

"Yes, but that doesn't require intelligence," Jimson countered. "Cleverness, ingenuity or resources, but not intelligence."

"Thurman was intelligent—*oh!*" She suddenly remembered a puzzle that Thurman had set her, and how much the late King had loved logic and riddles. "I think I have it!" She chuckled. "I think our Princes are not going to like it much, however. And we won't have to set aside anything other than a room."

Today, when the contest had been announced, everyone had been afire to find out what it was. When they were all ushered into the ballroom—a ballroom that had been refurnished with thirty-one desks or tables and chairs—no one had quite believed what the trial was going to be.

But when each of them was presented with a pen, a fat stack of foolscap, and a set of written pages—

Well it was clear that the contest was going to involve something that brawn could not compensate for.

Siegfried stared at the first lines on the first page of the stack of paper he had been given. At least it was in a language he could read. His own. That alone was amazing.

*A farmer is standing on one bank of a river, with a fox, a chicken and a bag of grain. He needs to get to the other side of the river, taking the fox, the chicken and the grain with him.*

*However, the boat used to cross the river is only large enough to carry the farmer and one of the things he needs to take with him, so he will need to make several trips in order to get everything across.*

*In addition, he cannot leave the fox unattended with the chicken, or else the fox will eat the chicken; and he cannot leave the chicken unattended with the grain, or else the chicken will eat the grain. The fox is not particularly partial to grain, and may be left alone with it.*

*How can he get everything across the river without anything being eaten?*

Leopold chewed on the end of the quill. This wasn't entirely foreign to him. He and all his brothers had gotten tested and schooled in a room not unlike this one. And to tell the truth, what they had been tested on was a lot duller than this sheaf of riddles he was being asked to solve.

*What is broken every time it's spoken?*

Siegfried worked out the business with the chicken after a lot of playing about with possibilities and the utter ruination of several sheets of foolscap as he drew out river, boat, fox, grain and chicken. It finally occurred to him that you could always take something *back* over the river, and that was the key—you always kept the two things that might eat or be eaten apart by hauling one back. But this puzzle...

*If I say, "Everything I tell you is a lie," am I telling you the truth or a lie?*

Leopold snapped his fingers as the answer occurred to him, and he quickly wrote it down. Of course! Speak the word *silence* and you broke the silence! Now the next—

Hmm.

*Food can help me survive, but water will kill me. What am I?*

Siegfried grinned. That one was easy. It appeared in the old sagas all the time. *If only some of the things are lies, then the statement that everything I tell you is a lie will always be a lie.*

He wrote down "lie." Now the next…

*The one who makes it sells it.*
*The one who buys it doesn't use it.*
*The one who's using it doesn't know he's using it.*
*What is it?*

Leopold snorted. A child could have figured that riddle out. It was fire of course, which needed "food" in the form of wood.

He had been worried at first. He wasn't worried now. If this was the worst they could do, he could get through this.

*A coffin…* thought Siegfried. That was…a rather too-morbid riddle. He did not like the way this was going.

At the end of the day, thirty-one men emerged from the room filled with tables, surprised at the amount of time that had passed. Some were elated. Some were in despair. All were happy to have the contest over and done with. They fell on the cold buffet laid out for them like starving wolves, and many were surprised at just how tired they were after a day of "only" thinking.

The astonishment came when they all started talking about the riddles and the answers, and compared what they could remember of the riddle test with each other. Because it appeared that no one recalled the same riddles.

No one.

"I don't believe it. Are you sure you don't remember that one?" Siegfried asked a particularly satisfied Prince Roderick, who was sure that he had done very, very well. The Prince shook his head.

"And you don't remember the wizard and the staircase?" the Prince countered. "I thought it was as morbid as your coffin one."

"I know I would have if I'd seen it, wretched murdering wizards..." Siegfried said, feeling more than a little confused now.

He wasn't the only one. No one was out in the garden tonight. The puzzle just grew and grew, as all thirty-one men conferred and cross-checked, and finally came up with the only possible solution there could be.

Each of them had answered an entirely different set of riddles. Impossible as it seemed, somehow thirty-one different tests had been assembled and presented to them.

As they separated, some to go straight to bed, some to drink, some to go straight up in despair and pack, Leopold and Siegfried elected to take the walk out to the King's Arms. They were such regulars there now that they had a preferred table, and the serving boy brought them their drinks before they even sat down. Everyone else that was a regular there knew they were Princes, and no one troubled them about it. Leopold said wistfully that it was just like that in *his* favorite tavern, back before he'd left his home. Since in Drachenthal, there were no such things as inns and taverns, Siegfried had merely nodded.

"That must have taken an immense amount of doing, making up all those riddle lists," Siegfried said, and shook his head. "I don't know how they did it. I don't know how I managed to get through it. That was one of the hardest things I've ever done, and I think if I had known in advance what we were going to do, I'd have packed up and left before trying. My brain feels worse than when Norbert dented my helm."

"Well, if nothing else would have convinced me that the Queen is the Godmother, this did. The only way you could do something like that is by magic. There weren't enough clerks in the entire Palace to have found and written up that many lists of riddles and never repeat one." Leopold drained his beer and signaled for another, then reached for a handful of the salted, toasted grain in a bowl parked between them. "And although no one said this out loud, I think we all know that the only reason to do it that way is to make sure no one cheated."

Siegfried chuckled at the idea of any one of the Princes knowing the runic alphabet in which the language of Drachenthal was written, much less the language itself. "I haven't seen that much of my own script written out at one time, ever. I think that test was bigger than every book in all of Drachenthal."

Leopold smirked at that; the very few times he'd seen Siegfried write something down, he hadn't been able to make head nor tail of how you were supposed to hold the paper, and never mind what was written on it.

"I supposed that eventually there would be a riddle contest, but I thought it would be just one fiendishly difficult riddle." Siegfried sighed. "And I thought it was going to be recited to us. I never thought I would spend a whole day answering puzzle after puzzle after puzzle." He rubbed his head. "Well, that's over. We might not have proved we're scholars, but we proved we aren't fools, either."

"I wonder how many of us were knocked out." Leopold sighed. "I saw quite a few long faces, and I think there are going to be more empty guest rooms tomorrow. Too much to hope one of them is Desmond."

Siegfried shook his head. "Not unless someone stole his paper and substituted another. He's smarter than he has any right to be."

"He's certainly smarter than I am," Leopold grumbled. "I couldn't get him to play cards with me."

The next day, there were, indeed, a few new empty guest rooms in the Palace, and there was no announcement of the next contest. It was one of those hot summer days that threatened rain without actually producing it, making people restless and listless at the same time.

Leopold managed to find himself a card game at last, and proceeded to fleece some of the other Princes.

At loose ends, Siegfried decided that, although he and Leopold were helping each other as much as they could within the competitions, there was nothing binding them to do so outside of the competitions. If there was any way he could manage to bring himself to the Princess's attention, well—it might not help him in the contests, but it certainly wouldn't hurt.

And he decided that Desmond was entirely too good at getting and holding the Princess's attention during the evening. It was time to do something for himself, without Leopold.

He resolved to get her attention in a different way, and maybe a way Desmond wouldn't think of. As always, when he needed to think something out, he took a long, solitary walk. By this time, he knew the Palace as well as any of the servants did, and there were plenty of places where most people didn't go. He just followed the lack of noise while he walked.

And after due consideration, guided in no small measure by the fact that, while he had been raised by aunts, those aunts had given him most of his early training in fighting, he thought he had a good idea.

And when Siegfried spotted the Princess alone except for her guards in an obscure hallway, he decided he was going to see if he couldn't give her something new to think about, as well.

The only reason *he* was here was because this hall was on the most shaded side of the Palace, for it led to a portrait gallery, and portraits were notorious for fading in sunlight. That meant it was cool—a good place for pacing. She was passing by the stairs going up to the gallery. He wasn't at all sure why *she* was there, but he was going to take advantage of it.

He bounded down the stairs and intercepted her, bowing comically, since he knew he couldn't do so gracefully. Her two guards first looked startled, then relaxed when they saw who it was. "Princess Rosamund!" he exclaimed. "Are you busy?"

She gave him an odd look and a raised eyebrow at his casual manner. Desmond was always formal, so Siegfried had decided to be the opposite. "I'm always busy," she replied warily. "Do you need something?"

"Some of your time." He looked the guards over for a moment. Stout fellows, yes, but from the way they stood—they'd had nothing but standard training. And they were woefully relaxed in his presence. That was a mistake. "Well let me—"

Just as he had been taught, he went from an unthreatening stance to a blur of action in the blink of an eye. The only thing that slowed him down was knowing that he didn't want to do anything permanent to either of these boys. He could, all too easily, leave them with broken bones or worse if he wasn't careful. A sweep of the leg knocked the feet of the one nearest him right out from under him so that he fell heavily to the ground, and a follow-up kick to the chin took him out.

"—show you—"

He grabbed the first one's pike—a stupid weapon in a hallway!—and rushed the second, pinning his arms to the wall with it at the elbows. Now he couldn't reach Siegfried or his weapons. Bar-fighting tactics, yes, but also the no-moves-barred style of his own people.

"—what I mean."

He felt the Princess behind him, and wondered if she was staring at him in shock.

"Now if this'd been a real attack on you, this lad would've been laid on the ground, too. Hit to his head with my forehead, then a knee to the stomach and then a kick to the groin, he'd be on the floor and you'd be unprotected." He stared into the stunned and angry eyes of his victim, and tried to convey that he was rather sorry he'd done this—but also not at all sorry, because these fellows were supposed to be protecting Rosamund, not making themselves victims.

"Not quite unprotected, I think," came the cold reply right behind him, and he felt the prick of a knife at his kidneys. He grinned.

"Good!" he said. Then he snaked his arm around, grabbed the side of her hand and twisted. The knife fell to the floor and she gasped a little, though he had tried to be careful. "I'm fair glad that you know to defend yourself. But I want to teach you how to be better."

He let go of her and her Guardsman at the same time, and jumped back out of immediate range of a punch or a weapon. The man instantly started to draw his sword, but Rosamund stopped him with an outstretched hand.

"No," she said. "I don't think Siegfried had any intentions of doing anything other than giving us a very pointed lesson. If he'd meant any mischief, you two would be dead, and I would be dead or on a horse by now." She massaged her wrist gingerly. "You have a strange way of trying to impress a woman, Prince Siegfried."

He shrugged. "I'm not trying to impress you." Then he grinned sheepishly. "Or—all right, I am trying to impress you, but I'm not trying to impress you like the others are. I wanted to make sure you could see that I know what I'm doing, and that you and these good fellows aren't really prepared to deal with a nasty scoundrel with no compunctions about anything. We both know it's not going to do me any good if something happens to you before this contest is over. So can I show you some low fighting tricks that a Captain of the Guard won't teach you?" He glanced at the red-faced Guardsman, and the one on the ground, who was starting to sit up, shaking his head and feeling his chin. "All three of you?"

The Princess eyed him for a moment, giving him the first really measuring look that he had gotten from her, then nodded. "All right. You may. I have a bit of time that I can spare, and it is clear it will be time well invested. Let me go and change, and I will send someone for you here."

He waited patiently, and in what he had come to think was a remarkably short period of time for a woman, a servant came to fetch him. The servant brought him to a room he recognized as a wealthy man's toy, a place indoors meant to practice sword work. Only a very, very wealthy person could afford a room with absolutely nothing in it but a pile of thick pads in one corner. Only the amazingly wealthy could afford the walls of mirrors. Or the multicandled things that lowered down from the ceiling to shed an even light at night. The Princess was waiting for him, with four guards this time; she was very sensibly dressed in buff-colored breeches and a linen tunic, a pair of sturdy boots, and with her hair braided up and pinned to her head.

The surprise was that the Godmother, in her guise of the Queen, was also there. She looked shockingly out of place in this very purposed room, in her elaborate black gown of the finest of silk and knitted lace.

He grinned, and bowed. He decided on the spur of the moment that now was the time to let her know what *he* knew. He walked up to her, where she stood apart from the rest. "Hello, Godmother," he said cheerfully, in a voice too low to carry to the guards. She probably did not want them to know what she was, and she wouldn't thank him for letting the secret out of the bag.

The woman's eyes widened, but she gave no other indication that he had surprised her. Instead, she granted him a slow smile. Good. She wasn't angry. It wasn't wise to anger a Godmother. Anyone who could casually distribute cursed objects the way she had was someone he did not want to cross. "And if I say that you are smarter than you look?"

"I'll thank you for it. Do you need any lessons?" he asked, with an inviting tilt of the head.

"Not really. I have magic." She flexed her fingers, and little crackles of lightning ran across the back of her knuckles. "But I am very interested in what you can show Rosa."

He nodded, and becoming all business, he turned back to face the waiting young woman and her entourage. "Then let us begin with the most common way someone is likely to attack the Princess. When she is alone, because she is in a great hurry, and in a passage she thinks is safe."

Rosa was not, and never had been, what anyone would consider fragile. She had gotten her share of bruises learning to handle sheep, she had fallen from jumping horses, she had gotten burns learning to cook over a hearth fire. But today she had learned that she was not nearly as hardy as she had thought that she was, and rather than making her feel frustrated, angry or afraid, the realization filled her with elation, because it meant that Siegfried was not holding back with her. He respected her enough and, for whatever selfish or unselfish reasons, wanted to see she was good enough to protect herself. If teaching her that meant that she got hurt, well, that was the cost of knowledge. She had known all her life that nothing in life came without a cost. She would far rather have a bruise now than face the Huntsman again and be unable to stop him or run from him.

One thing was certain. If the Huntsman ever attacked her the same way that he attacked her before, he was definitely going to have a broken instep, probably would have the most painful goolies in the history of the Kingdom and might even be choking on a broken windpipe, for those were the three moves that Siegfried had taught her to master today. They were shockingly simple. It had never occurred to her that simply smashing her foot down on his instep would break every bone in it—but he proved it by showing her how the same blow would break a thick bit of board, and foot bones were ever so much more delicate.

"If you're wearing a shoe or a boot with a heel to it, all the better," he'd added. "Like a riding boot. Concentrates all the force on a smaller place. And you might not think it, but I can tell you, there's only one pain that's worse than a broken foot."

Then he showed her how, when instinct and pain made the man bend over, to smash the back of her head into his nose. Even if she didn't break it, she'd give him more pain at the cost of very little of her own.

And then, while his hands were coming up to cover his face, how to pivot and bring up the knee, or smash the point of her elbow into the windpipe.

Then run.

"And shout while you're doing it," he told her, over and over. "Shouting keeps you from getting frozen with fear. Besides, you never know who might be about. This is a big place with a lot of people in it. You never know who might be taking a shortcut, or who might be where he's not supposed to be. If anyone hears you, even if they don't come to help you themselves, say it's a little lad or a scullion-girl, they'll probably run off to get help. And even if there are two to grab you, and you get carried off, people will know right away, and pursuit will be on your attacker's heels instead of an hour behind. Now, let's try this again, and shout this time."

Lily watched from the sidelines with a face thoughtful and approving. Rosa was rather amused at that. It looked as if Lily had decided that Siegfried was going to be worth cultivating after all.

When they ran out of every bit of time that Rosa could spare for the lesson, she was sure of one thing; she wanted another. In fact, she wanted a lot more than that. She wanted a lot of lessons.

"Think you can spare me more of your time again, Princess?" the Northlander said as she pinned her hair back up again and tidied herself. "We've only just begun what I'd like you to know." He eyed her Guardsmen again. "No disrespect to your men, Princess, but they're trained for war, not for fighting the sort of lawless scum I've been trained against, the kind that'd rather take you from behind. And that's the kind you've got to be wary of."

"I'll make time," she vowed. "And I'd like you to train my Guardsmen every day that you can."

Siegfried grinned. "It'll be a pleasure, and a change from play-fighting your other suitors." He waggled his eyebrows at the four Guardsmen, one of whom groaned, for Siegfried had not been at all gentle with them. Then he turned to Lily. "I'd like you to put a stiff leather or metal lining in a high collar in the Princess's gowns, if you haven't already," he said gravely. "Someone trying to strangle her will get a rude surprise, and a bit of surprise will give her a chance to squirm away, do a bit of harm and run."

"We will," Lily replied, and smiled slowly. "So far, of all the presents that have been given to Rosamund, I think that *I* like this one the best."

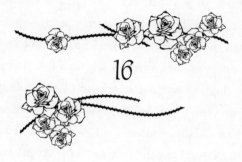

16

THE FOREST WAS COOL, DEEP IN SHADOW AND fragrant with the scents of leaf and herb. The only sounds were those of birds and the occasional rustle of something scurrying through the under-brush. It was, above all, peaceful. Exactly what Siegfried craved at this point. "What exactly are we doing?" Leopold asked Siegfried, as the latter sent his sturdy old horse ambling down another random path in the forest. The leaf-litter sent up the aroma of dead leaf and moss as the horses kicked it up, their hooves making dull sounds as they walked along.

"I'm not sure," the Northerner replied, taking a deep breath of the forest air and feeling a great deal of tension flow out of him. "I just couldn't stand being in the Palace or the city anymore. You can go back to the King's Arms if you want." He still wasn't sure why Leopold had insisted on coming along.

"And leave you to get eaten by bears?" Leopold snorted. Siegfried wondered if he was woods-wise in any way at all, or if the only thing that a forest meant to him was something to be gotten through as quickly as possible. "Or worse—run into your fire-circle maiden?"

Siegfried laughed and shook his head. "The bears are more likely to get eaten by me. I killed one when I was no taller than your waist. You forget I practically grew up in woods like these. This forest is more comfortable to me than any room in any building could ever be. As for the maiden, I think the Godmother might—" He paused, as a sound caught his attention. "Wait, I hear something." He held up his hand to keep Leopold from talking, and listened as carefully as he could. Yes, there it was again, a kind of scrabbling sound and a whimper. "Something's in trouble."

"Fine, if it's a some*thing* it can stay in—" Leopold began, his tone wary. But Siegfried left Leopold talking to the empty air as he slipped out of the saddle and followed his ears. The sounds led him off the path and into the deeper forest, where he had to pick a way among the bushes and undergrowth. The sounds persisted and he followed them, until he found himself very near a long bar of sunlight streaming down from above on a tangle of vegetation.

The canopy wasn't as thick here; an absolutely enormous tree had come down, probably in that big storm everyone was still talking about, clearing out a swath of lesser trees and bushes as it fell. Around the trunk, things were a mess, broken branches and debris surrounding it. Siegfried heard the scrabbling again, from up ahead, along the trunk. It sounded like whatever creature was making the noise was desperate.

When the tree had come down, it had made a tangle of the whole area; rather than fight his way through the mess along the trunk, Siegfried decided to see if he could find an easier path, moving back into the forest and paralleling the trunk. Still following his ears, with Leopold trailing cautiously behind him, he got as close as he could to the sounds before getting his axe off his belt and hacking the rest of the way in. In the quiet of the forest, he made a terrible racket; startled birds exploded through the branches above him, and a hare bolted away from practically under his feet. The sounds stopped then, but he knew where he was going, and at any rate the noise of his chopping was probably terrifying whatever poor beast was making them.

He emerged at the trunk, made a little cleared space, and as he looked around, it was obvious what the problem was.

Dug under the fallen trunk was a den. Four woeful little fox kits stared out at him from behind a screen of debris and branches. Claw marks showed where frantic digging had failed to free them. It looked to Siegfried as if a she-fox had made herself a den here after the storm, and then at some point today half a tree that had been left hanging above it had decided to come down, trapping the kits. The scrabbling and whimpering he'd heard must have been her, trying to get to them. Of course she was nowhere to be seen now.

"Well, if you want a present for Rosamund, there's some fur," Leopold said, pointing to the kits. The little ones couldn't understand him the way they could understand Siegfried, but he was looking at them, and they probably thought he was going to eat them.

"Don't be ridiculous. You don't kill kits for fur. The Princess would be appalled." The poor kits were nearly out of their minds with fear now. He whistled for the bird, which flitted through the trees and landed on a bit of the debris at eye-height. "Can you find the mother and coax her back?" he asked her. "Tell her I'm getting the kits out." He chirruped at them, but they ignored him. Even though they should have understood him, they were too terrified to think. They couldn't go much longer without feeding; their eyes were beginning to look a little glazed to him.

"Of course!" The bird flitted off. Siegfried examined the problem in front of him. There were a lot of branches piled up, and one log as big around as his thigh. The best solution would be to cut all that up.

He needed them to get away from the debris-choked entrance, because once he started chopping, an inquisitive nose in the wrong place could result in tragedy. He went down on one knee next to the den to explain, but as soon as he approached, they squirmed as deep as they could manage under the big log all by themselves, cowering away from him. Assured now he wouldn't strike them with errant chips or his axe, he raised the axe over his head and began carefully chopping away the debris, checking now and again to be sure he wasn't making things worse.

There was a lot of brush here, and the branches were springy. He was about halfway through the obstacle, when the bird flitted back followed by a trembling vixen. The little fox looked up at him with a terrified face, cowering when she saw the axe in his hand as if she expected him to rain blows down on her at any moment.

"It's all right, little mother," Siegfried said soothingly, looking, not straight at her, but off to the side. "You've nothing to fear from me. Give me a little more time. We'll have your children out."

"I hope so," Leopold said, sounding a little cross. "If we're going to wander about the forest, I'd prefer to do so in the saddle. I'm getting eaten to death by midges and mosquitoes." But he waded into the brush and started pulling the stuff that Siegfried had already cut, hauling it away from the mouth of the den so that Siegfried could get more easily at that last barrier.

The vixen slowly got over her fear when she saw he was doing what he said he would do. Her ears came up, her tail came out from between her legs, and she darted in to seize branches in her teeth and haul them away for him.

A short time later, while the vixen danced with impatience, Siegfried made the last cut through the thick branch lying across the entrance, Leopold pulled the branch away, and the vixen dashed inside. From within the darkness of the den, suckling sounds emerged.

"There you go, little mother," Siegfried called. There was no answer, but he didn't expect one.

"What, no 'thank you'?" Leopold said mockingly. "All right, let's get back to the horses and the King's Arms."

"Are you sure you want to?" Siegfried asked. "It's cruel hot in the city. It's nice and cool here." He shouldered his axe and made his way back to the path, listening to the life of the forest come back to normal now that he wasn't making all that racket anymore.

"It is cool here, as long as I don't have to chop wood or do some other insane thing you think you need to do. How can you tell where you're going in this maze?" Leopold asked.

"You weren't the one chopping wood, and I know where I am going because I follow the bird," said Siegfried with amusement. "All right, how about this. You were complaining that you couldn't find a gift for the Princess in the city that every other suitor would be able to duplicate. You will be much more likely to find something out here. As long as it doesn't require killing something that doesn't need to be killed, we stay here in the forest until we find something for you to give Rosamund to impress her."

He pushed aside some bushes, and there were the horses, waiting patiently, pulling up the few blades of grass they could find. Grass had a hard time growing where there was so little direct sunlight.

"What are we going to find here? It's a *forest*," Leopold asked incredulously. "There's no one out here!"

"That's where you are wrong, and that is why we'll find something. It's a forest. It's The Tra—" He stopped himself from saying "The Tradition" in time. "It's the way things work. Forests are full of magical things. The bigger the forest, and the more powerful the kingdom's Godmother is, the more magical things will be in it."

Leopold took up his horse's reins and fitted one boot into the stirrup. "Well if we find that frog who says he's a Prince in here, I am not bringing him back. I refuse to add to the competition."

They mounted, Siegfried cheerfully, Leopold impatiently, and Siegfried led the way deeper in.

They passed by the ruins of a cottage; it had once been carved and painted in a manner that was like nothing he had ever seen before. The door was off its hinges and on the ground, there were holes in the roof, and most of the trim had fallen off. They went inside and looked it over curiously, but could find nothing to tell who had lived there or what had happened to her. *Her,* Siegfried was fairly sure, because of the tattered remains of black dresses and skirts in a chest. Whoever it was had done a lot of baking, for there was an outsize oven in the yard. Maybe that accounted for why what was left of the walls and roof looked like a fancy wedding cake. It almost looked as if something else had been fastened over the wood, but whatever it had been was long gone.

"That place's almost morbidly cheerful," Leopold noted, as they left the cottage behind. "I think if I lived in a house that looked like you could eat yourself sick on it, I'd have to kill myself after a while." The path emerged from the woods and came out beside a pond. "Maybe that's what happened to the owner. She couldn't stand it anymore and jumped into her own oven. And why would you need a cottage to look like that out where no one could see it but you, anyway?"

"Maybe she used to be a baker in the city," Siegfried suggested.

If the cottage had been morbidly cheerful, this pond was just morbid. Despite the fact that the sun was high in the sky, there was no sign of sunlight here—it might have been twilight, not almost noon. It was surrounded by weeping willows that dripped their boughs morosely into the water, and a mist hung over most of the open area and wreathed in among the trees. The surface was covered with lily pads, but there were no lily flowers among the flat green leaves.

There was also no sound. Not a frog, not a bird, not even the plop of a fish.

Siegfried sensed something that he didn't like about the place. Something dark and dangerous. His skin began to crawl, and he felt the distinct urge to get away from there as quickly as he could.

And at that moment, the mist on the far side parted to reveal a beautiful, golden-haired girl, sitting with her legs dangling in the water, combing out her tresses. Except for the hair, she was absolutely nude. That was when Siegfried recognized exactly what the peril was.

"Now that's more like—" Leopold exclaimed, his eyes lighting up.

And Siegfried grabbed his friend's horse's reins, pulling them out of Leopold's hands, and spurred his own horse, plunging both of them into the green-scented forest gloom again. They needed to get away from there fast. Before she saw them and started singing.

"Siegfried!" Leopold snatched in vain for the reins, his face going red with anger. "Siegfried, what are you doing? What's wrong with you? That was a *woman* back there!"

"No it wasn't," Siegfried said shortly.

"Of course it was! I saw her with my—" Abruptly, Leopold remembered where he was, in the midst of a forest full of magic, and his mouth shut with a snap. Siegfried looked back at him, saw his face change and allowed the horses to slow. "If it wasn't a woman, then what was it?"

"That was a Nixie," Siegfried told him severely. "They're water spirits. They sing, and they like to take human lovers."

"They do?" Leopold grabbed for the reins again, eager to get back to the sensuous, nude spirit.

"They like to take them *underwater.*" Siegfried held on to the reins and waited for that to sink in.

"They like to...oh. Um."

"So unless you've suddenly gotten the ability to *breathe* underwater..." He let go of the reins. Leopold gathered them up again with a sigh.

"So far, we haven't found anything I could take to Rosamund," Leopold grumbled. "Can we go back to the city now?"

Siegfried grinned at that. The prince sounded like a sulky child.

But they hadn't gone five more paces before something suddenly appeared before them on the path, blocking their way. A beam of light lanced through the canopy overhead, illuminating it from above.

Not that it needed the illumination. It glowed from within.

Leopold blinked, as Siegfried blushed a brilliant crimson. "Siegfried, is that...?" he said, quietly, for once not a single note of mockery in his voice.

"Yes," Siegfried got out, in a strangled voice.

"A unicorn."

"Yes."

"I thought they were extinct!" Leopold exclaimed, drinking in the glorious creature with his eyes.

"Not...exactly..."

Siegfried didn't blame Leopold for being entranced. She was an exquisite creature, from the tip of her crystal, spiraling horn to the tip of her silken, leonine tail, she glowed with a pearly light that owed nothing to the sunlight she stood in. Her coat looked like the softest of plushy velvet—this mare clearly was of the same variety as in Drachenthal, which needed a thicker coat for the cold mountain winters. In his travels, Siegfried had also seen smooth-coated unicorns, with hides like satin. Her cloven hooves were a shining gold, her mane a fall of silver. Her eyes were gold to match her hooves, her tiny beardlette a dainty thing, as suited a lady unicorn. She moved like water flowing over a stream. There was nothing about her that was not perfection.

Except, perhaps, her brain.

She locked her gaze with his, radiating adoration. Siegfried groaned. Not again. Not another one...

Completely ignoring Leopold, the unicorn paced deliberately

toward Siegfried, each hoof leaving an indentation in the moss that glowed for just a moment. Siegfried watched her with the look of dread of a man that sees his inescapable fate bearing down on him.

Well, at least she wasn't trying to skewer Leopold.

With a sigh, as his bewildered and bedazzled horse stood stock-still, the unicorn lifted her chin and placed it firmly in his lap.

"Hewwo," she lisped. "I'm Luna. I wove you."

With a sigh of resignation, Siegfried bowed to the inevitable and scratched her forehead around the crystal horn. "I know you do," he said, with only a touch of bitterness, waiting for the truth to dawn on Leopold. "That's all right. I love you, too, Luna. You are a beautiful girl."

When the truth finally did strike him, his friend fell off his horse, laughing. By that point, Siegfried was crimson.

They rode out of the wood with a necklace of braided unicorn hair folded in a handkerchief and stowed carefully in Leopold's pouch. It had taken this bribe to get him to stop laughing. Siegfried wasn't angry—how could he be angry? It *was* funny. But he was deeply, profoundly embarrassed. Someday this would all be hilarious, he was sure. Someday he would sit at the fireside and tell the story on himself.

Today was not that day.

He hadn't been able to look Leopold in the eyes since his friend started laughing at him. Not even when he'd given Leopold the necklace. The ride back had been punctuated only by Leopold's smothered sniggers.

He did not regret going into the forest with Leopold today, and he was glad that they had found his friend a gift to impress the Princess, because he had been feeling a bit guilty about those lessons in defending oneself. He just wished that it had been some other sort of gift.

As they neared the gates of the city, Leopold finally rode up next to him; he seemed to have gotten himself under control at last.

"You are a fine fellow, Siegfried," he said quietly. "Most men would have punched me in the eye for laughing at them like that. I wouldn't have blamed you for riding off and leaving me there."

Siegfried sighed. "I don't blame you. It's funny. If it had been you, I would have been the one that was laughing. It had to look awfully funny, too, with that daft thing coming up and planting her head in my lap. At least you got a present for the Princess out of it. I told you something would turn up."

"Yes, but you were the one who suggested it, and you were the one who braided it. And you were the one who lured the—the—" Leopold's face twitched as he barely kept himself from laughing again. To Siegfried's relief, he managed to hold it in this time. "Anyway. If it hadn't been for you, I wouldn't have this, and I don't know too many people with a necklace of unicorn hair."

"Oh, there are plenty, they just don't come from a live unicorn." Now Siegfried *did* let bitterness creep into his voice. He honestly did not hate too many people, but there were exceptions. "Hunters get virgin girls to go sit in the woods, the poor stupid beasts come and lay their heads in the girl's lap, and the hunters kill them. You saw for yourself that in the presence of a virgin they lose what few thoughts they have, and they aren't the sharpest swords in the rack to begin with. That's why they're rare."

Leopold choked, which made Siegfried feel a little better about being laughed at. At least Leopold could see how vile the Hunters were. "That's horrible!"

He nodded. "So are the Hunters. They're vile, vile men. Only a really vile person would kill something like a unicorn, something that is literally purity and innocence incarnate."

"Then why do it?" Leopold asked, now bewildered. "I know the horn is valuable, but couldn't you just wait for it to fall off, or find where they go to die?"

Siegfried shook his head. "Unicorn horn can purify any poison. Nasty people that other people would like to see poisoned like to have a bit of it around, just in case, and unicorns are Fae, and if they don't live forever, they certainly live a very long time." Siegfried's voice was hard. "As for the hair—hair taken from a dead one protects from sickness, and it's so strong you can't break it."

"What about this?" Leopold asked, patting his pocket.

"It's better." Siegfried managed to smile. "Hair from a live one, especially hair given freely, is more powerful, though most people don't know that. It gives you insight into anything magical, it can ward off curses, and nothing inherently evil, like demons and demonic creatures, can come near it. I very much doubt the Princess has anything like that in her jewelry caskets."

Leopold nodded.

"Just don't tell anyone where you got it," Siegfried said, and winced a little. "Or especially how you got it."

"I promise," Leopold pledged. But he couldn't help himself, and Siegfried saw it in his face. "But how did you—I mean, why didn't you—why are you still—"

He had to ask. Of course he did. "Because up until I left Drachenthal, every single female I met was my aunt! My aunt, Leopold! Even at twelve, I knew better than that! In fact, the Shieldmaiden of Doom is probably my aunt, too, or at least my great-aunt!" He felt his face burning. "Why would anyone want to—with his mother's sister?"

Leopold waved his hands in the air to stop him. "Wait, wait, I'm confused here. I thought you said you were supposed to fall in love with the first person you see who is *not* your aunt...."

"I am. I'm supposed to fall in love with the Shieldmaiden, then I'm supposed to forget the Shieldmaiden and fall in love with the person who's not my aunt and then——" Siegfried let go of the reins to wipe his forehead "——then it gets very complicated and involves all the usual messy things like jealousy and retribution, and unusual things like murder and suicide and the death of gods and the fall of kingdoms and can we just not talk about this anymore?"

They rode on in silence for a good while longer. "Um...there *is* a way to fix that, you know," the Prince ventured at last.

"Fix what?" Siegfried turned in his saddle to stare at his friend.

"Being uni——" Leopold's face twitched, but he managed to hold in his hilarity. "Being unicorn bait. I know a lady. In fact, I know several ladies."

Siegfried thought that over for a moment. It was tempting. In fact it was very tempting. On the other hand——

"Let's just leave it for now," he said. "We know there's at least one unicorn in the forest now, and we might need more hair."

"If you're sure." Leopold's face twitched. Siegfried was pretty sure he had more things to say, and most of them would be funny someday. Just not right now.

"We have all sorts of tests ahead of us. Do *you* want to take the chance we'd need something like unicorn hair?" he asked. "Or unicorn blood? Or unicorn tears? She'll give me whatever I ask, you know. Unicorn blood cures any disease and most wounds. Unicorn tears mend broken hearts and broken minds. If we need either of those, the situation would be very nasty, and there are not many substitutes."

Leopold sobered.

"All right then. You go get a silver clasp put on that. *Don't* let it out of your sight. Wait while the jeweler does it. If you can help it, don't tell him what it is. That stuff is worth more than gold." Siegfried was not about to tell his friend that he had enough hair for several more necklaces in *his* pouch. No point in letting Leopold's greed get the better of him. He was going to braid one for himself; it might come in useful.

"How did you learn all these things?" Leopold asked, just before they split up inside the city gate.

Siegfried deadpanned, "A little bird told me."

Siegfried didn't particularly want Leopold around as he ran this lot of "errands" anyway. He figured that he had gotten enough teasing from his friend for one day as it was.

His first stop was at the market stalls. This late in the day, everyone was willing to sell him what he wanted at bargain prices, which was good, because it made his money go further. Granted, Leopold was very generous with his winnings, sharing them despite Siegfried's insistence that he didn't need them....

But Siegfried generally ended up giving the money away. According to the bird, one of the effects of resisting the Rivergold Ring that the dragon had guarded was that greed had no hold over him, and that made him particularly generous of heart. That might well be so, but he couldn't remember a time when he hadn't given things away.

In all events, since he had arrived here, he had done more, a lot more, than just help that one fox. Leopold had no idea, and Siegfried was fairly sure that he'd find what Siegfried was doing incomprehensible, laughable, or both.

His first stop, because he really wanted to get rid of that fish that was just going stale, was at an old warehouse. As he got off the horse, a cat and three lively kittens came running up to him. He had taken the kittens away from boys who were going to drown them, and rescued the mother from their confederate who intended to tie burning straw to her tail and then let her go, to watch her set fire to everything in her path as she tried to escape. He had taken them to this warehouse where they could earn their living catching mice, and stopped by whenever he could with old fish.

The entire little family spilled out of the warehouse when they caught his scent. The kittens greeted him with happy noises, and the mother cat bumped her head against his hand. "You have a good heart, BigMan," she said as he put down the fish. "We will remember you, you know."

He laughed, for this was the clearest thing she had ever said to him, and rubbed her head as she purred like distant thunder. Interesting! Maybe she was a Wise Beast? "Raise big cats to catch rats that make people sick," he told her. "That is all I ask."

When he saw that they had eaten their fill and he didn't need to stave off other cats, dogs or crows, he got on the horse and went on to his next stop.

This time, it was at a stable, where he made sure that an old, slow little donkey was still being cared for properly. The stable owner had a crippled child who was just the right size and weight to ride the tiny beast. He had rescued the poor thing from the enormous cart it was trying to pull. The cart was meant for a full-size horse or ox, not a donkey, but the skinflint drover was bound that the poor old beast was going to pull it, and had been beating her and goading her with an ox-goad. Siegfried tried to reason with him, and when the fellow tried to hit *him* with the goad, he knocked the man to the ground and beat him as he had beaten his donkey. Then he threw just enough money on the man's chest to pay for the poor old thing, cut the donkey out of the traces and took her away.

She was happy here. Her sores were healing, she was clean, her coat was shining, and she had something over her bones other than skin. And she loved the little girl; the two had formed an instant bond.

The stable owner loved her, too, not only because she was his child's favorite companion, but because she ate the thistles that plagued his pasture. Siegfried would have left money for her care, but the owner would have none of it. The donkey came up as he turned to leave, the little child on her back. "Thank you, BigMan," she said. "I will not forget your kindness."

"Just love and care for the child," Siegfried replied, smiling. "That is all I ask."

Definitely another Wise Beast. Then again…he was smack in the middle of a Kingdom, engaging in Traditional Trials, for the Traditional hand of a Princess.

Maybe he should be surprised he wasn't encountering *more* Wise Beasts.

Not long ago he had followed his ears to the door of another warehouse, where he had found a crowd standing around a crude arena, where a bear and a wolf were being forced to fight each other by a showman. The poor things were half-starved, covered with wounds and nearly mad. When he discovered them, lying on the floor of the arena, they were nearly dead.

He had treated the showman as he had the drover, then taken the animals. He had treated their wounds himself, not daring to entrust them to anyone else. At first, they had been too sick and weak to move, and by the time they had recovered their strength, he had won their trust. He kept them in roomy cages in a shed he had rented—in cages for their protection and not to confine them; bars meant no one could get near them to kill or steal them. Slowly, he was able to talk to them; they had been less than sane when he rescued them but with the healing of their bodies, their minds had also healed. He had known from the start, though, that he was going to have to get them out of the city, and as soon as he possibly could. Today would be that day. While not completely healed, they would be able to hunt—in the wolf's case, he would definitely find his pack, for he could smell them—and recover on their own, so today they were ready to be turned loose.

What he had paid for in the market were two short-lived charms of illusion in the form of cloth collars. They were meant for people who wanted to disguise a valuable animal as something less valuable. He would need those to get them out of the city. While the wolf and the bear would do nothing worse than run for the gate, their presence in the street would cause panic.

He opened the shed and stood in the quiet semidarkness. For days, this place had smelled of blood and fear and pain. Now it smelled of the musk of bear and the doggy-scent of wolf. "It is I," he said to the shadows in the cage. "Are you ready to leave?"

"We are, BigMan," rumbled the bear. The wolf yipped agreement.

He held out the collars and their ropes so that they could see and smell what he had. "I must put cloth about your necks and ropes tied to the cloth. These things will make you look like tame beasts that no one will fear, so that I may take you through the man-paths to the forest. You must not run ahead, but stay at my side like tame beasts. Will you permit this?"

He heard uneasy shuffling and knew why. The cruel showman had kept spiked collars around their necks to control them. But finally the wolf answered. "You have never said us false, BigMan. You healed us, fed us and protected us. We will abide this."

He opened the wolf's cage first, and collared him, then the bear. The illusions settled over them, making them look like a pair of goats. He took the ropes in his hand and led them to and out the shed door. And all was well. No one paid him any heed as he walked down some of the quieter streets to one of the city gates—although cats fled in terror, and dogs backed away, hackles raised, trusting their noses rather than their eyes. Perhaps one or two people might have wondered at the sight of a relatively well-dressed man leading two goats himself, but his clothing was modest enough that no one would realize he was one of the Princes unless they actually knew him by sight.

Siegfried took them well into the forest before removing their collars. The wolf, who had been sniffing the air hungrily for some time, gave a happy yelp and vanished into the trees, but the bear paused, turned and looked up at him out of dark little eyes.

"You saved our lives and our minds, BigMan," the bear said. "Wolf cannot wait to return to his kin, so I will say for both of us. You have a good heart. We will not forget this."

"Then when you see men, do not fight, but run," said Siegfried. "This is all I ask."

He walked back to the city, got his borrowed horse and headed for the King's Arms.

Leopold was waiting for him, with a finely carved wooden box in front of him. When Siegfried arrived in the doorway, he grinned and waved him to the table.

"Come see if this looks fit for a Princess," he said, as Siegfried sat down beside him. He opened the box, and the pure white braid glowed against the velvet interior. There was a simple gold clasp on it, and nothing more.

"I am no woman, but I think that will please her," he said gravely. "Did the jeweler know what it was?"

"He did, and he gave me the gold clasp for the cost of silver if I gave him a single hair. He means to braid it with silver and gold wire for a ring for his daughter. That seemed harmless enough to me." Leopold gave Siegfried a sharpish, sideways look. "I confess I took a few of the hairs that you saved. I thought they might come in handy. You never know, right?"

Siegfried shrugged. "You made a good bargain with them. But you should be sure that the jeweler either knows you are a Prince or does not know you at all now. There will be wizards and sorcerers who would pursue you for those hairs or that necklace, and you either want to be thought of as too high to dare to harass, or impossible to find."

Leopold nodded. "So, shall we head back to the Palace? I hope you have had your fill of running about in the woods for now. I, for one, would be glad not to see them again for a while!"

THE NUMBER OF SUITORS HAD BEEN PARED down, one trial at a time, over the past several weeks. From tournaments to hunts for odd items, to fiendishly complicated problems, the trials had been successful at eliminating most of the Princes.

But there were still ten left.

"I need more trials," muttered Lily, as she massaged both temples. "More than that, I need a long-term solution to keeping Eltaria safe. Thurman would still be alive if he hadn't been worn to a thread by running from one border crisis to another. Celeste might still be alive if he had been here instead of on the border."

"And *you* will be worn to a thread if you aren't careful, Lily," Jimson said with alarm and concern. "You do not need that many more trials. There are only ten candidates left. Three of them are the enemy Princes and two more are from Kingdoms flanking *them*. We are still safe. You can stretch this out as long as a year without any of them taking umbrage, I think."

"And I still don't have a long-term solution!" the Godmother said with despair. "I have been Godmother to this Kingdom for three hundred years, and I still haven't got a solution that doesn't involve sending the Kings to an early grave!"

There was no one to see her but Jimson, no one to be alarmed at her weakness, no one to wonder if she was no longer up to the task....

Even though she herself now wondered just that very thing.

For the first time in three hundred years, she felt inadequate to the job. She put her head down in her hands, and wept. The Fae, even the half-Fae, as she was, were not supposed, by mortals at least, to weep. Mortals didn't know. The Fae did not cry often, and never in public, but oh yes, they wept. When you lived as long as the Fae did, there was a great deal to weep over.

She had not wept in decades, but she was at the end of her proverbial rope.

"Lily—Lily—" Jimson sounded frustrated and helpless. "Please, do not cry—you are a good Godmother. No one could have managed better than you!"

She couldn't stop weeping, although she wept as the Fae did, quietly, the tears flowing from her eyes like rain. It was all, suddenly, too much. Even if one of the decent men won the right to Rosa's hand, it would all begin again. This poor little kingdom would be the tasty morsel that the neighbors all wanted to devour as long as there was no practical way to protect it.

Jimson continued to try and comfort her with soothing words, with reminders of several of the many disasters she had averted, and then just with "it will be all right," repeated over and over. But for the moment, she was inconsolable. Finally he burst out, "Ah, I wish I was in your world, my love. I could at least hold you!"

*That* stopped her tears. She looked up suddenly and saw in the eyes of her Mirror Servant something she had never expected to see.

"Jimson?" she faltered.

He flushed. "I should never have said that," he mumbled, and started to fade.

*"Wait!"* she called. He paused, halfway between *there* and *not there.* "Did you mean that?"

Slowly, he came back to *there.* "It slipped out."

"But did you mean it?" She stared at him, as if she was seeing him, really *seeing* him, for the first time. For three hundred years, he had been her faithful helper, companion and confidant. Everything, everyone else, would come and go—but not Jimson. When had her feelings crossed that line? When had his? They had been together so long...

Perhaps it had only been recently. It came to her now, since all this started, he had stopped calling her "Godmother," unless Rosa was around. That might have been the first sign, if she had just been paying more attention.

Maybe she hadn't wanted to know; maybe her heart had known, and her head had realized that it was impossible and protected her from the knowledge. Because it was impossible. He could not be here, and despite knowing mirror-magic as well as she did, his world was still somewhere she could not go, for it was inhabited only by spirits.

"Of course I meant it." He stared at her with naked longing, and for the first time ever, a hand joined the image of the face in the mirror, a hand pressed up against the surface of the glass as if by will alone he could reach into her world.

She pressed her hand to the same place, palm to palm. "I'm sorry—" she began.

"That you don't feel the same?" He smiled bitterly.

"No—" she replied. "I'm sorry it's taken me so long to notice that I do."

Prince Leopold's gift encircled Rosa's neck under her gown, lying cool against her skin; there was something extraordinarily comforting about the feel of the unicorn necklace. She very much appreciated the gift, although the giver had pushed himself forward just a little too much, kissing her hand and then starting upward before she pulled away.

She had heard of such things of course, but she had never actually seen one, much less owned one. As wealthy as Eltaria was, all the money in the kingdom couldn't buy what no one would willingly sell.

She wondered about the unicorn this had come from. Leopold had said the hair was freely given, which made it more potent, but she rather doubted that he was a virgin. How had he gotten it? Had he followed the unicorn at a discreet distance, picking the hairs off bushes?

More likely he had found some young girl to get the hairs for him. She smiled a little as she shook her head. That man! A more charming rogue there never was. And she liked him well enough— just not as a consort. He'd be very amusing as a friend; he was witty and had a prankster's sense of humor, but was not afraid to turn the joke on himself. However, he was not what Eltaria needed. She sensed that he was cavalier about most things, and not really that good at thinking ahead. He would probably be a very popular King right up to the point that he did something disastrous. She had felt a little guilty accepting his gift, but then again, that came with being courted, and she had accepted a great many gifts by now, some just as valuable.

The only one as practical, however, was Prince Siegfried's gift. And Siegfried's was priceless. Of all the things she had been given or offered, being able to defend herself meant the most to her.

It was also a gift that no one else had even thought of. Siegfried *had* thought ahead; he had seen the blind spot her guards had when it came to the Princes, and he had given her a tool to get herself free. The second lesson had been just as interesting; he had shown her how to pick up something, get its balance to know how to throw it and get it aimed, more or less, at a target. "Even if you don't hit someone trying to hurt you, you'll make him duck. If he's ducking, he's not grabbing for you, he's not chasing you, and he's not firing a hand-crossbow at you."

She was drilling herself in that now, to see everything as a potential weapon. It was going to take some getting used to, and she still had to remind herself to do so. It seemed for Siegfried it was automatic.

And she was also enjoying the quiet moments of conversation that occurred between them. Though they were surrounded by others—and often ended up sweaty and bruised—there was a tenderness and a wistfulness to Siegfried's glances that made Rosa linger after the lessons were officially over. Siegfried's stories about his home and his travels were so very different from hers, and his wry comments were both amusing and insightful.

"Between the two of us, Princess, you did Joffrey a favor by eliminating him. He has been looking for an excuse to do badly," he had said once.

"How do you know?" Rosa had asked.

He had looked her in the eye. "Because there isn't a man born who will admit he had to ask for directions unless he really doesn't want to be where he is supposed to be going. And Joffrey did. Three times."

The ballroom seemed empty now, with only ten suitors left—though of course, all her ladies in waiting and courtiers were still there, and still mingling with the remaining Princes. Things were going back to normal, insofar as they *could* be normal with the trials still on and the anticipation for the end building.

Three of the five "neighbors" were still in the running. She really did not want any of them to win. She really didn't want Leopold to win. That left six. Karl had been eliminated early on at the dragon trial. Not even his father was willing to protest that one. Not when he had tried to charge Sharpstone in defiance of the rules and had been picked up and dumped on his own doorstep by the dragon, in full possession of not only his own curse but several more.

Siegfried; a semischolar named Henzel who had done surprisingly well even in the contests that required strength; Caspar, who was *almost* old enough to be her father; Klaus, who approached everything in terms of strategy; Andret, who was here mostly to test himself; and Desmond.

As if the thought had summoned him, Desmond appeared at her side, moving fluidly away from a knot of admirers and giving her a little bow as soon as he saw she had seen him. "Good evening, Desmond," she said, smiling. "And what is the speculation about the next contest?"

"Most of us favor something spectacular—riding up a mountain of glass to fetch a golden apple, or something of the sort," he replied, with a charming lift of one corner of his mouth. "I was inclined to agree. With so much of the competition eliminated, it is a good time to—"

"—give my people something to watch and marvel over?" she asked.

"—I would have said, give them the sort of thing that tales are made of. This will be something that will be talked about for a hundred years, probably more." He raised an elegant eyebrow. "The tale will probably travel far, far beyond the six Kingdoms here, as your failed suitors return to their own lands, and probably exaggerate their own standings." His mouth quirked a little, in an ever-so-slightly-superior smile. "I would imagine every one of them will recount how *he* was in second place and only edged out by the winner at the last moment by some tactic either dubious or fiendishly clever."

Rosa waited for him to add something to that, and was a little disappointed. She knew that Leopold would have concluded with a crooked smile and "I know *I* will," and they both would have laughed. And Siegfried would have said something like "Everyone is the hero of his own saga," with a self-deprecating shrug and a chuckle. If

Desmond had a defect, it was that he didn't seem to find anything funny. Ironic, yes, or sarcastic. Not funny.

Part of the reason that the ballroom seemed so empty was that there was enough floor space for large open areas to form. Now that there was room to move in here again, the majordomo had brought evening entertainment back—not actually holding formal balls, but rather, evening gatherings with a small group of musicians, so that those who wished to could dance, and those that wished to merely watch and gossip could do that without musicians or talkers drowning each other out. The group of musicians that had been playing at the "dancing end" of the long room quietly struck up the chords to signal dancing was going to begin.

If there was one thing Rosa loved, it was dancing. And Desmond almost made up for his lack of humor with his ability to dance. He didn't ask her if she wanted to; he simply smiled and swung her into the first steps of the extremely lively dance called "Rupert Calantry."

Normally, the first dances of the evening were extremely energetic, and tonight was no exception. Desmond had to relinquish her to another partner for four more dances; Siegfried didn't know these dances and Leopold was at the gaming tables, and the other three suitors weren't quick enough to beat out Desmond. And then, right in the middle of a lively gigue, she found herself swung out of the door to the garden and into the shadows of some ornamental trees where Desmond swung her around and into his embrace, looked down into her eyes for a moment, then kissed her.

She closed her eyes and waited for…something to happen.

And nothing did.

It was pleasant. He was a little more forceful than she would have liked, but when she pulled back a little so did he. But…it was nothing more than pleasant; no spark, no excitement, just mild curiosity.

And...somewhere inside, a little disappointment that none of that was there.

Desmond reacted immediately to her lack of enthusiasm, smiling and releasing her. "Pardon, Princess, but you are so lovely and so adorable, I could not help myself." There was a flash of—something—in his eyes, but it passed before she could identify what it was.

"There's nothing to forgive," she replied, and he took her arm like the perfect gentleman, as if nothing had happened except that they had come outside for a breath of air.

Nothing, except that faint feeling of disappointment, and the growing feeling that there was something odd about Desmond.

"That's it," Jimson said suddenly, breaking Lily out of her trance. "That's it. The last trial. The contest will be to find a way to protect Eltaria permanently." He chuckled cruelly. "Our three 'neighbors' won't have a chance, since their solutions—which will probably consist of 'marry me'—will be unacceptable. The others will all be working on theirs for some time, I expect."

Lily dried her eyes and looked up. "Jimson, that is a very, very good idea. And it's the perfect trial. The young man that comes up with the best solution really *will* be the best one for Eltaria. And I don't mind at all keeping them here indefinitely...." She reached out her hand to the mirror and pressed it there. A moment later, Jimson's hand appeared on the other side of the glass. She smiled, a little wanly. "In fact, just to be fair, I will announce that the solution *cannot* be 'marry me,' since that is not so much an answer as an obvious case of not thinking far enough into the future, and the solution must hold well past when Rosa and her consort are long dead. You are a genius."

"Just desperate to stay your tears, my love," Jimson said tenderly. "Now, let us work together on the best way to phrase this announcement. We will want something that not even our worst enemies can

take exception to. You can tell them all at afternoon Court
tomorrow. Even the laziest will be awake by then."

There was silence for a moment after the announcement, which
seemed to take the Princess as much by surprise as everyone else,
then the chatter began. "Well, that's certainly an interesting and appropriate challenge," said Leopold after a while. He sighed. "I think
I will go find the gaming tables."

Siegfried blinked. "Shouldn't we be thinking of—"

Leopold interrupted him. "Siegfried, *we* should not be doing
anything. It's obvious that this is the last trial. You go think of your
way to answer the challenge, and I'll think of mine, and may the
best man win."

Siegfried was taken aback for a moment, but Leopold had not lost
his slight smile. Whether or not he actually intended to compete at
this, Siegfried couldn't tell. Maybe going to the gaming tables was
his way of thinking about it. But he was right. Now it was every man
for himself.

He nodded, and clapped Leopold on the shoulder. "Don't forget
your promise," he said. "When you win Rosamund, you help me find
a woman who will break my Fate."

Leopold laughed and punched Siegfried's bicep, swiftly reverting
to his usual cheer. "Siegfried, some of the women I've met down in
the city would set *themselves* on fire for enough money, provided they
didn't get hurt doing it. So don't worry. One way or another, we'll
break your Fate for you."

Feeling a little more cheerful, Siegfried headed back into the Palace
for Rosa's next training session. This one should be...interesting.

He met her at the door of one of the guest rooms, recently vacated
by one of the candidates for her hand, which the servants would be
cleaning thoroughly when he and she were done. All of the break-

able ornaments and furniture had been removed and replaced with things that didn't matter, or were already broken.

"Are you ready?" he asked. She nodded and went inside. He gave her a moment to orient herself, and then flung open the door.

And had to duck immediately as a huge, and incredibly ugly, vase came flying at his head.

From that point, it was sheer mayhem.

This was the test of what he had told her to practice over the last few days; to enter a room with an eye to what might become a weapon, and prepare to use everything that came to her hand.

That was exactly what she was doing. While he tried to catch her, anything that could be thrown at him, was, and with great accuracy. He wasn't going to trust this test to anyone else. Anyone else might get hurt; his reflexes were superb, possibly the best here, for he had certainly won the tournament *and* the archery contest. He was having a hard time dodging what she threw, too. She was good.

Her eyes sparkled with mischief and excitement as she aimed directly for his head with small objects he had only a glimpse of while he was dodging them. Her cheeks were very pink, and she grinned like a mad thing as she raced around the room, grabbing and throwing. It sounded as if there was a fight going on in this room, and he hoped there was no one nearby, other than her guards, to hear it, or a full-scale rescue party might come crashing through the door in spite of her guards.

Meanwhile he chased her, and she ran. They made three circuits of the room, and each time she passed the door she touched it quickly, as the mark that she knew it was there and if this had not been a test, she would have been out of it. She did the same at the window. He had taught her how to jump out of one without getting hurt a few days ago.

When she ran out of things to throw, she began finding things to turn over in his path, or knock over and kick at him. She picked up a shard of the vase to use as a knife. She picked up pieces of things still big enough to throw and threw *them* at him. Finally, when they had sped around the room too many times for him to count, she was getting out of breath, and he called a halt to the proceedings.

She put a hand to her side, laughing. "Oh the poor servants are going to hate me!" she gasped, and collapsed on an ancient sofa in the middle of the room, the only thing still standing. He plopped down beside her.

She was still laughing. "You looked so funny! It was like a scene out of a farce!"

He chuckled. "Leopold took me to a farce, so at least I know what you mean. Like the scene where the angry girl throws plates at the clown?"

"Exactly! Or her faithless lover." She patted his head. "Poor Siegfried! I hope you do not have too many lumps now!"

"Not too many." He grinned sheepishly.

Rosa's side hurt—and the corners of her mouth hurt from smiling so much. She knew this was *supposed* to be a serious exercise, but how could she be serious when Siegfried looked so funny, dodging all the horrible little ornamental things that people had bequeathed on the monarchs of Eltaria for the last hundred years or so?

She didn't think he'd been hit—the man had the dodging ability of ten cats!—but she patted his head to make sure. That shaggy blond pelt was softer than it looked, much to her surprise. She didn't feel any lumps.

But suddenly, she was seized with an impulse to—to—

Her hand seemed to snake to the back of his head without any conscious thought on her part, to pull it forward. His eyes went startled.

Then her lips met his.

The same physical sensations raced through her that she had felt when she had awakened in the grove and Leopold had been kissing her. And other things. Except that this time...this time, the sensations were more intense. All of her skin felt a thousand times more *alive* than it ever had. And there were fires burning everywhere inside her. And—

*Oh no—no I must not do this yet—*

She let go of his head with a conscious effort of will and moved herself back a little on the sofa. He blinked owlishly at her, then licked his lips, and did the same.

"If that is another weapon you threw at me, Princess," he said carefully, "it is most effective."

She laughed weakly. "Not...exactly."

*Well, I wanted sparks. Some sign. That was certainly a sign. Desmond might not have this, whatever it is, but Siegfried certainly does.*

He blinked again, and moved back as far as he could before he ran into the arm of the sofa. "I think I had better sit here, or I might— we might— It would not be wise," he finished, his voice strained.

She did the same, and folded her hands primly in her lap. Then she smiled, and felt her face flushing. He smiled back, then began to chuckle.

"Well I did tell you to use everything you had as a weapon," he said, his voice a bit steadier. "And as a weapon, that is a useful one. When your enemy is disconcerted, you can use the same techniques I taught you for being seized."

She was amazed that he was able to think clearly, because she was still a bit muddled. As if he had read her thoughts, he chuckled again.

"Also it becomes easier with practice, much easier, to keep at least part of your mind clear even when the rest of it is reeling with confusion." He ran his hand through his hair—oh, she wanted to do that!—and grinned ruefully. "This is useful when one has had a mighty blow to the head. As I can testify. It is a very good thing that my skull is very, very thick."

His bird, after landing on the windowsill and peering around cautiously, flew in and landed on her customary perch on his shoulder.

"You two certainly made a mess," she trilled. "It looks as if a bear went on a rampage here! Well, Princess, did you pass the test?"

"Oh, yes," Siegfried said first. "She certainly passed that test. Now all she need worry about is magic. I can do nothing to train her for that. Well, other than 'kill the magician before he can cast his power over you.'"

"Which is difficult to do if he is out of bowshot," the bird observed shrewdly. "Well then, Princess, even though your guards know what is going on and are listening for screams, the silence unnerves them almost as much, and I think you should go tell them it is all right before they burst in here with crossbows. Yes?"

"Oh! Yes!" Rosa leapt to her feet, grateful to the bird for breaking the awkward moment. "Yes, I certainly should. Thank you!"

Siegfried did not immediately get up, and when he did, she had already opened the door for herself. "Thank you, Prince Siegfried. I hope I never have to use your training, but I am so *very* glad I have it! This was the best gift anyone has ever given me!"

She had just enough time to see his face light up before she whisked out the door.

The guards were all huddled outside the door, faces strained and anxious. They, too, lit up when she saw them, then looked shocked when they saw the wreck she had made of the room. Siegfried gave them a little salute, and grinned.

"Do not annoy your Princess, gentlemen," he said with a laugh.

"Her aim is *very* good. Perhaps you might consider if your ability to dodge is as good."

They didn't reply, of course. It wouldn't be appropriate. But she could see that she had impressed them.

*Good. It won't hurt for them to know that I can defend myself. It might keep them on their toes a bit.*

With a little wave to Siegfried, she set off down the hall. After that workout, she needed a bath.

And it was in the bath, chin deep in hot water, that she was able to think.

There was no doubt that Desmond was wonderful. Unbelievable, in fact. But did that mean that he was in fact unbelievable? He saw her for no more than an hour at a time, less than that was spent alone in his company. He had *plenty* of time to study her, quiz servants about her, even use more esoteric means to find out about her. Then, all he had to do was be utterly charming for the short period of time he was with her, and guardedly genial when he was with anyone else, just to be sure that no bad reports got back to her.

Whereas Siegfried had every opportunity to lose his temper with her. Over the course of training, she had hit him by accident many times, quite hard, including once in his "jewels". He had never done worse than shout at her the one time she had very nearly done something stupidly dangerous to herself. He had lost his temper, yes, but never taken it out on her, and always apologized.

She licked the salty sweat off her upper lip and pondered.

She certainly had had the answer to her question of who she was attracted to. *No, do be honest with yourself. It is a great deal more than mere attraction.* And this was Eltaria, where Kings and Queens and Princes and Princesses actually fell in love all the time. It was not out of the question that she could be falling in love with Siegfried. He might not be the sharpest sword in the rack at times, but there was no doubt that he also wasn't stupid. And he was kind, brave, loyal...

But there was still the last trial to go.

*Damn you, Tradition!* she thought fiercely. *Do something about this!*

18

IT WAS WARM, TOO WARM. ROSA HAD TOSSED and turned in her soft, rose-scented sheets until the last sound faded from the Palace and the last servant went to bed for the night. Now she lay in her bed and stared at the patch of wall where a beam of moonlight, piercing through a parting of the curtains, slowly moved its way down the wainscoting. The too-warm air pressed down on her. She longed for a storm.

The moonlight was an irregular, pale slash on the wall. Crickets chorused outside the window, and once in a while she heard the steady footfalls of a guard patrolling the grounds. She was tired, and yet couldn't sleep. Her brain buzzed with thoughts. She felt as if she had been awake for hours. Judging by the position of that patch of moonlight, she probably had been.

And still her mind buzzed and chirped like the crickets and would not let her rest. She kept trying to think of a way she could covertly help Siegfried, and nothing would come.

It had been two days since the last trial had been announced, and so far, there were two dropouts. She hadn't expected more than that, but every man less meant more pressure on the ones still in the competition.

One was Andret. Andret had always been one of the more...enthusiastic and cheerful of the competitors. He had come to Lily all smiles immediately after the trial was announced.

"Majesty," he had said, after his bow, "in a sense, I came here under false colors. Frankly I never intended to try for Rosa's hand."

Lily, so she told Rosa, had been unsurprised, and a little amused.

She had asked why he was telling her now, though. "Because I have no good ideas for the defense of this realm," he had replied. "If I did, be sure I would tell you, but I do not, so I must bid you farewell. I have greatly enjoyed testing myself against your challenges."

It became obvious *why* he had never intended to finish the trials when his mother, the Sorceress Aubergine, arrived to fetch him away. With her, driving a second chariot, this one drawn by a pair of Gryphons, was a stunning flame-haired young female. Any thoughts that she might have been his sister evaporated in the heat of their greeting. It was quite entertaining for those who happened to be present to watch it.

The other dropout was the son of the ruler of Reritain, to the east. No one had been sorry to see him leave. He had been sullen to the point of surliness, and had made no allies here.

That left three remaining candidates from the neighboring kingdoms, which was enough to prevent anyone from deciding to invade, whether their candidate had lost the contest or was still in the running. At least, for now.

Rosa turned over again, trying to find a cool spot. Nothing. Her thoughts kept circling around the remaining competitors, trying to work out if there was anything she could do to keep them from quitting. The longer this trial went on, the better.

There were eight left now. Eight young men who had taken various approaches to the problem they had been set.

Leopold gambled. Every night he sat down at the gaming tables with her courtiers—and by day, she knew, he went into the city to a gambling club where he pitted his luck against that of rich young men of merchant families. He was winning, too, quite handily, and growing increasingly cheerful as he did so. She didn't know him well enough to tell if this meant he couldn't think of anything so he was glad he was making a small fortune at the tables, or if it meant he *had* thought of something, and he was cheerful and winning because of it.

As for Siegfried—well, Siegfried vanished from the Palace for most of every day. His bird told her that he was going out to the forest. She could sympathize with that; if you were used to being alone in the wild a great deal, then the Palace was not the best place to be able to think. But what if he was going to the forest to escape having to see her, knowing he had no ideas and was not likely to have any?

She intercepted him early one morning—getting up much, much earlier than she usually did, only to have him look at her with the eyes of a man cut off from what he most desires. "Princess," he had said, holding up his hand. "This is the hardest thing I have ever done. I am not good at thinking—but I will not give up and go away." He had paused then, looked at his feet and stammered, "And I wish you were a shepherdess so that there would be no contest over you, and I could put you in a ring of fire and awaken you and we would live happily ever after."

That had left her dumb for a moment.

"If you did not mind being poor, I would rather be wandering roofless with you, than living in a palace with anyone else."

Her heart thudded in her throat when he said that. But before she could muster the wits to reply to him, he had turned, striding rapidly away.

Desmond tried to corner her. When he caught her, briefly, he asked, framed in cautious words, if she would give him a boost over the pack. She was both angry and hurt by this—angry because he had asked her to cheat for him, hurt because of the way he had asked. Not that he wanted to win for her, but because he wanted to win, no matter what it took.

"This trial isn't a form of joke or the sort of test that the riddles were, Desmond," she had said gravely. "And there is no 'right answer' sealed away somewhere. This is a situation that needs resolving. Thus far, none of the best heads in the Kingdom have an answer for it, and whoever comes up with that solution will properly be the right one for the throne."

She had to give him this much: he took her rebuke well, as far as she could tell. He bowed over her hand, and had been pretty solitary ever since.

The remaining five closeted themselves in the library or in their rooms. Presumably they were looking for answers, too.

"She distracted you, didn't she?" The bird was keeping pace with him, flitting from branch to branch.

"Yes, and I cannot afford to be distracted. Do you think the Godmother could build a great wall around Eltaria?"

"I think if she could have, she would have. Besides, you'd need troops to man it, wouldn't you? Otherwise all it would take to get in would be a battering ram." The bird was quite good at picking holes in Siegfried's ideas—which he appreciated no end. An idea that was only a little good was not going to win him the girl.

The forest was a good place to think, and even Luna—who was, of course, pacing on the path behind him—knew enough to keep quiet while he was trying to come up with a good idea.

It didn't help, not at *all,* that there were rumors of mysterious sleeping women in rings of fire appearing in random meadows. Doom was trying to close in on him. And he knew how The Tradition worked. He was a stag, and The Tradition was the pack of hounds. Sooner or later it was going to run him into exhaustion, or into a dead end that he couldn't escape from.

Then again…

*If I can't win Rosa…I don't think I want to escape.* Doom would be preferable to going through the rest of his life knowing that he'd lost her.

"What about some sort of magical wall?" he hazarded. "One that won't let enemies in?"

Rosa had gone to bed unhappy, and her unhappiness had brought on insomnia. *"I would rather be poor with you…"* She might have thought it was flattery, but not with that haggard expression on Siegfried's face. Siegfried was known to stay out in the forest from dawn to dusk. She wished he wouldn't. She wished he was here. She was very much afraid that this was the last chance she would ever have to spend any time at all with him. One of the others, more clever, with better connections and resources, would have a plan that would save her Kingdom. And in a choice between her own needs and those of her Kingdom, Eltaria would win.

No matter how unhappy it made her.

She was sure of it now; she was, if not already in love with him, certainly falling in love with him. There was no doubt that he felt the same; when she intercepted his gaze—at breakfast, at supper—it was full of longing and frustration.

But he was not the sort who would give up. Not until the last of the remaining candidates offered his solution and he either had none, or had one that was rejected. And not because he wanted a throne; she had the feeling that if a crown was all he'd wanted, he'd have gotten one a long time ago. Not because he wanted her only to escape his fate, either. No…his feelings were quite clear. As clear as hers were.

Finally she got tired of lying in bed, unable to sleep a wink, running the same problems over and over in her head and coming up with the same lack of answers. She got up and pulled the curtains aside enough to flood the room with moonlight. This wouldn't be the first time she'd slipped out for a walk in the middle of the night; when she was younger, she'd often had restless nights. Thanks to her mother, she could do entirely without maids when she wanted to.

She delved into the back of one of the great wardrobe cabinets in her bedroom, dressed herself in the simplest of her clothing and carried her shoes, and easily slipped out of her rooms, past her sleeping maids. If she was seen, she'd be taken for a servant; she wore the gown and petticoat she had worn when her mother had given her lessons on how shepherds lived. She would have liked to have used the disguise cloak, but Lily had used it last, and it was in *her* room. Once out in the corridors that the servants used, she pulled on the shoes; a servant tiptoeing around the halls would arouse suspicion, not quell it. The gown still had the faint scent she associated with that happy time, of hay and clover blossoms, a little of the oily sheep smell, and smoke. When that scent was released from her gown, warmed by her body, she found herself suddenly overwhelmed with memories. She had to put her back to the wall of the servants' corridor and cry soundlessly a little.

Finally she fought her tears down and made her way out into the kitchen yard, between the Palace and the stables. She lost herself quickly in the passageways among the stables, the mews, the chickenhouses, the dovecotes, the rabbit-hutches—the Palace supported a lot of animals, more than most people might guess. Many of the buildings were brick and stone, even the chicken-houses, since stone and brick were easier to clean than wood, and easier to secure against predators and vermin. The stables, the kennels and the mews even supported living quarters for those servants who tended the beasts.

Once safely in the shadows, she put her back against one of the cool stone walls, and deeply breathed in the night air, only faintly scented with straw and horse and dog.

*Dog?* She realized with a start that she must be near the kennels. Not necessarily a good thing…the kennels were where the Huntsman had his quarters, and he was the very last person she wanted to encounter in the dark even if he didn't recognize her.

Just as that thought passed through her mind, she heard the voices. One was Desmond's.

What was Desmond doing out here so late at night?

She didn't recognize the other.

Impelled by concern as well as curiosity, she inched forward until she could hear the two speakers clearly.

"…the progress on hunting that unicorn?" Desmond asked, impatiently. Her hand went unconsciously to the necklace at her throat.

"Slowly, Prince." That was the Huntsman! "The beast is proving elusive. I find its spoor, but always days old. I took the bait—verified bait, I swear to you—out into the forest, and the unicorn never came near."

"I want that horn. I *need* that horn. Besides that, I need the blood, the mane and the hooves, but the horn is imperative." This was an entirely different Desmond from the one she was used to hearing. Arrogant. Demanding.

And ordering the Huntsman to kill a unicorn. Anger suffused her, and outrage. How dared he! This was *her* Kingdom's treasure, in *her* forest!

"As you say, Highness. Have you any other tasks for me?"

And then, after the anger, disgust. Kill a unicorn? Of all things, a *unicorn?*

When she told Lily—

"The Princess is proving resistant," Desmond was saying, snapping her attention back to the topic at hand. "I am going to need you to stand ready to take her at any moment."

Had he been the one giving the Huntsman his orders all along? Had he been the one who had sent the Huntsman in the first place?

"That won't be easy, sire," the Huntsman replied, and she could almost hear the frown in his voice. *Sire?* "She is well guarded these days."

*And I am going to be even better guarded now that I know about you!* she thought with a feeling of shock. The Huntsman she had been wary of, but Desmond? He was in no way related to any of the five enemy Kingdoms on the border! At least…they had thought he was not…

She calculated how quickly she could get help here if she just started running and screaming now—

*Not quickly enough. The guards won't know it's me. They might not even realize it's a human sound. It could be taken for one of the peacocks, disturbed, or some other animal. We are near enough the forest that anything could come into the yard and be killed by a dog or kill something else.* If she began running and screaming, Desmond and his lackey would have plenty of time to grab her and make off with her before help came. She knew then she was going to have to get away, get to the Palace, raise an alarm—

No, that would not do—it would be her word against his. Between this moment and when she finally organized guards to come after him, the Huntsman could be back in his bed, and even if Desmond was found outside of his rooms, he could say, well, anything. He could deny he was ever at the stables, and he *would* deny that he was talking to the Huntsman. He could claim that she was dreaming, sleepwalking. She would have no way of disproving him.

No, she needed to get back into the Palace, wake Lily and tell her what she had overheard. Her best bet to catch him was through magic. All this time, they had been watching the Huntsman, not him. Now that they knew what he was up to, they should be able to catch *him* at meetings with the Huntsman. At something, anyway—

She froze, as she heard a growl behind her, and smelled hot, doggy breath.

"What's that?" Desmond said sharply.

She knew not to move. That growl had been deep and menacing.

"My hound seems to have found a spy, sire," the Huntsman replied, in a growl not far removed from the dog's.

"Well that you set him to watch then," replied the Prince, and uttered a few guttural words in a language she didn't recognize. "Now you can call him off."

She heard a whistle, and the dog padded away. *Now!* she thought, ready to run for it, and—

Couldn't move. Not a muscle. She couldn't even make a sound.

She was barely able to blink and breathe.

"Let's see what little mouse we've caught," said Desmond, his voice full of cruel amusement. Two dark figures approached her where she was stuck, leaning against the stable wall. The light from a shuttered lantern flashed into her face, and she heard the Huntsman's swift intake of breath, and then Desmond's slow chuckle.

"Well, well, well. It looks as if you have managed to snare me my quarry after all," Desmond said. He tore off the magical bracelet Lily would have used to find her, and threw it on the ground before uttering another handful of words. And that was all she knew....

...until she woke up.

She was not in the stables of her Palace. This place was cold, and it was dank. It smelled like wet stone. It was so dark that at first she was in a panic, thinking she was blind, and she lurched to her feet, fell, smacked her head on stone and saw stars.

That was when a shutter in a door she could not see until that moment grated open, and a light shone in on her, proving that at least she wasn't blind.

"You're awake!" It was the Huntsman, and he sounded surprised. "His Highness told me you wouldn't be awake for half a day yet!"

"Well his Highness doesn't know everything, then, does he?" she snapped. Her head *hurt*. Where was she?

The Huntsman laughed. It was the sort of laugh that put cold chills up her back.

"Bold little Princess. Not that it will do you any good. Desmond is the best sorcerer in his generation. He is patient, and thorough, and *you* are where you cannot escape and cannot communicate with anyone or anything. Not even a mouse or a spider. Every way in which a magician can see at a distance has been eliminated."

She gulped, the pain in her head forgotten. So that was why they had never caught the Huntsman doing anything other than what he was supposed to! Desmond...

"Your Godmother will not find you a second time, Princess. And in case someone is listening as well, somehow, you may be sure that neither of us will say where you are within your hearing. I myself have been geased against doing so."

Her blood ran cold. It sounded as if Desmond had thought of everything.

"He is still at the Palace, of course. When your loss is discovered, he will be as horrified as anyone else."

*Of course he will.*

"I, of course, will be the logical suspect. When searchers are sent out, he will come here. No one suspects him of anything. Unlike some of the others, no one will demand he take a partner."

It was logical. There would be no reason to suspect Desmond.

"When he returns here, he will proceed to envelop you in magic.

He has specialized in the kinds of magic that—well, to put it simply, make it possible to control one other person. He has studied these things for years. Such spells take a great deal of time to cast, but that does not matter. He will have all the time he needs to make them work on you as there is very little chance that anyone will discover this place. If they do, there would be no reason to think you are here. If you are sought here, this cell is well hidden. His Highness will have sufficient time to wrap your mind in so many, many spells that not even the urge to eat and sleep will be your own. Then, when you are completely his thrall, he will 'rescue' you." The Huntsman laughed again. "Perhaps he will put you to sleep, and wake you with a kiss. You will be overjoyed to be with him by then, and he will reveal to your people that *he* is the answer to your problem, that his magic can control the enemies of this land and set them against each other instead of Eltaria. You will adore him, and be overjoyed to wed him. Who knows, you might even actually feel those things. You will probably be very next to an imbecile when he gets done draining you of magic, but that won't matter."

The slide clattered shut, then abruptly opened again. "There is a bucket of water and a dipper at the rear and to the right of this room. There is an empty bucket in the left. Food and water will be left here when you are sleeping."

The slide clacked shut, leaving her alone in the dark.

Panic rose in her, and she gave it room to run for a while. That was something she had learned from Lily; when things were at their worst, if you had the space, let the panic run out. Besides, they were expecting this. If she were calm, they would suspect her of being strong, or of having some secret way to get help. If she acted like one of the helpless things they expected, they would underestimate her.

*That,* she had learned from Siegfried.

So she screamed, cried herself hoarse, permitted herself hysteria.

The stone cell echoed with the noise of anguish. She sobbed helplessly as she felt her way around the stone cell on her hands and knees and begged the Huntsman to let her go. She offered immense bribes, and cried some more.

She knew he was out there, listening. She could hear him moving occasionally, or laughing quietly. And when the hysteria ran out, when her eyes were so raw she could hardly see, she felt her way to the pallet she had found and lay down on it.

She hadn't recognized the language that Desmond had used for his spell-casting...but that didn't actually matter. Lily had not been teaching her narrowly defined or restricted magic of the sort that those tied to rituals did.

Lily had instead been teaching her how magic worked.

She had learned how to see the constructions that magic made around the person or object a spell was cast upon. It was entirely appropriate to say that a spell was "woven," because that was what such things looked like, an intricate interlacing of something between thick yarn and thin rope. Desmond had been very careful and very clever not to weave *any* powerful magic back at the Palace, nothing that he could not have been given by some tame wizard to help him with the trials, or she and Lily would have seen it. Probably he had made arrangements to meet the Huntsman in the forest. Now, however, he was free to weave as many spells as he cared to.

She strongly suspected that The Tradition had a great deal to do with spells working. If it were only following exact ritual that worked, then how could the improvisational magicians get anything done? Yet exact ritual was much, much more powerful than extempore work.

Unless you knew the principles behind how magic worked. And unless you could see completed spells.

*"There are many more magicians who work by what they have memorized than there are those who work by knowing the principles of magic,"* Lily had

said. *"There are plenty who can't see it, and rely on the ritual to do the ma-nipulation for them, rather like a blind person threading a maze that he has memorized. All the Fae can, which is one reason why Fae magic seems so un-predictable to many human magicians. If they need to, the Fae can cast and unmake spells without using any sort of ritual at all."*

Lily *did* use spells and cantrips all the time, she said—and certainly Rosa had seen her do so. Was that because it was easier? Or was it because The Tradition said that they worked, so—they worked?

Did it even matter? *No it doesn't. My mind is spinning in circles again.* The point was, she could see magic. With patience, she could unravel it—

*Or maybe, apply what Siegfried taught me about squirming out of a hold. Don't resist, look for the weak point, then duck under it...Oh, bless you, Sieg-fried!* If magicians thought, well, like humans, they would model their spells, whether they knew it or not, on how humans bound things—grappling, ropes. Ropes could be unwound. The grappling arms could be squirmed out of.

She just had to keep her head...

Desmond had frozen her in place, then had the Huntsman carry her—up. She did her best to conceal her shock when she realized that underneath the cosmetic changes, she recognized that he had carried her up through the cellar to what had once been the Dwarves' cottage.

It had been heavily fortified somehow. Given how beautifully the stonework fit together, it had probably been the Dwarves them-selves who had been forced to labor on it. She recognized the kitchen immediately, although it, and the huge table and stools around it, had been cleaned until the wood of the furniture was a clear gray and the stone of floor and walls was almost white. The blackened beams of the ceiling remained, but the plaster between was snowy. The windows were gone; the entire ground floor had been encased in a layer of stonework, the original door replaced by a new, thicker one. That door stood open on what had been a garden, and now looked like a tangle of wicked thorns as long as a man's arm. As she *looked* for magic, they all glowed; they had been magically grown, then.

*Oh no...* Thorns? Tower? He was using The Tradition, too! The thorns that guarded the Beauty Asleep! No wonder he kept her sleeping most of the time! No wonder the Huntsman had laughed about awaking her with a kiss!

Everything but the table in the kitchen was gone, replaced by new fittings and utensils. The Huntsman carried her up a new set of stairs built along the outside wall in what had been that storage room to a second and much more luxurious room. The original cottage was now the base of a fortified tower.

In the center of the room on the second floor was a chair, covered, rather ominously, with engraved signs. The Huntsman put her in that chair—of course she still couldn't move, but as soon as she got over the shock of recognition, she began trying to see the bonds of the magic that held her. As she began to make them out, she saw that they were like heavy shackles, one on each arm, one on each wrist, made of braided bands of power. Experimentally, she tugged a little on one of the ends.

It loosened.

Yes! She could do this—

Then heavy footfalls above warned that someone was coming down. Her chair faced the staircase that slanted down the outer wall, and she knew it was Desmond from the moment she saw the too-shiny boots.

The genial manner was gone, replaced by a complete lack of expression. She had seen statues with more animation. By now, she had managed to ease herself free a little, and he didn't seem to have noticed, so she kept quiet and acted as if she was still paralyzed.

Meanwhile, he went to work.

He began to chant.

And within moments she knew this was going to be a real fight, for her mind, for her very self.

But in the same moment she realized that, she also felt something else. The necklace of unicorn hair lying around her neck began to warm.

Neither the Huntsman nor Desmond had taken it from her; for whatever reason, they hadn't noticed it. They probably assumed it was from a dead unicorn, not a live one, and couldn't do anything to help her—and of course, once she was bespelled, Desmond could have it merely by asking her for it. Strictly speaking, it couldn't help her, she supposed. But the bands of power that were snaking around her, trying to bind her, pulsed with a faint sensation of evil, and the necklace would not allow them to actually touch her.

She didn't know how long that would last…but the fact it was happening at all gave her the breathing space she needed. *I can study how these things are weaving, so I can unweave them,* she thought with a spark of anger-fueled energy. But she remembered what Siegfried had taught her about anger, and using it, and not being used by it. She throttled that anger down, letting it become the force behind her concentration, rather than letting it destroy her concentration.

Siegfried had taught her so many things—not just how to defend herself, but how not to be helpless. How to keep still and see a way out of what looked hopeless. He had shown her that, even if The Tradition was trying to steer your fate, you could push right back at it and change it.

She wasn't going to let The Tradition rule her, and she certainly wasn't going to let some arrogant Prince who fancied himself a great sorcerer do so. The very fact that he was depending on exact ritual meant he wasn't nearly as good as he thought he was.

So Desmond thought she was just some helpless little idiot, did he? Unable to stand up against his magic, and unable to help herself. He was going to find out exactly how wrong he was.

19

SIEGFRIED WOKE FROM A DREAM OF SHARPSTONE guarding the border, a dream that he knew in an instant was the key to his winning Rosa's hand. *Dragons!* He thought with elation. *Not all dragons are bad, but they all need a lot of feeding and safe lairs....*

But the dream was driven out of his mind by the agony that woke him, screaming, with twenty kitten claws impaling his left foot with red-hot needles of pain.

So much pain that for a crucial moment he was paralyzed. Then his reflexes kicked in—and so did he. The bedclothes went flying.

Fortunately the kitten had better reflexes than he did, and leapt off his foot and out of harm's way before his reflexes made him do something regrettable to it.

He sat up, eyes bulging, staring at the demon-in-fluff that had lacerated his foot. He tried to get words out, and failed utterly.

"*BigMan, BigMan, BigMan!*" the kitten mewed, bouncing like a demented ball of wool. "*Mama says get BigMan! Mama says BadMans take Lady!*" It repeated this in a high-pitched cat-yowl that cut right through his bewildered brain.

By this point, the bird, awakened by the screaming, was flying blindly around the darkened room, screaming *"Cat! Doom! Cat! Doom! Cat!"*

Siegfried hit the side of his head to clear it, but it was several moments before he managed to fumble a match onto a candlewick—by which time the bird had flown into a wall and knocked itself silly and had to be rescued from the kitten. It was longer before Siegfried could get any sense out of the kitten.

But once he did, he was into clothing and tearing down the hallway to the Royal Chambers as fast as he could go.

Of course, the guards there wouldn't let him in, but he was shouting so loudly before they grabbed his arms to drag him away that he made more than enough noise to wake Godmother Lily, who came to the door of her rooms herself. More to the point, he made more than enough noise to wake Rosa's maids, who discovered that she was gone about the time that Siegfried was insisting to Lily that she was in danger, which prompted more shrieking and shouting. Siegfried was at his wits' end by that point, trying to get *someone* to listen to what he had to say about the kitten—

Lily quelled it all by dropping her disguise of Queen Sable with a probably unnecessary thunderclap. When the stunned crowd fell silent, she began issuing orders. She pointed to the guards who had been at her door. "You guards—check on the remaining Princes. *Now.* Find out who is missing." She pointed to the ones that had come running at the fuss. "You guards—see if the Huntsman is gone." She turned to the maids. "You get back in those rooms, and if you can't calm yourselves, at least keep your hysterics *in there.*" And then to Siegfried. "Where is the mother cat?"

It was the kitten, clinging to the shoulder opposite the one that the wary bird claimed, that replied. "Mama outside! Mama see BadMans!"

"Put him down," she ordered Siegfried, who was perfectly happy to pry those twenty little needles out of his shoulder and put the kitten on the floor. "Take me to your mama," she ordered the kitten, who scampered off. "Find Leopold!" she called to Siegfried as she followed.

Siegfried ran back the way he had come, and burst in the door of Leopold's suite—for now that there were so few candidates, they all had their own suites again. Leopold was groggily clambering into his clothing, having been awakened once by Siegfried's screaming and again by the guards checking on the Princes.

"What in hell is going on?" Leopold demanded, blearily, looking haggard and a bit the worse for wear.

"The Princess is missing, an animal came to tell me someone had taken her, the Godmother is—" Siegfried began, only too well aware that he was perilously close to babbling, when Lily returned with the mother cat he had aided in one arm, the kitten in the other.

"Desmond is missing," Lily told them tersely. "He is the only one of the Princes gone. The Huntsman is missing, too. The cat says she was moving the kittens to establish them here at the stables, and she saw two men take Rosa. So unless the Huntsman has a confederate and Desmond followed them, somehow knowing when we didn't that Rosa had been taken, we can assume they were collaborating all along."

Siegfried snarled an inarticulate oath and headed for the door, but she stopped him dead before he got more than two steps. *"Wait,"* she ordered. "Just a moment. Think. What will you need?"

She was right. A moment spent now would be saved a thousand-fold later when he realized he was missing something. "My armor, my weapons, a horse—" he began.

"A direction," Lily pointed out. She jiggled the mother cat in her arm a little. "Cat?"

"Told kitten to wake you. Followed to market. Lost there," the cat said, tilting her head to the side and switching her tail rapidly. "Ran back here."

Siegfried thought about that a moment; from the market there were a dozen directions that Desmond could have gone, and at the moment he had no clear idea of which. Unless there was a witness…would the donkey have seen them? It was worth finding out. And if the donkey had not, perhaps he could start querying dogs. "There's a stable there. I might have someone in it who noticed them."

"I'll take care of the horses," Lily said. "You get down to the stable." She put down the cat and kitten and hurried off.

"I'm coming with you!" Leopold interjected, now fully clothed, and bundling up what little armor he had. Siegfried wasn't even going to try to dissuade him; first, it would be a waste of time, and second, Leopold had as much right as he did to join in the search.

"Come on, then," he snapped, and headed for his rooms at a run. Like Leopold, he only bundled up his armor rather than pausing to put it on. Speed was of the essence now, though it was unlikely that they would overtake Desmond before he got—well, wherever it was he was going. The entire Palace had been aroused now; people were poking their heads out of doors as they passed, and he could hear the steady tramp of booted feet that could only mean Guardsmen on the move. For good measure, he also grabbed his pack, which out of habit he kept ready to go. He'd lived out of it for months at a time. If he needed something, well, hopefully it would be in there.

With his armor and sword under his arm, he ran for the stables. When he got there, he discovered that there were two horses already saddled and ready. "Hurry up!" one of them whinnied, laying back his ears as he stamped with impatience. "We need to run! She has us so full of magic we are about to pop!"

"She" was undoubtedly the Godmother, and he was not at all unhappy about these being two of her mouse-horses. He tied his pack and armor onto the back of the saddle, then literally leapt into the saddle without using stirrups; Leopold did the same, and the two of them galloped out of the Palace grounds while the rest of the Palace was still buzzing in confusion after being roused from sleep.

At this hour the streets were empty, which meant they could gallop without encountering any obstacles. The occasional head popped out of a window, but otherwise there were no signs of life. He was still trying to think of what he was going to do if the donkey hadn't seen anything as they pounded into the silent marketplace— but the donkey was already waiting there for him.

"The men with the Princess!" the little beast brayed. "They came through here, riding straight for the Forest Gate!"

*Oh, bless you, little beast!*

With a wave of his hand to the helpful creature, Siegfried reined his horse over to the left and urged him down the street that led to the Forest Gate. Too late, he forgot that the Gate was probably closed and locked—

But the moonlight beating down on it showed that it wasn't. In fact, it stood wide-open. And the Gate-guards lay motionless beside it, on either side of the street.

He couldn't stop to see if they were alive or dead—and he couldn't help them either way. Someone else would have to take care of them, and he only hoped that all Desmond had done was to knock them out. Meanwhile, every moment that passed took Rosa farther from him, and that was all that mattered.

Leopold was right on his heels, though his friend probably couldn't imagine how he was getting directions. Still the open gate and the guards alone would tell him that they were on the trail.

The horse made straight for the forest without any guidance, but slowed as they neared it. The Forest Road paralleled the edge, with dozens of smaller paths and trails leading in and wandering off in wildly different directions. Siegfried peered at the forest, looking for a sign of where their quarry might have gone in. *Nothing...it's too dark...noth—*

The horse abruptly reared on his hind legs, screaming with alarm; Siegfried fought to stay in the saddle, his heart accelerating with alarm. What—he couldn't see anything—

*"Don't be foolish, mouse. I am not going to eat you."* What Siegfried had thought was a shadow detached itself from the other shadows and lumbered forward, further spooking the horse, who half reared again, then stood, trembling.

"Bear?" he said in astonishment, as Leopold's horse also danced sideways.

It was, indeed, the bear that he had rescued from the showman. A scar across the bear's muzzle identified the beast.

*"Wolf is tracking them. I will guide you, for I have his scent, and he will take care to lay it down thickly."* The bear whuffed at them. *"I told you that we would not forget your kindness. Now, follow me."* The bear lumbered into the forest, shoving his way into a game trail.

"Siegfried, what the hell—" Leopold sat atop his trembling horse, his own teeth chattering.

"The bear is a friend.... Remember, I can talk to all animals, not just the bird." He shook his head. He probably should have told Leopold about the animals he'd been rescuing, but he hadn't thought it was that important. "I'll explain later. We need to follow the bear, because a wolf that I know is tracking Desmond for us, and the bear is tracking the wolf."

"A wolf...a bear..." Leopold shook his head. "Friends. All right. I have either gone insane or you *did* just say that, and if you did just say that—" He paused. "I have accepted the Queen turning into the Godmother in front of my eyes, mice becoming horses and squash becoming carriages. What's so hard about you talking to wild animals as well as tame, and making friends of them?" He dug his heels into his horse's ribs, causing it to nervously leap forward after the bear. "Come on! Rosa is getting farther away from us all the time!"

* * *

Once she had magicked up the mouse-horses and their gear, Lily had transformed back into Queen Sable. It would be too much trouble getting the servants who hadn't seen her actually resume her real identity to obey her orders otherwise. She ran back up to her rooms, and from there, she sent out the servants to rouse the whole Palace. Desmond probably thought he had time to get back to the Palace before he was missed. Well, too bad for that plan; it had been disrupted the moment that Siegfried's cat saw him steal the Princess.

*That means either he has taken Rosa somewhere close by, or he has some variation on a spell of transportation.* She didn't think they would be lucky enough for the former, so it was probably the latter. She didn't think he'd have the "All Paths Are One" spell, since that was, as far as she knew, the peculiar property of Godmothers. But there were others, many others....

"Seven League Boots"—possible but unlikely; there were two of them, and neither of them would care to carry Rosa for very long. Probably they had left on horseback....

"Seven League Horseshoes" were possible. They wouldn't be restricted to paths...but they'd seriously disturb birds in their wake, and creatures with magic in them would sense the passage. But they were rare, and required not just a magician, but a blacksmith-magician. There were none here, and none that she knew of in the surrounding Kingdoms; most of them were up north—or Dwarves.

She also hadn't felt any huge perturbations of magic power, so he probably hadn't built anything as powerful as building a Portal.

Likeliest... "Pass Unhindered." That was an old, old spell, it was likely that Desmond knew it, and it would let the horses go at top speed through the densest of forest as if they ran on a smooth road. And if he was willing to kill his horses—which he probably was—he could layer on another particularly nasty bit of work, making it

"Pass Unhindered Swiftly," that would make them run at three times the pace that any normal horse could do. "Pass Unhindered Swiftly" absolutely required the life of the creature it was cast on, a form of blood magic that took the sacrifice at the end, rather than the beginning. A fresh horse at his destination, and casting the spell again, would get Desmond back in no time at all, comparatively.

Her head pounded as she dropped down into a chair. Their best bet would be if he came back and didn't discover that the Palace had been roused against him until it was too late to flee. She could get the location out of him—not easily, but unless he was extremely powerful, she could, if only because she could bring in as much help as she needed to.

But catching him by surprise wasn't likely.

So they would have to hunt for him.

"Jimson," she began.

As usual, he practically read her mind, answering her question before she asked it. "There's a pair of mirrors in Siegfried's saddlebag, and a second pair in Leo's. I'll speak to them through one of them at the first halt."

"Is Desmond—"

"There is nothing shiny on his harness or his person." Jimson's face swam into view in her mirror; he looked positively haggard with worry. "We have to assume he knows about mirror-scrying at least, if not mirror-travel. If he is in league with the Huntsman, that would be how both of them evaded my scrutiny. So there will be no mirrors where he takes her."

She swore. So at the moment it was all in the hands of Siegfried and Leopold, and whatever other searchers went out.

"Lily, the cat was not the only friend that Siegfried has made." Jimson paused, his head cocked to listen. "The animals he has helped saw Desmond pass, and they are showing Siegfried the way. A wolf

is tracking him, and a bear is tracking the wolf and leading Siegfried."
He smiled wanly.

"He is?" Lily nearly went limp with relief. "Desmond won't have
thought of that."

"No, he won't. Typically that sort doesn't think much of animals
except as something to eat and something to hunt." He paused. "Also,
may I point out that if the wolf can track them, they are on the ground
and not traveling by any other means. That is good for us."

It was, very good news. It meant that one or the other variation
of the "Pass Unhindered" spell was likely what he was using. Unfortunately, she could not leap ahead of the young men and join the wolf,
because she didn't know the wolf herself.

"He's a sorcerer or a wizard," she said aloud. "He knows magic.
He never let slip a hint of that while he was here except for the
simple charms and spells that anyone could have gotten. He probably
knows about mirror-scrying, as you pointed out. We have to assume
he has defended his stronghold."

Jimson nodded grimly.

She drummed her fingers on the arm of her chair. There were so
many ways that he could defend that stronghold...but there was one
that was very, very likely. Especially if he kept Rosa asleep. The Tradition would only aid him.

She could get through almost any defense that wasn't an army.
But... "I can't do anything until they get there and lay out a mirror."

"Exactly so."

She needed to give him an aid, a very special helper. Short of a
dragon or a unicorn, this would be the best possible help he could
get. "Except...one thing. And I hope that I can do this at a distance."

When the bird had taken a bath, a single brown feather had been left
in the saucer. As any magician would, Lily had kept it safe. Just in case.
Well, this was just in case...and the spell was very, very complicated.

At least it would keep her mind occupied.

But when it all came down to it, everything rested on Siegfried. Exactly as The Tradition required.

"We have...to rest...a moment," Siegfried's horse puffed. Beneath his legs, the poor beast's sides heaved. He suspected that the Godmother's magic had finally run out, which was hardly surprising, considering the pace they had set. "Please. And water."

The bear looked over his shoulder at them. He was not in nearly as bad a case, but then, as Siegfried knew, bears could go for immense distances at a fast pace. "I need the same. There is water ahead."

Siegfried would have very much liked to tell them to press on, but—no. Desmond might be willing to kill his mounts, but Siegfried was not going to exhaust his friends. Never mind that they had not yet caught up with the villain. They would. "We'll pause there until you are ready to go on," he said, trying not to feel as if the words marked defeat. They were not defeated; they hadn't even fought yet. They *would* find Desmond, and Rosa, and they would rescue her.

At the promised water, a small forest pond sheltered by trees, green with algae and tasting of old leaves, but otherwise good, he dismounted, to let the bear and the two horses slowly sip, pause for a moment, then sip again. They needed the water, but—thank goodness—they were all three intelligent enough to know not to drink their fill at once. Their sides heaved, and the horses were dark with sweat.

He put a comforting hand on his horse's rump—and jumped as he heard a muffled voice not a handbreadth from where it rested.

"Siegfried, we must talk. Open the saddlebag, Siegfried. This is important. I'm speaking for Godmother Lily."

"What the hell—" said Leopold, staring wide-eyed.

"You've been saying that a lot." Siegfried cautiously opened the saddlebag. A glowing green face looked up at him from inside.

*"Yah!"* he yelped, and jumped back, dropping the flap.

"Oh!" said the bird, flitting down through the branches to land on his shoulder. "That's just Jimson. He's the Godmother's Mirror Spirit. It's all right."

"Mirror—there's a mirror in that bag?" Siegfried blinked.

"There's two, in case you drop one," said the muffled voice. "Leopold has two, as well. Please open the bag."

Once again, Siegfried raised the flap.

The face looked up at him, brows furrowed with anxiety. "That's better. Siegfried, when you find Rosa, put this mirror on the ground, and put the others you have left next to it—if you have all four, make a square. We are going to try something dangerous then, and we will only have one chance. Meanwhile you can talk to me through the mirrors, and Lily through me." He transferred his gaze to the little bird. "Bird, how fond are you of being such a small plain bird?"

The bird cocked her head to one side, considering the question. "Not all that fond, I wouldn't mind being an ea—"

"Good."

A brilliant, flame-colored light enveloped bag, bird and Siegfried's head, blinding him. Leopold shouted. For a moment, all that Siegfried could see were flashes of color. He knuckled his eyes, blinking away tears of pain and hoping he hadn't just been permanently blinded.

Odd. The bird had gotten a *lot* heavier. And…warmer.

His vision started to come back but—it was strangely bright on the side where the bird was. As things around him blurred and swam back into focus, he turned his head to see what was so bright, and so big.

What was on his shoulder was a bird, still. She was easily eagle-sized, though not eagle-heavy. She had a tall curving crest of flame-like feathers, bright gold eyes, red-and-gold wings now held open with delight, and a pair of scintillating tail-plumes that trailed down his back and ended in a pair of peacocklike eyes. *All* of her feathers were red and gold, and glistened and sparkled like living flames.

"Bird?" he said incredulously. The bird was craning her long neck around and looking down at herself in astonishment.

"I—you made me a firebird!" she exclaimed in delight. "You made me a *firebird!* Is this permanent?"

"Unfortunately, yes, I'm sorry," Jimson said apologetically. "There was no time to do anything reversible."

"Oh, don't be sorry! I'm not!" The bird lifted her head and gave vent to a joyous trill. If anything her singing was sweeter. "I don't mind dodging a few feather hunters to be able to look like *this!* Do I turn into a human girl, too?"

Jimson shook his head. "Unfortunately, no, I'm—"

She caroled with delight. "Even better! No clumsy old men wanting to marry me and sending people to catch me so they can!"

Jimson coughed. Evidently he had not anticipated how pleased she would be. "Erm, well, good. I'm glad you approve. I apologize that we did this, but Siegfried may need your new powers when—"

*"Siegfwied! Siegfwied! Wait!"*

Once again, Jimson was interrupted. This time it was from a bell-like voice that rang through the forest. The face in the mirror looked frustrated, then resigned. "You had better deal with that," he said. "I'll talk to your bird while you do."

The bird hopped down onto the horse's rump and stuck her head into the bag. Muted mumbling came from it.

"Siegfwied!" A crystalline horn shoved the undergrowth aside, and to Siegfried's dismay, though not his surprise, the unicorn leapt through the gap. "Heah I am!"

*Oh, no—*

"Luna, we're going into danger," he said, as gently as he could. "We don—"

"I *know!*" said the unicorn, stamping one hoof impatiently in the dead leaves. "I aweady know that! I'm coming wif you!"

Siegfried's mouth opened and closed several times without being able to get a word out. This was going to be dangerous...and Luna was such a delicate little thing. She would probably be more hindrance than help, but how to tell her to go without crushing her? Leopold said it for him.

"Uh, pardon, unicorn—"

"Luna," said the unicorn.

Leopold flushed, and tried to find the same words that Siegfried had been unable to muster. "Luna then—you don't—I mean, it's very sweet that you want to help, but I don't know how you could—we're going to be fi—"

It seemed that being interrupted was the order of the day. Leopold's words stuck in his throat, as Luna reared up, lashed the air a fraction of an inch from his left ear with her forehooves, pivoted before he could wince away, sent her rear hooves flying through the air a hairbreadth above his right shoulder and pivoted a second time to drive her horn deep into the trunk of a tree just under his right arm. She wrenched it loose with a splintering and creaking of wood, then stood back from him, lashing her tail triumphantly.

It was Leopold's turn to stare with his eyes gone round and his mouth open, and Siegfried was in almost as much shock.

Siegfried cleared his throat carefully.

But Luna wasn't done yet. Still swishing her tail, she trotted down to the little pond they had all been drinking from. She knelt beside it and dipped her horn in the water.

Something like softened lightning laced across the surface of the pond as the tip of her horn touched the water. When she stood up, the water, which had been a little murky and green with algae, was now crystal clear.

"Dwink fwom that," she said imperiously.

Without hesitation, Siegfried, the horses and the bear all did. Leopold waited a moment, then, when Luna's eye flashed angrily at his hesitation, he gulped and joined them.

The moment that the first sweet drop slipped down Siegfried's throat, he started to feel energized. By the time he had finished drinking his fill, all his energy had been restored, and more energy heaped atop that. He had never felt so good in his life. Looking at the others, he could see that they felt the same.

"I will do that each time we stop," Luna said with a toss of her horn. "I can heal you. I can make you feel good. I can fight! You can't do wifout me."

"You are right, Luna." Siegfried caressed her neck, and her eyes softened with infatuation. "We need you. But it's very dangerous—"

"I know," she said again. "I *know*. You think I don't but I do! Wosamund is in the hands of the Huntsman. He has murdered many of my bwovvers and was twying to murder me. I am coming because I wove you. I am coming because Wosamund needs us. But I am also coming for me. For my own weason." Her eyes flashed silver. "I am coming for wevenge."

Somehow, even with her lisp, she did not sound ridiculous anymore.

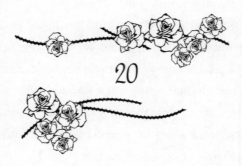

20

THE SECOND-FLOOR ROOM OF THE SORCERER'S stone
tower was, for the moment, still. As Rosa had guessed, Desmond was
what Godmother Lily had called a "ritualist." He probably didn't have
more than a few simple things memorized, and he managed all of his
magic by repeating, with painful exactitude, what he had written out
in his "grimoire," or spell-book. Everything in this tower room—at least,
everything that she could actually see—had been carefully positioned.
There was a long, waist-high cabinet behind him; on it were a candlestick and his sword, which he had spent some time positioning. He had
taken various things from the drawers with each spell, and put them
back when he was done. To her right was the hole in the floor that gave
access to the staircase. To her far right was another cabinet with another
candlestick. To her left, the same. Circles had been inlaid in the stone
of the floor, and symbols inlaid inside the circles. As he had worked,
he had walked around her, chanted, burned various incenses and done
things behind her that, from the sounds that she had heard, she was
rather glad she hadn't been able to see. He had almost certainly killed
several small animals after torturing them. It all turned her stomach.

At least she had found out all this *before* he had won the contest.

She was almost certain that he would, indeed, have won. If he hadn't done so legitimately, he'd have found a way....

Then again, this was probably the way that he had found.

*Bah.*

And it was obvious that he could not see magic as she could—or sense it in any other way, except when the spells were completed and he got the results he was looking for, or when the spells themselves caused effects that anyone could see. If he had been able to, he would have known by now how much she was interfering.

"You returned sooner than I expected, sire," the Huntsman said, as Desmond paused between spells. The Huntsman might well have been thought handsome by some, if it had not been for the coldness of his expression. Facially, he could have been Desmond's relative.

Perhaps he was. It would not be the first time that a bastard son had ended up as the legitimate son's right hand.

Rosa could tell that Desmond was between spells, because the woven bands of sinister murky-yellow magic around her were— well, *finished off* was the best way she could describe it. The ends were precisely tucked in and the whole looked neat and complete. Desmond really was a patient and thorough sorcerer. He had pronounced each syllable of the spell exactly, had been painstaking with his diagrams and had taken his time over it.

He was not, however, as observant a sorcerer as he was patient, or he would have noticed that she was not as bound as she should have been. No sooner had he finished the work, than she began unpicking it, having paid careful attention to where those ends were tucked in. The necklace of unicorn hair kept the things from affecting her, and once she started unpicking them, well they might just as well have not been there. The magic wasn't that hard to break when you could see it. She wondered if he had any idea that there were magicians who *could* see magic, and just undo so easily what he did. If he didn't—he was probably thinking smugly that unless someone knew the spells he had been working, it would be impossible to get her free of them.

*Ha.*

"Someone saw us taking the girl," was the terse reply, as he leafed through his book. "The entire Palace was aroused. I couldn't even take a horse from the stables for my return journey. I had to steal one from outside."

*Oh, that made him angry. He wasn't counting on his plans being disrupted.*

The Huntsman's frown deepened. "Is that likely to be a problem for you, sire? If they send out searches, which I am sure they will—"

Desmond laughed. Clearly he had no idea the resources that the Godmother could call up. Which actually relieved Rosa; she was a lot happier with the idea that he was overconfident. "Not likely. The wretched Dwarves kept this place a secret even from their own kin. I doubt that they will muster a search that goes beyond the city very soon."

"They could track you," the Huntsman said, looking dubious. "You will have left a scent."

Desmond shrugged. "I will grant you that Queen Sable is a clever woman, but even if they can get your hounds to obey without you being present, do *you* think they could track us all the way here?"

The Huntsman shook his head after considering this. "The trail will be cold and muddled by the time they get the hounds to track, and it is too far. You cannot keep them on a cold track forever, especially if I am not there."

*Unless, of course, you are a Godmother who knows Magic Beasts,* she thought angrily. *Then—well I don't know what she can do, but I imagine that she can persuade them.*

"What about the Godmother?" the Huntsman asked. "She's the one who rescued the Princess the last time."

Desmond smirked. "She has to be able to find the girl in the first place. I have made sure no one can scry what is in this tower. *Perhaps she is clever enough to realize that a place so warded must have something interesting in it, but I doubt it. She is only a woman. But even if she does, she has to get here. Then she will have to fight through my defenses. Godmothers are many things, but I have never heard that they are adept at combative magic, and certainly not at physical fighting."

The Huntsman nodded, and Rosa wanted to slap the self-satisfied looks off both their faces. *Only a woman! She's cleverer than both of you put together—which is just not that hard. And combat? She'll bring help. When Siegfried gets here—and he will get here—I hope you remember that he's bested you in combat at least once.*

That is, assuming she left enough for Siegfried to fight once she got loose. Right now she was angry enough to tear Desmond's handsome head off his body and stuff it down his neck.

She used that anger, just as Siegfried had taught her, as the lever to pry the magic encircling her apart. She had left the paralysis magic alone for now, since it was loosened, and it would take no effort at all and little time to unravel it. She was more concerned with the things Desmond was concocting that were designed to manipulate her mind and emotions. Those were the things that most worried her. The necklace kept them from touching her but only because of the faint taint of evil about them. If he used something that hadn't come from a tainted source...

Well, so far, he hadn't. She just hoped that her luck would continue in that regard.

The wolf still had the trail. Siegfried only hoped their luck would continue in that regard. If it had not been for Luna, they could never have pressed on as fast as they had, but they had still been pushing through the forest for most of the day. He was beginning to think that they would have to find a place to camp for the night—which would not be good—when the bear threw up his head and stopped.

*"The wolf is near,"* he said. Then he took a deep breath and let out a roar to signal to the wolf that they were close behind.

Every hair on the back of the bear's neck stood up when he roared...and every hair on Siegfried's body did the same. He had never been this close to a bear when it made a noise like that—the bear he had killed as a child had been too busy fighting him off to make anything other than growls. The sound actually vibrated Siegfried's chest and awoke a deep and primitive fear in his gut. It made his heart suddenly race, and from the way that the horses jumped and Leopold's eyes widened, it did the same to the others. Even the bird fluttered her bright new wings nervously. Only Luna was unaffected.

A howl in the distance answered the roar.

"Uh, won't that tell Desmond that we're out here?" Leopold asked, patting his horse's neck to try to calm it.

"It will tell Desmond that there are animals out here," Siegfried replied. "And this *is* a forest, after all. One would expect animals in a forest. I doubt he would recognize that the wolf is answering the bear."

"But the Huntsman—"

"The Huntsman will expect animals to behave as wild animals usually do." Of that much Siegfried was certain. "Wolves and bears don't work together. If anything, he'll assume that one challenged the other."

Since the bear wasn't moving, they all waited patiently; evidently the wolf was going to come to them. Now that they had stopped moving, Siegfried was very conscious of the forest around them. The presence of the bear was probably keeping most of the wildlife nearby very quiet. Bears were known to eat whatever they could catch, after all. But in the middle distance, there were rustlings and the occasional call and the even more occasional sound of something falling from the trees. There was a great deal of birdsong, above and around them. This was a very, very old forest, as evidenced by the girth of the trees; late-afternoon sunlight pierced the thick canopy from above, making slender shafts of light that only served to emphasize how gloomy it was beneath the branches. In fact, he realized he'd passed this way when he first arrived in the Kingdom.

"So I had this idea," he said quietly to the bird. "Dragons. Are there a lot of good dragons out there? All I ever saw were the killers. And Sharpstone…"

"Lots," the bird replied, looking at him as if he had lost his mind. "But is this the time—"

"And what do dragons need besides their hoards?" he persisted.

"Safe lairs and lots of food they don't have to risk their necks for. Sometimes the Godmothers can help with that. But we haven't time to wait for Godmother Lily to fetch a dragon!" The bird fluttered her magnificent wings.

"That's all I need to know." The idea was forming up quickly in his mind. If they rescued Rosa—

*When* they rescued Rosa, damn it all! They would! He had to! He was not going to let that damned fop Desmond take her!

Just as he was wondering exactly how near the wolf was, the animal himself pushed his way through some bushes to the side of the path. He looked up at Siegfried, but there was no sign of good news in his scarred face.

"*The foul one is clever, BigMan,*" the wolf said. "*First, he cleared back the forest. Then he has put some sort of bad magic between the forest and the stone place he built in that clear place. Then he made a terrible thorn tangle to grow about the stone place. All that is before you even enter it.*"

"But the Princess *is* there, right?" he asked, as Leopold fidgeted, looking baffled.

*"Oh, yes. I smell her."* The wolf paused. *"The bad magic smells like bones and dragons."*

Well that didn't sound any notes of recognition. He turned to Luna, the bird and Leopold. "The wolf says there is magic that smells like bones and dragons. Does that mean anything to any of you?"

"Not me, I don't know much of anything about magic," Leopold replied.

The others were still shaking their heads when Jimson's muffled voice came from the saddlebag. "The Children of the Dragon's Teeth."

Siegfried twisted around and flipped back the flap. "The what?" he asked, looking down into the dark bag.

"The Children of the Dragon's Teeth. Rather nasty, dark-tainted magic. Necromancy, of a sort." The green face looked up at him. "The *spell* is called 'The Children of the Dragon's Teeth,' but in actuality, the sorcerer in question sows the finger-bones of warriors in the ground. When the ground is trodden upon, the warriors spring up out of it to fight. Or rather, their skeletons do. Of course, they can't be killed in the usual manner."

"That...doesn't sound good." Leopold frowned.

"Well, it's not, if you go in there in the usual manner!" Jimson snapped, sounding exasperated. "Don't slash or stab at them, break them apart. Staves, clubs, the flat of your sword, shield bashing—" He looked up at Siegfried again, clearly impatient. "You're a barbarian, that sort of thing ought to be natural to you!"

"I'm not—" Siegfried began, feeling insulted. But Jimson was already gone. The mirror was blank again.

*"We can help you in this, BigMan,"* the bear said, and the wolf nodded his head. *"That sort of fighting is natural to me, and the wolf can break their leg bones with a snap. They cannot fight if they cannot stand."* Siegfried was not too certain of that last, but the first—oh, yes. He had seen bears fight. And this one was huge. He didn't think that there was a warrior born who had the reach of this bear.

"All right then. Take us there, brother wolf. And my thanks to both of you."

*"We told you we would not forget your kindness,"* the bear said gravely. The wolf made a whuffing sound, and turned to lead them in.

They stopped at the edge of the cleared area—and the wolf had been less than accurate when he said "cleared." The trees, the bushes, everything had been taken down to the bare soil, and the soil itself had been plowed up. Mindful of what Jimson had told them, Siegfried took all four mirrors out and placed them faceup on the ground. Then he and Leopold armored up, Leopold pausing to cut himself a stave rather than using his sword.

Siegfried looked at the bird and Luna. "I think you had better stay back," he said, cautiously. "You two are not well suited for fighting something like this. Luna, I think they will stay well away from you, so I would appreciate it if you would guard the mirrors, the horses and the bird."

The bird trilled agreement. Somewhat reluctantly, Luna bobbed her head. He looked over at Leopold, who nodded.

"Try to stay back-to-back," he said. "I don't think these things will be like living fighters. I think they will just keep throwing themselves at us until they are all in bits. If we can keep our backs protected, we can just let them do that."

The wolf looked up at him. *"I am not suited to that. Let me run the outside, breaking legs."*

"Agreed." Siegfried took a deep breath. "It will probably take them a little while to come out of the earth and attack us. Let's try to get halfway there before they do. Ready. Set. *Run!*"

The moment he and Leopold set foot on the churned-up soil, there was a strange, moaning sound, followed by the appearance of bony arms sprouting all over the field, punching through the dirt like some macabre crop. The three of them sprinted for the center of the area, but the arms were quickly followed by the rest of the bone-bodies, as the things got a grip on the loose surface and hauled themselves up. Before they had gotten a quarter of the way there, the creatures had shoved themselves up out of the dirt and turned the empty eyeholes of their skulls toward them.

They were all armed, and armored, though the armor hung loosely on them and looked as if it would be more hindrance than help. Most had round shields, though a handful had shields of other sorts. Most had helmets of wildly varied design. None had any weapon that would give them any reach, and Siegfried gave silent thanks that they were not going to have to deal with rains of arrows. No, the weapons they faced now were swords, axes and the shields themselves. If they could manage to not be overrun—they could do this.

What seemed like hundreds of dark eye sockets glared at them. Then, from all directions, the reanimated army charged.

"Form up!" Siegfried shouted; the bear reared up on his hind legs, and he and Leopold put their backs up against that furry bulwark just as the first of the skeletal warriors reached them.

If they had not been warned of how to fight these things, Siegfried and Leopold would certainly have been cut to ribbons in the first moments. But they had been, and instead of trying to stab or slash the monsters, both he and the Prince concentrated on smashing down the skeletal arms. Leopold's reach with that staff was tremendous, and Siegfried's strength was definitely his best asset in this fight. The bear roared, and when Siegfried took a sideways glance, he saw that the great beast was sending skulls flying, leaving the bodies to flail their weapons in random directions, connecting with their fellows more often than not.

*So they need the heads—*

"Leopold!" he shouted. "They need the heads to see!"

Leopold's answer was a swipe with the staff that took off at least four skulls.

There were *hundreds* of the things. But as Siegfried had suspected, they were essentially mindless. Breaking their arms or heads off was the best tactic, since there wasn't much they could do to attack or defend themselves with no arms, and leaving them headless meant they attacked whatever was nearest. The ones with shields held out a bit longer, but eventually either a blow from the flat of Siegfried's sword, or from the bear's paw, would break the shield-arm, and at that point the warrior had fundamentally lost.

As the ranks thinned, Siegfried could see the wolf darting into and out of the mob, snapping legs with a single bite of his tremendous jaws. That took them down, but not out. His stomach twisted with nausea as he watched the downed skeletons continue to crawl toward them—until they got within sword, staff, or paw-reach, and were reduced to fragments.

And then...it was over. The field was covered with twitching bits of bone, all of them trying to get to where the three of them stood. The bear dropped to all fours, and looked up wearily at them. The wolf limped in, a couple of shallow slashes across his ribs. They were all wounded—but not badly. Nothing like as badly as they *could* have been.

"*We will leave you now, BigMan,*" said the bear. "*We have done all that we can for you. Your fate lies within the stone place. Farewell.*"

"Thank you!" he called, as they turned and padded back into the forest. "I will not forget your kindness!"

The bird flew to him, followed by Luna, as the bear and wolf vanished into the undergrowth. The twitching bone fragments attempted to roll away from Luna as she paced near them. Most of them succeeded.

As one, they all looked toward the tangle of black, bare thorn-vines, most of which had thorns as long as Siegfried's arm. The windowless stone tower rose above the thicket, grim and gray. There was a terribly long distance from where the thorns began to that tower.

"Let me get my breath," wheezed Leopold.

\* \* \*

"This is very, very dangerous," said Jimson.

"I know that," Lily replied tensely. "I'm just glad that all four mirrors survived. We can lose two, and this can still work."

"I'm not trying to dissuade you—" Jimson swallowed. "All right, I am trying to dissuade you. I wish you wouldn't do this."

"And you know very well I have to."

He sighed. "Alas, yes. I do."

"All right, then." She concentrated on the image within a tiny crystal ball. It was all she had the power to spare for. It showed the four identical mirrors lying together on the ground outside Desmond's stronghold. Now she deeply regretted that she had taken her travel-mirror away when she had made off with the sleeping Rosa, for if she had just left it there, she wouldn't have to do this now.

"This" was a calculated adaptation of the sort of spell used to join two objects, except that this adaptation was not meant to join them, but to *merge* them, and do so seamlessly. The sort of mirrors that you could pack on a horse's back, even though she had enchanted them to allow her to pass through them, were not big enough for her to travel through. Two of them together would be big enough for her Brownies to attempt to bring a bigger mirror through. Attempt, because no one ever had successfully done so to her knowledge; she had the feeling that the problem was that it was like trying to transport a horse on the back of a horse. She didn't want to try that unless she had to.

Three of them *might* be big enough for her to squeeze through.

Four would be perfect. Although doing so was going to require some flexibility on her part....

*Concentrate, Lily!*

She wove delicate strands of magic through her spell, inching the first two mirrors together bit by bit. The frames touched. The frames butted against each other so tightly you could not have gotten a silk thread between them. With little stroking motions, she suggested to the frames that they should be one.

Reluctantly, the frames obeyed her.

With further motions of her fingers, she suggested to the frame bar in the middle that it should move to either side and allow the glass to merge. The bar didn't care for that, but eventually—it flowed, sulkily, off to either side. Both sides thickened. She tickled the mirror that had been beneath it.

The mirrors were not as reluctant as the frames. They rippled a little, then merged.

She let out the breath she had been holding. "That's one and two," said Jimson.

"I'm going to do three and four first," she said aloud. "It occurs to me the symmetry will be better."

"I—" Jimson began, then stopped himself. "No, you are the magician. I am not. Just be sure you are ready. We won't get another chance."

She refrained from telling him that she knew that, and bent her concentration on the second pair of mirrors.

The four companions stared at the wall of thorns. "We aren't getting anywhere trying to stare a hole into it," Siegfried said finally. With a stiffening of his back, he walked toward it, sword at the ready, prepared to start chopping his way through.

But the hair on back of his neck rose when, as he neared it—the vines started to move. They uncoiled like sleepy snakes just aroused, then they reached for him. Slowly at first, then—

With a yelp, he leapt back just in time, as a vine with one of those evil thorns on it whipped through the space where he had been, and buried the thorn all the way into the dirt where he had been standing.

He looked at the huge tangle of the things—hundreds of vines, thousands of thorns—he tried to imagine himself chopping through them and fending them off at the same time.

It wasn't possible.

He had to try.

"*No*," said Luna sharply. They all jumped, and turned to stare at her. She took a deep breath and dipped her horn. "No. It is our turn, I fink. Yes, bird?"

"Definitely," trilled the firebird. "Why else would the Godmother have transformed me?"

"Then fowwow," Luna replied with immense dignity, and walked forward, her horn leading, as if she was planning on battering her way through the tangle.

The vines seethed and writhed, as if they weren't quite sure what to do about her. As she reached the edge of the tangle, several of them reared back to strike—but then reversed themselves, and buried themselves in the mass of their fellows. It was clear that they didn't want to get *anywhere* near Luna, her horn, or both.

She stepped right into the edge, confronting the thicket with her presence, and they withdrew from her in what looked like a panic, leaving her standing in a hollowed-out alcove of thorns. Luna moved in deeper, her horn glowing faintly in the gloom, then deeper still. The thorns slowly began to move to close in behind her.

That was when the bird moved in.

With a trumpetlike call, she dived after Luna, and when she got just inside the wall of thorns, she hovered and burst into flames, a fire so intense that Siegfried winced and looked away for a moment.

That was when the vines screamed. They sounded like mice screaming, a thin, high-pitched keen.

The firebird continued to hover, and burned brighter. The vines turned themselves into knots in an effort to escape the fires. In vain. They caught and burned with a sullen green flame and an ugly green-black smoke that gave off a stench like burning carrion. When the vines around the firebird were truly dead, she hovered forward a little, deeper into the wall of thorns, following Luna.

*Luna keeps them away, and the firebird can kill them without getting hurt!* Siegfried was astonished. It was brilliant! The firebird moved deeper still, into the wall of thorns, leaving behind her a charred tunnel. Soon she was nothing but a ball of fire at the end of the long, blackened expanse.

Then—suddenly, the fires vanished.

"Siegfried!" cried Leopold, but Siegfried was already racing for the thorns, his heart sinking. But it rose again when Luna emerged from the tunnel of char, head hanging, the firebird clinging exhausted to her mane. She was sweating as badly as the horses had at the end of their run, and it was clear that she and the bird were at the absolute end of their strength.

"Luna! You are *brilliant!*" Siegfried cried, throwing his arms around Luna's neck. With a sigh, she rested her chin on his shoulder. He could feel every muscle in her body trembling with exhaustion.

"We know," sang the bird. "It took both of us—Luna to make the tunnel, me to burn it in. The thorns can't cross the threshold of their own purified dead."

Luna pulled her chin off Siegfried's shoulder and tapped him with her horn. "Now go," she said. "Wescue your Pwincess. We'll fowwow when we can."

Siegfried kissed her nose, then turned and ran into the tunnel of dead, crackling thorns, Leopold beside him. And the sudden thought that he was off to rescue a Princess by crossing what had been a ring of fire gave him a sudden burst of hope that the Tradition might once more be moving in his favor. And just as he thought of this, he looked up at the sound of flames. There was still fire up there in the thorny canopy, fire that winked out just as he crossed beneath it. Just as the magical ring of fire around his Aunt would have. Hoy-yo toho!

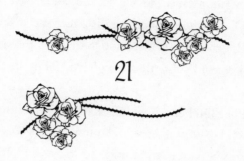

21

LEOPOLD REACHED THE DOOR FIRST, AND stopped—
he held out his hand and Siegfried all but ran into it. Outside the
tunnel of burned and dead thorn-vines, the still-living ones had recovered and were trying in vain to get to them. The burned "bower"
above their head shook and rattled, and little bits of ash and burned
wood rained down on them. Both of them glanced up. There was
no telling how long the protection would hold.

Leopold put his finger to his lips, signaling for quiet, and pressed
his ear to the door. Siegfried nodded, and held his breath, wishing
there was some way he could get the vines to stop making noise.

"They may not know we're out here," Leopold whispered, his eyes
narrowed in concentration. "Better if we can surprise them."

Siegfried nodded again, and waited. Finally Leopold shook his
head. "I can't hear anything," he whispered. "But we aren't doing Rosa
any good out here." He grimaced a little. "The man who trained me
always told me to try the door before I tried knocking it down—"

"I'm ready," Siegfried breathed, and watched as Leopold carefully
tried the handle. To his shock and disbelief, it began to turn. Leopold

eased the door open as slowly as a snail crawling, while Siegfried held his breath expecting a loud creaking at any moment. When it was open a mere crack, Leopold put first his ear, then his eye to the tiny gap.

"I think they're upstairs," he whispered, and eased the door open farther. "I can barely hear them at a distance, and it sounds *up*."

When the door was open just enough to allow them to slip inside, they did so, Leopold first, then Siegfried. They both paused and looked around.

They were in a kitchen; the windows here, which had never been large, had been covered over with stonework. It was lit by candles stuck in their own wax in the middle of a great table. There were shelves around the walls that looked old, a cupboard against the wall to Siegfried's right that had once had a window that looked just as old, a stone sink next to it, chairs around the table that looked new. To Siegfried's left was a blank wall with an immense stone chimney and a huge hearth. Opposite him was another wall with a rack for kitchenware that was mostly empty. The kitchen was unoccupied, but there were signs someone was using it; a pot hung over the hearth, covered, giving off the aroma of rabbit stew, and there was an empty bowl with a spoon in it, and an equally empty bottle on the table. There was a doorway without a door at the far end, and an open door in the wall opposite them, halfway along it. That open door gave out into darkness; there was light coming from the doorway without a door in it, and that was where the voices were coming from.

Siegfried inclined his head at that dark door, and Leopold nodded; moving as quietly as possible, they eased along the wall until they came to the open door. This time Siegfried stuck his head inside—he could just make out a set of crude stone steps that went down into darkness. He toyed with the idea that Rosa might be in a cellar or dungeon or something below, then decided that whatever was down there didn't matter right now. If it was Rosa, she could stay there until they eliminated the threat. Nothing was going to happen to her that hadn't already. If there were reinforcements of some kind he could make sure they didn't get a chance to act. With a nod to Leopold, he eased the door shut, and then gently let a bar down across it, to keep whatever was down there from coming up. Then he slipped up to the next doorway and peeked around the frame.

The next room was also unoccupied, but contained a single bed, a stool and a wooden chest. The windows here were also walled up, and it was lit by more candles stuck about randomly.

Siegfried signaled to Leopold, who slipped past him into the room. Siegfried followed. They kept their backs pressed firmly up against the wall. Desmond might be a magician, but he had certainly put no magical guardians or alarms inside this place. He had put rather too much trust in his external safeguards. That, in Siegfried's opinion, was never a good idea.

The voices were definitely coming from the next room, and above. It looked as if the tower was in the shape of a rough square; the kitchen and this room formed half of the square, with this room leading into the other half of the square.

In the wall to Siegfried's left was the door to that other half of the bottom floor, and this door also stood open. This time it was Leopold's turn to peek his head around the frame, and Siegfried's to slip inside at his signal.

Light for this room poured down the staircase going up the wall. It looked like something added recently; the stone was a lighter color. It also looked as if this had once been divided into two rooms. And there were some dark brown stains on the floor that Siegfried did not like at all. Signs of the previous owners?

Siegfried slipped back to the bedroom, and motioned to Leopold. "They're definitely up there, and Rosa is either in the cellar I barred or up there with them," he whispered. "We need a plan. We can't just rush up those stairs and hope everything comes out all right."

Leopold nodded. "We're definitely at a disadvantage if we come at them up that stair. We need to get them down—"

He was interrupted by a shout from the other room.

Their heads swiveled toward the open doorway as if they were on the same wire, and there was the Huntsman, standing in the middle of the staircase, staring at them. So much for plans.

He and Leopold nearly collided in the doorway trying to get to the man before he could get off the stair, in the hopes of blocking Desmond from coming down, too. But the Huntsman was quicker than either of them; he leapt off the stair and charged them before they could get clear of the door and get their swords up. He hit them without drawing his, shouldering them into the bedroom. Leopold hit the floor and tumbled back up to his feet; Siegfried staggered but didn't fall, his heart pounding and his focus already narrowing to the fight. He backed away from the Huntsman and shifted his grip on his own weapon, just as Desmond leapt from the second story, disdaining the use of stairs altogether.

With a single glance and a nod, Leopold jumped for the Huntsman, while Siegfried charged Desmond.

He came straight at the magician in his usual style, and Desmond parried him easily. Then Desmond closed, and he pivoted out of the way. Within the exchange of three blows, Siegfried, at least, knew he was in trouble.

Desmond had been holding back in the practice bouts they'd all had. The bastard had even allowed himself to lose once in a while. If he'd actually exerted himself, he'd never have lost at all. Desmond was not just good.

Desmond was unbelievable.

* * *

Rosa's mouth was dry, and she thought longingly about a drink of water. After leafing through his grimoire twice, Desmond had found the spell he was looking for, and the Huntsman, seeing this, retreated down the staircase to the first floor. But he did not get far.

*"Sire!"* came the startled voice from the stair. *"Intruders!"*

Her heart leapt. There was the immediate sound of scuffling, the sounds of bodies impacting and grunts. Desmond tossed his book aside, grabbed his sword from the table where he had left it and charged down the stairs himself. Then there came the clash of metal-on-metal, grunts and curses, as the fight began in real earnest, and her heart didn't just leap, it raced with excitement and the need to get free.

Rosa fought the paralyzing magics in a frenzy of impatience, attacking them with everything she had in her.

She had loosened them, yes, but no more than that. They weren't undone, not even close to being undone. She still had to pick the ends loose and unweave them. She tore at them with mental fingers, her heart racing, her chest aching with the urge to swear at them. All the time she fought with the bindings, she could hear the sounds of fighting below, and *thought* she recognized Leopold's and Siegfried's voices.

And it sounded as if they were in trouble.

She had to get free! She concentrated all of her strength on the unraveling bonds. She didn't know what she could do, but she was going to do *something!* But first she had to get loose!

She was able to physically struggle a little—then a little more—

Was there any untainted magic around here anywhere that she could use? She could see the magic that Desmond had been using, lying around her like stagnant, repellent puddles, but was there anything *she* could use? Because there was no way she was touching that stuff.

The necklace pulsed gently, and a bit of power flowed into her from that. With a last push of impatience, she shattered the remaining strands of the magic, grabbed the nearest thing she could see—the candlestick standing on the same cabinet where Desmond had left his sword—and scuttled down the stairs herself with one hand on the stone wall for balance.

The fight had moved into the kitchen. She sprinted to the doorway in time to see Desmond about to get past Siegfried's guard. She heaved the candlestick at him in a fury, glanced around and grabbed a bowl from the cupboard beside her.

The candlestick struck Desmond a glancing blow to the shoulder. Startled, he turned, giving Siegfried an opening. She flung the bowl at the Huntsman, who had pinned Leopold's arm and blade against the wall. It hit the wall beside his head and shattered. He whirled, giving Leopold the chance to get away from where he'd been pinned.

The look of rage in Desmond's eyes would have made anyone less angry than Rosa start running. Instead, as he took a single step toward her, forgetting about Siegfried for a critical moment, she dashed over to the kitchen cupboard, wrenched the doors open and seized a frying pan. It was heavier than it looked, but she picked it up with both hands, whirled, and threw it anyway, making him duck, and giving Siegfried a chance to move in on him.

The cupboard had quite a few things on it and in it. She emptied it out, then moved to the shelves, and threw everything she could get her hands on, keeping both Desmond and the Huntsman distracted from what should have been their main concern, the men with swords in their hands. Meanwhile Siegfried and Leopold kept Desmond and the Huntsman from coming after her. It was stalemate. And it couldn't remain that way for long.

The Huntsman swore, bound Leopold's blade with the flat of his own and sent Leopold's sword flying out of his hands. Leopold dropped and rolled, bowling into the Huntsman's legs and knocking him over. Leopold got to his feet before the Huntsman did, and he came up with—

The frying pan.

Holding it like a short club, he ducked and moved in under the Huntsman's thrust, came up inside his reach, swung hard and bashed him in the side of the head with the flat bottom.

The Huntsman went down like a stunned ox.

But now Rosa had run out of things to throw. And the sound of the frying pan hitting the Huntsman, and the Huntsman dropping, momentarily distracted Siegfried. Siegfried glanced to the side to see which of the two had gone down. Desmond saw his opening, and took it. His face full of savage joy, he, too, bound Siegfried's blade with his own and wrenched it out of Siegfried's hand. Siegfried tried to evade him but ran up against the wall. Rosa screamed as Desmond moved in for the kill.

Leopold turned and saw at a glance what was about to happen.

Leopold lunged forward, moving faster than Rosa had ever seen him before.

Not for Desmond; Desmond was out of reach. Leopold lunged for Siegfried. He flung himself between Desmond and Siegfried. And the blow intended for Siegfried plunged into his body instead.

Rosa's heart all but stopped.

With a curse, Desmond wrenched his sword loose as Leopold slumped to the floor, hands clasped involuntarily over the wound, blood pouring between his fingers. He turned to find Siegfried.

But Siegfried had already rolled to the side and found his sword, and Siegfried's face was contorted into a mask of fury. An animal roar came from his throat as he charged Desmond. The first blow would have been countered by Desmond's parry, except that Siegfried shattered the sword to the hilt in Desmond's hand, and all Desmond could do was try and scramble out of the way. As he dodged and overbalanced and fell to his hands and knees, he spotted Leopold's sword on the floor and scrabbled for it desperately. He reached it just as Siegfried reached him. Again, Desmond tried desperately to parry; this time it was his sword that was knocked from his hands like a toy as he backed into the table. His widened eyes stared at Siegfried in utter disbelief.

With another roar, Siegfried actually drove his sword down with both hands into Desmond's undefended chest, impaling Desmond to the table like a beetle pinned to a display board.

Desmond shook once, then was utterly still, a look of disbelief still on his cruel, handsome face.

Freed from her shock, Rosa ran to Leopold, undoing the useless light armor, tearing open his shirt with her bare hands, which were soon blood-covered. Grateful that she was wearing her peasant clothing, she pulled up her skirt and began ripping strips off her petticoat.

"Leave it be, Princess," Leopold croaked as Siegfried joined her, and grimly pressed his own hands against the wound while Rosa fashioned a bandage. "Looks like the contest is over. Hell of a way to get eliminated, but you got the better man. We wouldn't have suited each other anyway." He tried to laugh, but it came out as a moan. "Just give me a big fancy funeral."

"Shut up, Leopold," said Siegfried. But Rosa glanced at his face, and her heart sank as she read the truth in his expression. Leopold's wound was fatal.

And to prove it, at that moment, Leopold slipped into unconsciousness, his face gone gray and pasty.

"It's now or never," Lily said, putting Jimson's mirror in her pocket. She had suspended her travel-mirror facedown between the back of a chair and the table. Crouching beneath it, she invoked the spell, hoping that combining the four small mirrors wasn't going to scramble her, or leave her quartered as she came through.

Slowly and carefully, she stood up, passing through her travel-mirror at the oddest angle she had ever taken.

She found herself waist-deep, as if she was in a pool of water—except, of course, she was in a mirror at the edge of a churned-up field. Beside her, there was an exhausted firebird, and a very surprised unicorn.

The unicorn yelped and jumped away. The firebird's eyes pinned in startlement as she fluttered her wings and trilled with alarm.

She ignored them, getting a grip on the frame and pulling herself out, exactly as she would have pulled herself out of a pool of water, getting her rump up on the frame, then swinging her legs out. That went better than she had any reason to believe. "Jimson?" she asked.

"Still here, Lily, and much relieved," he said from her pocket.

She turned to the unicorn and firebird. The stared at her as if they could not believe their eyes. "Where are Leopold and Siegfried?" she demanded.

"In the Tower," the unicorn said promptly, the first of the two to recover her wits. "They told us to stay here."

"And you obeyed them?" she asked incredulously. "Come on! Let's go! They might need us!"

The unicorn blinked. "You have a point, Godmovver." And as Lily dashed across the field to the tunnel in the thorns, she shook herself and followed at a weary trot.

It was not easy ground to run across. Every step threatened to turn her ankle, and the gown she was wearing was not exactly constructed for running in. *I should have taken the time to change—* She thought about transforming what she was wearing, but that would take too much time. Illusions were one thing. Actually changing—that was something else entirely.

Halfway across the field, she heard Rosa scream. Cursing the encumbering skirt of her gown, she reached down, grabbed the hem in both hands, and hauled the mass of fabric up to run faster.

As she entered the tunnel through the thorns, she heard a bestial roaring that sounded more as if it had come out of a bear's throat than a human's. And just as she was within sight of an open door—

The vines shrieked in a high-pitched cry that sounded like nothing she had ever heard in her entire life.

She had to clap her hands over her ears, and she bent over double; the terrible sound cut through her head like a knife, bringing tears of pain to her eyes. The vines shook with a convulsion that nearly brought the entire tunnel down around her.

For a moment her heart leapt into her mouth as the vines thrashed uncontrollably. Something was killing them—but if they broke through the barrier of their own dead, they could still impale her and the unicorn.

Then the scream cut off abruptly, leaving behind an echoing silence.

And with another convulsion they all straightened, pointing skyward. Then they abruptly shivered into black, bitter dust.

The dust went everywhere, and she found herself coughing desperately to rid her lungs of it. Dashing her hand across her eyes to clear them, Lily ran the last few feet to the open door, and froze at the gory vision that she had stumbled into.

The first thing she saw was Prince Desmond, quite dead, grotesquely pinned to a table by a sword. His eyes stared sightlessly at her, his face bearing a strange expression of surprise.

The second thing she saw was Siegfried cradling a near-fainting Rosa in his arms, touching her face and kissing her, both covered in blood. Her heart nearly stopped.

Then as they both looked up, she realized it was not *their* blood, and her heart started again. "Godm—" Rosa exclaimed, reaching for her.

And the Huntsman rose up from beyond the table, face mad with rage, a sword in one hand, a meat cleaver in the other.

Lily froze. Siegfried had his back to the Huntsman and couldn't see him. Rosa was looking at her. In another second, the Huntsman would—

The unicorn shouldered her aside and charged the Huntsman, uttering a high-pitched scream of fury.

The Huntsman laughed and dodged, so that the unicorn hit him with her shoulder instead of her horn. She whirled on her hind feet and charged again. He neatly stepped aside at the last minute and parried her horn with the sword. This time the cleaver came down on her neck, inflicting what had to be a mortal wound. The unicorn made a gurgling sound and went to her knees, scarlet blood pouring down her neck, and the Huntsman turned on Siegfried, who flung himself between the Huntsman and Rosa, searching frantically for a weapon.

"Lily! Throw me! Throw my mirror!" Jimson shouted from her pocket, breaking her paralysis. Without even thinking, her hand went to her pocket almost of its own accord, and as the Huntsman raised the sword for another fatal blow aimed at Siegfried, she threw the mirror with a snap of her wrist, sending it spinning for him.

She hit the Huntsman squarely in the face with the edge of the mirror. And it was the Huntsman's turn to scream. The mirror shattered into a cloud of coruscating motes and a deafening explosion, half blinding her for a moment, and the Huntsman went down on his knees.

Then the cloud condensed back into the shape of the mirror again; the mirror clattered to the floor. But—it was not Jimson's mirror, with the clear glass and the gold frame. It was a mirror with a sinister, tarnished black surface, and a frame of rotting wood and verdigris-greened bronze.

Lily ran for the mirror and snatched it up. "Jimson!" she whispered, her voice catching in her throat with fear. What had happened?

But what looked back at her out of the mirror was not Jimson.

It was the Huntsman. The Huntsman, as she had never seen him. His face was contorted in a rictus of terror, his mouth open in a silent scream, as two skeletal black *things* seized him by the shoulders. He glanced at one of them, and turned his gaze back to her, clawing at the surface of the mirror frantically.

His captors were inexorable. His face receded into the black depths, mouth still open in a scream she was glad that she could not hear, as they hauled him down, down, and at last, were gone. Then there was only the mirror, black and empty. "Jimson?" she sobbed. Where was he? What had happened to him?

"I'm—here, Lily," said a hoarse voice beside her, and she looked down, startled. What looked up at her might have been wearing the Huntsman's clothing, his body even—but the face?

The face was Jimson's.

Before she could even begin to react to that, Siegfried's frantic call dragged her attention back to the three against the wall. "Godmother! You must help Leopold! He's dying!"

She stumbled over to them, but from the Prince's pallor and his shallow, catching breaths, it was obvious that there was nothing she could do in time. "I—I'm not a healer," she said helplessly. "He's hurt more than I can mend—I can't help him—"

"I…can…" coughed another voice. Bleeding terribly from the wound in her neck, the unicorn lurched to her feet and staggered the three steps it took to get to them, falling to her knees beside them all. With a last effort, she flung her head across Leopold's chest so that her own wound bled into his.

"Fweewy…given…" she gasped.

As the light in her beautiful golden eyes faded, she sighed once. Then she was gone.

Leopold opened his eyes with an effort at the sound of hoarse sobs. It was not something he had expected to do, actually. He should have been dead. He couldn't imagine why he wasn't dead. He knew he had taken a fatal wound, and a moment ago the world had been fading away around him. He couldn't imagine why now he was feeling better by the moment.

"Lie still," said the Godmother—how had she gotten there?—with a firm hand on his shoulder. "You're still healing." Healing? And then he saw past her.

He could only lie there in bewildered wonder, watching Siegfried cry with terrible grief as he cradled the head of the dead unicorn in his arms.

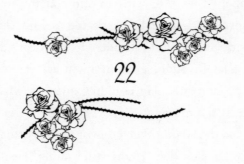

22

THE BALCONY WAS A GOOD TWO STORIES above the
crowd, and as Lily looked down on the sea of faces below her, for
the first time in her life she experienced a great deal of trepidation.

She glanced to the side, where Jimson stood in a uniform the
Brownies had designed especially for him. Not overornamented, not
overelaborate, and, she hoped, not uncomfortable. In black, of
course, to match "Queen Sable's" ubiquitous black, for Jimson was
the Queen's personal Guardsman so far as anyone other than Siegfried, Rosa and Leopold knew. His slightly pointed ears, that betrayed
him as some form of Fae, were hidden beneath a helmet.

Lily still was not sure what had happened when the mirror hit the
Huntsman. Jimson just got thin-lipped when she asked, and said,
"Let's just say that under certain rare circumstances, someone evil's
fate can catch up with him—and that allows for an exchange between
our world and yours. I hadn't planned on that, though. I had only
planned to drag him over into my world, where he couldn't threaten
you anymore."

Well, whatever had happened, she was grateful for it.

She should have known that Jimson was Fae of some sort, though. After all, he had been alive longer than she had.

She held up her hand where he could see it, and they both watched it shake.

"It's called *stage fright,* my love," he said, quietly. "Don't worry, everyone gets it."

Well, that was comforting. Sort of.

This was her own fault, really; she had wanted to address the largest number of the people of Eltaria that she could to cut down on rumors and wild stories, and this was the result. She would just have to tell the butterflies in her stomach to settle down, grit her teeth and get through it.

She took a deep breath, and with a gesture hidden from those below, invoked the spell that would allow her voice to project to the farthest point of the crowd. It was a good thing that the Palace had been built with a view to making mass addresses like this, because otherwise she had no idea *where* in the Kingdom it could be done. But she, Jimson, Rosa and Siegfried all stood on the seldom-used East Balcony, and there was nothing in this direction but acres of practice fields and lawn. Not that long ago, those fields had held a small army of adventurers vying for Rosa's hand. Now they seemed to hold every man, woman and child in Eltaria.

"People of Eltaria," she said. *Oh, heavens. Do I sound nasal? I sound nasal. I sound like I'm whining—* "We thank you for coming here today. This day, this moment, marks a turning point in the history of our Kingdom. For centuries, we have lived in fear of the surrounding lands, for Eltaria is small and rich, and a tempting morsel for others to swallow up. For centuries we have worn out our Kings, sending them to early graves, forcing them to confront invader after would-be invader. For centuries our bravest warriors have spent their lives dashing from one trouble spot to another. But today, that is at an end."

That was the signal for Jimson to toss the firebird, who had been sitting quietly in his cupped hands, into the air. She arrowed upward and burst into flame, causing oohs and aahs from the crowd, and surely some people were wondering how on earth this little creature, potentially dangerous though she was for her size, could defend a kingdom.

Of course, it wasn't the firebird that Lily was talking about. The firebird's flare signaled something quite a bit more impressive. And a very great deal more dangerous.

From where they had been waiting, soaring in slow, lazy circles high above the palace, hidden by the glare of the midday sun, the dragons came.

Four of them.

This was the culmination of Siegfried's plan, the one that had fairly won him Rosa's hand. Oh, how she had laughed aloud when he told her, because it was perfect. And as the years went by, the defenses would only get stronger. Kings and Queens would come and go, even Godmothers—but the Dragons would remain, increasing in numbers with every century until not even an army of Dragonslayers could defeat them.

The people below were already looking up at the firebird; beyond the firebird, four little dots of color came slowly spiraling down out of the sky. A few people in the crowd, keener eyed than most, spotted them first. As they drew nearer, more and more folk noticed, began pointing, murmuring. Then as it became apparent that these winged things were not, in fact, birds…as it became obvious that they were bigger than folk originally thought…as it became *very* obvious that they were much, much bigger than folk thought, and that they were, in fact, dragons, the murmurs increased to a dull roar that sounded like a distant ocean.

The dragons backwinged and settled to graceful landings on the peaked roof of the palace, spaced out equally behind the royal party.

Then, as one, they lifted their heads and blew out huge plumes of flame that joined into a canopy of many-colored fire above the heads of those on the balcony. The roar of the flames and the heat were just a little bit uncomfortable, even fifteen feet below.

The murmuring cut off abruptly. Every eye in the field was fixed on the dragons and their flame. Before anyone could take it into his head to panic, Lily spoke again.

"People of Eltaria, I present to you the Guardians of the Border."

She paused, as the dragons cut off their flames and gazed benignly down on the crowd.

"You will have heard that Prince Siegfried of Drachenthal, here beside us, won the hand of the Princess Rosamund with his answer to the final test of the competition—the question of how to best protect our land, not only now, but well into the future. Finally we can reveal his brilliant answer." She did not stint on the warmth and approval she projected into her words. Siegfried had gotten the idea just before Rosa was kidnapped, but had not been aware just how many dragons the Godmothers knew. Nor how many were ready to jump at the chance for secure homes where they wouldn't be harassed by treasure-hunters. When he suggested it tentatively, Lily had nearly proposed to him herself.

Siegfried blushed crimson. Fortunately, he didn't have to say anything, or she was fairly sure he would have stuttered.

"As Guardian for the East, we present Beryl of the Clan Buchenwurm. She and her kin will dwell in the caves of the mountains of the east."

Beryl, a dragon who had made Sharpstone's eyes fairly pop out of his head with desire when he first saw her, was a slender and graceful creature of emerald green, with wingwebs exactly the color of young beech leaves. She nodded her head to the crowd, a glint of amusement in her eyes. Sharpstone's interest had not been lost on her, and as Beryl herself was a young dragon with no hoard yet to speak of, and Sharpstone was not bad to look on and had quite the impressive hoard…well Sharpstone was a very attractive prospect to *her,* as well. So far as Beryl was concerned, Sharpstone's presence only sweetened an already-honeyed bargain.

"As Guardian for the West, we present Thundershrike of the Clan Windrider. He and his mate and their kin will dwell on the ledges of the western border. They will have the additional boon that as they protect us, so we will protect their eggs and young with a permanent detachment of the Guard stationed with them. That detachment, of Eltaria's finest, will henceforth be called the Dragonguard."

Thundershrike was an old dragon, enormous and proud, the color of blued steel. His Clan was rare; dragons did not usually like to lair in the open, and their nests were vulnerable to attack. He inclined his head to Lily, every line of him expressing gratitude.

"As Guardian for the North, we present Kukris, of the Clan Parbellum. He and his kin will dwell in the mines that the Dwarves have emptied of their treasures, and in addition, will serve as guards to the Dwarven convoys conveying their precious cargo to our capital."

Kukris was everything that people thought of when they thought of a dragon. Red and gold, fierce and strong, his ornamental spikes were particularly long, his teeth particularly large and sharp. He had been the first to accept, for Parbellum had long ago made their peace with the Dwarves of their homeland, and their numbers were putting a great deal of stress on the available lairs. This was an opportunity they would never have refused.

"And as Guardian of the South, we present Precious Peony, of the

Clan Wazashi. She and her clan are new to these lands, but are long in friendship with the peoples of their own. They will dwell along the river canyons, and above Lake Arrowhead, in the wind- and water-caves there."

Precious Peony looked very different from the others; her snout was shorter, her wings more ornate, and she was more snakelike. Her scales shone like opals or pearls in the bright sunlight, and she bowed rather than nodding her head. Unlike the others, Peony's sort of dragon was as much at home in water as in the air. It had been the idea of the dragon champion attached to Godmother Elena's Kingdom to recruit her and her clan; like Clan Parbellum, they were beginning to feel crowding in their island home and welcomed the chance to split the Clan and make a new home here.

"This is the treaty we have made. The dragon clans are to act as our defenses on the borders and protect the Dwarven mines in the mountains. In turn, we are to provide them with food, which the Crown will pay for out of the Privy Purse, in the form of special herds and flocks which will be pastured nearby. We are also to help them defend their lairs and nests from attack. And in return for the special protection they afford the Dwarves, and the gift of shed skin, the Dwarves will supply them with ten percent of the production of their mines, with which to build their hoards. We believe this treaty will be of immeasurable value to the Kingdom of Eltaria and lead to a firm foundation of alliance with dragonkind that will only strengthen our security as the years pass. People of Eltaria! What say you?"

The acclaim was slow to start—these were, after all, *dragons*—but after a moment, a few started to cheer. More joined them, cheering or applauding, and more still, until at last the entire crowd roared its approval, and the dragons lifted their heads and roared back until the roof shook.

Lily waited patiently for the cheering to stop, which it eventually did. When she had relative quiet again, she took another deep breath. She had been looking forward to this part for *months.*

"As you know, the Prince and Princess were wed two months ago. His solution was discussed, negotiated and, as of today, is in place. Flocks have been moved to their new homes. The dragons are today picking out their lairs. The Prince and Princess have been administering to the day-to-day needs of the Kingdom under the eyes of the Council and us. And now it is time. This day, we, Queen-Consort Sable, do hereby abdicate all pretensions to the crown, giving over the rule of Eltaria to King Siegfried and Queen Rosamund. Long live their majesties! Long live the King! Long live the Queen!"

This, of course, was completely unexpected for everyone but the four on the balcony, and after a moment of silence, as she placed the Royal crown on Rosa's head, and Jimson took the State Crown from its box and put it on Siegfried's, the roar that went up actually rocked the balcony under their feet.

Then she stepped back into the Palace, to let the new King and Queen properly greet their subjects.

"Someone is likely to have a polite tiff at usurping the coronation," Jimson observed, as they made their way back to the Queen's suite. Everything that Lily wanted had already been sent back home to her Castle. It only remained for the two of them to leave.

"Someone can have all the tiffs he wants," Lily retorted. "The last time we had a coronation, there was nearly a war amongst the priests and clerics over who was going to get to perform it. Now they can all blame that 'foreign interloper, Queen Sable' and unite in their umbrage."

Jimson threw back his head and laughed. She loved that laugh. She loved to make him laugh. She had always known he was witty, but she had never known what a good sense of humor he had. The past two months had brought many revelations.

"Now, have we gotten everything taken care of?" she asked as they passed through the doors of the suite and closed them behind themselves.

"Well, let's tick off the list." Jimson marked off the needed tasks on his fingers. "Dragons, abdication, coronation."

She nodded.

"Rosa knows the mirror spell, so any time she needs to consult with us or have a lesson in magic, she can just step through."

"And Siegfried has the firebird to advise him on magic and whatever the Tradition is going to try to sneak by him."

"We've cowed the Council into acting as a Council should, and not trying to bully them."

Lily laughed. "Or Siegfried has. That one day he roared at them, it was all I could do to keep from laughing out loud." She ran through the list in her mind. "There will still be problems. And Eltaria will *still* need its very own Godmother. It's too wealthy and too full of magic not to."

Jimson snorted. "Eltaria will still need the Godmother, the Queen-Godmother, and the—what would you call me?"

"Utterly captivating. I cannot wait to get back home so we can drop all the 'Queen and her guard' nonsense. I was so tired of stepping through mirrors every time I wanted to seduce you!" She gave him her "look" through lowered lashes.

"And here I thought *I* was the one doing the seducing!" He kissed her nose. "All right, then—"

For the last time, Lily discarded the persona of Queen Sable, and with it an invisible burden she was only too glad to set down. She and Jimson each picked up an identical hand-mirror from the table beside the "traveling" mirror.

"Mirror, mirror, in my hand," they chanted in unison—and a green face appeared in each. Now, of course, she realized that the green color was just the result of the image having to pass through the veil between their worlds.

"Godmother Lily!" said the one in her hand, and "Master" said the one in Jimson's.

"Is everything ready for us at home, Apprentice?" Jimson asked, a little sternly.

"Oh, yes!" they both said. "And the Brownies do not wish you to leave like this ever again, Godmother," added the one in Lily's mirror.

"Well *I* don't want to, either," she replied fervently, and turned to Jimson. "Well, my love, shall we?"

He bowed and gestured to the mirror. "After you, my dearest."

Swiftly they stepped through, leaving the suite silent and empty, waiting for its new occupants.


Rosa was perfectly happy to put her new crown in the hands of the attendants who were hovering nervously beside her, waiting for her to give it over. She really had no idea how Lily had put up with that much weight on her head. She was already getting the signs of a headache.

Siegfried seemed just as happy about being rid of his. "Are they gone?" he asked, as the attendants took the crowns away to be locked up. Even in a kingdom as wealthy as Eltaria, the two State Crowns were priceless, every gem—and there were exactly one hundred gems, large and small in each crown—matched and flawless, and enough gold in them to stagger the imagination.

"Let me check." Rosa took out her own little mirror, and the face of Jimson's third apprentice appeared in it without her prompting.

"Sylvie, are the Godmother and Jimson gone from here?" she asked.

"Not only gone home, but retired to the bedchamber and locked the door!" giggled the Mirror Spirit. "Shameless!"

Rosa slipped the mirror onto the hanger on the wall and laughed.

"Indeed! You would think that after three hundred years they would have some decorum!"

"I don't know about that," Siegfried replied, slipping his arms around her from behind and kissing the top of her head. "We don't have anything pressing, you know. That sounds like a good idea to me—"

"We still have to say goodbye to Leopold, so he has some daylight to travel by," she reminded him, and he mock pouted.

"All right. Let's go say our farewells to the rogue so we can get back to more important business." At her raised eyebrow, he retorted, "What? Making an heir *isn't* important?"

"Shush, you." She batted at his hands, and he released her with a laugh that made her shiver a little at the promise in it.

They made their way out to the garden—closed off from the public, and for once, empty of the courtiers. The public were being feted in tents out in that enormous field—after all, it wouldn't do for them to say they had been cheated of a coronation celebration!—and the Court having a celebration of their own in pavilions in the orchard.

Which left the garden free for someone who needed space to say his farewells. Like Leopold.

And Leopold's new wife.

Who was currently berating her father and getting the best of the argument.

As Rosa and Siegfried entered the garden they could already hear her. She had a very impressive voice, and the lungs behind it to make sure people got her point. Siegfried held out his hand, and the royal pair stopped just out of the immediate vicinity of the three. The stunning and statuesque blonde woman in the gold armor had her hands on her shapely hips and, from the look of it, had been dressing her father down for some time. "…and did I, or did I *not* do exactly what you *wanted* by helping Sieglinde escape?" she asked the old, white-bearded man acerbically. "And never mind what you told Mother about her! And never mind what Mother told *you*. Goddess of the hearth and marriage be damned, she has no right to go around trying to murder poor pregnant girls who got *wyrded* into falling in love! That makes no more sense than punishing a fish because it can't breathe air!"

He rubbed at his eye patch uncomfortably. "Well—yes—but—Brunnhilde—"

"So since I did what you wanted, *why* was I punished for it?" she demanded.

He fidgeted and wouldn't look at her. "I—promised your mother—"

"Promises you had no intention of keeping! And you *knew* what was going to happen! You knew very well that once Siggy woke me, the whole wretched saga was going to play out. Erda told you. And I know she told you, because she told *me* she told you!" Brunnhilde actually stamped her foot at him. "Half of your problems are because you keep too many secrets, and the other half are because you bring them on yourself. So why punish *me* for them?"

Leopold stood to the side, arms folded, lips compressed as he tried not to smile. And when Brunnhilde's father turned to him for help, clearly counting on a man to support another man, he shook his head.

"I have no idea what you two are talking about," he replied. "So don't ask me to take sides here."

Brunnhilde had gotten the bit in her teeth and was not going to be stopped now. Clearly she had been saving this up for some time. "So. You lie to Mother, you manipulate me, you manage to lay the blame for everything that happens on *me* and set *me* up to be the instrument for everything that is going to go wrong! You set me up to fall in love with my *nephew* of all the perverted things, *and* put everything in motion to make my life total misery and end in—"

*"Dooooooom!"* trilled the firebird from the tree above their heads.

"Exactly." Brunnhilde glared at her father. "And now *you* actually have the nerve to come here, think you're going to force me to give up my husband, and take exception to me for wanting to keep doom and destruction and the end of the gods from happening?"

"Your mother——" the old man said feebly.

"My mother is a manipulative idiot," Brunnhilde said bitterly. "You're another. And you two deserve each other, and you should just go home and slap each other to sleep. *I* am not going to repeat your mistakes." Then, out of nowhere, a slow, sly smile crept over her face. "And by the way, *Father,* I made sure you can't repeat your own."

Alarm contorted the old man's face. Leopold snickered.

"Brunnhilde—what did you do——"

She turned her attention to her nails, examining them critically, then buffing them on the leather strap of her breastplate. "Oh, nothing much. I just got that ring and returned it to the River Maidens."

The old man's eyes bulged. "You—*what?*"

"Well, *I* didn't renounce love!" she snapped. "And Siggy was smart enough when the bird warned him to leave it alone! No one else knew where Fafnir was. So Siggy told me where he'd left it, and I got it and gave it back to them. No more cheating and lying over it. No more trying to barter away the other goddesses over it. *And no more betraying your own children over it.* It's back in the river where it belongs and now there's going to be no downfall of the gods, either. There's no escape from the consequences of what you do now, Father. You're just going to have to face Mother and learn to *deal* with each other now."

"I—she—you——"

"What's more, my sisters have decided they aren't going to be so quick to jump to your orders anymore, either. They're tired of picking up dead men. They'd like some live ones of their own. What are you going to do, put *them* on rocks with circles of fire around them?" She sniffed. "Siggy and Leo will find *them* Princes if you do. Niffleheim! *I* will find them Princes if I have to! I'm sure there are entire marshes full of frog princes that would like to find a sleeping princess that can't run away when they try to get a kiss! So there. This whole cycle of family drama is *over*, Father. You just get on that thing you call a horse, and ride back to Mother, and *deal* with it."

She crossed her arms over her chest, in a pose uncannily like Leopold's, and glared at the old man. Rosa and Siegfried hung back— in no small part because Siegfried really would rather not have had his grandfather notice him—

Alas, too late. In the vain attempt to look at anything but his daughter, Wotan glanced to the side and spotted both of them.

"You!" he blustered, pointing a finger at Siegfried. "This is all your fault!"

"Because I didn't want to marry my aunt?" Siegfried must have decided to face the god down, because he waggled his eyebrows at the old man. "You really do need to get your sense of proportion straight."

Wotan stood there with his mouth hanging open. Clearly he had expected to intimidate Siegfried, at least.

But the last straw was when a raven, one of two that was up in the tree with the firebird, snickered, breaking the stunned silence.

He glanced up sharply. "Which one of you did that? Hunin? Munin?"

They both snickered.

He threw up his hands. "Bah! Ungrateful! All of you! Go ahead, discard your *Wyrd,* see if I care! I'll be sitting on my throne in Valla-halia, drinking mead, while you are—are—are—"

"Alive?" suggested Brunnhilde. "Enjoying ourselves? Seeing the world? Having adventures? Having families? Ruling a peaceful kingdom? Which none of us *would* be thanks to that *Wyrd?* I'll be going into adventuring, and I'll have you know that Leo thinks I make the perfect fighting wife!"

"Bah!" He turned to his—well, it was hard to call something with that many legs a horse. Mount. He hauled himself up into the saddle, and kicked it in the side, unnecessarily hard. The thing took a few moments to sort its legs out, then it began lumbering clumsily up an invisible slope of air, as if it was lumbering up a steep hill.

"Oh and by the way, old man? Besides my having a job on my own? *Leo makes love like a tiger!*"

"*I—can't—hear—you—!*" came the desperate reply on the breeze. Then Wotan, his beast and, finally, his two ravens, vanished into a cloud and were gone.

At last they could all let go of the laughter that they had been holding in.

When they all got control of themselves, Siegfried clapped his friend on the back. "Are you sure we can't persuade you to stay?" he asked.

Both Leopold and Brunnhilde shook their heads. "Too dull!" Leopold said cheerfully. "Things are going to be far too peaceful around here. Poor Hilde has been sleeping years away, and before that—"

"Before that it was the same damn thing, day after day. Fly to the battlefield. Pick up the dead man. Ferry the dead man to Vallahalia. Play serving wench to the dead man, his dead friends, his new dead friends, and my father and his drinking buddies all night long," Brunnhilde said with disgust. "Next day, do it all over again. I was nothing more than a transportation service and barmaid. I *know* how to fight, but I never got a chance to! Now I do."

"Uh—I think I've had all the fighting I ever want to see," said Siegfried.

"Boring! We're going to get into as much trouble as we can, aren't we, lover?" Leopold smirked. "First thing we're going to do is drop in on my father and brother and scare them into thinking I've come to steal the throne. And from there?"

"I know of a really evil dragon that needs killing," said Brunnhilde. "Whoever kills him and takes a sword and helmet in his hoard is supposed to save a Kingdom for its rightful heir and topple the usurper from the throne. That Dwarven chain mail you gave both of us as a wedding present is going to come in very handy for that." She beamed at the King and Queen. "I don't think we can ever thank you enough for sending Leo to wake me up."

As Rosa recalled…it had been quite an awakening. Leo hadn't learned his lesson about taking liberties, but Hilde not only hadn't minded, she'd been pretty enthusiastic about her awakening…ah…kiss. If it hadn't been for the armor, it might well have turned into a lot more than just a kiss.

"See, now that's more like it—dragons to kill, heirs to restore!" Leopold nodded. "You just keep track of us in those mirrors of yours and warn us if we're getting into any doomy situations, all right?"

"We will," Rosa promised as Brunnhilde put her fingers to her mouth and gave a shrill whistle. Two stunningly beautiful snow-white horses appeared from another part of the garden and waited patiently for them to mount.

"All right, we're off," said Leopold, as their mounts curveted restlessly.

"You're *sure*—" Rosa persisted.

"Of course we're sure." Leopold beamed at them, then as his new bride spurred her horse off into the orchard, followed after her, calling back over his shoulder, "You two are going to live happily ever after! Where's the excitement in that?"

"I don't know, love," Siegfried said, shaking his head. "You make happily ever after exciting enough for me."

And that was exactly what Rosa wanted to hear. "We have some time before we have to show ourselves at the celebration," she pointed out. "Wasn't there something you wanted to do?"

He grinned. "I'm so forgetful. Remind me?"

And so she did.

\* \* \* \* \*

*Don't miss the next*
FIVE HUNDRED KINGDOMS *novella*
*to be found October 2010 in the*
HARVEST MOON *anthology*
*featuring Mercedes Lackey,*
*Michelle Sagara and Cameron Haley*